HOLED UP

A Novel by
Eric Green

2d7. 338. 5583

To my old friend Jake MacKenzie
who might know mill towns better than I do.

HOLED UP

Belfast, Maine, 2019

HOLED UP
Chapter One

Scoggton (March 28)—A Scoggton woman escaped injury late Tuesday night after her car plowed through the front window of the IGA and ended up in the meat department.

Dolly Kimball, 73, who was wearing a fur coat over her pajamas, was uninjured, though her older model Buick was totaled. Kimball told police she was about to stop when the car went "Zoom!" Officer Packett surmised that she must have mistook the accelerator for the brake. "It could happen to anyone," she said. "After all, they're right there next to each other."

Store manager Daniel Rondeau estimated the damage to the building and its contents at $24,500. Police said Kimball, who had a clean driving record, would not be charged.

Jimmy watched her arrive up aisle 6—blasting through a pyramidal display of bright yellow bats and plastic balls, past TV dinners for every size of appetite, frozen vegetable medleys, fifty kinds of ice cream. It was the only aisle that could have possibly accommodated the width of the sedan.

Jimmy had been picking up a package of pork loin during the store's midnight lull when he heard wrenching metal and exploding thermopane. At the advance of headlights he didn't drop the meat or run; he merely stepped aside like a bullfighter, and the car slammed into the refrigerated case next to him. He stared at the incomprehensible union, the steaming hood, one sealed beam illuminating a jumble of glass-covered cellophane. He rubbed his free hand across his shaved head. "*Jesus!*" he said to himself, sensing the jolt now that it was behind him. "We never know when the dark blade is coming through the tall grass, do we?"

Slightly weak-kneed he walked over to the driver's window and peered in at the woman. She was screaming, both wrinkled hands gripping the wheel with obvious intensity. The speedometer needle registered a little over 70 miles an hour; she was still blindly accelerating, her foot locked against the gas pedal, the rear wheels shrieking as loudly as her voice, spinning insanely against the waxed linoleum. He could smell the acrid rubber smoke, exhaust, the leaking antifreeze. Jimmy leaned in towards her, and she stopped screaming. His tattooed arm reached for the ignition key. The roaring engine and rear wheels ground to silence. A silence that hummed sweetly in his ears.

"What?" he said to her, trying to think of something cheerful to say. "No drive-through? Fuck it, right?" Though he waited for an answer, she didn't respond, so he tried again, feeling sorry for the old girl. "Since you're here, you wanna steak or a chop or something?" He held up his packaged pork to entice her, but again nothing. Other than her immobility she looked okay; he supposed the woman wasn't in the mood for conversation at that moment, which was fine with him—he needed to get out of the store before the cops arrived anyway. So he lumbered toward the check out, employees and a few stray customers rushing past, some yelling.

Jimmy Hakken left the IGA with the loin unpaid for—no one was at the register—and passed through the automatic doors. Outside he hunched against a cold rain as he walked to the corner of the parking lot where he'd left his station wagon. Even though it was past midnight, there was some mayhem in the lot, people running, idling cars stopped with the drivers gawking, a distant siren or two. He opened the door and tossed the meat onto the bench seat, got behind the big thin wheel, keyed and roused the motor. It was only on leaving the lot that he remembered the rack of Ballantine pounders, his reason for being in the store in the first place.

He drove past the approaching sirens in the late March rain, the flaring blue and red gumballs prismatic in the wet windshield. The heater began to warm his steel-toed work boots, so he cranked up the fan to high, the smell of damp leather rising. Since he wore only a quilted black leather vest and a T-shirt, the heat felt good on his bare arms. Eventually he turned onto Acadia Avenue. The avenue was virtually empty, hillocks of dirty slush between the sidewalk and the two-lane one-way street.

He drove past the commercial bakery, the wonderful smell of hot bread the main reason he took this route home, motored past the windowless plywood doors of a dozen social clubs, a fancy name for bars that excluded outsiders. He had no problem with that: *Fuck 'em.* He passed at least six pawn shops full of guitars, stereos, and guns; a taxi stand; a smoke shop and lunch counter, the mostly faded sign showing a dapper gent smoking a billiard briar. He rumbled by block after block of empty store fronts, empty five and dime, empty banks, empty drugstores, boarded up or black windows decorated with the now limp and wrinkled watercolors of grade-school kids, all over-illuminated by clusters of street lights looking like giant electrified ping-pong balls on curved wands, the city of Scoggton's attempt in the seventies to brighten and revive the downtown.

The rain changed to snow and he cursed. He'd taken the wagon out of storage too soon; he should've kept the rental another week. But what did he know about Maine winters? He hadn't been back to New England since he'd left home at sixteen. Santa Cruz had weakened him, made him forget. End of March and it was still snowing. The oversized random flakes were very white in the harsh streetlight. The flakes flew at the car's wipers like crazy beings with no sense.

The 1965 arctic-blue Impala wagon had been a gift, but for Jimmy Hakken it was more than that. The car had belonged to Chevalier, and Jimmy felt about the car the same way a mother grizzly regards her cub. He'd received the wagon from the woman who'd inherited all of Chevalier's possessions, and Jimmy had asked her for the privilege of adopting his two cats as well. They were still with him, and he looked after them the way he protected the car.

Waiting at a red light, he idly watched a bum in a listing orange tuque about to cross Acadia in front of the Impala. Just as the bum stepped off the curb, about two feet from the car's front fender, he slipped in a mound of slush and disappeared from sight. Jimmy rolled down the window. "You," he called.

The bum ignored him. Got up slowly and slapped angrily at his filthy pant leg, mumbling.

"Hey, you," Jimmy tried again.

The bum glanced over, seemed finally to register something, and negotiated around the hood.

The flying snow turned green but Jimmy didn't move the car. "There a bar still open around here where I could get a quiet drink?" he said. Though he'd been in town four months he drank at home. Tonight, in the absence of the Ballantine pounders, he decided to risk a bar. He couldn't return to the IGA and didn't feel like searching out another market for the beer; not everyone carried it. He knew he was wasting his time questioning the bum and didn't care. The death sedan had him in an unusually good mood, and he felt like some human interaction, a rare thing during the last months.

"Bar?" said the bum.

"Yeah, *bar*—alcohol served by surly assholes, TV blaring the latest skunkshit."

The bum hesitated. He swayed, and to steady himself his hand—

"Don't touch the car," said Jimmy. The bum jerked straight almost falling again.

Jimmy dug into his pocket and cupped a roll of bills. He fidgeted one loose and held it out. The bum hesitated a moment, blinking, then took the bill. No one ever turns down money, thought Jimmy. Doesn't need to be a reason, you hand anyone money, they take it every time. At least the bum said, "Damn me if dis ain't a twenny."

"Make sure you spend it all on drink."

The bum didn't reply. Not a town of conversationalists. So Jimmy drove off.

Through a red light.

Chapter Two

The smell whacked him in the face. Humanity. Not just any humanity—years of layered humanity; a smell grown and mutated in neglected crevices by all the pathetic secretions of loneliness, loss, disappointment, lust, anger, boredom and alcoholic joy, not to mention the caged breath of endless cigarettes, stale spilled beer, rank perfume, one lingering molecule of cleaning fluid. My people, thought Jimmy.

He'd located the bar on looks alone. Two opposing doors, flat roof, hand-painted wooden sign *The Den*, a Pabst neon burning in a window; low ceiling varnished black by smoke; dim light over a row of narrow upright booths as rigid as church pews where every nick and burn over seventy years had simply been painted in forever, the last color an attempt at matching tobacco spit, with powder-blue and yellow a séance at its edges; another beer neon brazen in its competitive cheeriness; two pinball machines squawking and soliciting near where Jimmy entered. Place was a carnival-colored burl growing out the bottom of a turn-of-the-century Victorian. Or what had once been a Victorian.

When he opened the door, there was the usual bored swivel from the four or five patrons, yet on seeing him, they quieted. He ignored the hush and mounted the end stool at the window side of the bar, left the snow to melt on his head, on his shoulders. Though it was too cold outside not to be wearing a long-sleeved shirt or a jacket, he—

"Pabst draft, small glass, two of 'em," he told the bartender.

"*Two?*"

Jimmy didn't answer. The bartender turned to get the beers, pulling two classic tulip-shaped glasses from a frozen locker, angling each in succession under the streaming tap. He set them down. "Two dollars."

Hiding his roll in the shadow under the bar, Jimmy evicted a twenty and slid it onto the bar top. The bartender made change as Jimmy downed the draft in a long swallow. "Again," he said as the five bills were laid out. The bartender glanced at the untouched second beer, then refilled the other glass, lifted a dollar.

As Jimmy expected, when he looked down the length of the bar, he was being surreptitiously examined, mouths moving. It was the usual orthodontist's nightmare. One way you could tell status—the wealthy never had missing, crooked or yellow teeth. Because of his stare they went back to the TV, their talk, their drinks. All but one big red face. A face that had seen too many tanning bulbs. Jimmy figured it was just this skin color that had turned the upper classes pale again. When we toiled in the fields, *they* were pale. We were herded into the factories, *they* tanned. Now, with electric browning beds, they were white as lard again. The fucks always had to make sure to differentiate themselves from us. It was like when the blacks and Italians were able to afford Cadillacs, the rich bought German cars. Now the drug dealers had those and *they* shuttled around in those dorky Volvos and Saabs or even worse those boring boxes on wheels, those Limey Range Rover SUVs—pay more and look even dumber. It had gotten embarrassing, this quest to appear separate. He ignored Red-face and sipped his draft, glanced at the hockey game. Red-face was drinking a Red Eye—beer mixed with tomato juice. Maybe that's what stained him so red? Jimmy had no smile for his joke.

The door opened again, the sleet-infused wind reaching him for a refreshing second. And in walked somebody special because everyone greeted enthusiastically. Jimmy didn't turn, he listened.

"Hey, Claire, whatsup?"

"Josh, we missed you earlier. What's going on?"

"Can't kick, can't complain."

"Ain't that the truth."

"—You get it?" This from a new voice.

No answer.

"*Did* you get it?"

"I couldn't find him."

"You got to be shitting me."

"Look, I couldn't find him."

"Give me the damn money then and I'll find him."

"All right, calm down."

"Give it."

"Hey, come on, Slag, leave it alone."

"Josh, stay the fuck out of it."

"Who's that?"

It was the female, in a different tone of voice.

Now they whispered and he could only make out a few words, one jabbing him. That's who they thought he was? But after a few minutes everything went back to normal. He glanced over, but she was hidden behind the men, so he returned to his beer. A few minutes later he smelled some kind of perfume or scent and knew she had to be beside him.

"This for me?" Her hand reached for the untouched beer, the head flat now, only a few bubble lines hesitating up the inside of the glass.

"Don't," he said, nastier than he intended.

Her hand stopped. "Just a little bit touchy, aren't we?"

He turned to face her and was surprised. Her features were delicate, eyes almost vulnerable, her hair very black and full with the buoyancy of a fresh shampoo. The smell must come from that. Best smell in the place, but that was easy.

She smiled. "What's with you?"

He offered no response.

"Quite the talker, aren't we?" She continued to watch him. "Where ya from?"

"I live on the hill."

"Brackert?"

He nodded.

"Staying awhile?"

He shrugged.

"You're not from around here, are ya?"

"Nope." He was more than willing to give her that.

"So . . . you going to tell me?" She flipped her hair in the careless way women can have. The gesture irked him.

"No," he said again.

She was unruffled. As if to prove it she reached out with the tip of her finger and poked his bicep. "Nice tats. You sure as hell couldn't fit any more on your arms, could you?"

He grunted.

"I've never seen anyone wear sideburns *and* shave their head. Least not around here."

"Did they send you over to check me out?"

"What're you talking about?"

"You think a narc looks like me?"

She examined him more fully. He could almost feel it, as if she were touching all his imperfections, from his scalp where the crowbar had marked it; a hesitation at his irises, a washed-out sky color that always reminded him of a sled dog; down his broken nose to the too sensual lips; and worst, settling on his chin, which no matter how many times he checked never seemed quite strong enough. He grabbed for his beer and found it empty. There was nothing worse than being stared at by someone like her.

"Listen," he said. "Give it up. I'm not a narc."

"Yeah—you're *way* too touchy to be a cop."

"Did I ask you over here?" A pause now, a stalemate of eyes. "You got a name?"

"Claire."

"Bob."

"Bob? You don't look like no Bob."

"Yeah . . . what do I look like?" *Jesus*, he was doing it again.

"So if you're not a cop, whaddaya do?"

He turned from her face and signaled the bartender. Noticed that Red-face was glaring at him—a too obvious attempt at intimidation. Too many steroids. These assholes never realized posturing was a giveaway.

"He isn't your husband, is he? That big guy?" It seemed unlikely but you never could tell.

She glanced at the group of men. "I've never been married."

The bartender set down two. Jimmy passed her one.

"So . . . what's with the extra beer?"

"You can't say thanks?"

She took a sip. "Thanks. So why did ya move here?"

"People can't move to Scoggton?"

She shook her head, the hair again dancing like in a shampoo ad—more fragrance. "Everyone tries to get away from this place, not to it."

Red-face was headed their way, husband or not. Probably over thirty yet still dressed like a college kid, he towered over the woman, his massive arms folded across a Patriots sweatshirt. He rocked on the balls of noticeably new running shoes, insisted on the intimidation stare again until Jimmy was getting bored. Then he turned to her. "What do you think you're doin', drinking with him?"

From her change of expression, Jimmy knew he had something on her.

"Slag, I'm just having a beer. Since when can't I have a beer with who I want?"

"I can see what the fuck you're havin'."

"You," said Jimmy, waiting for the red face to focus on his. "You always this grumpy when on empty?"

The guy puffed up even redder, veins showing in the thick neck, the shoulders bunching, and Jimmy was curious if he'd make a move. If he was going to, it would be now.

"Who the hell're you?" he said instead.

"Bob," Jimmy said evenly. "And you're . . . ?"

"Come on," Red-face said to the woman. "We're goin'." He grabbed her arm and yanked her away, beer sloshing down her jeans and onto the dirty linoleum before she could gain her balance and set the glass on the bar top. "You!" He pointed at Jimmy. "Find some other fuckin' place to drink."

Red-face snatched their jackets and pulled her toward the door. Jimmy almost came off his stool. He forced himself quiet. When they were halfway to the door, he noticed her walk. Her right leg looked shorter than the other, that foot pigeon-toed. The sight of her limping revealed too much in one uneasy instant, like when he saw a hurt and struggling animal, and he realized he might have been wrong about her. It increased his dislike for Red-face all the more. The door slammed and they were gone. Jimmy downed his beer, and leaving the untouched one untouched, he picked up his change minus a deuce.

"Nice friendly place you got here," he said to no one in particular. Then he lumbered out into the driving sleet.

Chapter Three

Jimmy punched the metal box, the red light blinked to brightness, the apparatus began to throb. He grabbed the wand out of the metal holster and started rinsing. No soap. He moved back to the display to verify that the rotating selector was on soap, clicked it back and forth, still no soap. And the water was cold. He cursed but kept spraying, the digital clock running down. Lack of time could be like that—make you do things against principle. But as he hosed off the filthy sides of the wagon, even without soap or hot water, he felt an almost therapeutic wellbeing. His thoughts strayed to the detail shops in Santa Cruz mostly run by Mexicans. Those guys knew how to treat your ride. Swarms of guys washing, vacuuming, polishing, massaging in tire balm, all for something over a twenty. Jimmy shivered more and more. He didn't know how the hell Chevalier had done it. It was too damn cold in Maine not to wear a jacket.

Soon enough, with the heater on high again, he was headed home. Steering gingerly, he attempted to stay in the cleanest part of the road. It was a personal affront every time a nasty amount of salty slush chattered into the wheel wells. Even though the squall of wet snow was past, it had not been the night to wash the car. He didn't care. It was the gesture that mattered—towards the wagon, but more importantly, towards Chevalier.

At the dead-end of True Terrace he turned in behind the fieldstone foundation and carefully slotted the Impala into the far left of the three narrow bays of the doorless carriage barn. It wasn't an ideal place for the car, but it was what his landlady, Doris Callahan, provided. The other two bays were piled high—an ancient tractor, ladders, sleds, the usual mismatch of rusting gardening tools, spreaders and mowers; clearing a berth for the Impala had been an effort. Usually Jimmy slid across the bench and got out the passenger side of the car, but tonight he used the driver's door and squeezed through this narrow gap along the bead-board planking. He wasn't sure why he changed his routine and blamed it on meeting Claire. He couldn't seem to get her out of his mind. Staring up at the dark building, he wished he was cradling a rack of pounders; he might be in for another bad night. He hadn't slept well for months, ever since Chevalier had been murdered, though it certainly wasn't the fault of the house. The Callahan Victorian was three floors of towering clapboard and ornate trim from which a sharp scraper could generate poisonous confetti for an entire summer, the tall stone foundation and turret lending a castle-like atmosphere that he cherished. Doris's grandfather had built the place, and it must have been something back then. Now it looked as forgotten and bedraggled as Doris.

Jimmy had first met Doris Callahan on Acadia Avenue during his second day in Scoggton. As he'd driven around town, deciding whether it was the right place to hole up, he noticed a diminutive woman yelling and pointing. Guided by her quivering finger, he saw a guy running up the sidewalk, clutching a large handbag. Jimmy accelerated the station wagon, drew parallel and examined the bag—lemon yellow daisies on white plastic. The runner, on noticing him, shot up a narrow alley. Jimmy took the next side street, pulled up to the edge of a park, got out. Rows and rows of huge oaks, paved paths dashed every so often by crumbling cement benches, a litter of newspapers and fast-food wrappers, and there—the guy was behind some bushes next to a chain-link fence by the empty town pool. Jimmy walked up quietly from behind. The guy was digging around frantically in the bag, tossing everything onto the pavement.

"I want that," said Jimmy.

The thief snapped around, hesitated for an instant, then threw the bag at Jimmy and sprinted off. He gathered up the sad contents and went to find the old woman. She was still waiting for a cop.

"My goodness," she said, her eyes searching him up and down. "You certainly are an odd-looking thing to be my savior, aren't you?" Then she must have noticed his expression. "Oh my, I wouldn't worry about it. I've never been all that much to look at either, and it hasn't harmed me a bit. At least you're good and tall, and I must say I'm pleased to get back my bag." She hesitated. "I suppose you want me to pay you something. Would you like some tea instead?"

And so it had started.

Jimmy looked up now at Doris Callahan's black windows. She went to bed early and was obsessed with saving electricity, refusing to leave on even a hall light. With the package of pork loin under his arm, he walked past the monolithic white posts of a porte cochere, their bases brown with rot. One bare bulb hung in the center of the sagged ceiling, a clumsy star of shadows on the ground and stone steps. It was Doris's single lighting extravagance, and he'd had to beg for it. He closed the elliptical-paned front door with a tender click, entered the dark hall, thumbed on the newel post light, an acorn of amber, and mounted the wide stairs. The house had that smell of age. Dust, wax, varnished wood, molting curtains, worn-out stair runner, dry air breathed a thousand times—who knew? Halfway down the second-floor hall he managed to unlock his door by feel with an iron key. On the bottom step, a massive yellow tom with a missing ear arched his back in greeting, letting loose a hoarse baying as Jimmy reached down to scratch him. Together they tiptoed up the steep stairs to his rented rooms. His heavy boots weren't ideal for this, but Doris insisted on quiet, so he did his best.

He entered his sanctum. Four small gable windows and a windowed turret at one end that peered over the city. Jimmy was always drawn to this view like a knight on his ramparts. The dark river bisected an undulating drape of lights organized into bright lines leading to the two bridges, a few dots of taillight and headlight even this late meandering up the main streets, the storm clouds saturated by an orange glow as if by fire, though nothing like the icy January night he'd watched a neighborhood of tenements burn to the ground. Near the river hulked the embattlements, the tomblike fortresses of textile and shoe factories, long bitter rows of abandoned brick and steel skeleton like a monstrous freight train shunted to a river siding and forgotten. The black heart of the town. A couple of these buildings had recently been renovated into commercial space by optimistic developers but remained unrented and lifeless. Over weak tea at her kitchen table, Doris Callahan had told Jimmy the story of the mills closing. But he'd only half-listened. The plight of Scoggton wasn't his concern. Actually, he didn't give a rat's ass about it. He was only holed up here because it was a lost town and because Chevalier had been from Maine.

Jimmy shoved the pork loin into the electric icebox. He'd dragged the appliance up from the basement strapped on a rusted cobweb-laced dolly. About killed him. Afraid of marks on her casements, Doris had directed him like a drill sergeant as if she expected men to be that strong. Now the cats rubbed against him. He called them Yellow and Black. No one knew what Chevalier had called them, and the cats didn't seem to mind what they were named as long as they were fed. Jimmy petted and scratched them behind their ears, filled their bowls.

Now he craved a beer more than ever. Instead he fed a video into the quirky player and settled on Doris Callahan's reject Victorian sofa, an errant horsehair quill spining him as usual. They'd furnished his entire apartment from her basement and attic. She'd even supplied sheets, linens and towels, dishes and tableware, commenting on each item with a mixture of regret and pleasure, explaining where each object had come from and when—as if he could possibly care. He focused his attention on the ancient mahogany-cased black and white TV, also dollied up three floors.

An image expanded to life.

From opposite sides of the screen, across a barren gray field cloaked by an impending gray storm, two men on gray horses approach each other, each towing an entourage of mounted soldiers. The two groups soon face each other, drawing up their horses in a wasteland of cinematically oversized boulders, and it's apparent that confrontation is inevitable. The one chief, a scarred giant with a ferocious-looking plume exiting his steel helmet, represents the evil interloper, having recently seized the throne from the rightful king. The other leader, modestly attired, with a tall but slim build, bareheaded, and a nose like an anteater, is the wronged knight of the slaughtered king, unwilling to yield to the new regime. Plume's men outnumber the other knight's three to one, and are generously appointed in shiny armor, weapons and plumes, though none is as daunting as Plume. He glares at the modest knight and his crew of misfits.

"So," says Plume, "you insist on continuing this stupidness of yours."—Jimmy read the white subtitles because he couldn't understand the French, though he'd watched the scene enough times to have it memorized—

"My loyalty can not change," says the knight.

"You are a fool," responds Plume.

"Sir, I must take issue with being called a fool."

"You are not only a fool, your dead king was an idiot."

At this, the knight jumps gracefully from his horse. "Sir, you have offended my king's honor. I must take exception to such words."

Plume now dismounts as well, needing some assistance from his henchmen. He clanks down. With a malicious smile he examines the other knight clad only in a leather chest plate and clinging leggings. He unscabbards a sword the size of a battleship. "I accept your challenge."

"But," says one of Modest's band, "Sir Fragonard is not in battle dress."

This comment falls on deaf ears. Everyone's, even Jimmy's. He considered this part embarrassing overkill but forgave it because of what followed.

The modest knight now grimaces miserably for the camera, a look that the French have perfected, and slowly unsheathes a modest but serviceable blade, allowing the weapon to tip toward the hard tundra as he bows solemnly.

Instantly Plume lunges, attempting an ungentlemanly kill as Modest leaps back. He glances at the wound in the leather chest protector, his expression saying it's merely a trifle. He raises his sword, his other hand stemming the flow of blood. Plume, a sudden dervish of sword thrusts, works his advantage, puffing and panting as our knight quietly parries the blows, backing up from the fierceness of the attack. Those watching, however, become progressively uncomfortable because he's entirely on the defensive; he's exhibiting a kind of medieval rope-a-dope. After a few minutes of this effort, Plume wheezes to a stop.

"Fight, you coward," he bellows in French.

"Sir," says Modest. "I am compelled to advise you at this juncture that it would be foolish for you to continue."—Jimmy loved the use of *fool*ish here because it harkened back to the original insult.

"What?"—though out loud Plume said *Eh, merde alors*. "Are you such a coward you will not fight?"

"On the contrary. I have just learned all your weaknesses, so I must warn you that it would be futile for you to continue. I can kill you quite easily now, and if you commence, I will be forced to do so." At this he gives another slight bow, lowering his sword.

Plume is enraged, and seeing another unguarded chance, lunges. Modest steps delicately to the side and skewers Plume just under his outstretched arm straight into the heart. Plume staggers to a convulsive halt. The screen is now filled with his stunned face. He topples like an oak, raising dust even on that barren gray field.

Modest bows chivalrously once again, over the dead body this time, an expression of sadness on his noble face more dramatic because of his large nose.

Hakken leaned forward and blackened the set. A dot of light remained, winked out. He sat for a moment without moving. Then his fist swiped dampness from each eye, and he renewed his vow.

Chapter Four

Unlike many men, Hakken didn't fully believe that most women were an alien species and therefore dangerously incomprehensible. He did however worry about beautiful women. They tended to be trouble. And why not? How can someone who's been told how precious she is, fawned on and doted over since preadolescence, come out normal? But their need to cash in constantly on their looks bugged him. Which brought him to Claire again. Her hair, her large vulnerable eyes, that voice, and how it had felt when she poked him with her finger. Like a branding iron. And then there was the leg. Maybe that changed things? But he'd spent too much of the night thinking about her, and she probably wouldn't be interested in him anyway. She might even be involved with that red-faced moron for all he knew, though somehow he doubted it. But there was certainly something between them.

Then he almost slapped himself: he had something to finish and thinking about Claire wasn't going to get it done. He threw off the covers—the two cats stretching from different locations on the bed—and wandered over to the turret, checked the morning view. A clear day, the sun melting last night's squall, the streets already mostly dry, the roof dripping an uneven rhythm. He listened for Doris Callahan below him though she'd only climbed his steep stairs twice in four months. In a back closet were his mushrooms. He gave them a spray of water. The balance of aeration and moisture was imperative. The mycelium required rapid growth over the rye host or contamination could set in. Green and putrid, he loathed the stray molds that destroyed his efforts. To avoid them, he sterilized the rye by pressure-cooking, the whole apartment reeking of boiled grain like a brewery. During the procedure Doris had banged on his door. "What in heaven's name are you making up there?" she asked. "Soup," he'd said. "Well, Robert, it's simply awful smelling! If you're going to cook for yourself, you'd better get a cookbook and follow the instructions. Or better still, open a can." She'd left it at that. One or two of the jars offered mature fungus—ruptured veils and silky ivory caps. Pulling the stems from the soil he set the yield on the drying rack, tempted to toss a few down for breakfast. But there was work to do.

First he did his hundred pushups and sit-ups, then he fed the cats, made himself a grilled cheddar sandwich sided with a few dill pickles, washed the dishes. He always cleaned up immediately after eating. He hated the sight of unwashed dishes. At his desk he roused his computer. E-mail:

H—The more I look at it the more the C option is out. To much security. I say F. L

Luke Delamar had been Jimmy's right hand back in Santa Cruz. He was the older statesman, tactician, and weapons expert of the crew. Besides Chevalier, Luke was the only man Jimmy had ever trusted. Even so, he knew partners were a risk. Crime had two smart rules, the two *N*s: No partners, Never talk about it. Nonetheless, Luke he needed. Jimmy had slow-mailed the code, knowing the Internet wasn't secure. *C—Connecticut, F—Florida, A—Alden*, etc. He checked the rest of his e-mail. Penis-enlargement and porn site spams needed deleting; one in German stood out, inviting him to view Lillian's Livecam Botschaft; he wasn't sure what that meant and was tempted before he zapped it. Discipline. Then he wrote back to Luke.

L—Puts us months behind. I was hoping to move within the week. J

He opened his Word program and popped his novel onto the screen. He wasn't sure why he was writing. It annoyed him that so many people tried to write or believed they could if they only had the time. And here he was doing the same damn thing. His was strictly autobiographical as he'd learned most first ones are. Why make things up when you didn't have to? All these guys who'd never left college were forced to do that. He'd read them and knew they were inventing— easy to tell. He liked what was true. Or at least what seemed as though it were true. If the reader couldn't tell, he supposed that might be okay, as long as the writer had lived some of it. Those college professors probably just wrote for each other anyway. It wouldn't matter to them a wink that most of their stuff bored him. Writers seemed to be an odd lot. He'd read about this one French guy who went on a three-hour walk to decide about a semi colon. Fine—but why the hell tell anyone? He looked over what he'd written. It had taken him almost two months to get this far.

My Life
     by Jimmy Hakken
The night I planned to run away from home my stepfather caught fire. Here's what happened.

I get out of my sleeping bag to pack some stuff for my trip, pissed I got to leave it behind (big black and yellow cotton thing, covered in flying ducks, I'd gotten it two years ago on my fourteenth birthday, the bag was a gem, but no good for the road). My mother cries out from the other end of the trailer. I run. There in the bathroom is my stepfather passed out cold on the toilet with his pajama pants bunched around his ankles and the side of his bathrobe burning up. My mother's trying to splash water from the tap into the flames and yelling: "Harold! Wake up, wake up!" Most of the water though is going between her fingers onto the floor. So I grab a towel and put out the fire. Then I take the Camel from his one hand and throw it in the sink. Fucker gives a last hiss. My stepfather never dropped a drink or a cigarette, no matter what. Got to give him that. Mom is still throwing water at the smoke, saying, "Oh, my God. This is why I check him every night. Oh, my, God." He'd set the bed on fire twice.

"It's lucky the flames didn't reach higher," I say. "Whiskey fumes probably burn like gasoline. He coulda burnt down the trailer."

My stepfather is still out cold, his bony knees sticking from the smoking robe, his face with the mouth hanging open, and his false teeth missing. He'd lost his teeth really young, and the new teeth never fit right, or so he told us. The bathroom is full with smoke and a bad reek I could never get out of my mind. Not something you wanted as a last memory of anyone. And then he starts to snore. And I mean, loud. Mom and me look at each other and start laughing like crazy, so at least I had that of her.

I leave while it's still dark, letting myself out like a ghost, though I could hear them both snoring away. Poor mom, she'd be tired at work. It hadn't been easy dragging my stepfather onto the bed and then we'd talked afterwards together. I was only grateful he hadn't woken up and started in again. I'd had enough.

The trailer park is dead when I pass the Happy Acres sign. The night air and the wet grass smell good after the stench of the trailer. As I head down the street toward town, my pack digs into my shoulder. I like the feeling. Mist from the Androscoggin River surrounds the paper mill down there, its stacks going no matter what the hour. Another smell I'll always remember, chemical pulp. My stepfather worked that mill his whole life until six months ago.

As I walk into town and under where the streetlights are, I see my reflection is in the shop windows. I feel like a hero out of fiction. I'd been sick a bunch as a kid, and I'd spent my time reading. There hadn't been much else to do. Mom got me books from the library though my stepfather was pissed about that, too. He said the reading was what

ruined me, put stupid ideas into my already dumb head. Maybe he was
right. Who ever really knows about anybody?

The Shell station is all dark, except the one light above the
counter and cash register that was always on so they didn't get robbed.
The bus wasn't going to be there for another ten minutes. Though I don't
want to waste any of my money, I figured I'd get a paid ride south and
then get to hitching. My mom showing up in our old Dodge as I stood
by the side of the road was a nightmare I'd already seen in my head. I
felt bad enough leaving her without that scene.

The bus shows up out of the mist, makes this wide turn the way
they do, and stops. The door jumps open with a hiss and the driver hops
down. In that cool way they have, he tosses my pack below in a locker
and sells me a ticket. The whole thing makes me want to be a bus driver.
Of course, so many things look good from the outside in.

Most of the other passengers are dozing off as I head down the
aisle and get a seat toward the rear. Somebody already has the far
backseat, the long one. Out the window, the only town I know whips
past in a matter of minutes. Every damn building whacks me with a
memory and they hit my stomach in a funny way. Though it's cozy on
the Greyhound with the diesel engine and a few people whispering, I
can't stop thinking of Mom and I get all sad. My note is hardly going to
help, but I hope she'll understand that staying around my stepfather
wasn't negotiable anymore.

Jimmy was proud of the *negotiable*. For him the word fit exactly
what he'd felt. When words did that they gave him a thrill.

I suppose my stepfather wasn't that much of an asshole. He just
hated me. It happens a lot with stepfathers and step kids. Nothing new
there, right? And he was this big healthy handsome fucker, and I was
pretty much the opposite. At night when he was drunk, he had this thing
he did. He'd come out of his room slamming the door. (If you've ever
lived in a trailer you know what slammed doors are like.) Then he'd
head into my mom's room and give that door a good whack. Now he'd
yell something at her for a few minutes and return to his bed with two
more banged doors. Within ten minutes he'd be raging back out again.
Once I stood in the hall and said, "Hey, I got to get up early for school."
Didn't do any good. He only knocked me down and then added my room
to the loop, which made it six slams per cycle. A bunch of noise. It
could really wear on you day after day.

So the bus stops at one of its stops, and I watch a girl about my
own age get on. I kind of pray silently she'll sit beside me, and I kind of

pray she won't. As she walks down the aisle I point my face out the window. I have this discoloration, as it's politely called, and I always sit so it doesn't show. Because of it, a kid at school called me Scarlet Pimpernel, probably thinking about pimples and not

Jimmy stopped reading. He'd made that part up and it bothered him now. The truth was that he had pimples, not a discoloration. *See,* invent stuff and it sounds wrong. He'd loved that book as a kid but it sounded stupid used in his novel. He removed those sentences and started to peck with one finger. Two hours later he had condensed the many paragraphs he'd written to this:

The bus stops in a town, and I watch a girl about my own age get on, half praying she'll sit beside me, half she won't. As the bus starts moving again, she walks down between the seats. She seems to slow at the sight of me and I look down. I can hear her slide in across the aisle. After a few moments I look at her, but she's looking out her window. So I look out mine at the mountains, the orange sunlight shining on their peaks, getting kind of lost up there. I jump when she speaks.
 "Where're you headed?"
 She's leaning across the aisle, her hair half over her face, her mouth in a know-it-all smirk. Her face and dress make me think of a big summerhouse on a river with hand-cranked ice cream on the porch, but her dad probably pumps gas for a living.
 "West," I finally say.
 "You're going south right now, in case you didn't know." She tosses her hair back.

As he wrote the sentence, Jimmy thought of Claire in the bar yet again. The vision stalled him. Annoyed, he jolted out of his chair. He walked around the apartment and then stared out the window. After a while, he returned to the computer and proceeded.

 "You're headed south right now, Smarty, in case you didn't know." She tosses her hair back.
 "I know where I'm going."
 "Well, aren't you something."
 "No. But I know where I'm headed."
 "Where then?"
 "I'm going to find my father."
 She hesitates at this. "Where's he?"
 "West Coast."

"Why so far away?"

"Not sure. He left when I was three."

Jimmy got up again and went to the fridge, opened the door and peered in until he remembered there wasn't any beer. Thinking about fathers made him thirsty.

He tiptoed down his staircase and then the front stairs, keeping to the wall side to minimize creaks. Even with these precautions, Doris shot around the corner of the front hall to ambush him, her form bordering on troll-like, her eyes icy as pale marble behind wire-rim glasses. She sure wasn't any advertisement for spinsterhood. He was forced into these collisions almost every day, as if she listened for his tread and pounced. He was safe only at night.

"Robert!" She refused to call him Bob, and had a way of pronouncing Robert as if she knew it couldn't be his name. "Have you seen the papers?"

He shook his head.

"It's horrible. That Dolly Kimball almost ran down a dozen people at the IGA last night. She drove right through the market—right plum through it." She seemed delighted by this. "She insists she confused the foot pedals or some such silly nonsense. Now how in the world could a person do such a thing?" She eyed him incredulously as if it were his fault.

"Couldn't say," he finally said.

"She was always trouble. Always nasty in school. Dressed like a hussy even then. Three husbands and buried them all. Each one with more money than the last. Awful woman!"

Jimmy continued down two more treads, hesitant.

"You didn't shovel the steps," she said accusingly.

"They didn't melt?" The massive, stone and cement steps were mostly protected by the porte cochere, but she insisted he clean off anything that blew in.

"My newspaper was sopping."

"Wet?"

"Well—the edge was certainly damp."

"They forget the plastic bag again?"

"They did."

"I'm headed into town, want me to grab a dry one?"

"I suppose not. I've read it by now anyway. Why are you going into town?"

"Beer."

"You drink too much," she said decisively. "You think I don't

27

notice all that clanking every time you take out the garbage?"

"Beer isn't like drinking."

"*Humph!*" It was more of a snort than a word. He was relieved when she made that sound. It usually meant she was about run down, like a wind-up-toy spring when it gives a last spasm.

"Remember I showed you that article," he said, "about how beer helps cure all kinds of disease?"

"It was most certainly paid for by brewers."

"Doris, brewers have families too. Someone's got to support them. You want me to let their kids starve?"

"Oh, you." She spun and stomped off, if a woman as light and bony as her could stomp. Doris was pretty agile though, he had to admit that.

Jimmy opened the front door and stepped into the day.

Chapter Five

Hakken left the hill and drove into town, rolled down the driver-side window. The sun was warming the air, and that feeling of spring one gets in New England, which was completely different than in California, leapt twenty years and he remembered. Maybe it was the contrast after the long winter? The edge of the breeze had that quality of freshness, of renewal. Even the river didn't smell too poisonous. He considered the IGA for his beer but decided it was time for another source; someone there might recognize him or the car from the night before. The IGA was already under construction, a three-foot-high brick wall being built to guard the front so no one could ever roar down an aisle again. Doris would be disappointed.

Locating the Ballantine's took a while, but eventually he found two racks of pounders lurking in the cooler of a corner store and suggested to the guy at the register that they order more. A grunt for response. Unaffected, he walked back to the car and breathed the air again, settled behind the wheel, aimed the blue hood down the street. If he returned now, Doris would be lying in wait. Better to drive around town for a while.

Suddenly a red SUV pulled out right in front of him. He stood on the brakes, the wagon diving and fishtailing. Less than a block later, the SUV veered off on a side street, tires squealing. Wasn't that always the way? Drivers have to pull out, almost tear off your front bumper, and then within a block or less, they turn again. Where was the logic in that? He snapped open a can and took a long pull, pointed the Impala wherever it wanted to go, trying not to get annoyed. The weather was too damn nice for being upset.

Jimmy didn't drink and drive. He knew that could be a mistake. Instead he drove and drank. A good combination as long as you got the order right. Without meaning to—or so he told himself—he found himself passing the Den. He couldn't see inside, but with the hope that Claire might be there, he tried. When he glanced forward again, he was about to run up over the curb into a telephone pole. He wrenched the wheel left, the ale soaking his crotch.

The weather continued to warm, everything melting. Up the

opposing hill, across the river from Doris Callahan's house, meandering dark tongues of runoff backed out of driveways and swirled into storm drains. On this side of the river, the factory side, which surrounded the downtown along Acadia Avenue and the park, multi-family tenements, clapboard four- or five-story boxes with sagging porches and scaly cornices, rubbed shoulders, row after row. Most had been vinylized, the plastic strips bulging and gapping as the building rotted and settled underneath. Like many mill towns, one side of the river had housed the workers, the other the managers and owners, but as he climbed even the houses on the laborer's side became progressively fancier, although these days every building in town was in disrepair and depressing looking. Any kind of wealth or civic improvement had long abandoned Scoggton.

He hated that America was no longer a manufacturing nation, and that his birthright, the northern mill towns, had suffered the worst. Chevalier had opened two factories in California, bringing some manufacturing back into the country, even hiring Jimmy, trusting him to run one of his factories. But Chevalier had been murdered when he wouldn't sell out, when his technology threatened the preordained order of their world—Wendell Alden and his corporate cronies. It was all Jimmy could do not to punch the dash. *Fuck*, here he was after twenty years, back in another dying New England mill town, getting more and more pissed off every day, just like his stepfather.

He turned and headed for the graveyard, hoping it would calm him. During last November and early December, just before the snow closed it, he'd spent time there as if it were a drive-in bar. Wherever he'd lived he had searched out overlooks. Maybe it was from where he'd grown up. For a trailer park, Happy Acres had had quite the view—the monstrous paper mill with the mountains rising up steeply behind. He drove through the iron gate of the graveyard, slowed on the humped narrow road between massive maples reddening at their tips, the Impala threading carefully around muddy puddles to his special spot between the moss-sponged gravestones. Grabbing a rack, he stood a moment beside one of the stone markers. A foot taller than Jimmy, it was carved from granite to resemble a dead tree trunk, complete with an anchor and a twisted drape of rope, granite ferns bowing in from the real ground, and a stone tablet with a page edge blown back eternally by the wind. The tablet read:

> *Death's hand did drown this seaman so fair,*
> *Those dark depths of ocean have claimed his body thar,*
> *But may his soul find peace and take my hand,*
> *To hold it under this stone tree anchored to Thy land.*
> *—In memory, his loving wife.*

If someday Jimmy had a gravestone, that would be it.

He brushed a place dry on another rough granite surround and settled his back against the cold slab. He looked out over Scoggton, and beyond the many roofs, the hospital, church spires, the trees of the park, the octagon of points from the massive Catholic cathedral, the factory boiler-house smokestacks, he could just make out the Callahan house across the river in the distance. He opened another can of ale, hoping his pants would dry in the breeze. As he searched the sky, he decanted the beer onto the damp ground. A beer poured out for the dead. He hoped Chevalier sensed it, knew that he remembered, knew how he felt. Then he tabbed one for himself, his face to the sun.

He squinted at the bone-white stone of the cathedral as he drank. Doris had asked right off if he was Catholic, and then, without showing the least bit of interest in his answer, she'd launched into the restoration of the cathedral story—three years and a fortune, the one isolated stamp of civic pride and renewal in Scoggton. Apparently a woman had created a stir with a letter to the newspaper insisting the money be used to feed the hungry and house the homeless instead. But he knew the Church was more interested in architecture than in feeding poor people, and they did have lovely buildings. Doris had complained about the French Canadian Catholics in Scoggton. The Irish Cs had feuded with the French Cs for generations. Each went to different churches on opposing sides of the river. Doris hated the cathedral, which was the superior domain of the French and many times the size of the Irish church. Just to make her mad, he'd attended a service there. When he went, the main body of the building had been closed, open only in summer, and in the heated basement the priest had spent half his sermon complaining that putting Canadian money in the plate was cheating the church by the current exchange rate. Jimmy had no use for organized religion. He had his own.

On his third pounder he reached into his vest pocket for a Percocet. He broke the pill along the scribed line and chewed half, rinsed away the bitter taste though he never minded it, actually liked it somehow because of what it meant. Soon some of his aches and tensions would recede, at least contract to a manageable level. Luke sent the pills, fortunate to have a consistent supply from the VA hospital because of his Vietnam wounds. Jimmy considered it damn nice of him to share. Sometimes he mailed up plain Oxycodone, sometimes Percs, always with a false return address. Leaving the return blank was a flag. Headaches had bothered Jimmy ever since the crowbar opened his cranium ten years ago, and after Chevalier's death, they'd gotten that much worse. He could probably get his own script, but then he'd have to go to a doctor. Because of his afflictions as a kid, he hated doctors, so he self-medicated through Luke's generosity.

He felt rotten about Luke being stuck in Connecticut. Luke didn't complain—actually, Luke rarely spoke about himself—but someone had to run the recon down there and it couldn't be Jimmy. Wendell Alden lived in one of those gated communities, which made Luke's task harder. Jimmy drew his cell phone.

"Hey," he said.

"Hey, brother, what's up?"

"Not much, just sitting in the sun, waiting for Doctor P. We can't move?"

"I say no way. A's paranoid. The place is like a barracks."

"Fuck."

"Yeah."

"Okay then. F it is."

"Later, Hack."

And that was Luke. Luke would never be mistaken for an accountant biker. Jimmy'd known him for over a dozen years and still had no real knowledge of his past, his torments or his dreams. He wondered if it was because Luke was sixteen years his senior, but that probably had nothing to do with it. Maybe Luke felt the same way about him? He knew he didn't give up much either. Why should he?

He topped another pounder and looked over the graveyard. He'd read an article about the super wealthy freezing themselves submerged in nitrogen just in case science eventually found a way to revive them. Pickles in a barrel. They'd been doing it for years. Had they considered that they'd all be awakening at the same time? A herd of egocentric monsters, half of them bodiless, brought back into a culture that would have no use for them. Talk about the dawn of the living dead.

As he motored back down the hill, Luke's pronouncement whacked him. He'd have to spend the entire summer in this damn town waiting until Wendell Alden II, Mr. investment banker, decided to return to Florida for the season. Why couldn't the bastard be in West Palm Beach now, as he should have been? Jimmy had promised himself Wendell Alden would confess before he executed him. He wanted the man to know why, needed to see the realization in his eyes. It wouldn't change anything, but Chevalier deserved at least that. It wouldn't be difficult to get the confession if he had enough time—he knew that about the rich, they'd do anything to stay alive—but he needed the ten or fifteen minutes it would take to break Alden. Maybe less, but he couldn't rely on that. And there was something more. His death would send a message. The privileged had to learn they weren't immune, that they couldn't just order a great man dead and get away with it! He rubbed his temples, so enraged he grabbed another Doctor P out of his pocket and took such a pull at his can that beer soaked his chin and vest. And his pants had barely dried. He cursed, glaring at the pristine pulsing cobalt of the afternoon sky.

Jimmy stayed off the cops' normal flight paths. It was habit as much as anything; besides, he liked back streets. On an empty stretch of pot-holed puddled road along the abandoned textile factories and railroad tracks, he heard something and glanced in the rearview mirror. A red SUV loomed right behind him. He thought he recognized it vaguely from somewhere. The vehicle started honking, then nudged his bumper. It was with the bump that he guessed who it was, cursing himself for becoming so distracted that he'd begun making mistakes.
"Why now?" he muttered. Should he try and outrun them? Lousy timing for that. The Doctor P was mixing energetically with the ale and the combination hardly favored a car chase. Besides, attracting cops was one situation he must avoid. To prevent any further scrapes to the Impala, and using the blinker just to rile the shadowy faces behind the SUV's windshield, he pulled off onto the dirt and crept to a halt.

Jimmy hopped out and shot back to check the rear bumper for damage. The SUV's massive plastic prow had marked the chrome in two spots. It could probably be buffed out. At least no dents. He intentionally ignored the four guys exiting the SUV like storm troopers, all four doors wagging on their hinges. As the group got close, he turned, his arms loose at his sides, his back to the tailgate.

"Slag," he said. "You always drive around with an army?" The other three were red-faced Slag clones, the same team shirts and sneakers. They bulked around the original as he sauntered up beside Jimmy.

"Always the wise ass, aren't cha?" said Slag, folding his arms across his chest, bobbing on the balls of his shoes.

The others spread out so Jimmy was surrounded, two on each side of him, only his back protected by the car. He couldn't keep his eyes on all of them. A dangerous situation, particularly since it would be unwise to attack first.

Slag again: "Just thought we'd take this opportunity to welcome you officially to Scoggton. I've been checking on you, Bob. You live on Brackert hill with that crazy dwarf Callahan. You two must make a lovely couple. The tattooed totem pole and the ancient dwarf. Maybe you can get yourself a few more old dwarfs, though you're the ugliest fuckin' Snow White I ever seen." The group laughed; nobody on empty today, at least one of them sure to have leftover white smut in a nostril.

Slag was obviously baiting him, wanting him to fight.

"You got nothing to say, Bob? You were so talkative when you were coming on to Claire like a dog with its carrot out. What's wrong? Maybe you can only talk to girls?" He looked around for approval again. Got it. "Wanna know how we found ya? This piece of junk here"—he kicked in the rear quarter panel, forming a football-sized dent in the blue metal—"makes you real easy to find."

Enraged, Jimmy left the protection of the tailgate and faced Slag, but Slag backed quickly away. Jimmy immediately sensed his mistake: he'd been suckered. Attachments, even attachments to cars, are always trouble. He was attempting to rotate behind him when a dull blow struck the base of his skull. A spike of numbing pain and his legs began to waver. *Fuck*, nothing worse. Once he was on the ground, they'd use their expensive sneakers, hopefully not break too many ribs or damage something internally. The wet dirt and gravel rose up to meet him, the jolt of the fall distant and remote. He told himself to cover his head with his arms, attempt a fetal position. That was all he remembered.

Chapter Six

Ten minutes later, Jimmy came to. The sky pulsed strangely, an anemic slice of moon above the silent mills, Slag and crew gone. At first he didn't move, just concentrated on carefully filling his lungs with air. He was shivering uncontrollably, but at least his lungs seemed to be okay, no broken ribs after all. His left forearm, however, was another matter. He groaned with the stupidity of what had happened, rolled onto his side to vomit and felt slightly better afterwards. To be taken out so easily really irked him. Red-face, the sucker puncher, would of course get someone else to do his fighting. The setup had been so obvious. He really was growing careless hanging around Scoggton.

By the time Jimmy had leveraged himself onto the bench seat of the Impala, he knew his arm was broken. It reminded him of Chevalier with his gunshot wing, so at least that cheered him. Anything that compared him to Chevalier pleased him. But the situation was a mess because he couldn't go to the hospital. Too risky. Could he fix the broken arm himself? He didn't know a thing about setting a bone, but it couldn't be that complicated, could it? The bastards had kicked him everywhere, but he bet it was Slag who'd done his arm trying to get at his face. As he sat sprawled on the blue cloth, he reached into the paper sack with his good arm. They hadn't stolen his beer. He managed the can's tab with the one hand and the ale tasted wonderful, like a first hot meal after days in a boxcar. If only he had another P he could probably make it. He clamped the can between his legs and rummaged a few pockets, distinguished the familiar shape, swallowed the pill greedily. This was how Popeye must have felt sucking up the spinach. He finished the beer slowly, waiting for his dizziness to pass, then he caressed the car to life.

He steadied the Impala up Brackert hill, avoiding his reflection in the rearview mirror; no point in knowing what the damage was yet. He never thought he'd be so glad to see that turn onto True Court. She was waiting for him in the dim hall next to the lit acorn. "Robert, why are you walking funny? Are you drunk again?" She came closer. "My Lord, what happened to you? Did you have a wreck?"

"Fender's dented." At the memory of the kick he almost vomited again. He'd left the Impala under the porte cochere, which he knew she didn't like, but at the moment he didn't give a damn. Driving to the house had exhausted him.

"The car? Who cares about that old rusty thing." She looked him over. "The point is you're not all right. You're shivering. Good gracious, look at your head. You're bleeding profusely. Why are you holding your arm?" He couldn't respond. "Come into the kitchen." She spun around in her nervous way and shot off.

He didn't think he could make it up the stairs to his rooms, so he followed her, worried he might faint.

"Oh Lord," she said, examining him in the overhead fluorescent blaze as he slumped into a chair. "Robert, you really are hurt." She flicked the gas up under the kettle and wet a dishcloth with warm water from the tap. "I'll make you a good strong cup of hot tea."

That was bound to cure him. "Doris, you have any whiskey or brandy?" He'd stupidly left the beer in the Impala.

"I believe tea will be much better for you."

As the kettle began to hiss, she stood in front of him, gently wiping at the blood on the side of his head with the cloth. Even with him sitting, she was at his eye level. He saw real concern and tenderness in her face. It reminded him of his mother, the whole experience making him very uncomfortable.

"Now just sit still," she said. "What in God's name *did* happen to you?"

"Scoggton's Welcome Wagon."

"What are you talking about?"

"You know a guy named Slag? Big and burly with a salon tan, mullet hairdo"—Doris looked blankly through her glasses—"short on top, hangs long in back. He said he knows you."

"What's his last name? A bunch of those boys around here look like that."

"Drinks at the Den. Hangs around with Claire, long black hair and a slight limp—" He immediately felt disloyal describing her that way.

"Raymond Cloutier. That idiot! His father is even worse. Has the same name. How a man with no sense and the personality of a slug could end up owning half this town is just beyond me. He's nothing more than a common thug. His son ran into you?"

"Something like that."

"They all drive *much* too fast around here in those big cars. Let me see your arm."

He tried not to wince as she felt along it, but when she reached where the lump of bone protruded, he yelped. "Robert, this arm is definitely broken. And your head needs stitches; it's still bleeding. I'm afraid you don't need tea, you need a doctor immediately. I'll call Fred and have him take us to the hospital." Fred was her cousin the cabby. A wheedling and overly inquisitive guy with nervous eyes who sniffed constantly and must've considered bathing sacrilege, Jimmy had avoided him since the first dead-fish handshake. Doris used him for transportation, his malodorous taxi a place Jimmy refused to contemplate.

"Not going. Just need something to drink. Come on, don't you have *anything*?"

"You know how I feel about liquor."

"This is an emergency, no time for a temperance talk."

She scowled at him and went to the oak built-in. "One and then you're going to the hospital." She shuddered. "My Lord, I think I might need a drink too. All this ruckus and fuss is rather unsettling."

Doris removed a dusty bottle of Irish whiskey and poured two into juice glasses, half-filling them. She passed him one, then gulleted her three fingers as if it were cold tea. "Did you hit your arm and head on the wheel when he ran into you?"

"Wasn't driving."

"Who was driving then?"

"I was outside the car."

She stared at him. "You should learn to stay clear of moving vehicles. I'm always very cautious when I'm walking in town."

"Unavoidable."

"I still don't see how Cloutier came to run you over. It looks like you fell out of the car onto your head. It's all rather strange." She adjusted her glasses. "You should sue him. His father is loaded. Now I'm going to ring Fred."

He started to shake his head but it hurt too much. "Wait."

"Robert, don't be an absolute fool."

"Not going."

"You must."

"Can't. Believe me, not possible." He tried with his look to convince her. "Don't you know how to set an arm? It can't be that tough. Tape it to a broom handle or something. Whaddaya say?"

"I think those tattoos have leached into your blood stream."

"Let's have another pop." He held out his glass. If he kept her drinking she was bound to give in and do arm surgery.

After the second healthy pour, thrown back by Doris in the same professional fashion, she agreed to work on his arm, seemed to forget about Fred and the hospital. He heard her clamoring around on the back porch with her hatchet, whacking away at something, and she soon returned with two trimmed pieces of kindling and a roll of silver duct tape. She called it duck tape. "Oak," she said, holding up the stick like a baton. "A damn good wood." He wasn't sure he'd ever heard her swear. She sizzled off about a yard of tape and bound his arm tightly between the two sticks. "Robert? What made you color up your skin in this awful way?"

"To distract from my good looks." He attempted a grin.

"You know, you're sort of funny for such a gloomy person."

"This is good whiskey."

"My father's brand. When he died I found a couple full cases in the basement. He liked a glass now and then. It is pretty damn good though, isn't it?"

After the third glass, Doris wound down to a halt. She stared into his face, her eyes behind the glasses bleary with seriousness. "Robert, I've decided to go to bed. I'm feeling a mite dizzy, but I want to say something to you first. Stay away from those Cloutiers! They're no damn good. The son about ruined Claire Constantine, and she was such a nice girl, if a tad plain. She won some state spelling contest when she was sixteen, but when Cloutier got hold of her he dragged her into the muck. Now, I think I need to retire to my room. Good-night." And off she went, steady as a Pullman coach on rough track.

Jimmy managed to get to his feet, pulled the string on the overhead, and the kitchen shuttered into warm darkness. As if on cue, the ancient boiler thundered on and then settled to muted life below him; the chime of heating pipes and the impatience of steam would soon rise through the house. He was tempted to steal the rest of the bottle, but left it on the table. It had been her father's after all. Slowly and painfully—his muscles were seizing where bruised, and that was about everywhere—he ascended to his rooms.

The cats cried out when he opened his door. Poor fellows, he'd forgotten to feed them.

Chapter Seven

Jimmy awoke in the middle of the night and knew he'd been wrong. Doris had been right. His arm had expanded, the skin bulging around the duct tape and splints, throbbing from his fingers to his brain like a sparking short circuit. The rest of him didn't feel much better, a fever basting him in his own sweat.

Yellow was sleeping against Jimmy's head. Cats, he thought, they knew when you were hurt and attempted to soothe by smothering your eyes and nostrils in fur. Yellow started to purr and stretch, nudging Jimmy's wounded head with his club-ear, letting out one of his rooster-like cries. At least someone was glad he was alive. Jimmy managed to get his feet on the floor, got himself upright, and staggered through the dark into the bathroom. He flicked on the light with his good hand and glanced down at the bowl, praying for no red. He sighed: college boys, they always leave you to fight another day.

Right now what he needed was Doctor P. He turned on more lamps, but as much as he searched, wincing with every clumsy motion, the fever increasing his dizziness, he couldn't find any. Whenever Luke sent up a fresh lot, Jimmy played a game with himself, hiding the individual pills in different places all over the apartment. That way he'd have one hidden somewhere when he really needed it. "One," he muttered. "Come on, baby, just one goddamn pill."

His stomach began to lightning and thunder. And no wonder, he'd had nothing except P, beer, whiskey, and the light breakfast since yesterday. He'd read how early settlers utilized ale for over half their diet, but what he needed now was something besides ale. He knobbed on the electric burner, the fluorescent tube built into the old stove sputtering to brilliance. Cast-iron pan, pork loin from fridge, condiments. At least his hangover wasn't bad. Negotiable. He judged hangovers at three levels: negotiable, non-negotiable, and nuclear. Negotiable you could drink again that day. Non-negotiable you could still work but definitely not drink. Nuclear he hoped never to experience again.

The loin sizzled and snapped as he shook on some Worcestershire sauce. "Worcester sauce," his mom had called it, kneading it into hamburger meat with chopped onion. The cats skittered and nuzzled at his legs, but it was too early to feed them. He grilled a few heels of bread and tossed all on a plate, settled at his enameled table, trying to ignore how sick he felt.

But by halfway through the meal he knew something was seriously wrong that a sandwich wasn't going to fix. He had to head for the hospital, whether someone alerted the cops or not. The only thing that bolstered him was the possibility of more P.

He creaked down both flights of stairs and passed Doris's distant snores echoing from the hall. For a small woman, she could really churn out the decibels. Maybe she was having wonderful whiskey dreams. He hoped so. Spinster whiskey dreams, what would they be? Jesus, the damn fever must be percolating weird thoughts. Holding his throbbing arm, he exited the house and angled around the front of the Impala lit by the hanging porte-cochere bulb. He went that way so he wouldn't see Slag's dent. Inside the car he noticed the paper bag and considered a Ballantine pounder but knew he was too nauseated; the loin had landed like a dead pig. Although the pre-dawn air was near freezing, sweat dotted his forehead and upper lip. He wondered if he could make it. For once Jimmy navigated straight down the main thoroughfare, took the center bridge, and headed up the hill to the hospital. Not a soul was out now anyway.

As luck would have it, the only person in the empty waiting room was Claire Constantine. He almost turned and disappeared back out the automatic doors, but she'd spotted him, signaling with a raised arm. Jesus, he'd never felt uglier—like a glistening, unshaven, taped-up cadaver. And under fluorescent lights that would shield nothing. At least he'd brushed his teeth. Hadn't been easy getting the toothpaste on either. Flossing, however, had been out of the question. She by contrast was ravishing, her raven hair pulled back into a ponytail, her face even more beautiful than he remembered from the bar. As he drew closer with each step, his stomach knotted tighter, and although he was tempted to ignore her, magnets must have been hidden somewhere.

"Hey, Claire." He used his best cool, flicking his good hand at the wrist, trying to stand straight.

She examined him, and he cringed. "What the hell happened to you? You don't look so hot, you know that?"

"Run over by a Welcome Wagon."

"How's that?"

"Just a dumb joke. I fell out of a tree. What're you doing here?"

"A tree?"

He didn't answer.

"It's Brandon. He woke up with severe stomach cramps. I was worried it might be his appendix."

"Who?"

"My son."

"You have a *son*?"

"Would you prefer I didn't?"

Jimmy glanced over at the admittance desk, not knowing how to answer that. Of course he preferred she didn't. Never married and she has a fucking son? "Is he gonna be okay?"

"For tonight, yeah. It wasn't appendicitis."

"How old is he?"

"Fourteen."

"*Fourteen?*"

"Oh, now he's the wrong age?"

He felt too lousy to deal with all this. "It's not that. You just seem way too young to have a kid that old."

"Things happen."

"Look, sorry if I pissed you off."

"You're too smashed up to be sorry." Her lips parted and her perfect teeth laughed at him. "That must have been some tree. You better see the nurse. Did you do that to your arm? Duct tape?" She shook her head. "Bob, you're a strange one. You should at least remove the tape. The swelling might go down some."

"Didn't do it to myself."

"So who did then? Your girlfriend?"

"Doris Callahan. I rent from her."

"You let *her* work on your arm? She's been tweaked since her father bankrupted the family." Her expression retreated. "That's not fair. Her father was a decent guy. He just thought he was a lord of the manor and couldn't accept that times had changed."

"What happened to him?"

"She didn't tell you?"

He felt even dizzier. The tornado in his stomach was accelerating, heading right for him. His knees were beginning to falter; he needed to sit down but didn't want to appear weak in front of Claire.

"Maybe Doris should tell you," she said.

This slowed the conversation.

"Doris is okay," he said to break the silence.

"She's pretty weird. Now head for the nurse. Your lips are pale blue, and besides that purple bruise on your head you're white as birch. Very colorful, I admit, but you look like you're going to faint any second."

He swayed a little.

"Bob, I'm serious." She started to stand up as if to steady him.

"I don't faint." Suddenly he wasn't so sure. He turned and aimed at the nurse's desk, reaffirming for the hundredth time that Luke should have gotten him a different alias than Bob. Anything would be preferable to Bob. He hated being called Bob, especially by Claire. As he neared the desk he knew he was going to be sick. There was no way in hell he was going to allow Claire to witness this. He dashed past the nurse, vaguely hearing her call out, burst through some double doors, and lunged into a hallway. A trash can!

When Jimmy came to, splayed on the hard linoleum, the nurse was kneeling next to him, checking his vital signs. While unconscious, he'd been skinny dipping with Claire through azure surf and was reluctant to surface into the merciless glare of a hospital hallway. His body was so soaked in sweat he might as well have been swimming.

"A stretcher is coming," said the nurse. "Don't try to move."

"Bym-fin," he said, but it didn't sound much like "I'm fine." As they loaded him on the gurney, his one thought was that he had to get out of Scoggton before it killed him.

Chapter Eight

Hakken was released from the hospital that afternoon. His continued insistence that he was fine eventually worked although the doctor suggested more rest and the nurse told him he appeared quite ill. "Just my natural color," he said. "If you said I looked healthy, I'd be scared." Antibiotics had singed the edges of an infection, and he'd convinced the young doc that Tylenol 3 bugged his stomach, that only Percocet didn't. They'd given him brand name, heavenly blue, unlike the generic white Luke sent. That morning, they'd pumped him full of IV Demerol, added another row of stitches to his head, examined his bruises, and prepared him for surgery where a specialist set his arm. The removal of the duct tape had not been pleasant. Jimmy almost expected his tattoos to be missing in two-inch-wide swatches, the hair certainly was.

He limped out the front doors of the hospital into an icy March drizzle, sucked the chill air into his lungs. Even mill-town stench was preferable to antiseptic stuffiness. Two soggy parking tickets were under the Impala's wiper. He unlocked the car and flung them into the backseat. Now he reached into the paper bag and snaked out a pounder—snapped, sipped. It had been a long interval getting to that second rack of beer. Maybe it tasted better because of this? But everyone feels good when getting out of the hospital. His mood improved even more once he got the car rolling through town, the heater purring.

The young doctor—why must they always be so annoyingly rational and crisp?—had asked who had beaten him up and if he'd notified the police. Jimmy stuck to the tree story, saying he'd hit a lot of branches on the way down.

"What were you supposedly doing in the tree?" said the doc.

"Bird watching, what else?"

Claire had asked to visit, but he'd refused to see her as he was—groggy, wrapped in bandages, with his teeth unflossed and unbrushed, especially after throwing up. Usually he carried a toothbrush with him, but when he'd pulled up to the hospital, fuzzy with pain, he'd forgotten to get one of the half dozen brand-new spares out of the Impala's glove box. He promised himself that next time he saw her he'd be at his best. And what was that? And why would she want to see him? Or he, her? What would be the point of it? On top of everything else she had a kid. Not to mention that moron Slag, someone his feverish brain refused to think about. He'd deal with Slag later even if he couldn't figure out how at the moment.

But her face had kept floating at him from the ceiling of the ward. The eyebrows that seemed to race outward in surprise or perplexity that life was really like this, the dark vulnerable eyes above those incredible cheekbones, the skin glowing like burnished hardwood, the smile with that sexy gap between her two front teeth. He had thought of his own blanched almond of a face and moaned.
"Are you okay?" a nurse had called over.

Jimmy docked the Impala in the Callahan carriage barn and slid across the seat and out. Walked slowly up the drive with his beer and pills, preparing for Doris. She was waiting in the doorway.

"Well! There you are," she said. "You should have gotten me up. I would have telephoned Fred to drive you. Robert, that was plum foolish driving yourself. You might have crashed and killed yourself or hit someone else. Claire told me how sick you were. Didn't I tell you—"

"Claire?"

"—we needed to bring you in to the hospital? If you hadn't gotten me drunk on whiskey I never would have even considered attending your damaged arm. See, I told you liquor was evil."

"Claire?"

"Claire Constantine. We discussed her yesterday evening. She brought you some fruit."

"Fruit?"

"Yes, fresh fruit, Robert, which you are going to eat. It was very nice of her to bring it. Of course she feels terrible about that idiot Cloutier beating you up and feels responsible in some way. And you lied to me and insisted it was a car accident, embarrassed and unwilling to accept the truth. I *knew* it wasn't any car accident. Didn't I say so?"

"Claire knows about Cloutier beating me up?"

"Cloutier is bragging about it all over town apparently. Everyone knows. He's just like his father. A braggart and a savage." She paused to frown at him. "Frankly, Robert, I thought you looked a mite tougher than you are, but I suppose looks can be deceiving. No wonder you try to hide behind those ghastly tattoos. But if you ate better and drank less, perhaps you could learn to defend yourself."

Jimmy just shook his head and slid past her into the house. What a goddamn town!

"And Robert." He turned reluctantly. "I fed your cats. They

were putting up just an awful ruckus." He nodded thanks and started up the stairs, feeling as if a drain plug had been removed from his toe and his lifeblood was pouring out.

"One more thing."

He slowed.

"Why are you trying to grow mushrooms up there when they sell perfectly good ones at the store? I was going to throw that whole muck out; those mushrooms are all blue and strange looking anyway. I could tell Fred to pick you some up if you care for them so much, but I suppose it's your business if you want to save money that way." She snorted and darted off down the hall.

The fruit was on his kitchen table in a wicker basket. Apples, pears, oranges. They looked carefully chosen, beautifully ripe, as unblemished as her skin. He didn't think he'd ever be able to peel or bite into one. A note was attached. *Bob, I'm so sorry about all this, Claire.* But Jimmy wasn't sorry. She'd added her phone number. That had to be a good sign.

Chapter Nine

A last cold snap gripped Scoggton the following week. The snow fell like Hakken's grandest frozen wet dream of Claire. He shoveled with one arm, pushing the snow around awkwardly, the hardened filthy tongues of leftover slush neatly hidden in a tarp of white. He was relieved the Impala was under the cedar-shakes of the carriage barn although some snow had blown past the doorless front, mounding around the rear tires.

Doris fired the kitchen stove with oak, and the steam pipes clanked at three-hour intervals. Jimmy settled in with her around the kitchen table; she had insisted on feeding him, saying it was too difficult for him to prepare meals with only one arm. She had the paper open, dividing her attention between his breakfast progress and the news. She insisting on highlighting worthy items out loud.

"There was another car accident yesterday morning on Route Sixteen. That black ice again. The sheriffs went out and flagged the spot after the first crash, but a second vehicle drove plum round the sheriff and slid off in the same spot, plowed smack bang into the first car. It was probably that Dolly Kimball." She laughed madly at her own joke, slapping her thigh. "But I'm sure the police took her license away for running down all those poor innocent shoppers in the IGA."

He was surprised that by now she didn't have Dolly Kimball in jail on multiple manslaughter charges. He struggled with a second biscuit. No wonder she'd never landed a husband. How could anyone take normal store-bought ingredients and turn them into this? After suffering the first of her meals, a mere breakfast, he'd coldly rejected her offer to cook for him. Her lips had tightened and she'd snapped, "As you wish!" and bolted off. She wouldn't speak to him for the rest of the day. The next morning he'd knocked on the kitchen door, told her he'd changed his mind and would join her for supper.

And so wished he hadn't. Doris was obsessed with fixing him mushrooms. First off, he hated the taste of mushrooms and would never have eaten the things unless they were psychoactive; and secondly, she managed atrocities with the innocent little fungus that could have toppled empires; and third, there was nothing he could say to convince her otherwise. Vegetables in general weren't a favorite, but lima beans, Brussels sprouts, okra, squash, eggplant, and mushrooms were the worst in his opinion. He just prayed she didn't start telling Fred about Robert's ugly mushroom garden on the third floor. It wouldn't take much for Nosy to figure it out. Jimmy told her he'd stopped cultivating for now because she was fulfilling *all* his mushroom requirements, and as a precaution had thrown out the evidence. He hinted that he was even losing his taste for mushrooms, that too much of a good thing was bad, which only fired her scowl. She was set on feeding him mushrooms and that was that. The woman was way stubborn.

Her other specialty was New England boiled dinner. Turnips, potatoes, carrots and corned beef metamorphosized into a uniform mush only vaguely distinguishable by color and only to a discerning eye. The salt content would have turned a small pond brackish. *And*, served along side, her famous one-box biscuits akin to newly batched plumber's putty. Doris was very proud of her biscuits. This was her signature dish and she passed them out with abandon. They landed on the plate with a damp thud. He had to get the cast off soon, even if it jeopardized his arm.

Jimmy sat in his garret, looked out the window at the melting white roofs, and considered the past week. He was losing his edge, his discipline, his focus; that was all too obvious. He had to admit that he wanted to call Claire although getting involved with anyone in this town was against his code and the task at hand. But the idleness and depression of the winter had driven him slightly nuts, and the possibility of female companionship was blindingly tempting. But look at the mess his little bit of wandering into the town—just a few beers in a bar for Chrissake—had already generated, and besides, she had a kid, not to mention that moron Slag hanging around. Why would she have anything to do with that bastard? Not a good sign. These factors added up hugely and helped cool his ardor, but not enough. What was the kid's name? Melvin, Kevin, something like that. Could it be Slag's kid? That would make things even worse, though regardless of the father, he didn't want anything to do with a kid. Basically he couldn't stand kids. It was odd how someone could both draw and repel you, but he supposed that like magnets, people had two poles. You just had to locate the right end.

After he'd gotten out of the hospital, he'd decided to postpone calling her until he looked a little better. Although he intended only to thank her for the fruit, what if she asked to get together? He wanted to be presentable. And not with his head mottled in Technicolor bruises and Frankenstein stitches. On top of everything else, a nasty pimple had ballooned on the tip of his nose. He'd been tempted to hide it under a

Band-Aid, but it was hardly a place you could cut yourself shaving. Even Doris, squinting through her glasses, had said, "My lord, Robert, what happened to your nose? I hope it wasn't my cooking." Jimmy had just groaned and choked down another forkful of mushrooms. Today his face had finally found some sort of equilibrium. Telling himself he shouldn't, he picked up his cell and dialed, annoyed that he could suddenly feel his heart thumping.

"Claire? It's J—Bob."

"Jumbo?"

"Naw, just Bob, Bob Gray." Over the phone he heard noise in the background.

"Oh hey, Bob. Can I call you back?"

"Sure."

"Later then."

After the click he closed his eyes. It was ridiculously obvious that she didn't care a rat's ass about him, and here he'd been thinking about her constantly for no reason, imagining all kinds of stupid things. What a fool he was. He felt like pounding something. Instead he moved to his computer and brought up *My Life*. Maybe it would take his mind off Claire. Lately, while he waited to heal, he'd been working on his novel constantly. What else was there to do?

Chapter 4

I'm leaning up against an abandoned railroad station, the sun on my face, looking west. The Great Plains are flat, different than I'm used to, the railroad tracks are two straight lines touching at the horizon. I've never been this far west before and everything seems different. The sky is bigger and bluer with giant clouds, the cornfields smell sweeter, as does the wind that I imagine travels all the way from the snow on top of the Rocky Mountains. A diesel horn is blowing in the distance. I've never hopped a train before, but I'm going to try now.

He stopped reading. He hated it. This writing stuff was a lot more difficult than he'd figured. How was the reader supposed to know how he'd felt from that? Or care? That he'd stood on the weedy cement slip of the station, the cool early-autumn wind fragrant from the fields, the light crystalline, the hot sun on his face, that much was true; but how about his hope that the sun might burn up some of his blemishes after he'd washed his face from his canteen, or how his body and mind were humming with excitement because he was finally going to hop his first freight and ride it through the West—*The West*—of which he'd only dreamed, and then the headlight approaching, the wailing of the diesel horn same as the shout in his throat, the train drawing closer, the rumble intensifying, his mind at a perfect junction of poetry and reality, freedom and pure joy mounting to a pitch until he thought he might explode. And then the engineer waving, and he, uncertain, waving back, and then the boxcars, some empty, flooding past in a rust-colored wall, and he leapt from the station platform, sprinting madly beside the train along the uneven gravel roadbed, slinging his pack onboard an empty boxcar, his palms on the rough wood floor—he'd practiced so many times in freight yards, but now, he's doing it for real, like the first time you ease your penis into a woman and you can't believe it's actually happening, which at sixteen hadn't, so this would have to do—and he's in, lying on his back, his heart and lungs hammering with the cadence of the wheels under him, then he's sitting up and he's riding a freight train. He, Jimmy Hakken, was riding a freight headed to the great West! That the train stopped after about a mile and backed up, what did that matter?

How could he write all that? Certainly not by describing some wind gliding down an imaginary mountain. He felt like chucking the computer through a window.

His phone chimed.

"Yeah?"

"Bob?"

"Yeah."

"Sorry I cut you off before. I couldn't talk right then."

"Surrounded?"

She laughed, and he loved the sound of it.

"Hey, thanks for the fruit. It was very nice fruit. Great fruit, actually. The best."

"No problem."

A pause, Jimmy wondering what to say next. Analyzing each of her words to find out what she felt about him, if anything. And how did she get his number? She must have caller ID.

"I'm still sorry about what happened," she said. "You okay now?"

"Fine."

"Bob?" And she started to giggle.

"Why are you laughing?" he asked, sensing a pothole.

"Sorry." Another giggle. "Really."

"What's funny?"

"Bob."

"That's me, onboard."

"No, I mean, it's the name Bob. When I was a kid our dog was called Bob. He was part basset hound and had this huge belly and these big droopy ears that dragged on the ground. 'Basset Bob,' my dad called him. I'd laugh every time Bob walked into the room. He'd sit in front of you and make this mournful baying sound. Telling him to shut up just made him do it more. He was a really, really dumb dog."

"Great."

"Are you upset?"

"Maybe you should call me something else."

"Like what?"

"How 'bout Jimmy?" *Shit*, he thought, what the hell was wrong with him?

"Why Jimmy?"

"Just like the name. To be honest, never liked Bob so much."

"Remember I told you you didn't seem like a Bob?"

"The night you thought I was a narc."

"Listen, Jimmy . . . you know, it does sound better. Listen, let me try and make it up to you. Why don't you let me cook you dinner?"

"Mushrooms?" he mumbled.

"What?"

"Nothing. Why don't you let me take you out instead?"

"You want to?"

"Any place you wanna go."

"But I feel like I owe you a favor, you know, 'cause of what happened. He never would of come after you if I hadn't come over to talk."

"You don't owe me nothing. There a nice place in town?"

"The Broadway is pretty nice. You mean for a fancy dinner?"

"Sounds great. When and what time?"

"I'll have to see what's up with Brandon, but how's tonight, or is that too soon?"

"Great."

"Okay, I'll ring you back and let you know."

"Cool," he said and clicked off his phone. *Cool?* He never said cool.

Chapter Ten

The Broadway Restaurant, lost among all the abandoned storefronts of Acadia Ave, was two round-edged windows that had long been closed off to the street, the black tile facade surrounding them chinked and missing in places, the heavy oak door in-between bisected by a worn brass bar that whispered push. Only the elaborate neon sign—half the tubes broken, all of them dark—jutting out above the doorway was remarkable, so the Broadway was easy to miss. Nevertheless, Jimmy was annoyed he hadn't noticed the place on his many drives past. Although it may have appeared forlorn from the outside, inside was another matter.

Jimmy and Claire waited by a glass-topped cigar counter and an ornate antique register. The narrow dimly lit room was bordered by booths on each side, white tablecloths individually illuminated by shaded sconces, a bar at the back shimmering in colored light. After a moment, a gold apparition greeted them in a hushed voice. "Two? For dinner?" From her bun of hair to her earrings, glasses, long dress, nylons and shoes, even to her skin and expression, everything was a monochrome of gold. She looked like someone in a wax museum. Claire nodded, and a slim wrinkled hand with gold bracelets and gold fingernails picked up two enormous burgundy-clad menus.

As the hostess led them into the restaurant, he watched Claire in her plaid skirt. Her limp was a slight wobble to the right with each step, her calf muscle under the navy blue stocking like a young girl's on that side. She seemed unselfconscious about it, but who knew? He wanted to remove her plain brown leather shoe and fondle the misshapen foot with its inward twist, massage it carefully in his hands. Was this how it was? With the right woman you just liked everything about her.

Settled in a booth, he felt a sudden surge of emotion, and it took him a second to identify what the sensation was because it had been dormant so long. He was ridiculously happy and shook his head to clear the feeling.

"What is it?" said Claire.

He didn't know how to answer so he said, "This place."

"You don't like it?"

"Fuck."

"What?"

"Love it." He glanced around. "It's a fucking time warp. I don't even feel right swearing, like it's a church or a temple or something in here."

"Slag hates the Broadway. He calls it the Formaldehyde. He'll never come here, and I mean never. You really like it?"

"Are you kidding? It's the best." Had she told him that on purpose, so he wouldn't worry Slag might show up?

"Not many people eat here though. I don't know how they stay open."

"Rent must be cheap."

"It's been in her family for generations. She probably owns the building. But I can't imagine they can last much longer. But maybe Phyllis doesn't need the money."

"The gold one?"

"Even her Cadillac is gold."

"How's the food?"

She frowned. "You'll see. Nice jacket by the way."

Was she teasing him? He rubbed his bicep through the cloth. One cuff covered about two-thirds of his tattoos, the other was bunched around his cast. Doris insisted he wear it. She'd steamed and aired it for him, but it still reeked of mothballs, and it had been tedious inching the sleeve past his cast. He should've dumped it but didn't want to disrespect Doris after all her efforts. "It was old man Callahan's. Lucky the style was loose back then."

"It's getting warmer outside, so now you're wearing a coat?"

"Can you smell it?"

"Just barely." She rolled her eyes.

"Doris seems to like you since you brought the fruit."

"I shouldn't have called her tweaked, though she really screwed up your arm."

"My fault. I got her drunk."

"You did?"

"Had to. She wouldn't have done it otherwise."

Jimmy noticed something emerging from the shadows. The guy arrived at their booth, a skeleton dressed in a white shirt and bow tie, his hands behind his back. On such an old guy, Jimmy expected a stain somewhere, but there were none. Henry's milky eyes appraised him as well. "Perhaps a cocktail before dinner?" he asked them in a harsh whisper, as if his vocal chords had been sandpapered.

"You want anything, Claire?" Jimmy said.

"My usual, Henry."

"Very well. Anything for you, sir?"

"You got any beer?"

"What is your preferred brand? Perhaps we stock it."

Jimmy told him. No acknowledgment.

"Would either of you care for a glass of water?"

"Who needs water when there's beer?" said Jimmy.

Henry didn't blink. "Very good, sir. Miss?"

"Maybe later."

Henry nodded and shuffled off.

"Place can't be real," he said. "It's like you set this up for me, like I'm in a dream."

She smiled, and he glanced down. The attraction of her face simply overwhelmed him.

"You're letting your hair grow," she said.

"It wasn't going to be easy shaving over them stitches."

She leaned forward. "My God, if you aren't a dirty blonde. I wouldn't have suspected it with those reddish sideburns."

"Finnish blood. Or maybe the Irish on my mom's side." He opened the menu and hid.

It was three pages of carefully described appetizers, entrees, and cocktails. He realized whoever had written the damn menu wrote better than he did. Actually, it was better written than a lot of stuff he'd been reading lately. One item caught his eye. He couldn't believe it. There could be no doubt about his order. He just prayed they still served it.

"You know what you're gonna get?" he said.

"I always take the trout with slivered almonds. Jimmy?" He set down the menu, her face springing at him anew. "God it's a relief calling you that. No one's signed your cast." She reached to touch it. "I still feel really bad that Slag had to beat you up."

"*Had* to beat me up?"

"He said you attacked him, and he was forced to hurt you."

"Forced to hurt me?"

"Said you accosted him on the road and made him pull over."

"You believed that?"

She shook her head. "I know what he's like now. What gets me is you look like you'd be a lot tougher. That night in the Den I took you as someone who could really handle himself, even against Slag."

"You too, huh?" Here he was wanted in California for almost killing someone, the guy was a vegetable they had to feed through a tube, and *this* was what the only two women he knew in Scoggton thought of him.

"What do you mean?" she said.

Henry set down a dark mixed drink with a swizzle stick in the shape of a pikestaff and a bottle of beer with a glass ringing on top. The Ballantine's label looked different, but it was Ballantine's. Jimmy couldn't believe they carried it. Henry took a long church key from his back pocket and opened the ale. With a shaky hand he poured a splash into the glass, managing not to spill too much on the tablecloth. Off he went.

"Jimmy, what did you mean? 'You too.'"

"Doris also thinks I'm a wimp."

"I didn't say that."

"Tell you what, forget it. Here's a toast. To you. By far the best thing in Scoggton." He almost added: "If not the world," since the best thing in Scoggton wasn't much as far as he was concerned. He picked up the bottle, touched her glass, and they drank. He almost spit out the beer.

"What's wrong?" she said. "You changed your mind about me already?"

"This." He pointed. "I thought the label looked different. Stuff must be ten years old."

"So?"

"Beer is like bread, it goes bad."

"Rotten?"

He nodded.

"You're really strange, you know that?" she said.

First a wimp, now strange. "I'll get something else."

"See that button under the sconce? That'll bring Henry."

"You gotta be kidding me." He pressed. Heard nothing. "That works?"

"You don't trust much, do you?" She nudged the bottle cap along the tablecloth, then picked it up. "Hey, there's something printed in here." She handed it to him. "Looks like a puzzle."

After a long moment, he handed it back, annoyed that he couldn't solve the thing, something to do with a playing card and an animal's ass. "So what."

She examined it. "I think it means, 'No place to go but up.' The ace of hearts forming *place* with the *P* and then the cow's butt in the air."

She was probably right, and he grunted.

Henry appeared. "Sir?"

"You got any dusty bottles of whiskey back there?"

"Sir?"

"You know, stuff that maybe nobody has ordered in a long time.

All dusty, special stuff, expensive." Did Jimmy notice a twitch of a smile? He was beginning to like this old guy. Man had his own style and stayed with it, couldn't be ruffled.

"I believe the Haig and Haig might be what you're looking for, sir. It's a Scots whisky, old."

"Bingo."

"Bingo, sir?"

"Glass of that, on ice, with a twist."

"Very good. Any thoughts on what you might like for dinner?"

Claire ordered her fish. Jimmy held the menu up and pointed. "You still have this?"

"Oh, definitely. Excellent choice, sir."

"And another one of these," she said, rattling the ice in her glass. Henry took Claire's empty, leaving the beer. Jimmy hated to tell him it was undrinkable. The bottle was probably collectible though.

"What did you get?" she said.

"Surprise."

"You're one big mystery, aren't you?"

"What do you mean?"

"Well, you don't share much about yourself. I really don't know anything about you."

Here it comes, he thought. He looked for Henry in the shadows, and spotted him in the bar's tinted light, decanting a cocktail. Jesus, a guy that old still working, shaky as hell but doing all right. And the man had style. The bus boy and another waiter, younger, were discussing something back there. Two other couples had wandered in, and the gold one had shown them seats. Both groups sat on the other side of the narrow room, the center empty, a row of two-person booths with small Greek columns extending to the fancy tin ceiling. He faced Claire again.

"You still working in the frame shop?"

"How'd you know that?"

"Doris."

"For a city this size, it's like a small town. Everyone grew up here, no new blood."

"Then I arrive, attacking all the best citizens and getting beat up."

She gave him a look, straightened the cuff of her shirt though it had looked perfect to him. "A few years ago, two guys came to Scoggton and opened a really nice antique shop. I was even thinking of working for them. They'd asked me. You know what happened?"

He shook his head.

"Somebody threw them off the railroad bridge. Into the falls."

"Murdered them?"

She nodded.

"Why?"

"Probably 'cause they were gay." She was watching him. "The cops never found out who did it. Bungled the investigation on purpose. Then some state newspapers got all riled up about it and the FBI was called in, but by then it was too late. Everybody sticks together against outsiders here, no matter what. The cops never do anything in this town except give traffic tickets, unless they don't know you. One cop was just busted for selling steroids to high school kids, but they probably wanted him off the force for some other reason."

"But you stay here."

"My dad's around, my girlfriends, and Brandon has his friends. Or his one friend. He's not very popular."

"Not?" He didn't want to discuss her kid; he wanted to ignore the fact that he even existed.

"Brandon's never been healthy. He has severe allergies and his immune system doesn't function normally, so he's stayed home a lot from school and doesn't know how to mix with other kids. He's not very good at sports either, and in this town that's a big deal. He hated gym class so much. It took a while, but at least I was able to have him excused from going. Not easy but I managed it. He's smart though. *Real* smart. But lately all he wants to do is play pool, but I don't like him hanging around the poolrooms. It's dangerous, but he loves it so much I can't bear to take that away from him too. He wants me to buy him a pool table, like I could afford one. Are you a pool player?"

"Tried it. Wasn't much."

Henry whispered in and dropped off their two cocktails, only slightly wetting the cloth. They sipped, the peaty burn of the Scotch filling Jimmy's mouth like a young kiss. Once again he was reminded why he couldn't keep bottles of this stuff around.

"So, Jimmy, what do you do?" she said.

"Besides get beaten up?"

"You should get over that."

"You asked me before."

"What?"

"In the Den? After you decided I wasn't a narc?"

"I guess I remember vaguely. I was pretty high that night. So, you ever going to tell me, Jimmy Bob?"

He sipped his Scotch, looked into her eyes, which did all those things lovely female eyes can do— times four months of winter alone in a turret. "I'm writing a book," he said, surprised how it just popped out.

But what was he going to tell her? That he was holed up in Scoggton waiting to avenge a murder? That he was about to execute one of the richest most powerful men in America. Somehow he didn't think that would be appropriate on their first date.

"So what's it about?" She sounded skeptical.

"My novel?"

She nodded.

"My life."

"You have a title?"

"*My Life*." He waited. "Why are you laughing?"

"I just wouldn't have taken you for a writer, Jimmy, that's all. Have you published anything?"

"Naw. Just starting out. Not so easy as I thought."

"That's what I've heard. You going to let anyone read it?"

He shrugged.

"Can I? Maybe I could help you with it."

"Not ready yet. I'm only up to chapter four and it sucks."

"Have you taken any writing classes?"

"Me? You kidding? I quit high school at sixteen."

"There's this writers' group that meets at the library. Maybe you should join?"

"What is it?"

"What do you mean?"

"Whadda they do there?"

She sipped before answering. "Four or five writers get together every week and read their work to each other, then critique it."

"Critique it?"

"You know, say how they feel about the writing, what it might need to make it better."

"You in it?"

"I usually show up, though I only critique, I don't read anymore." She glanced away for an instant. "They have one published author in the group, Eliot Barclay, a novelist. He's very well respected and reviewed. I've done some copyediting for him."

"Copyediting?"

"Yeah."

"What's *copyediting*?"

"I read through his manuscript and look for mistakes. Kinda like what I just offered to do for you. I take in copyediting from a New York publisher as well. Helps pay the bills, and it's something you can do at home, which is nice."

Jimmy took a long pull, the ice tumbling to his lip.

There was the squeak of a dinner cart, and Henry arrived with their meals. Claire's fish was served on a big plate, with a mattress of rice and a nest of split green beans. Jimmy's meal was another matter. He'd ordered a shish kabob. What intrigued him was that it came on a sword. *Served by our waitstaff, flaming on a sword*, the menu read. The meat was skewered on a steel rod, one end approximating a gilded hilt. The sword rested on a special metal plate with a bracket to elevate the grip, the entire unit set in a recessed wooden board with handles at each side. The setup must have been manufactured during the forties or fifties.

Henry glanced at Jimmy, then back at the bob. "It has been some time since this particular dinner was ordered, sir." He proceeded to douse the grilled lamb liberally in a clear fluid from a squeeze bottle, his trembling hand sending the liquid everywhere. He set the bottle down on the cart and extracted a battered Zippo from his pocket.

A click, a flick, a flame.

Henry moved the jiggling lighter toward the bob and with a *whoosh* everything ignited. Bright blue and yellow flames danced. And it wasn't a waltz, more of a jitterbug.

"Good Lord," said Claire. She was right—it was burning rather energetically.

Jimmy was transfixed; his whole life he'd wanted to eat something flamed on a sword.

Henry, his face even more skeletal illuminated from underneath, picked up the board by the handles to transfer it in front of Jimmy. The flames were further excited by his quivering hands, the burning sauce sloshing like a pond in an approaching storm. When the meal was mere inches from its destination, Henry yelped and dropped one side, then the other. He leapt back, moving well for his age, as the blazing liquid ran onto the tablecloth.

"Shit," said Henry.

"Oh my God," said Claire, sliding quickly toward the wall.

There was a hot pause.

Jimmy grabbed the beer bottle and splashed it into the rising flames. The ale quelled some of it, his napkin choked out the rest. When he removed the large napkin, like a magician at the completion of a trick, his bob was a charred beer-soaked ruin, smoking feebly, reeking of dead ale and burnt meat. A trickle of liquid wandered to the edge of the table cloth. He stuck the wet napkin there as a dam, looked up. "Henry, you okay, buddy?"

"I'm so sorry, sir. My hands are not what they used to be. They seem to have a life of their own."

"It's really lucky you didn't drink that beer," said Claire. "Henry, is your hand okay?"

"Nothing worth mentioning, miss."

The other diners were bright-eyed. The bus boy and the other waiter advanced cautiously. Phyllis bore down on the smoldering table like an irate general.

"Henry, good God, what have you done now?" she said. "What a horrible mess!" And in a shrill whisper, supposedly only to him, "This will have to come out of your paycheck."

"Phyllis, I'm sorry." And he looked sorry, his head and hands hanging, the fingers continuing to tremble.

"This is simply *too* much. You know what this means. I've warned you." She rotated to address Jimmy and Claire. "I do apologize. This is the last time something like this will happen." She glared at Henry again.

Everyone seemed at a loss.

"Hey," said Jimmy, a lot louder than he intended. All three of them, along with the busboy and the other waiter, stared at him. "I'd like another one of these flaming things." He extracted his roll, thinking, you would too if you'd been eating Doris Callahan's signature dishes for weeks. "I'd like to pay for this, and also buy everyone in the house a drink. I think we need another table though." He stood. "Claire." He gestured with his hand. As they moved from the booth he passed a Ben into Phyllis's hand. With her gold obsession, he figured she never missed a trick when it came to money. She noted the size of the bill and smiled.

"Doug," she said to the busboy. "Get this cleaned up." She turned to Jimmy. "I'll tell the chef to bring two fresh meals. And you'll need another waiter."

"Ma'am," said Jimmy, and she stopped, attentive. "I don't think I ever had a waiter I liked more than Henry."

She raised her eyebrows.

"And don't forget those drinks. Everyone gets thirsty after a fire."

Soon Jimmy and Claire were repositioned at a fresh booth, finishing the new cocktails. Claire was looking at him differently. "Aren't you full of surprises."

"What do you mean?"

"I didn't think you had it in you."

Jesus, here he'd run a crew of over a dozen workers for Chevalier, and she didn't think he could handle a small table fire. He couldn't respond; her impression of him kept revealing itself as worse and worse.

"Sorry. I don't mean to hurt your feelings. I was just impressed, that's all. It was so kind and considerate what you did."

"Kind?" What was kind about putting out a fire?

"You probably saved Henry's job."

He shrugged, embarrassed. "Want another pop?" He was beginning to realize it was the best Scotch he'd ever drunk.

She nodded. "I'm being too honest. One of my problems. Everything just jumps out."

"I like that about you." He spotted Henry, attentive in the shadows. He held up two fingers.

"You do?"

"Yeah."

"Can I write on your cast then?"

"What do you think?"

"Stick it out here." She rummaged in her purse, small and plaid, and came up with an eyebrow pencil. She looked at the ceiling, tapping the pencil between her teeth.

Henry slid them cocktails, not spilling a drop. "These are on me, sir," he said quietly, and was gone.

Jimmy lifted his. She set down the pencil and lifted hers. "This one's to you," she said. "You're a very interesting guy, Jimmy."

They drank.

Chapter Eleven

That night Jimmy couldn't sleep. There was no blaming it on the whiskey. Or the inexplicably tough lamb of his shish kabob, which he'd guessed was more than likely pork. The reason he couldn't sleep was the gut sense that he was fucking up. He shouldn't be seeing Claire. And knowing that, what was he doing? He had the Alden thing to get done. He'd given his oath, and nothing, nothing was more important.

But was going out to eat with her that big a deal? The long summer stretched in front of him—nothing to do but read, drink, jack off, and work on his stupid novel. The endless waiting was driving him nuts. He wasn't used to inactivity. Maybe he could convince Luke to move on Alden sooner? Take the bastard out in Connecticut, the hell with the security problems. But he knew that would jeopardize everything. The possibility that he wouldn't make it had always been there, but he still wanted to minimize the risk, give himself at least half a chance.

Yellow stretched and nuzzled with his damaged ear, his purr chugging like a diesel locomotive idling in a freight yard. Sometimes Jimmy couldn't believe he'd actually ridden freights. As he lay there, the dark room cozy with the steam heat ticking, a siren passing over Scoggton's center bridge, he remembered how it had been. That vastness of land. He'd never imagined the country could be so huge and so barren. He closed his eyes and saw the wheat fields of Minnesota, the burnt fields' black stripes against the blazing yellow of the ripe grain. And the wind. He heard the wind banging the boxcar door, felt the car sway. And the resonant silence between the blusters of wind, the freight waiting on a siding for the passage of a faster through-train, a hot-shot. He saw the black grid of the telephone poles that paralleled the rail bed and collected at the horizon. The immense blue sky stretching like a clear sound over the earth, a few thin clouds like passing whispers. He'd never felt so alone. Not lonely, just small and alone—his mom in the White Mountains probably worrying about him, his blood father supposedly on the West Coast, and Jimmy in-between. He'd been so excited by his own courage, by the image of himself in that boxcar in the middle of nowhere. He was afraid too, but the feeling that he was really doing something, taking control of his life, eclipsed everything else.

James Hakken? Who was his father? Hakken. All he really had was a name. Hakken. Like *tomato* everyone pronounced it differently. Hakken. It was like chopping something up. And wasn't that part of who he'd become? Someone willing to kill. He wrenched off the covers, cats leaping, then staring at him, eyes cautious. He went to his turret and looked out over the dark town. Maybe a beer? No, he was drinking too much. Instead he went into the tiny bathroom, brushed and flossed, brushed again. Then he moved to his computer and opened his book.

One afternoon, a harsh wind is blowing across the plains, the boxcar door banging, the freight waiting on a siding. Tumbleweed rolls by, a grain elevator wavers in the distance.

Jimmy loved the *wavers* because that's just how it had looked, as if the sunlight were a thin liquid, the flat horizon a mirage lake.

I smoke my corncob pipe in the doorway, the smoke whipping out of the pipe's bowl. Way up the line, along the gravel roadbed, I see someone walking toward me. As he gets closer, I see he's carrying a battered suitcase and a plastic jug. He wears an orange wool hat, a "tuque" we call them in New Hampshire. His busted up cowboy boots are outside his pants, and his padded nylon vest has holes, his stubble white. I've never seen a hobo clean-shaved and never with a beard.

Jimmy still didn't understand how they'd managed it. It wasn't as if they had those electric stubble razors that became so popular from the Miami TV show.

He slows for a moment when he sees me, then stops under me as I stand there.

"Got any smoke?" he says.

I nod. Every hobo I meet wants tobacco, but for it, I learn things.

"Mind if I come up?" he says.

If he hadn't asked, and he tried to get in, I could've kicked him in the head. That's hobo code. Your boxcar is your home. He hands me the suitcase and jug. The car rides so high I got to help him up. His hand is like a piece of bark.

"Thanks, son. I was riding forward a few cars backa the units, the exhaust was bugging me. Where you headed?"

"West," I say.

"Me, too." This is obvious stuff, but all part of polite hobo code. Hobos are different than bums and tramps. A few days later I watched two men almost kill each other fighting over who was a hobo and who was a bum. Class systems are everywhere.

I get out some pipe tobacco from my pack and offer it to him. He grins with no teeth.

"You don't have a pipe?" I ask him. "Or papers?" I get him my cigarette papers. There is no way I want that mouth on one of my pipes. He makes up a smoke. Guy doesn't even have a match. Once it's lit, he puffs the thing with great pleasure. Hobos love booze and smokes. He works it down until his fingers must be burnt. But maybe his bark don't burn.

Jimmy decided that last line was stupid though it had seemed funny when he first wrote it. He highlighted and deleted it.

He works it down until his fingers must be burnt. "Gettin' cold," he says. And it is. We're just under the Canadian border.

We hear a diesel horn and I look out the door at the approaching headlight of the highball. The hobo tugs on my sleeve. "Stand back, son." I do just as the other train roars by. After it passes he turns to me. "You can get sucked right out the door if yer not careful. Seen a man die that way."

In a few minutes the hump comes down at us, and we brace ourselves for the jolt. A long freight starting up has a wicked hump as the slack gets pulled out of the couplers. Getting ready for it becomes second nature after a while, once you've been knocked on your ass a few times.

Jimmy stopped reading. These pages sounded a little better to him, but it was so difficult to tell. Maybe he should join that writers' group Claire had suggested? And then his mind jolted to Alden again. The guy was like a cancer.

He opened his e-mail. Went through deleting the spam. Penis size and credit, was that all anybody cared about? Again Lillian's Botschaft tempted him, but he figured it would be some half-assed pay site, just in German. Nothing from Luke, so Jimmy wrote:

Hey L—Any new news from C? Any chance for an earlier move? Sorry I been out of touch. Broken arm, which would probably hold us till this damn cast comes off. It sucks up here. Snowed a week ago and I mean snowed. Did you get the scratch I sent? Thanks for the P shipment, as always, they come in handy. Best—J

Usually he didn't write Luke so much silly stuff. Luke would think he was weakening. And wasn't he? Letting Slag set him up like that. He flushed at the thought, but sent the e-mail anyway and just sat staring at the screen.

When he'd gotten the job at BioTel, after the first three months he'd asked Chevalier to hire Luke. The factory needed more security and muscle, and no one was better than Luke. Chevalier hadn't allowed guns, but he also didn't have any prejudice about what Luke and Jimmy had come from. Everything had worked out great—until everything ended. It was Luke who'd arranged the alias and helped him get out of California after Chevalier was murdered; Luke who'd found out that Duncan Henlic—the guy who'd ratted out Chevalier and tried to destroy BioTel and hand it to the Aldens—was still comatose, could die at any moment, and Jimmy implicated. Henlic was so terrified when Jimmy confronted him that something must have exploded in his brain. Along with wetting himself. The lard ass had fallen over in a puddle of piss and just lay there, twitching. Jimmy hadn't even touched him, but how was he going to prove that in court? With his past, he knew how that shit would work.

After a few minutes, he headed for the fridge, grabbed one, sat down again. He opened the ale and a porn site. Jimmy didn't like porn; he relied on it. With the way he felt, he figured it was easiest. He liked this one site run by Terri. Terri Coal had started a billion-dollar empire with her set of natural breasts. He thought of them as the greatest working-class tits on earth. Her perfect pendulous curves looked as if they'd calmed a hundred crying children, her birch leaf-sized aureoles and bud-like nipples looked as if they'd been chewed by coal miners. Her breasts were so full it made him laugh, but what he particularly liked was Terri. She had a slightly bulbous face, redhead pale and freckled with a large pointy nose and chin, her small body spotted with freckles and a few moles. Not pretty, but somehow he felt as if she would talk to him. Terri's site was oddly wholesome, had a family atmosphere, if a bunch of naked women with shaved genitals could be a family.

Jimmy went back to the icebox and retrieved a jar of mushrooms from the freezer. The jar was partially gripped by encroaching ice; no defrost on this ancient machine. He helped himself to a few and slid the jar back into the igloo. Returning to Terri, he sipped the ale and watched a few Busty Joke of the Week clips. Terri was smart to tempt all these women with acting. The results were mostly embarrassing, but who cared? Many of the models were Czech or Russian, and their English was clumsy, but the women seemed to be having a great time, were probably hauling in nice salaries, and could dream about becoming actresses if they cared.

As the mushrooms began to tingle through his body, the images grew increasingly real. The breasts filled, the nipples elongated and reddened, lips moistened, the down on the inside of thighs lifted, and he could almost smell the skin. He tapped open his collection of still shots, programmed his desktop to shuffle the images, then moved to his archive of Naked Dance of the Week clips. He liked almost every physical variation in women and wasn't obsessed with a specific size, height or hair color. The only thing he disliked were obvious silicone implants, which simply made him sad, so he avoided them if he could.

There were a lot of Veronicas. Veronica Vanno, a mulatto; Veronika Zemalovala, who was too ideal to be sexy, but beautiful as a sacrament; Veronica Zdrot, who spoke perfect English, a lawyer who found porn earned much more than law. There was blonde Shauna Saint, who didn't appear very saintly. Adele Michaels with a cockney accent who'd become slightly plump, and he wondered if he didn't like her more that way. Although he never would have admitted it to anyone, didn't even want to admit it to himself, he felt close to these women in a strange way.

And then just as he was pulsing at a fevered pitch, he was interrupted.

Claire.

He closed his eyes and her thin, polished beauty rose before him. He saw her delicate chest, her lost and tender eyes, her torrent of midnight hair, her imbalanced walk, and then that horrible purity of spirit, that he couldn't help but sense in her, whacked him like a vision of everything he'd ever been scared of. His eyes blurred and he bit his lip as the cry of anguish and ecstasy tore out of him.

Chapter Twelve

The old hobo calls himself Bill. I tell him my name is Cody. Everyone on the road probably uses a made-up name. We're sitting in a rail yard in Minot, North Dakota, trying to cook some green tomatoes over a fire we made.

"Amazing the things people'll leave lying around," Bill says.

"What's at?"

"Well, these tomatoes for instance. Perfectly good."

There was a pile of them in the gravel as we walked up the stopped freight. (When a train blows its air, you know it's not going anywhere for a while.) Bill immediately gathered them up, which I never would have thought of since I've never eaten them. We're frying them in bacon grease on a piece of metal we found. Bill had a peanut butter jar of it in his suitcase.

"Cold!" he says, rubbing his hands near the flames. "You got anymore fixings?" Bill calls my tobacco that.

"You keep smoking it, there's not going to be any." Still I toss him the pouch.

"Watch that one!" Bill points at a tomato slice that's getting burned. I flip it over with my knife. He watches the food intently, even telling me how thick to slice the tomatoes. "Little thinner," he kept saying. "They crisp better that way." He had a few stale crackers we crushed up, or I crushed up based on his instructions, and I pressed the slices in them. After Bill rolls one up, he loosens a stick from the fire and lights the cigarette with it. I've never seen a guy enjoy a smoke more. Seems he loves pipe tobacco, but he'll probably smoke anything as long as it has nicotine in it. I only smoke a few bowls a day, and if I'm honest with myself, I know part of doing it is just for the idea of it, the style of it, and I don't inhale. But Bill just wants to be a chimney like my stepfather, though my stepfather never seemed to enjoy anything.

"Cody."

"Yeah."

"I'm givin' her up." He gives a big exhale of smoke. He smokes cigarettes like a pothead.

"Giving what up?"

"Ridin'."

"Hoboing?"

He nods.

"What're you gonna do?"

"I'm goin' home, son, back to Billings, find a fleabag, see if I can get on the dole."

"How come?"

"Too old. Winter comin'. This cold just kills my bones, she gets right in me, and I never could stan' the heat. Tried it down south, but it weren't for me. I just sweat like a pig. Hey!" He points at another burning slice. The food is cooked and I slide some on a tin plate I carry in my gear. I pass it to Bill. My half I slide onto a flat board I rubbed clean. Bill uses a stick and I use my knife. I'm not going to let him use my knife.

"Hey, these are good."

"Told ya," he says, though he hadn't.

The tomatoes are so good we slice up the rest of them though we're out of crackers, and I get my last can of beans out of my pack. I hate to use them up. B&M baked beans from Maine. Bill's eyes light right up when he sees the can. After the beans bubble I serve them with more fried tomatoes.

"Damn, son, this here is one fine meal. Wish we had some whiskey or wine to wash her down."

We finish and Bill licks my plate clean which sickens me. Fuck, I figure I might as well give him the damn plate now. But he seems so happy I don't say nothing. I know he wants tobacco and though I'm almost out, I fill my pipe and toss him the pouch again. We light up from the fire and I toss on some more scraps of wood.

"If it wasn't so cold, she'd be perfect," he says. "Son, I been thinkin'. You've been mighty nice to me these last two days. I know yer pissed I smoked up all your fixings. Way I am now, I take what I can get. Never know when she's gonna end. You get as old as me, you might think the same way. But I'm gonna give you something in return. Bill always pays his way. Just the way I am." He has another big toke. "I'm gonna give ya something I've carried with me for many years waitin' for the right time. I was hopin' to use her myself, but now I see I ain't goin' to make her. Maybe you will. That's why I'm given et to ya."

Just as the harvest moon rode into the eastern sky and iced the barren yard out on the plain with an eerie greenish light. Just as the haunting stillness wrapped around them both, touched only by an occasional snap from their fire, Bill's face now excited in the glow of the flames—

There was a loud noise.

It vaporized everything.

Doris was banging her dinner gong.

"God damn it," muttered Jimmy. The ringing rose through the house like a fire alarm. Time to face another Callahan culinary horror show. He jumped for the fridge and downed a B pounder. Since the arm-binding night, Doris was adamant against alcohol. But sober, her food was an impossibility. He had to get the cast off—soon, no matter how his arm suffered.

"So . . . are you going to tell me about it?" Doris said when they were settled around the kitchen table. She never used the dining room.

"What?"

"Your date with Claire, of course."

"Why would you want to know about that?"

"Robert! Don't be impertinent. It's not becoming."

"The jacket worked out nice. Thanks."

"You looked handsome in it—for you. At least it covered those awful tattoos. Where did you have supper?"

"The Broadway."

"Phyllis, the gold whore!" Doris turned red and looked down at her plate. He noticed she didn't eat much of her own cooking. "I didn't mean to say that. I apologize, Robert."

"We all do it."

"Does Henry still work there?"

"Our waiter. You know Henry too?"

"He used to work at Martin's before it closed. It was a men's shop at the end of Acadia Avenue, across from the jewelry store. My father bought all his clothes there. I'd go with him sometimes when I was a girl. I loved it in there, all quiet and dark and masculine with those high ceilings and the smell of wool and wood. He'd let me choose his ties. Henry started there just before . . . before my father passed away."

"Is he your age?"

"Henry? Heavens no! What's wrong with you, Robert? He's a full twelve years older than I am."

"Sorry."

"Well I'd think so."

They picked at their food for a moment, Jimmy forcing down a few more bites. The hardiest of one-eyed scar-faced swabs couldn't have managed her biscuits, and they'd knocked the weevils out of theirs. Even bugs wouldn't try to burrow into this cement. On his initial attempts at eating the things, he'd gotten biscuit wedged in the roof of his mouth, and unable to dislodge it with his tongue, and without beer to lubricate, he'd been forced to stand and turn, not wanting Doris to witness him prodding madly with a finger. By now he'd learned techniques for getting the things down without too much trouble. Man is amazingly adaptable when under duress.

"That Cloutier give you any more trouble?"

"Still in one piece, aren't I?"

"Very funny, Robert. At least you have a sense of humor about it."

"What's with Claire and Cloutier anyway?" He tried to say it casually.

But she perked right up. "What is it that you're asking me?"

"Why does she hang around him?"

She watched him for a moment. "It's said around town that Claire's son is his. But the rat never married her and never owned up to it. She was underage at the time, and I think the father, the older Cloutier, paid Claire off, but no one really knows for certain. Claire's like that, she wouldn't blab. Her boy is a rather sickly pathetic child."

He said nothing.

"And she buys drugs for Cloutier. His father will cut him off if he gets caught again. He's kept him out of prison about as many times as is humanly possible. You should tell Claire to stop doing it. She's going to get herself into real trouble, and she's had enough trouble in her life already. Her mother's in the nut house, you know? Claire visits her all the time, though who knows why. I doubt her mother even recognizes her." Doris seemed delighted to tell him this.
"How do you know all this stuff when you never go out?"

"Fred. Cab drivers hear everything."

That sneaky stinking weasel. It figured. Probably knew every secret in the whole city. Another reason to stay clear of him, as if he needed one. So her kid was Slag's. He guessed that explained why she had anything to do with the moron. Nevertheless . . . the whole thing couldn't have been messier. How could she have fucked Slag? He felt even sicker at the thought.

"Who wrote on your cast?" said Doris. "Oh, I bet it was Claire. Let's see." She leaned across the table. Jimmy had no choice but to show her, so he stretched out his arm. She adjusted her glasses. "Well, I can't make that out." There was a long pause. "You didn't ask me to write anything."

He stalled, but saw there was no way out. "You want to?"

"Could I? At least you'll be able to read it."

She reached into the catch-all basket she kept on the table and grabbed a pen. It wouldn't write. She tried another, scribbling it on a scrap of paper first—no luck either. The pencil she found had no point. "Not meant to be," he said happily, standing, ready to flee.
Muttering to herself, she dug deeper into the basket, all manner of junk spread onto the table, and came out with a large magic marker. It would have to be red.

When Jimmy got back up to his apartment he headed directly for the fridge. Finding reasons to drink was a Hakken credo, and he firmly believed beer helped dissolve Doris's cooking, hops soothed the stomach. Tonight he wondered if beer dissolved red magic marker. He doubted it. Doris had probably used the indelible kind. Most evenings he worked on his teeth first, but the toothpaste disturbed the taste of the ale, particularly since he scrubbed his tongue, so sometimes he chose the beer first, then the brushing. It was a dilemma. After two ales he sat in front of the computer again. The e-mail envelope was pulsing.

H—I bailed on C after our phone call. I'm in F. Got a plan. Water. Easy access. You need more than 1 arm? Got the G. Thanks. L

He smiled; Luke was the best. But water? Boats? Jimmy hated boats. He got seasick just standing on a dock.

Chapter Thirteen

A week later, Claire called and invited him to dinner.

"It's only fair," she said, "since you took me out."

"Let's go to the Broadway again. My treat."

"What, you don't trust my cooking?"

"Not that."

"What is it then?"

The kid, he almost said. "Nothing. Wanted to show you something."

"Jimmy, come on, let me make you supper. I'm not that bad a cook, you'll see, and I really want you to meet Brandon. I told him about you."

"You did? Why?"

"He was interested. I told him you had tattoos and he thought that was cool. Well, at first he wasn't impressed; he said, 'Yeah, so what, everyone has a tattoo,' but then I told him your arms were covered with knights and shields and swords and stuff, and he thought that was 'way cool.' He even looked up your car on the internet to see what it looked like."

"He did?"

"It's a sixty-five, isn't it?"

"Yeah."

"See? I described it and he found it. He wanted to know what engine it had."

"Really?"

"*Jimmy*—he's a very bright kid."

"Brandin."

"Bran-*don*."

"Right, Brandon."

"So, will you come?"

He sighed away from the phone. "What time?"

"Six."

They hung up. Jimmy went into the bathroom and flossed.

Claire lived on Cartier Street off Atlantic Avenue in a large turn-of-the-century apartment house. A quiet neighborhood, the buildings actually nicely kept. Jimmy parked at the curb, retrieved two packages from the backseat and locked the Impala, struggling to balance everything because of his cast. He frowned at Slag's dent. It wasn't that the car had been blemish-free before; it was that the worst of its dents had been his fault. He'd failed to protect the car and therefore failed his mentor again. Chevalier had prized the original paint. Maybe someone could pull the dent out without repainting? He'd have to check around and see if anyone did good bodywork in Scoggton. In Santa Cruz it would've been easy: he'd had his people. He gazed up Cartier Street.

Trees, lots of trees: they were probably maples, the buds swollen and red, a few on the south side of the street beginning to flower, the narrow borders of grass along the sidewalk showing some vibrant green patches. In the fifties and sixties, America's shady tree-lined streets were reduced by Dutch elm blight to tight rows of old houses in need of roofs and paint. No longer hidden by leaves, there was nothing for them to do but glare nakedly at each other. No wonder so many people had moved to the suburbs. Cartier Street must have been one of the few streets that had been replanted because most of Scoggton was bare.

When Jimmy had first moved into the Callahan house, one of Doris's neighbors, a burly guy with a blue jaw who rented one of the many apartments next door, had walked over. "Who're you?" he said for a greeting. "You should tell her to cut down those trees there," referring to her prized oaks. "They only make the leaves. Too much raking. The leaves, they blow over here."

Number 67 Cartier, the numbers in brass script on mustard yellow shingles. He walked up onto the porch and struggled with the door, trapping his gifts with his good arm. Each floor was its own apartment—Claire was on the third. The same as his. He trudged up and stood a moment before her door, wishing he'd checked his teeth again in the rearview mirror. A warm smell of cooking surrounded him, and he sent up a silent prayer. Then he knocked and the door sprung open.

"My goodness. Are these for me?"
He had decided on six in every color just to make sure. Turned out to be four-dozen tulips. Roses had seemed too forward.

"They're lovely."
It amazed him how women got excited by flowers. "Could you take them?" He was about to drop the beer.

She gathered them up, the white paper crackling around all the stems and pointed leaves. "So many. No one has ever given me so many flowers."

He renewed his grip on the bag of pounders. "Didn't know what color you liked."

"They're all so lovely." She seemed genuinely pleased. They stood a moment, Jimmy feeling awkward, her hair its usual wonder. "You mind taking off your shoes?" she said.

"My boots?"

"If you don't mind."

He set down the beer and started on the laces, trying to remember what socks he'd worn.

"I'll just put these in water."

As he worked at his boots, he noticed someone lurking, slumped, hands deep in his pockets. His clothes were ill fitting as if handed down from a much larger brother, his hair long and stringy. He had none of Slag's robustness or bluster, which was in the kid's favor. Claire was apparent in the delicate features and the wary brown eyes, but the skin was paler, almost chapped in places—the kid probably washed his face too much.

"Hey," said Jimmy, standing up in his socks, flicking his hand in his understated way.

The kid shot forward and nervously pulled a hand out of his pocket. "Hi. I'm Brandon Constantine. It's *really* good to meet you, Mr. Gray." The kid's grip was so gentle Jimmy retracted his hand immediately. "We watched you park. That is one awesome wagon. What's it got in it?"

"Three twenty-seven."

"Sweet!"

Jimmy nodded, reached down and picked up the beer, looked for Claire. When did boys go through the octave change anyway? Wasn't it way before fourteen?

"Wow," said Brandon. "My mom said you had tattoos, but these are totally awesome."

Jimmy had worn his black leather vest over a black T-shirt. As he'd dressed he couldn't help but think of the kid. Although he didn't even want him to exist, he still wanted to make an impression. "One guy did most of 'em. Pinto. He was the best artist out there. Really knew his sh— stuff."

"Out where?"

"West."

"California?"

"Around there."

Suddenly, the kid starting sneezing. And he didn't stop. Jimmy glanced uncomfortably around the apartment. The floors were urethaned hardwood and the few pieces of furniture modern—bright fabrics with spindly legs, a chrome and glass coffee table, cheap-looking after Doris's antiques. There was a huge bookcase along one wall, the rest unadorned off-white. It wasn't his style, but it excited him somehow. Everything was very neat, and he wondered if she'd cleaned for his arrival or if this was the way they lived.

"You okay?" he asked after about the tenth sneeze. *Jesus*, what a fucked-up kid.

"Just"—*sneeze*—"allergies. This time of year gets me, with the tree"—*sneeze*—"pollens and . . ."

Claire finally appeared with a vase overwhelmed by tulips. She set it carefully on the dining-room table. "I could only fit half of them. I need another vase." She moved toward them. "Brandon, did you introduce yourself to Mr. Gray?"

"We were talking tattoos," said Jimmy. What was with all this Mr. Gray stuff?

"Brandon, if you're going to keep sneezing, please use a Kleenex."

The kid muttered, "Sorry," sneezed once more, and slunk off.

Now that he was alone with her, in her apartment, his excitement rose again. He held out the bag. "Beer."

"Ballantine's? Are you sure it's fresh?" She took it from him and walked into the kitchen. He followed.

"Something smells good," he said.

"Baked potatoes. And I made a pie earlier. You want a beer?"

"I always want a beer. Don't always have one, but I *always* want one."

Her delicate hands found the pull-tab, and she opened and passed him a can. "I suppose you never use a glass."

"You teasing me?' He loved that she opened it for him. The slow sound—she tabbed it much more carefully than he would've—and the way the ale foamed slightly from the hole.

She picked up a glass of white wine. "Are you always so serious?" Her look was unreadable. He took a long pull from the beer, glanced out the window at the dusky light filtering through the trees. Her kitchen was as neat as the rest of the place.

"Did I upset you?" she said.

"Not sure you could upset me."

"I mean that little to you?"

"What do you think?"

She put the rest of the six-pack in the fridge. "I hope you like lobster? Brandon insisted I get them for tonight. Kind of a Maine supper."

"I like them," he said, though he couldn't remember ever having eaten one.

When they had walked through the dining room, he'd noticed the table

was set for three. It annoyed him. He wanted her alone, badly. As if on cue, the kid appeared, puffy eyed and flushed at the edges. "Sorry about that, Mr. Gray. I just get these fits like that and there isn't much I can, like, do about it. I know it's annoying for others to experience."
"No problem."
The kid grinned. "Are you excited about the lobsters?" He didn't wait for an answer. "I talked Mom into getting them. Our cousin from Spruce Head used to lobster, you know? We went to the coast once when I was a kid and I rode in the lobster boat with him pulling traps. That's what they call it, 'pullin' traps. Oh, we was just out they-a pullin' traps.'" He imitated a coastal accent. "Have you ever fished, Mr. Gray?"
"Not much."
"But you have?"
"Not big on boats."
"But cars, you're big on cars. And tattoos, of course."
Jimmy nodded. Jesus, the kid talked a lot and waved his hands around even more. He looked at Claire and noticed delight in her eyes, but had no idea what from. He sure wasn't delighted. "Let's go into the living room," she said.
"Need another beer." He set the empty on the counter.
She pulled one out of the fridge, tabbed it again. He could watch that forever. After she filled her wine, they all moved to the other room—the kid walking right next to him, glancing up repeatedly like an affection-starved mutt—and they settled.
The kid leaned forward. "So, Mr. Gray, my mom told me you're a writer. I've never met a real writer before. What are you writing?"
Jimmy worked the can, hard. Had the kid prepared all these questions? "Just a book."
"What kind of book?"
"Novel."
"What's it about?"
"About?"
"Is it like what we read in school? Like John Steinbeck or something? Like a book about the culture problems of the working classes?"
The kid continued to stare at him with those earnest eyes. Jimmy took another long pull. "I'm not a real writer. It's just this thing about my life. Stuff that happened to me when I was younger."
"What kind of stuff?"
"Let's wait till it's finished. Okay?"
Brandon nodded and glanced nervously at his mom, then back. "Hey, maybe after dinner you want to see my model collection? I make plastic car kits. I've got a whole bunch of them. No sixty-five wagons but I got

some fucking totally kickass street rods."

"Brandon!"

"Sorry." His attention was back on Jimmy. "Or maybe you want to see them right now? They're in my room, right over there." He pointed down the hall.

"I think Mr. Gray might want to just sit for a moment."

"Okay. Hey, can I get you another beer, Mr. Gray?"

Jimmy drained it and held out his empty can. "Now you're talking."

The kid leapt up. "You got it."

"He really likes you," said Claire when Brandon was out of earshot.

"You think so? I didn't do nothing."

"I can tell. He won't talk to Ray at all."

"Ray?"

"Slag. His father. I figured Doris told you." He heard the fridge door click. "Did she tell you?"

"Some of it."

"He's always ignored Brandon. A few years ago he attempted to make contact. Brandon wouldn't have any of it."

"In his favor."

"What?"

"Just mumbling."

"No, tell me. What did you say?"

The kid shot back with the beer. "Here you go. Can I open it?"

"I got it." He saw disappointment in the kid's eyes, but he still wanted to open the can himself.

Jimmy was standing next to her in the kitchen. The kid was finally in his room.

"My cousin Mitch taught me this." She was holding up a struggling lobster and gently massaging it with the index finger of her other hand, rubbing between the eyes along the nose bone. Jimmy felt every stroke. "This hypnotizes it," she said. He couldn't have agreed more. "This way when it hits the water it's calm and doesn't secrete bitterness into the meat. Makes it sweeter tasting." The lobster stopped squirming, the claws no longer snapping, and it drooped becalmed in her hand. He felt himself relax. When she suddenly dropped it into the raging pot of boiling water, Jimmy cringed.

"You want to try it?" she said.

He stared at the two remaining lobsters.

"Come on, be quick. They have to go in together."

He grabbed one, the greenish shell cold and hard, but not slimy as it looked. The lobster attempted to reach back and nip him—Claire had removed the rubber bands. Earlier she'd shown him how a claw could almost bite through a pencil. She was toying with him and he knew it, probably continuing to doubt his toughness. He started rubbing the nose of the writhing beast, and sure enough, it quieted. He dropped it in. Did the next one.

"You're becoming a Mainer," she said. She leaned over, and for a moment he thought she might kiss him, but instead she reached for the pot lid. He smelled her soap and hair over the aroma of the cooking lobsters. He wanted to kiss her now more than ever. Had she done the move on purpose, to tempt him? He couldn't tell.

"I'm from New Hampshire, not far from the Maine border."

That stopped her. "Where?"

"Northern."

"There you go again. Are you ever going to tell me anything truthful about yourself?"

"It's true."

"Yeah, right."

She turned, reached into a drawer, took something out, held it up to him. "You want some of this?"

He shook his head. Her eyebrows arched and she shrugged. He could tell she was suddenly upset but had no clue why. She flicked on the burner beside the boiling lobsters and leaned over the stove, straightened, inhaling. "God, I used to live on this stuff. I don't smoke much anymore," she said, her voice constricted.

"How about the kid knowing?"

She exhaled. "In this town? Are you kidding? But I do try to keep him from seeing me. You sure you don't want any? Worried you might get stoned and actually tell the truth about something?"

It was as if she'd slapped him. "Claire, I really was born here. In the White Mountains."

"But you don't talk like a New Englander, and what's with the California plates?"

Fuck, he kept putting off getting them changed. "I spent some time on the West Coast, but I was around here until about Brandon's age."

"Jimmy, you can be mysterious if you need to be. You can do whatever the fuck you want. I stopped giving a shit about most things a long time ago." She said it so nastily it went through him like a burning sword. She took a last puff and threw the tiny roach into the sink. Then she ran the cold water, and they both watched it swirl away.

They worked on their lobsters: Claire and Brandon were devouring theirs, Jimmy struggled with his as if he were removing a knight from his armor. He wasn't enjoying himself for a number of reasons. When he tried to slice open the tail with his bread knife, Brandon said: "Mr. Gray?"

He looked over at the kid.

"You just need to twist off the bottom of the tail. These little flippers here." Brandon pointed. "Then push the meat out with your finger." Jimmy tried it and had to admit, that made it much easier. He dipped it in butter and bit off a hunk. It was chewier than he expected and not as tasty as Claire and the kid professed. More like butter-soaked rubber. At least he'd had no trouble with his baked potato, showing the kid how to cleave it four ways in a cross with a fork and then press it open with thumbs and two fingers. It was one of the few things his stepfather had taught him, not that he mentioned that. He didn't feel like talking.

After most of the tail and the second limp-tasting claw, Jimmy got even quieter. The kid tried a few questions, and Jimmy just mumbled quick answers. He was thinking about what Claire had said and it bothered him; it changed his whole impression of her. Here she said she didn't give a shit, yet her apartment was immaculate. And the kid, she obviously cared insanely about the kid. Why wouldn't she believe anything he said? Why was she fishing for information anyway? What was she up to? His mind was churning these facts like a clothes dryer. She couldn't fool him. He knew who she didn't give a shit about. He started to worry he was being set up, that she'd found out about him. He was—

"Jimmy?"

It was her. "What?" he managed.

"Is your lobster okay?"

"Yeah, why?"

"Nothing."

He ate the narrow wiggly part of the last claw.

"Are you okay?" she said.

"What do you mean, *okay*?"

"You just look so glum."

"I'm fine." He went back to work on the lobster, sucking on the legs like the kid showed him, walking his teeth along the thin shell, though it tasted nothing but salty and there wasn't any meat.

"Are you sure you like it?"

"Of course."

"Don't finish it if you don't want to."

He ignored her and downed the last bit of tail. Chased it with a welcome pull of ale.

"I'm sorry you don't like it."

"I'm eating the thing, aren't I?" He said this a bit louder than he intended, but lobsters were damn overrated as far as he was concerned. He still planned on finishing the beast if it was the last thing he did, only some greenish slime inside the belly left. He'd show her he was tough, but why didn't she give a shit about him? And to think he'd been crazy about her.

"Don't eat the tomalley if you don't want," she said.

"What?"

She pointed at the green stuff.

"Maybe not." There were limits. He'd reached his.

"Are you sure you're all right?" she said again. Her voice seemed to echo slightly. The kid was staring at him too, but at least the little shit was motionless for once.

"Why do you keep asking me that?"

"Well," she said, "you're all red, and your eyes look weird. They're bugging out."

"So?" He also felt dizzy and his skin itched insanely, but he'd be damned if he'd tell her.

"And you're sweating."

She was right, his T-shirt was soaked right through to his vest. He hadn't noticed it, or how extremely odd he felt—it was amazing how deeply women could hurt you, more than you ever knew. One damn nasty comment and look at him. Jesus, his whole body was reacting.

"Listen," he said, jerking to his feet.

"Are you going to be sick?"

"'Course not!"

"If you are, the bathroom's right down the hall, last door on the left."

"What're you talking about?"

"Jimmy, you said you'd eaten lobster before, didn't you?"

Had he? He couldn't remember what he'd told her. Now all he cared about was getting out of there. "Listen," he said again. Was he going to fall? All the room's colors pulsed and swirled, the light much too bright, and he was having trouble breathing. "Think I better get going. Thanks for supper."

"Mr. Gray, you don't want to see my models?"

Models? Oh, the kid's plastic things. "Next time."

"And there's pie. My favorite. Mom's homemade lemon meringue." As if that changed anything.

Claire was standing too. "Jimmy, I think you should lie down. You really don't look so hot."

"I'm fine."

He made the door, negotiated the knob, found himself on the stair landing. He wanted to run but couldn't. He gripped the railing, headed down the staircase, his cast bouncing off the occasional wall. His strides reverberated into his brain, sounding like *Not a shit, not a shit, not a shit.* It wasn't until he reached the porch that he realized he'd forgotten his boots. Fuck 'em!

He was attempting to unlock the Impala when she appeared on the porch. She limped across the grass toward him as he got the key in and the lock snapped up. At least she was holding his boots.

"I think you're allergic to lobster," she said.

"Lobster?"

"You've never eaten it, have you?"

He shook his head uncertainly.

"Some people are highly allergic. I should drive you to the hospital."

He looked at her, and she touched his shoulder. His whole body short-circuited. Why was she touching him? He opened the door clumsily and fell onto the bench seat.

"You definitely shouldn't drive."

"Right." He sat up and started the car.

"Jimmy, please, don't drive. At least come back upstairs and lie down for a minute while I call the emergency room. *Please.*"

"Hey, I don't give a fuck about anything either," he said, and wheeled out of there. This wasn't good, he muttered to himself, this wasn't good at all.

On top of everything else, she still had his boots.

Chapter Fourteen

Claire had been calling his cell for the last two days, but he couldn't answer. What was he supposed to say, that every time he got around her he just happened to dash off and vomit? He didn't cherish facing the kid either, though he told himself this kind of thing could happen to anyone. But it kept happening to *him,* and in this damn town. Even Doris had held back that evening, not saying a word as he'd hobbled up the stairs in his wet socks.

Now he was stationed in his garret, glaring out over the town, trying to find what was missing. He rotated his arm awkwardly and squinted at his cast again. Claire's eyebrow pencil was scrawled in small spidery letters in a location that required a mirror to read. When he'd first made it out, he'd figured she was teasing him. Now he wondered. It said:

When you really love something, you can understand the desire of squeezing it to death

There was no period. Had she come up with it, or was it a quote? Was she trying to warn him about herself? Once again he didn't have a clue. Not a single clue about Claire—period. And there was Doris's giant red smiley face and her THIS IS BETTER THAN THEM TATTOOS! That was easy to read and understand. He had to get this cast off. The doctor had said three more weeks, but he was tempted to remove the thing this morning. He needed to get back into a gym—craved working out, punching a heavy bag again. This writer's life was weakening him. At least he'd finally told Doris he was going to cook for himself for a few days. She'd humphed, but after the lobster poisoning, his stomach wasn't strong enough for the Callahan diet. He'd been making sandwiches— grilled bacon, sausage, and cheddar on rye—and his strength was returning. He grabbed his cell phone. No matter what he did he couldn't get her out of his thoughts.

"Claire?"

"Jimmy!"

"Can you talk?"

"Hey, I've been worried about you."

"Thought you didn't give a shit about anything?"

"I shouldn't have said that. You took it too personally, and it wasn't meant like that. We all have issues, you know? Things we're trying to work through. I get overly emotional sometimes, and I suppose I have a lot of baggage. I try to hold back, but it doesn't always happen. I warned you about things jumping out of me, and you said you liked it. Remember?"

"What did it mean then?" He waited. He wasn't going soft around her ever again. He knew how the game was played. He'd been a fool to allow himself to be so vulnerable and open.

"I can't tell you that now," she said finally.

"How about over dinner?" What the hell had he just said? Was he already softening? But there was no reason not to see her; he just had to maintain fierce caution and resolve.

"Maybe," she said slowly.

"The Broadway?"

"Tonight?"

"Pick you up at six-thirty."

"I'll be ready."

I bet you will, he muttered as he hung up. At least she hadn't mentioned the kid this time. He wondered again if she sensed or knew certain things about him, if he was being set up. Women knew stuff and could be bizarrely intuitive. That had been proven historically. Men had to accept that they were always at a disadvantage in these realms and prepare accordingly.

He decided to get back to work on *My Life*. He needed to do something with his afternoon besides drink. The beer had been calling a little too loudly lately. He opened his Word program and began to write.

Bill takes a wallet out of his jacket pocket. It's long and cracked and worn round on the edges. After a long stare at the thing, he removes a folded piece of paper that looks worse than the wallet. He holds it up like a winning lottery ticket.

"Son, I've carried this for a dozen years. It was given me by a little Mexican fellur who said he was some kinda medicine man, but he spoke good English and rode the West. We caught the same flatcar one morning ridin' along the Rio Grande. Guy looked a hundred years old. I had some beers in a bag, a little cool from the night air. And when I shared the beers with him, he give me this paper. So it's being passed along. I don't know where he got it. Feeling I had was that he wrote her up himself."

His face all serious in the fire light, Bill hands me the dirty thing.

I unfold it and it almost falls apart. On it are some numbers in a grid and a diagram. I keep looking, not wanting to putdown Bill's gift, but I have no idea what it is.

"That, son, will make you a fortune. You see them numbers at the top? Them's dates. You see them others? Them's addresses. Next row? Them's times. Then comes the key ones. They're roulette numbers on a roulette wheel. The diagram shows you where in the casino the tables are. You know how roulette works?"

"Little bit."

"Well, you hit a number it pays big-time. You see that number there, eight-five? Well, she's coming up, as you know. Next year. And then you got yer month and yer day. Then you follow her down, and you got yer address. Them casinos is all in Las Vegas, Nevada. You hearda the place?"

I nodded. Who hadn't?

"They're all on the same big street. They call her the strip. You go there, find yer table, wait fer the exact time. She's gotta be exact now." He snapped his fingers. "Then you play yer number. She'll hit, and yer a millionaire just like that."

Bill is looking at me with his toothless grin like he just made me rich.

"But you never tried it?"

"Son, you got to raise at least a hundred to put on yer number. Now, I raised her one time, and I headed fer Las Vegas. No doubt about that. Trouble was, the thirst outran me fore I ever got there. And I ain't raised that kinda money since."

"But you think it'll work?"

"You can't be certain about nothin', but I'll tell you what. I asked that little Mexican fellur the same thing. He looked over at me and says fer me to watch. He takes an empty beer bottle. Now the freight, she's flyin' along past a rock wall on one sider us. He throws that bottle at the rock cut." Bill made a throwing motion like you'd toss to home plate. "And you know what?" He waited until I shook my head. "She bounced. That there bottle didn't break, she just bounced." Bill shook his head and started laughing. "Damndest thing I ever seen."

Jimmy stopped and leaned back in his chair. That next day, he'd ridden with Bill as far as the freight yard in Billings. He could still see the old hobo walking toward his hometown, the warm afternoon sun on his back, a tired gait taking him over a couple dozen track rails until he was lost from sight. He'd been surprised at how sad it was to see him go—the loss of all his tobacco and food aside. After waiting in the empty boxcar for a lonely hour, Jimmy had decided to head into town himself, at least buy a few things; he was starving. He'd lied to Bill about money, telling him he had none when there was some hidden under the inner sole of his shoe. At the time he didn't realize everyone hid money there.

As he'd walked into town with his pack, through neat rows of nearly identical suburban houses, he'd come upon a small park. On the bright green September grass raked by afternoon sun, a dozen girls had danced in differently colored leotards, all turning in unison. To his young eyes they were prismatic angels. He'd stood and watched, fantasies accelerating in his mind like a freight train with a green board. The dancing women were so surreal it made everything seem possible. He'd find his father in California. They'd go to Las Vegas together. His dad would have the money to place on the roulette table, the wheel would turn exactly on the specified hour, and the little steel ball would lock onto their number. It could work; against all odds, it would work. And why not? Didn't everyone have an even chance at being lucky? His dad would slap him on the back, tousle his hair. His dad would love him for being a hero. And beautiful girls in leotards would fall at his feet, him, the unwanted mill-town kid.

Jimmy jerked to his feet and headed for the fridge. Now the beer was shouting.

When he arrived on Cartier Street, he was only slightly drunk. Fifteen minutes early, he parked and sipped a Ballantine, the May evening breeze strumming through the car with a seductive wink. Occasionally he glanced up at the apartment. He didn't honk, but eventually there was a face at the window. Brandon. The kid waved madly as if he'd found someone lost, and Jimmy cringed. Soon Claire appeared on the porch; she had his boots. He set his can on the floorboard and got out of the car.

"Hey."

"Hey," she said, making that gesture with her hair.

"You look great." And she did. Black pants and a dark leather jacket, as if she'd dressed just for him. But he wasn't going to let it weaken him. He'd show her he could play the game just as coldly as she could.

"Brandon said to say Hi. He wondered why you didn't come up."

"Next time. Come on." The first bruise of evening was dimming the tree-lined street; they needed to hurry.

He opened her door and she thanked him. Manners and flowers, a cliché but it seemed to be true. He would be polite but remain cold.

"You wanna beer?"

"I'll never finish it in time."

He opened her one anyway. Twisted the key and had them headed downtown. He'd checked on the drive over and knew it was on. Suddenly he worried she'd already seen it. But she would have told him. As they turned onto Acadia Avenue, the light was perfect for it—that bluing of spring dusk, the rest of the street deserted, the ugly streetlights not lit. He slowed the Impala a block away from the Broadway and pulled over to the curb.

"Look," she said and pointed, turned quickly to him, then back. "My God, Jimmy. It's been fixed. I can't believe it."

"Nice, eh?"

"I can't believe Phyllis spent the money. She's always been as tight as a tick. I never realized it was so beautiful. Look at those colors. That flicking arrow is the best."

Claire sipped her beer as Jimmy swamped his. The neon *Broadway* was the orange of hot coal, the restaurant white-blue. A green arrow on the leading edge and along the bottom of the sign elongated in four quick gestures toward the door. The moment swirled around him, Claire's quiet presence making him so aware he almost tingled. For a moment he almost put his arm around her but stopped himself in time. The beers were hitting him harder than he'd anticipated; he probably should've eaten some lunch. And then the streetlights started to blink on, those ugly ping-pong balls on wands, ruining everything. He wished Scoggton had the ones that glowed like fireflies before they flared bright.

"Wait'll Brandon sees it," she said. "He loves neon. I wonder when Phyllis got it fixed?"

"Come on, I'm hungry."

"I'm not even part way done with my beer."

He grabbed it from her, opened the car door and poured it out.

"Hey," she said, glaring at him.

"Come on."

They walked under the neon, and the glow of it lit her face. He stalled opening the door just to watch her. Inside the restaurant he felt that rush of emotion again. Phyllis was there, gold as ever.

"Mr. Gray. How lovely to see you. The sign looks great, doesn't it? Two?"

They followed her down the aisle, past another couple. Even on a Friday evening the place was basically deserted. Henry motored forward from the bar.

"Mr. Gray, good-evening, sir. Miss," and he nodded to Claire.

"Henry, let's have no accidents this time," said Phyllis.

"What's a tiny table fire amongst friends," said Jimmy, winking at Henry.

"Claire, beverage?"

They ordered and Henry went off but Phyllis continued to hover.

"Thanks, Phyllis, we'll take it from here," said Jimmy.

"If I can help you with anything, you let me know." She went back to the front.

"Why is she so obliging? She's never like that. You're like long-lost family now or something." She searched him, and suddenly her expression changed. "You paid for the sign, didn't you? You had it fixed."

"Kinda."

"Christ, it must've been expensive."

"Kinda."

"A thousand?"

"Round there."

"Why'd you do it?"

For you, he wanted to say. "To see it lit up." He'd ordered the neon repaired after their first dinner together, by way of commemoration.

"You have that kind of money?"

There it was. Did she know? "Some," he said. "Stuck it on my DEA expense account."

She gave him a resentful look. "Are you ever going to tell me anything? I mean, there you are living with Doris, you say you're writing a book, you don't seem to have to work, and now you fix Phyllis's sign at great cost just to see it lit up."

"Writing's not work?"

"You know what I mean."

Henry dropped off their drinks. Jimmy asked him to wait a second, drained the Scotch and handed back the empty glass. "To women, Henry."

"To women, sir."

"Another."

"As you wish." Henry whispered off.

"I like that guy," he said. "Pours one hell of a drink."

"Can we stay on the subject?" She sipped hers, watching him with an uncertain expression that pleased him immensely. He'd show her: "Why should I tell you about me? Have you told me anything?"

"What haven't I told you? I work in a frame shop part time. The pay sucks. I help old ladies pick out frames for pictures of their cats. 'Doesn't that turquoise matte set off Frisky's eyes just perfectly?' I take care of Brandon and I do some copyediting. I read a lot. That's about it—my boring life."

"And Cloutier?"

"He's Brandon's father. What was I supposed to do? I was very young."
"Why didn't your family get a lawyer? The Cloutiers are rich."
"I suppose Doris thinks she knows what I settled for. I'm starting to dislike that woman." She pulled her hair back and let it fall again. "You don't know my family. My parents had me when they were older, and my brothers had their own lives by the time I was a teenager. My dad is a quiet nervous guy, not the type to confront the Cloutiers. He worked his whole life at Scoggton Shoe until they closed. Now he just putters around in his workshop at home and goes to church constantly."
"And your mom?"
She took a long pull from her cocktail. "Jimmy, why are you doing this?"
"Just wanna know about you."
"Something's changed. What is—"
Henry appeared and set down Jimmy's drink. "Have you decided on something?"
"Escargot," Claire said. "And the trout."
"And for you, sir?"
Jimmy worked his Scotch. "Lobsters. Two of 'em."
Claire jolted slightly, Henry unmoved. "I'm sorry, we don't have lobsters tonight. We used to, but there wasn't much call for them and they tended to die in the tank."
"Can't have that, can we, Henry?"
"No, sir."
"Tell you what. How 'bout a steak? Phyllis got any meat back there that didn't die in the tank?"
"I suggest the T-bone, our finest cut."
"No horse in it?"
"Sir?"
"Just horsing around." Jimmy laughed at his own joke. He had to admit his laughter sounded odd, as if he needed practice. "And another one of these babies." He rattled his ice.
"How would you like your steak cooked?"
"Burnt and raw."
"Sir?"
"Dealer's choice."
"French fries, twice baked, baked, or—"
"Twice baked, wedger of iceberg with that blue cheese. An' that Zee-Nine sauce."
"I'm afraid I'm not familiar with that particular condiment."
"Just the A-1 then." He felt a bit put out. Try to make a funny joke and nobody gets the damn thing.

"Very good, sir."

After Henry left, Claire said, "You okay? Did something happen? You seem strange."

"Whaddaya mean?"

She worked at her drink, looked away.

"Tell me just one damn thing," he said. "Why me?"

"Jimmy, what are you talking about?"

"Why would you want to go out with me?"

She examined him, which still made him uneasy, new icy attitude or not. "Because you're interesting, you're nice—most of the time—and you have really beautiful eyes."

"What?"

"You do. Even Vicky thought you were very attractive in an unusual—"

"Vicky? *Who* the hell is Vicky?"

"Vicky Lattrell. We grew up next door to each other."

"Why would she know how I look? You have this woman spying on me?" That slowed her, but he couldn't read her expression.

"I told her about you, and she noticed you at the grocery store."

"How'd she know it was me?"

"You do have a distinctive look, you know, especially around here."

He thought that over. "What's *she* look like?"

"Lots of blonde hair—though it's not natural like yours—and a curvaceous figure."

"H-m."

"The opposite of me." She glanced down, but he wasn't going to take the bait.

Henry brought his iceberg and her escargot. Eight of them in white ceramic shells, rattling in an indented matching tray. Jimmy wrinkled his nose and ordered another Scotch. Claire started eating.

"You know about snails, don't you?" he said, not touching his salad. She didn't look up, but he continued anyway. "The French had the things crawling all over their country. It was a real fucking problem. They were everywhere, sliming things up. Not the French, the snails. So this one guy says, 'Hey, Zoot allors, let us make a new dish, with the snail. The garlic, the butter, we serve them to the dumb Americans. Charge the big monee.' And they got rid of their snail problem."

Claire set down her fork. "Jimmy, are you going to tell me what's up or not?"

"You said I was too serious. Just making a few jokes." He was really starting to feel the whisky collide with the beers; he'd drunk it way too fast.

"*Please,* stop it and just tell me what's wrong." Her face, her eyes, cut into him.

He reached for his drink. The ice tumbled over his lip, some falling into his lap. The glass was empty and he set it back down. "You know about me, don't you?"

"Know what?"

"That's why you're going out with me."

"Jimmy, *please*, what are you talking about?"

"You know I got money."

"Money? *You?*"

"How'd you find out?"

"Find what out?" She leaned toward him. Her face was slightly blurred, and he tried to focus on it. "Do you really have money?" she said.

He nodded his head very solemnly.

"How much?" Her eyes lit up, he noticed that.

"Lots. Fucking piles. Wouldn't think so, would ya?"

"You're a criminal, aren't you?"

"A criminal? Fuck no. I made a bundle in the market."

She started laughing. "Jimmy, I don't believe this."

"You didn't know? Not why you're going out with me?"

"You're too much. Here I thought you were on the lam from a robbery or something. But none of it really fit. Now you tell me you were a broker. In California?"

"A broker? Hell no! Ran a factory—high-tech. Got all these stock options and the stock went nuts, up and up. Then everything went fucking bad." At the mention of Chevalier he suddenly felt teary but pulled himself together.

"What company?"

"Not important."

"Jimmy, you actually expect me to believe any of this?"

"True!" He said it too loudly.

"You mean it?"

He glared at her. "You can't tell nobody."

"For some ridiculous reason I'm starting to think you're serious."

"And I mean—*nobody*."

She nodded.

"Promise?"

"All right, I promise."

Chapter Fifteen

The first thing Hakken did when he woke up was moan. As he surfaced, bits and pieces of the evening fell in on him until he was covered, suffocated. How could he have? Those inane jokes, and actually confiding to Claire about his money. And bragging on top of everything else. He was acting like a rank beginner, breaking every rule he'd ever set for himself. What was it about this damn town anyway? Why couldn't he just stay holed up?

Then his pounding brain locked onto Chevalier and the oath of revenge. He had to get back on track. There was no way Alden could remain unpunished. Soon the cast would be off, he could get into a gym, cut down on his drinking, get tough again, make up for this lapse. He was wandering completely out of control.

His stomach was too riled for breakfast, and his hangover teetered on non-negotiable. If Claire hadn't insisted, it might have been nuclear. All that thinking about his father had set him off, and his fears about Claire had magnified it. At least she'd gotten him out of the Broadway before he'd done too much damage. He had to give her that. Henry had looked all wrong as he left, but he was too drunk to interpret his expression. Phyllis had been a gold blur. His feelings for Claire were weakening him, making him act like a fool, no matter how he attempted to harden himself against her. It was all too obvious that there was only one thing to do: stop seeing her. He'd call her in the afternoon when he could think better. It wasn't going to be easy to say; he needed a clear head to make a clean cut.

He fed the cats and then settled at the computer. He weeded his e-mail and opened his only message:

H—Back in SC. Boys at the Office say hey. You need anything you know where I am. Limb better? L

Jimmy wished he was back in Santa Cruz, just sitting around with Luke, talking about bikes or sports. His decision to break it off with Claire had made him instantly lonely. He forced himself to work on *My Life*.

I ride into the mountains. I'm alone again and I can't keep my thoughts off Bill. The freight climbs and climbs and I can sometimes see the caboose below me. They cut diesel units into the middle and end of the train to help get the thing over the summit. As the freight heads back down, through big pines and streams of fool's gold, smoke starts to pour from the journals. There is the smell of burning metal and the smoke gets blacker.

He read it over twice. It didn't improve. The second sentence wasn't even about Bill. No one would want to read this stupid book. Why was he wasting his time writing it? God, he felt awful. Everything had gone so damn wrong. Instead of being on track, his whole life seemed shunted onto a remote siding and abandoned. He should have protected Chevalier better, should've had his guys in place no matter what. He'd offered it many times, never actually believing Wendell Alden would resort to murder. He'd underestimated the enemy, an unforgivable mistake. Chevalier wouldn't sell the company, and Alden had him killed. Chevalier wouldn't let Jimmy protect him either; he simply wasn't like that, never would have permitted it. The guy had been completely fearless. Jimmy pounded the desk, yelped as pain shot up his arm. It'd be just like him to break his wrist. Doris would be feeding him forever. His phone chimed. He picked it up without thinking.
"Yeah."
"Hey, how're you feeling?"
"Great. Working on my book."
"About growing up in New Hampshire?"
"I get out of there pretty quick."
"I'll bet."
"You *still* don't believe me?"
"Should I?"
"What do you want me to do? Drive you there and show you where I grew up?"
"Okay. When?"
He hesitated. Here he was supposed to tell her that they were through, and now he was driving her to his hometown? "Look, you just got—"
"So it isn't true! Is anything you tell me true?"
"Claire, come on."
"I don't get you at all. Why can't you be honest with me?"
He didn't say anything, feeling worse by the second. "Okay," he said.
"Okay what?"
"I'll drive you there." It just seemed to come out of his mouth. He cursed silently. He'd have to call her later and cancel, try and explain.
"How about today?" Her voice back to normal now.
"Today?"

"Oh, changed your mind already?"

"What about the kid?"

"Brandon'll be at the poolroom all day. All he does every weekend now is hang out there."

"Too long a drive. Probably take hours. Have to check the map."

"Jimmy, it's like an hour to New Hampshire. We can even take my car if you want."

"That junker?"

"It's not a junker—it runs good and gets great mileage." She sounded put out, and he figured it best not to answer. "Do you want to go or not?" she said. He couldn't seem to answer that one either. "Forget it then. Listen, I just called to see how you were, and to thank you for dinner. I got to get going."

"Wait a minute."

"What?"

"When would you want to leave?"

"Anytime. Hey, you want me to pack a picnic? It's a perfect day. We could stop somewhere along the way."

"Don't worry about any lunch." He wished his stomach down.

"What do you think I'm going to bring—lobster rolls?"

"Okay. An hour?" *Jesus*, what was wrong with him?

"I can't wait. It's been *so* long since I've gotten out of this damn town."

Jimmy looked in the mirror. His face was a week-old fish fillet, gill-colored beneath the eyes. The eyes Claire had said were beautiful. He sure couldn't see it. He flossed and brushed, working extra hard on his tongue, wondering again if he shouldn't get his teeth straightened and whitened. The money was sure as hell there, but somehow it would be a desertion. All those perfect white celebrity smiles gloating from every magazine and TV sickened him. He didn't trust those self-satisfied grins. There was a falseness, an ugliness under there. But Claire had similar teeth, even with the slight gap and the more natural white. Nothing was ever clear-cut, was it? Anyway, not the day to worry about that.

He went to the fridge and moved a Ballantine to the freezer. *And another thing!* Here he was a slave to this damn Ballantine just because Chevalier had told him about the stupid beer once. When he'd arrived in Maine, he'd thought it was the best, now he wasn't sure he even liked the damn stuff. "Hakken," he muttered, "you're just hung over and fighting the horrors. Get past it!" He felt in the freezer. The can of ale hadn't chilled even a little. He poured it into a glass anyway although he liked them very cold when he was hung. "Hey, Claire, see?" He held it up. "Even I use a glass once in a damn while." With a raw egg floating in the bottom, the foam salted, he sipped, then tossed it back, hoping for the best. He could almost track its descent. And in a matter of minutes, like a miracle, his hangover stumbled toward negotiable. "Drinking your way out of hangovers. You know what that's called, buddy? Alcoholism. Just like the stepfather." Now he was talking to himself. He never did that. Silently, he reaffirmed his promise to tell Claire he couldn't see her anymore. But he'd tell her after the trip was over. It really bugged him that she thought he was lying about Irving, and he'd be damned if he wasn't going to prove at least that to her.

To nurse his headache, he sent down half a Doctor P, added a few to his vest pocket as backup, and headed out of his apartment. As he tiptoed down the front stairs, his stomach wondered if Claire had packed a lunch. A good sign. He was almost to the front door, his hand on the—

"Robert."

He turned reluctantly.

"You made an awful lot of ruckus last night. You woke me up."

"Sorry."

"It's fine for you to apologize now, but I could *not* get back to sleep."

"Doris, I said I'm sorry."

"Did you fall down the stairs?"

"Slipped once." It came back to him. That explained the knee.

"Where were you?"

There was no point not telling. "At the Broadway."

"Again? I suppose you prefer Phyllis's food to mine?"

He almost said, "Damn right, you poisoning old bat," but instead, "Just felt like a change."

"You were there with the Constantine girl?"

He nodded.

"And what was all that banging this morning?"

"Swatted a roach."

"*Robert*, that is beneath even you. There are no bugs in this house! It may be rundown, it may need painting, I know it needs a spring cleaning—but *bugs* we do not have."

He placed his hand on the knob. "Got to get going."

"But I'm in the middle of talking to you."

"I'm late."

"Will you be here for supper?"

He shook his head, twisted the knob.

"But I was going to make your favorite."

He could only guess. "Not tonight. See ya." He opened the door and escaped, heard her snort as he clicked it shut.

Claire was radiant as they headed out of town. There was something about the way she sat on the bench seat—her posture so straight, her pale blouse shivering in the breeze, her breasts just denting the ironed cotton, her pony tail resting along the top of the seat—it killed him. She'd been right about the weather too. As they left the mills behind, made the transition from tenements to big rundown Victorians, to modern split-levels, to farm fields, the expanse of the grass increased until the greenness was almost a shock. Dry sand from the snowplows lined the shoulders of the road, but the apple trees were overwhelmed by white, and leaves were beginning to open everywhere like verdant moths escaping cocoons.

"Hey, what was that?" she said.

"Nothing."

"Come on, don't start already. I saw you sneak something into your mouth."

"Just something." *Jesus*, she had eyes in her ears.

"Why don't we make a deal? On this trip we only tell the truth. We'll call it the Truth Trip."

"And you'll hold to it?"

"Maybe." She started to giggle. "I guess you're right; it could get complicated. But, come on, what was that?"

"Doctor P."

"A pill?"

"Percocet."

"Where'd you— Oh, from your arm. Does it still hurt?"

He shook his head.

"And here I didn't bring any pot."

"You want one?"

"What's it like?"

"You've never done one?"

"People at the Den are always eating those. That or Oxy. Then they start doing heroin 'cause it's so much cheaper."

"These aren't heroin. Just good with beer." He handed her a half. "Chew."

"*Chew?*"

"Won't bug your stomach that way."

She made a face. "Tasty little bastards, aren't they?"

He pulled in at the next store and bought beer, returned to the car, startled to see someone so pretty waiting for him, she matching the Impala in some special way as if from a famous scene in a movie.

"No Ballantine's?" she said once they were rolling.

"Didn't have it. Lady said she hadn't seen it in years, thought they didn't make it no more, so I figured I'd try this one."

"My dad used to drink this. It's Canadian. You like it?"

He nodded, feeling only a slight betrayal.

The country surrounded them—sunlight like Morse code through young trees, small towns huddled between hills with old men raking dirt from lawns or raising pendulous clouds of dust as they broomed their driveways, teenage girls strutting with purses and cigarettes, a dog bark caught in the breeze, two kids tossing a football, a motorcycle screaming past, a sawmill with stacks of twenty-foot logs kept wet by spraying wands. As they got closer to the mountains, the trees held back their blossoms and leaves, just the occasional yellow blare of forsythia beside a porch. He tried to rein in the memories; a mixture of fear and excitement kept his hand on the wheel, his foot on the gas pedal.

"Why are you tapping the dash?" she said.

"Car just rolled another thousand." His fingers kept counting, his lips helping.

"You do it every thousand miles?"

He nodded. "Here—one for good luck." He waited until her hand joined his.

They talked back and forth. It was so easy with her today, just as smooth as the big wagon rolling through the curves and bends of the highway.

And then a careless question jumped from him:

"Why do you buy drugs for Slag?"

He felt her deflate. "What are you asking me?"

"Sorry, none of my business."

"You want another beer?" she said, and he signaled. "Oh, that's right—you always want one." She opened two, took a long sip, her lips rimming the bottle end. She turned to him.

"I do it for the money. He pays me."

"Is it worth the risk?"

"I don't make much—the frame shop sucks and copyediting is inconsistent. Kids are expensive. Hey, you have another one of those things? They're kind of relaxing."

He reached into his vest, handed her another half.

"Doctor P," she said. "I'm chewing like a good girl."

"Guess I don't get you and him."

"You don't, huh?"

"No."

They drove in silence, the perfect day having changed somehow. Even with the P his headache was back, and he was pissed he'd brought this stuff up. What was the point? He had to end the whole thing later anyway. But maybe that's why he could bring it up?

"You really want the truth?" she said suddenly. "The story no one knows?"

Did he? Something in her tone worried him. It was so open, so flat; nonetheless, he said, "Tell me."

She studied him for a moment and then stared out the windshield. "When I was sixteen, I was this timid kid. I thought everybody just noticed my leg and it made me very shy. Of course I couldn't do sports. Instead I was smart like Brandon. But what good was that going to do me in Scoggton? It hardly made me popular.

"There was this other timid kid—Jeremy Miller. Good old Jeremy. His father was some kind of financial closure expert they brought in when the mills were going out of business. Jeremy was new in school, lousy at sports, kind of goofy looking, and everybody picked on him. I knew how that felt. He never made fun of my leg. Not once. He even asked me about it kindly and seemed truly sympathetic when I told him."

She took a sip. "Jeremy was in the spelling club, so I joined too. And surprise—we were two of the best spellers in school. We went to the state finals. And guess what?"

Jimmy kept driving. The tone of her voice, self-derision added to the flatness, was worrying him.

"You're not going to guess? Oh, well. Nice Jeremy forced himself on little Claire. It started innocently enough, but then he pushed up her dress and ripped down her panties. And though Claire tried to get him to stop—first she pleaded, then she beat at him—Jeremy wouldn't. It wasn't even a minute and it was over. And a couple months later when she told him she might be pregnant, he must've confessed to his parents, or made up some story, because he was missing from school a few days later—he was supposed to be home with the flu. By the time Claire decided to go to his house, it was empty. His family just up and moved away. She never saw him again. So, what was Claire supposed to do? She was so desperate. She was going to have a baby, and she was terrified. She needed someone to help her. But who? Her dad, the withdrawn devout Catholic who wouldn't begin to understand?" She shook her head violently. "Her mom who was in a mental institution?" Again. "So, you know what I did, Jimmy?"

"No," he managed.

"I seduced the richest boy in school, who was two years older and who every girl, including little lonely Claire had a crush on. You didn't know Ray then; he was pretty magnificent before the coke and all the mistakes and failures. But he was so dumb he never realized, though I was nearly a month and a half early. At least Brandon was way late. But it was all horrible and so misguided. Ray never married me anyway because his family simply wouldn't have it, even if I was underage. That's the way things are in Scoggton. They sent Ray to college and paid my hospital bills and that was the end of it. But you know, I screwed up Ray's life, and I'll never forgive myself. And though he might be an asshole now, I still feel sorry for him. After a few years he must have sensed Brandon wasn't his—I mean, look at the two of them. Could they be any more different? So that's why I do him favors. To try and make some kind of amends for the unforgivable thing I did." There were two wet lines on her cheeks. "Do you hate me now? Now that you know I was a scheming bitch? Though all I really was was terribly confused and frightened. So very alone and frightened."

He could hear her crying, but he didn't look at her.

"The truth. You wanted the truth. Or maybe I did? Was it me? Did I want it? The Truth Trip, wasn't that what I called it?"

He saw a pull-off beside a row of birch trees. The tires grumbled on the dirt; a stone kicked up into a wheel well. He stopped the wagon, got out and walked around the car. At the edge of the birches he could hear a stream below, full of snowmelt from the mountains. Then he sensed her behind him.

"Jimmy?"

Her voice bit into him, but he tried to keep his attention on the rush of the water.

"Don't hate me. *Please*. I've hated myself for fourteen years."

When he swiveled and saw her face, all he could do was take her in his arms, or his one arm, the other with the cast sticking out behind. "I don't hate you," he said. *My God*, hate her? Tears wet his neck and her body trembled against him, her hands caressing his back. He smelled her hair, always the same as that first night in the bar, but so much more complex this close. The whole warm scent of her took him. And then his penis began to grow. *Damn*, he thought, trying to think it soft. That her stomach was pressed against it, moving in and out with her emotion, didn't help. He tried to shift, but her body followed his. Suddenly, she backed up a little, her hands leaving his back. He didn't know what to do. What would she think? She tells him her secret tragedy, and he gets an erection. But her hand found him and rubbed through the cloth, her body against his again. He felt her stretch, and then her mouth touched his, her tongue breaking the seal of his lips. Her tongue felt delicate and gentle just like the rest of her, her lips surprisingly soft, feeling much fuller than they looked.

A car honked from the road as it went by; someone yelled.

"Come with me," she said, and took his hand, leading him down toward the water. "Sit down." He obeyed, stumbling onto a leaf-covered boulder, the torrent roaring beside them. She kneeled before him, reached back and took her hair out of the ponytail, shook it free, started to unzip his pants. He moved to stop her, holding her wrist. "No," she said. "Let me." She opened his pants, pulled them down until he felt the damp leaves and smooth stone against his ass, the sunlight on his penis. He still wanted to stop her but he couldn't move. Her fingertips rotated along the ridge of the head and he shivered. Almost immediately a bead of clear liquid appeared, increased in size, quivered like mercury, and dropped glistening onto her palm. She massaged it into the tight skin. He moaned. She leaned forward, her lips open, her hair touching it. "Don't," he said.

She straightened, her hand gliding up and down.

"Please," he said. "I want to look at you." He reached out and touched her hair, his fingertips along her cheek, her mouth closing over one of his fingers and sucking the tip gently, releasing it.

She used both hands. At his moment, his eyes squeezed shut, he felt as if the icy stream were running through him, the whole inexorable power of it.

When he opened his eyes, she was laughing.

"You're too much," she said. She leaned over and kissed him, rubbing her sticky hands along his biceps, over his tattoos.

"I ruined your nice shirt." He felt terribly awkward now.

"I don't care."

"I'm sorry."

"It looks kind of like a butterfly. Maybe I'll never wash it." She stood and almost fell.

More like a deformed moth, he thought, as he jumped up to catch her, almost falling himself, his pants still around his calves. "You okay?"

"My leg. It was that position. It gets stiff sometimes." She glanced down. "Why's it still hard?"

"Just the way it is sometimes." He closed up the best he could, leaving the top button undone.

"Come on. I need a beer. My God, I sound like you."

"Claire?"

She stopped. He couldn't say it, so he just stood there. "I . . . "

"Oh shut up."

They walked back to the car together and rolled west again.

Mount Washington was snow-clad in the north-facing ravines, the smoke from the cog railway just visible toward the summit as a dark calm plume. The mountain looked so immutable and serene. Jimmy, on the other hand, was a rampage of emotions, his mind churning. He kept seeing Claire kneeling in front of him. How the hell had he let *that* happen? At least he'd managed to hold himself back. He sensed once they fucked they would be connected forever. But he'd resisted, and he wasn't sure what that meant, or if she even desired him that way. And Claire, setting up Slag. But he knew how easy it was to do careless things when you were desperate. It was only arrogance that allowed someone to criticize from a distance. Things were always different when you were in the middle of them. He wondered what Slag had really been like as a teenager. Did believing he had a son change him? He sure didn't seem to care now. Regardless of what Claire had said, Jimmy knew most assholes aren't formed by circumstance—as much as people like to believe that—but who could know? And then Claire had been so young, so scared and damaged, and without anyone to turn to. We all do things we regret; he sure knew about that. Then she'd spent years trying to make it up to the guy, but never disclosing the truth to him. The whole thing was confusing and his brain hurt. Too many times reality isn't what you want it to be. Jesus, he felt depressed. Part of it was drinking on a hangover, but everything else was boiling over, and on top of it all he was still horny for Claire, and worse, terrified of heading home for the first time in almost twenty years.

"You okay?" she said. "You're very pale."

"My usual look."

They continued in silence, but he could almost feel her restraining herself.

"Are you upset? About what happened?"

"What do you think?" he said. She seemed uncertain what to do with that, but he didn't know what else to say. This was the woman he planned on telling, "I can't see you again," at the end of the day.

He accelerated on a straightaway, passing a motor home with a Massachusetts plate. Jesus, early May and the tourists were already starting to clog the road. There was another slow group ahead, clustered together like a funeral procession. Soon he'd turn north and lose them. Tourists never ventured to his hometown.

"Are you upset about what I told you? . . . Are you? I don't blame you if that's the way you feel."

"Thinking about where I'm going."

"Oh."

"Beer."

"What? Oh." She handed him one, opened one for herself.

And there was the turn, heading up the valley between the mountains, the pavement full of potholes, the road joining the river now, the high water gnawing at the dirty banks.

"No smell," he said.

"Smell?"

"Stink's gone. Used to stink along here. The pulp stench hung around if there was no wind. Sometimes, in the summer on a hot day, you could barely breathe and it could make you gag. We lived up on the hillside, which helped a bit. Funny thing is, you could only really smell it after you left and came back."

They passed a series of manmade ponds slightly higher than the river, the stagnant water a hideous chemical green, passed two auto parts stores with lurid signage tucked in crumbling brick warehouses abutting the road, and another sign, welcome to irving. It was as if the car were floating. He wanted to stop, but it kept driving somehow. And then, on the other side of the river, there was the mill. It didn't look smaller than he remembered. Not at all. It was still the same enormous labyrinth of filthy buildings—some brick, some cement, some metal, acres of endless pipes and rusty grids of iron, rows of stained silos. But the multiple smoke stacks were quiet. It was like seeing an invincible dragon finally lying dead. "Jesus, they've shut the thing down."

Only once had his stepfather taken him to see the mill. Jimmy had snuck onto the grounds many times, but this was different. This was inside and official. He was thirteen, and after his stepfather's lecture on how to act, he'd been escorted into one of the huge buildings, the one that housed the newsprint machine where his stepfather worked. The hardhat he'd been handed was too large, and he knew he looked stupid in it. "No hat, you ain't going in," his stepfather said. Inside, the whole place had hummed and vibrated, even the cement floor seemed to be shaking. Dozens of giant steel rolls, any of which would barely have fit in the trailer, spun at a blur. At one end, wet pulp poured in a long even drape onto a flying screen, and then the wet sheet was squeezed and pressed, the drying paper wide as a street and infinitely long. His stepfather told him that keeping the sheet from breaking was the big deal. Every time it snapped, the company lost money, and a new sheet, narrow to start with, had to be rethreaded at a crawl through the maze of rolls until the machine could be cranked up, the sheet widened, everything run again at full velocity. "But there's tricks," he said. "Lots of dummies lose their hands, but not this guy"—he tapped his chest—"I'm too smart." Jimmy had been impressed, proud to be there, and then his stepfather had looked to the few men standing around and pointed, "This is Sue's wimpy kid, I'm trying to toughen him up."

Less than two years later, half his stepfather's arm was gone, and the real trouble had started.

"Christ," said Claire. "And I thought Scoggton had mills. It's like they

haven't torn anything down in a hundred years. It must be miles long."
They crossed a double set of railroad tracks, the wagon complaining,
drove past a large wood construction on four posts. "I think it's supposed
to be a moose," she said. It was a new addition, and he wanted to
comment, but he couldn't seem to speak. They bumped along the main
street that hadn't been repaved in many years. Among the boarded up or
empty storefronts was a music store with the usual window curtain of
guitars and an open flag, a plywood sheathed candlepin bowling alley
with one curved glass-brick corner, a bank with its digital time-temp
indicator stuck at -12, a candy and flower shop bannered in gaudy Easter
colors, and a pizza joint. The Shell station where Jimmy had taken the
bus out of town so long ago was vacant, the pumps and advertising gone,
only the barren husk remained.
"This is even worse than Scoggton," she said.
He glanced at her.
"Well, it is. I mean, I don't want to upset you more, but look at it."
He *was* looking at it. "Beer," he said again and headed up the hill.
Of course, Happy Acres had to be there. A new sign, but the same basic
horseshoe of trailers propped to the slope on cinderblocks. Crescent Hill
Homes was the new name. His stepfather's trailer was gone. He turned
the car around and parked by the sign and just sat there, drinking his beer
and alternately holding the damp bottle to his cheek.
"Why are we stopping here?" she said.
"You wanted to see it."
"This is it? Where you grew up?"
"Bingo."
She didn't answer. Instead she slid over on the bench seat and pressed
against him, her head on his shoulder, her smell again, almost familiar
now. At first he didn't move, then he put his arm around her, but it felt
like lead, too heavy for anyone to bear.
"Is any of your family still in town?"
"Stepfather might be. Who knows."
"Your mother?"
He shook his head.
"Is she alive?"
Shook his head again.
"I'm sorry."
They worked their beers.
"Is that why you left home?"
It took him a minute. "Naw." He paused, his throat tight. "But the first
time I call home, I get my stepfather." He took a sip to clear it. "He tells
me she's dead. He was driving."

She moved even closer to him. Tried to get her arms around him, held him awkwardly.

"Aw, fuck," he said.

Chapter Sixteen

You don't get things done by being a nice guy. Jimmy knew there were exceptions, but there weren't many. So—had he told Claire anything like he'd planned as they drove back to Scoggton, her warm body nestled against his on the bench seat, her eyes closed, his good arm around her as he carefully steered the wagon through the spring dusk? When they'd left Irving, she'd asked him, "What do you really care about?" and he'd said, "Work. Getting my work done." He hadn't, of course, told her that his work was executing Wendell Alden. When he dropped her off at her apartment, he'd said, "Need to get some stuff done. Call you when I can."

Almost a week had gone by. A long week. He felt particularly crummy ignoring her after what she'd confessed to him. No wonder she was kind of jittery about relationships. But what could he do about it? *Jesus*, his life had been so straightforward when he was working for Chevalier, and now it seemed to get messier and messier on a weekly basis. The conflict between his vow to Chevalier and his feelings for Claire kept plaguing him, and he didn't know how to resolve it. He hoped dumping Claire would solve everything—he'd be on track again— but instead he just felt frozen in place, unable to decide anything. She'd rung several times, and he'd forced himself to ignore the calls, but that hadn't helped one way or the other.

Yellow was brushing against him, and Jimmy gave him a scratch. Transporting the cats across the country had been such an annoyance. They'd jumped around in the car, sometimes onto his shoulder or head at the worst moments; they'd hidden under the seats, cried out incessantly, particularly Yellow who sometimes seemed to be channeling roosters. And then he'd had to sneak them into motels. When he got to Scoggton, he'd vowed never to drag another damn litter box into or out of a motel room again. But what was he going to do with these guys when he and Luke headed south? No one brought cats along to kill someone. Maybe Doris would take them? But it was too soon to worry about that. He drifted over to his computer. He had only a vague interest in *My Life* these days, but he opened it anyway. He needed to do something, besides drink.

There is the smell of burning metal and the smoke gets blacker. I'd heard about freights breaking loose in the mountains. (When the brakes can't hold them, the metal gets so hot that the grease burns up in the journal boxes.) The train gets going faster and faster, and the smoke is all I can see now. I wonder if I should jump, but what am I going to do in the middle of the Idaho wilderness, even if I survive the fall?

Once again his writing failed him. All these emotions, all these memories, but none of it seemed to solidify in the type. How was he to convey being alone in a boxcar, standing in the middle of a seemingly vacant train of hundreds of cars, thundering down a mountain, the wheels and brakes screaming, the hot acrid smoke stinging his nostrils, the adrenaline of fear overlapped by excitement, his hands gripping the metal edge of the door so he wouldn't be pitched to the floor, or worse? He didn't jump that day. When he did, the train was moving a lot slower and he'd still gotten hurt.

Those many years ago he'd arrived in Pasco, Washington after riding through the desert night. His father finally felt close—all he had to do was get to Portland and head down the coast to San Francisco. His mother had told him that his father had once shipped out of there before their marriage. It was a long shot, but to him then, it seemed a certainty. He just needed to find the docks and ask around. Somehow, he knew his dad would still be a sailor. Maybe they could ship out together, travel around the world, father and son. Jimmy'd imagined the two of them lounging on the deck of a tramp steamer, south sea islands in the distance, an overflowing goblet of a moon, smoke from their pipes corkscrewing into warm air. Of course, this would be after they'd cleaned up in Las Vegas.

In Pasco, Jimmy'd left his train and walked along the tracks.

There is this scarred, abandoned icehouse with a bunch of hobos under it. They're drinking wine. As I walk by, one of them waves. I realize they take me for a tramp, which secretly pleases me. I stop and go over. The guy who'd waved says, "Got any smoke?" There's four of them so I shake my head.

"Where you headed?"

"Portland."

"Ain't a train till this afternoon."

"You going to Portland?"

"We're all headed there. You want some wine?"

It's Thunderbird, and the thought of drinking after these guys is not pleasant. I shake my head.

He liked *scarred* because the timber frame of that ancient structure might have been recycled from the ark, but his drinking after the hobos—their gapped-tooth mouths, their scabbed lips, their rotting gums—*not pleasant* hardly matched his disgust. And the dialogue about tobacco—though it always happened that way, the reader already knew it. If there were ever going to be any readers. Why would anybody want to read about some poor kid trying to find his father?

He got up and circled the apartment. He couldn't shake the memory of that day. It was the first time he'd watched someone die, and the worst part—he hadn't tried to save the guy.

He'd joined the hobos in their drinking, surreptitiously wiping the bottle neck with his shirt. By afternoon everyone was drunk. Someone who claimed to be a bank robber tried to befriend him. Wearing unsoiled khakis and a fairly new jacket, the guy had teeth and seemed more intelligent than your average hobo. The oddest thing was his clean-shaven jaw, so blue it might have been in a cartoon. After demonstrating to Jimmy how to steal wine and beer out of a trackside grocery, the thief explained in detail how to crack safes—which drills, which chisels. He doubted the thief knew what he was talking about but listened anyway. Then trouble started. He was soon to learn that drinking among bums usually led to violence.

Two guys began arguing. A sledgehammer of a guy with hair that looked as if it mopped floors, was insisting he was a hobo. Another tramp was shaking his head. "You ain't no 'bo—you're a bum." He said it as calmly as a judge with a verdict. "You never travel, you never work, so you're a bum." Sledge staggered upright, yelling. The tramp stood as well, his ill-fitting overalls hanging on his tiny frame. "I don't give a damn what you say—you're a bum, and that's the end of it." In response, Sledge grabbed a scrap of lumber and whacked the tramp in the head with it. The tramp tried to cover up with his childlike hands, but the second blow brought blood. No one seemed to care. Jimmy got to his feet, and coming from behind, wrenched the weapon from the large man's grip. Sledge turned on him now, bellowing. Jimmy held the stick ready like a baseball bat, his hands shaking.

"Leave the kid alone." It was the thief.

"Git out-a my way. This got nothin' do with you."

"You heard me. Leave it." He turned to Jimmy. "Come on." He gathered his bedroll and battered suitcase.

Jimmy backed away from Sledge and shouldered his pack.

"I'll fine ya, ya punk," called Sledge to their backs. "I'll fine ya, and I'll kill ya. It won't matter where ya hide, I'll fine ya and kill ya."

"Ugly drunk," said the thief. Jimmy tossed away the stick.

As they walked, a long row of freight cars began creaking and moving a few tracks over. The thief turned to him: "We can catch it. We better get you out a here 'fore he starts lookin'." There weren't any boxcars, so the thief grabbed the ladder on a hopper car and pulled himself onboard. "Come on," he yelled, his hand outstretched. Jimmy just made the train. It was ten minutes later when they tracked into the desert that he realized what was wrong.

"We're headed east."

"Don't matter."

"When do you think this freight will stop?"

"No idea." He opened the suitcase and pulled out a pint of tequila, offered it.

Jimmy shook his head.

The thief shrugged, tipped the bottle, licked his lips.

The car they rode on was a massive cylinder that held dry powdered cement, poured in at the top through hatches and released out the bottom through hinged doors. At each end were diamond-grated platforms under the sloped angle of the enormous drum, one taken up by brake machinery. It was on the other end that the thief and Jimmy crouched, only a six-inch lip of metal around the perimeter protecting them from rolling off onto the roadbed and under the wheels. As the freight reached speed, it became too noisy to talk. He was miserable—headed away from his father, his temples pounding from the cheap wine and beer. Evening brought cold and the thief got drunker. He opened a second pint. His suitcase seemed to be filled with them and little else. When night left only a brutal red blur at the horizon, the thief sidled up next to him and mumbled something, the foul alcoholic breath, spit-covered lips touching his ear. With the clatter of the rails and the car, he couldn't understand at first. But when the guy reached toward him, grabbed him by the thigh and tried to pull down his zipper, he did. Jimmy punched him in the throat. The man fell backwards and just lay there on his side. Then, like a wounded animal, he retreated on hands and knees to the other side of the platform, his eyes wet in the last light. Jimmy stayed wary, but the thief just muttered to himself and kept pulling at the pint. The freight left the black desert and entered the outskirts of Spokane, slowing only slightly, the city lights and the red swirl of crossing gates reassuring. Suddenly the thief staggered to his feet, stood a long moment, swaying, Jimmy barely breathing. He pointed oddly at Jimmy, mumbling something. Then he turned clumsily and simply stepped into nothingness. Jimmy leapt to that side of the car. The body was still tumbling along the gravel as if it would never stop, and then it whacked soundlessly into a steel electrical box. All he could do was throw out the man's meager belongings after him, the pints probably shattering when they hit the roadbed. In seconds it had all vanished in the darkness, but never in his memory.

The freight is still going kind of fast. I head into the Spokane yard, but it doesn't seem to be slowing much. I think of spending the night in the Idaho mountains, and I decide I might as well jump as freeze to death. At that point I didn't know the secret of jumping off a moving train, which is to run like crazy when you're in the air. I jump like I'm leaving a porch step. When I come to I'm looking at the night sky. My head feels wet. It's blood. But I figure I did better than the other guy.

All that, he thought, standing again and walking to the window. He'd gone through all that to find his father! But the big reunion, the big conclusion, the big moment? He'd have to change it in his book. Who the hell would want to read that truth? He'd made it to San Francisco all right. He'd found the docks all right. He'd asked around—no one knew or had heard of a James Hakken. It was cold and foggy down by the water, a tug or something moaning way out in the bay. And then he'd spotted a payphone. He'd opened the damp, swollen phonebook hanging in the filthy booth. Why had he never thought of that? He couldn't believe it. There it was:
Hakken James 441 Douglas Ln.................285-4856
And with his heart hammering melodramatically, echoing every freight mile he'd ridden:
"Hello, is this James Hakken?"
"Who's this?"
"The James Hakken who was married to Susan Quinn?"
"Listen, who the hell is this?"
"It's Jimmy."
"Jimmy who?"
"Hakken. Your son."
There was an endless pause. So many things roared through him like a train into a tunnel. The light on the other side was blinding.
"Oh. . . . Where are ya?"
"Right here, in San Francisco, by the docks."
"Oh."
Another long pause started, so he said: "I just got here . . . from New Hampshire."
"So you're still living there are ya?"

"No, not really. My mom is still there though."
"Oh."
He squinted out across the mostly invisible bay, the murky light wavering, his knees going weak. "You want me to call back some other time?"
"Well, kind of. Listen, I'm shipping out, uh, soon. I got a lot ta do, ya know . . . before I leave."
"Yeah."
"Maybe when I get back, or something."
"Yeah." It barely came out.
"So, you're doing okay? You out here visiting?"
"Sorta."
"By yourself?"
"Yeah."
"And your mom?"
"Yeah."
"She doin' good?"
"Yeah."
"Great. Take care, kid, all right?"
"Yeah."
And his father hung up.
All right? No it wasn't fucking all right.
When he'd called his mom the next day, slotting all that change into the same stupid machine, he'd gotten his stepfather. Nothing was ever going to be all right again.

Chapter Seventeen

"Bob Gray?"

Jimmy was reaching for a rectangle of cheddar cheese in the long refrigerated case. The sharp kind with the plaid label, the one he liked best.

"Aren't you Bob Gray?"

He felt something prick his bicep and he straightened, turned, faced a huge nest of hair dyed an unnatural yellow, arranged in some complicated incomprehensible logic. He almost expected a miniature squirrel to pop its head out and wink. Her body, however, he understood at a glance.

Her voice was in no hurry. "You're Bob, aren't ya? I'm Vicky, Vicky Lattrell, Claire's friend." She held out a hand, the nails long and glittering in the IGA's fluorescents.

He shook the fingers reluctantly.

"I work right next door." She pointed. "I come over here to get lunch. You know, they have a pretty good salad bar if you get here before it's all pawed through." It was around five o'clock. And she didn't look as though she ate only salads. "Claire has told me *so* much about you, I feel like I already know you." She smiled, and her bottom teeth were crooked. Her uppers were fairly straight and so white they were almost blue. Her upper lip didn't seem quite able to cover her teeth although her bottom lip was overly full. Everything about her was large, except her waist, which was surprisingly slim. She stepped forward, the hand in motion again. It touched the side of his head, and he pulled back. "You have nice hair. I wish I had your color. If you ever want it styled, come see me. My salon is Taboo Cuts, right over there." She pointed again, gave him a last look over her shoulder, and moved down the aisle with a walk that held his eyes all the way out of the grocery store. He shook his head and went back to shopping.

Jimmy headed across the parking lot with his beer and paper bag of eats. He glanced over at Taboo Cuts, one of four businesses in the mall attached to the IGA. The evening was finally warm, the leaves fully formed, a soft California-like tone draped over everything. But it was different here. Here, the warmth seemed to bubble through him like sap.

He felt as if he'd earned the temperate weather, as though he deserved it. In Santa Cruz it was just expected. As he lowered the bag onto the seat of the wagon, there was a loud honk and he almost banged his head against the roof liner.

"What're you doing in that old heap?" she said.

Vicky had pulled up next to him in a neon-violet convertible with its rear sticking up suggestively; it looked brand new. Her hair color vibrated against the car paint. "What is that thing, like a fifty-nine or something?"

"Sixty-five."

"No shit." She leaned across the seat, the shoulder belt dividing her breasts. "Hey, you want to go get a margarita or something? There's this new Mexican place out by the interstate."

"I should be getting back."

"To Callahan's? Oh come on, what's the big deal? Aren't you *thirsty*?" The way she said it, it suggested everything.

"Got some stuff to do."

"Are you sure?"

He nodded.

"Whatever." She flipped her hair, which barely moved—though the jerk of her head would have dislodged the squirrel—and backed up with a chirp of tires.

The whole way through town, up Brackert Hill, even at the entrance to True Terrace, he couldn't get her image out of his head. She stuck there like a sloppy wet kiss to his forehead, drying slowly. So that was Vicky Lattrell—Jesus.

There was a brown sedan parked under the porte cochere and the house door was ajar. Doris must have company, which was unusual. Besides that scurvy cousin, Doris never had visitors. Jimmy dumped the wagon in the carriage barn, grabbed his groceries, and headed for the house. As he turned the corner, he heard:

"I assure you ma'am, this is *not* going to go away. The city has allowed you every consideration because of your family's history, but the next step is the sheriff."

Jimmy stopped.

"Young man, you know it's not right! My grandfather and my father built this damn town."

"Mrs. Callahan, *that* has nothing to do with it. Our hands are tied. I've explained it to you over and over."

"Humph!"

"Being stubborn like this is counter-productive."

"There is no reason to be rude, young man."

"Ma'am, I'm sorry, but you're just going to have to face reality."

"I want you off my property."

Jimmy showed himself then. The chubby guy in the ill-fitting suit turned.

"Problem?" Jimmy said.

The guy started backing toward his car, his briefcase in front of him, his eyes on Jimmy.

"It's all right, Robert," said Doris from the top step. "He's just some salesman who won't take no for an answer."

The guy unlocked his car and slid his belly behind the wheel. "One more week, Mrs. Callahan. That's your final warning." He eased the sedan forward and drove off, shaking his head.

Jimmy joined Doris on the steps. Her face was beet behind the glasses. "What's that all about?" he said.

"Nothing. Just what I told you."

"Come on, Doris, what's going on?"

"You mind your own damn business." She spun and shot off into the house.

He followed her, setting his groceries on the stair landing. She was in the kitchen, slumped in a chair. He took a seat next to her. "If someone's bugging you, tell me."

She rotated like the cannon on a tank. "And I suppose you're going to fight the whole city."

"Tell me who it is."

"I'm going to have to ask you to leave."

"Leave?"

She nodded.

He stood. "You need a few minutes alone, no problem."

She looked up at him, her glasses catching the window light. "Robert, you're going to have to move out. I'm sorry."

"*Move?*"

"By next week."

"Doris." He placed a hand on her shoulder. It surprised them both. "What the hell is going on?"

"There is nothing you can do. There's nothing anyone can do." The tears wandered down her wrinkled skin, her white hair so thin at the crown.

He was embarrassed now. Her voice sounded painfully miserable: "How could my father have done that to me?"

"Doris, you okay?"

"Please, Robert, just leave me alone."

He waited, not knowing what to do. But what could anyone do with a crotchety spinster who's crying? He had no clue.

She covered her face with her trembling hands. "*Please.*"

The word sounded so desperate and certain that Jimmy walked out of the kitchen, grabbed his bag and beer, and headed up the stairs.

In his garret, he cracked a Ballantine and glared at the cell phone resting on the desk. He never took the thing with him unless he needed to call Luke. As far as he was concerned, it looked too dorky talking on cell phones when you were walking or driving around; a man had to have some dignity in life. He picked it up and finger-tipped in a number. Jesus, they must design these things for teenage girls with tiny hands. He'd promised himself he wouldn't call her, but he needed to find out what was going on with Doris.

"Claire," he almost shouted.

"Hey, how's the work going?"

"Sucks."

"So, you coming outside to play again?"

"I need your help."

Her voice changed. "What's up?"

"It's a long shot, but do you know a guy, balding, little goaty beard, paunch, wears a dumpy suit and drives a brown Buick, probably works for the city?"

"Not offhand. What's this about? You get beat up again by a little fat guy?"

He was silent. There it was again. And to top it off, she sounded as if she hadn't missed him at all.

"You there? Christ, I'm only kidding."

"Any reason the city would be after Doris?"

"Not that I know of."

"And the father, what happened to her father?"

She didn't say anything for a moment. "Can I call you back?"

"Yeah, I guess."

"Let me make a few calls, okay?"

"Yeah."

"And Jimmy?"

"Yeah."

"It's great to hear from you, whatever the reason."

He slapped the phone onto the desk. Her voice went right into the center of him, and her face appeared as it had looked that day beside the icy stream, as it had looked in the dusk driving home from Irving. He wanted to smell her again, press his face into her hair. Instead, he put away the groceries and snapped open another pounder. The can was almost empty when his cell warbled.

"Yeah."

"Okay, I talked with my dad. I knew he'd remember the story better than me, though he never worked at Callahan Shoe."

"Tell me."

"Remember I told you Callahan bankrupted the family? What I forgot was that his wife left him before that, when Doris was at college. He took the loss hard, and Doris quit school, came home and took care of him. It went on for years, just the two of them living in that huge house, Doris with no life except her father. According to my dad, what ruined Callahan was that he wouldn't unionize when everyone else did. Even so, he had loyal employees and kept the business going for at least ten more years, but the union was really pissed and started putting pressure on his workers, threatening their families, beating people up, stuff like that. He couldn't hold on. The factory was probably refinanced a bunch of times anyway. That happened to a lot of businesses in Scoggton during the seventies. So the bank foreclosed, and the morning they came to take the building, they found Callahan hanging in his office."

"Shit."

"Sad, isn't it?"

"And Doris has been there ever since? By herself?"

"She's been pretty much in seclusion since his suicide."

"And the mother?"

"She never even showed for the funeral. Who knows what happened to her. I was like seven years old when the whole thing happened, but I still remember it. The Callahans were a big deal back then. Their factory employed a lot of people."

"Anything on the other?"

"The other?"

"Guy with the Buick?"

"You want me to check more?"

"Hold off. I'll look into it tomorrow." He could feel her waiting for him to say something more. It took everything he had just to thank her and hang up. He didn't mention running into Vicky Lattrell.

First thing in the morning, he went to his secret hideaway, an unfinished tunnel between the roofline and the plaster wall, with an odd-shaped door. In the darkness were two suitcases, the vintage kind made out of vinyl-covered cardboard with leather along the edges, worn to an orange felt on the corners. He pulled one out, tossed it onto his bed, lifted up the false bottom he'd fabricated, and slid out a carbon fiber case. He aligned the lock and popped the lid. Inside were neatly stacked hundreds. Thousands of them. Removing about half an inch, he fed the bills into a black leather wallet. The wallet was so long it stuck out of his back pocket about three inches, which is why he chained it to his belt. He raced through his dental routine and headed down the stairs.

For once there was no Doris. No dinner bell last night either. He never imagined he would miss her front hall assaults. But she had pride, and that was something he understood. He opened the front door to rain, a hard soaking downpour. The storm had woken him early when it started and he'd listened to the monotonous threshing against the slate roof until he'd drifted back to sleep. Now he stood under the porte cochere a moment, could almost feel the earth absorbing the moisture, that cold clean smell of ozone. By the time he was behind the wheel of the Impala, his leather vest was wet, his cast damp. The cast was coming off today anyway, he decided. To hell with the damn thing. He'd removed the stitches in his head himself; the cast would be easy after that. The one visit to the ER had been annoyingly expensive. He should've sent the bill to Slag.

With the wipers thrashing, Scoggton a gray and brick blur, he found city hall, its stone tower bleary with fog. Doris had said he couldn't fight the whole city, so he'd start there. He walked up the granite steps, annoyed that his stomach still reacted to these kinds of places—court rooms, police stations, jails, anyplace official where cops clustered. He pulled open the heavy door; there weren't any cops in the hallway, just groups of people waiting, hands clutching papers, raincoats dripping. He moved past them, figuring he'd try a few closed doors farther down the hall, not ready to stand in line yet.

The second door he tried opened. A woman looked up from her computer, the rest of the office empty. "Maybe you can help me?" he said.

Her plump hand returned a powdered-sugar donut to its box; the arm moved as slowly as a railroad crossing gate going down. "I doubt it."

He entered, leaned against an elbow-high counter of dark wood, her dull eyes continuing to watch him. "Just a bit damp. I dry up pretty good." A barely perceptible upward movement of lips. "What do you want?" "I'm looking for someone. Maybe you know him."—he described the guy, leaving out *fat*. "Was up at Doris Callahan's yesterday. Dropped his pen. I got his pen for him."

"Paul Bilinear, his office is upstairs. Room two seventeen."

Bingo. "Thanks."

She picked up the donut again.

The door to two seventeen was closed. He knocked. Waited, tried the knob. Locked. He headed back downstairs and slid into the office again. The empty donut box was in the trashcan beside her desk. He stood at the counter until she glanced up from her computer.

"Wasn't in. Any idea where he is?"

She studied her watch. "He's at home today until noon. Something to do with his dog. You can leave the pen with me." She might have mentioned that earlier.

"You wouldn't know what he was doing at Callahan's, would you?"

"Of course I know."

He waited. "And?"

"And what?"

"What was he doing there?"

"Trying one last time to get her to pay at least something on her taxes."

"She hasn't paid her taxes?"

"Not for almost four years."

"That's all?"

"That's *all*? The city owns her wreck of a house now, and we hate being in the real estate business. The sheriff comes in one week to evict her. I'd say that's something."

"The city owns her house?"

"Didn't I just say that?"

"How do you know all this?"

"I'm Bilinear's assistant, who do you think I am?"

He paused. "What's it take to get her house back?"

"Money."

"How much?"

"You've sure got enough questions. Who are you anyway?"

"Her nephew. Tell me how much."

"Her nephew, huh?"

He nodded though he could tell she didn't believe him. "How much does she owe?"

"You expect me to look it up?"

"Would you?"

She stared.

"Please."

She muttered something to herself and began tapping at her keyboard. It might be the one place she moved fast, her fingers a blur. "Eleven thousand, four hundred and fifty-two dollars and sixty-eight cents. Satisfied?"

Jimmy reached for his back pocket. His hunch had been correct, not that it was much of a hunch: money solved a lot of problems. He snapped the wallet open, started counting hundreds, and then stopped. *Damn*—he should've grabbed an inch. He cleared his throat. She glanced up.

"Listen, you gonna be here for the next twenty minutes?"

"Where do you think I'm gonna go, the Bahamas?"

He headed back down the hall past the dripping raincoats, out into the fog, wipers beating, under the porte cochere, up the steps, two flights of stairs, suitcase out, case open, another half inch—he made sure this time—and then he was tapping on the door and walking into the office.
"Back from the ATM already?" she said, chuckling.
He pulled the wallet and began counting. "You got a receipt or something for this?" He held up the wad. "I want proof she'll get her house back."
She hesitated for a long moment, then struggled to her feet. Powdered sugar dusted her bulging lime-green front. She wobbled over to the counter. "You have *got* to be kidding me." She stared at the money, then looked all around suspiciously. "Is this one of those America's Funniest Video things?"
"Now that was funny."
She gave him a fake smile. "I try."
"What's your name?" Why did fat women so often have such lovely skin?
She pointed to the plaque on her desk.
"Can't read it from here."
"Rebecca Hines."
"Can we make a deal?"
"What kind of deal?" Her vague smile wilted instantly.
"You keep the change on the eleven-five large, and you don't tell anyone who paid this."
"I'm a city employee; I can't take bribes."
He tossed another hundred beside the pile. "That's not a bribe, Rebecca, it's a gift. Maybe you want to go out for dinner, do something nice for yourself? The city owes you that."
"Are you serious?"
He nodded.
She looked around carefully again, though the office was still just as empty, and slid the hundred off the counter and into a fold somewhere. "Why you don't want everyone to know is beyond me. I mean, you could get in the paper for something like this."
Jimmy shuddered. It struck him how stupid he'd just been. But sometimes you just had to say Fuck it.
Rebecca hobbled back to her desk and went to work. Printers hummed, papers fluttered forth. She gave him the forty-seven dollars and thirty-two cents change.
"You're not from around here," she said.
"New Hampshire."
She nodded as if that explained it.

Jimmy headed back out into the rain.

Chapter Eighteen

"I need a gym."

"What kind of gym?"

"Free weights, heavy bag, and a steam room."

"There are a few in town." Claire's voice sounded different again—kind of distant this time. Only yesterday she'd been amused when he told her about removing his cast himself. She'd even laughed when he confessed to doing the stitches in his head with a mirror and tweezers. Something had changed.

"Where does Slag work out?" he said in quick retaliation for her tone.

"Don't worry, I wouldn't send you to *his* gym."

"Why not?"

"Why *not*?"

She was beginning to upset him. "You ever gonna tell me what's *really* going on there?"

"What do you mean?"

"You know what I mean."

"What're you asking?" She sounded even colder.

"You with this guy or not?"

"Hell no! We've never been together. What happened, happened long ago. It was a horrible mistake—I told you all that. Didn't I tell you everything? Jimmy, you think I would've let happen what happened at the river if I was with Ray?"

He didn't know what to say.

"Well?" she said.

"But he acts like he owns you."

"He acts that way with everyone. He's become an ass. Coke changes people and not for the better."

"You still buy drugs for him."

"I told you, it's only sometimes, and he gives me a hundred every time. I need the money."

"How 'bout I give you two hundred not to?"

"Are you serious?"

"What do you think?" Jesus, how had he gotten into this position? What was it about her? "You telling me the truth?"

118

"About what?"

"Slag."

"Shit, Jimmy, you think I'd lie about that? I'm an honest person."

"Don't get so pissed."

"And talk about lying, you didn't tell me about running into Vicky, did you?"

He was silent.

"Or that you asked her out. Were you going to take her to the Broadway? I mean, you could, of course, that's up to you, but—"

"—She said that?"

"You think she wouldn't tell me? Were you embarrassed she turned you down?"

He was silent again. This was too much.

"Seriously, if you want to take her out that's—"

"Where does Slag work out?"

A long pause. "Super Flex." She said it like, Fuck You. "Why don't you go there and see what happens." And the phone slammed down.

"I will," he muttered to himself, irate, wanting to punch something. God damn her! And God damn that lying skunk Vicky Lattrell. And to hell with that old bat Doris, costing thousands, poisoning him with those soggy biscuits, and saying she thought he was tougher, blinking at him with that condescending look of spinster scorn. God damn all women! He knew he was overreacting. A message flickered in his brain like a weak radio signal, audible but incoherent. It said: "Accept the beating, the dent, and the red-faced moron," but Jimmy wasn't listening. Once again he saw himself sprawled in the cold mud beside the damaged Impala. It made him furious. And then the months of ridicule from these damn women with nothing to do but peck at his stupid novel as his arm healed. And what was his book about? His fucking father who hadn't given one rat's ass about him. Not once! Even after he'd traveled three-thousand difficult miles to find the unfeeling bastard. And there was Brandon, that sorry-ass pathetic sneezer without a dad as well. Jesus! He pounded the desk so hard an empty beer bottle clattered to the floor and rolled clumsily into a corner.

But what did he care if Claire and Doris thought he was a wimp? What did he care what anyone in this goddamn useless town thought of him? Why give a moment's emotion to any of these losers? He was just holed up here for a few more months, then he'd be gone forever. But he did care, and that made him even angrier.

His rage expanded like blood in water. Against everyone in Scoggton. And then it targeted Wendell Alden again. How could that rich slime kill the only great man who had ever lived? And Jimmy unable to protect him. He wanted to strangle Alden with his bare hands until his tongue stuck out a like a foot-long hotdog. If that arrogant bastard hadn't murdered Chevalier, he wouldn't even be in this goddamned lost excuse for a town.

Super Flex was off Acadia Ave toward the river in one of the abandoned mills. There were a couple dozen cars in the parking lot, Slag's red SUV not one of them. He locked the wagon and entered the building, bitter momentum moving him forward like a breakaway freight train.

A young woman behind a shiny blue counter looked up. He disliked her on sight; she might as well have been one of those fitness trainers on TV who jump and stretch provocatively, grinning at the camera, giddily counting reps, self-satisfied and oblivious to anything real in life. "Hi there," she said. "Are you here to work out or to tan?" Her blonde ponytail and her gum kept rhythm with each silly word, her lipstick only slightly redder than her skin. She was exactly the type who had consistently disdained him in California.

The room was large, panels of mirrors below iridescent yellow walls, the maroon carpet covered by grids of blue workout machines, loud pop rock pumping up the brightly clad exercisers. This was tough-guy Slag's gym? It looked like something suited to a bargain-basement cruise boat for maladjusted singles.

"You wanna like, look around first or something?" she said.

"Ray Cloutier work out here?"

"You know him?"

He nodded.

She brightened. "He's like, one of the owners. Did you see our special in the paper? Three hundred for like a *whole* year. It's a *really* awesome deal."

"Cloutier ever stop by?"

"He's usually here by like three."

"Every day?"

She nodded.

Jimmy checked the clock—twenty minutes.   "How much for a month?"

She reached over and shuffled some laminated sheets.

"Got any free weights?" he said. "Boxing stuff?"

"In the other room. Are you a boxer?" The gum continued to keep the rhythm.

"Sometimes."

She glanced up, smiling uncertainly, finally getting it that he wasn't being all that friendly. "Here it is. It's like, eighty-five for a quarter year. I'm afraid we don't do months and you don't, like, get the special for that."

He pulled out his roll, filled out the few sheets of paperwork, signed as Bob Gray. She passed the change. "I'll have your card ready by the time you leave. Now I'll show you around." She stood, athletic in her lime and blue spandex. "You've worked out before, haven't ya?"

"Once."

"No way. You look like you're in really good shape."

"Got any bag gloves?"

"*Bag* gloves?"

"Leather with a metal rod." Still nothing. "For training on the heavy bag."

"You mean for boxing?"

"Bingo."

She turned and opened a metal cabinet, searched among stacks of Super Flex sweatshirts, knee supports, and towels. "Like these?"

He paid her for the gloves and stuck them in his back pocket.

"You're not from around here, are you?" she said.

"New Hampshire."

Her ponytail bobbed, the gum moved to the other side. Around Scoggton, that answer seemed to explain everything. She waved for someone to take over the desk and told Jimmy to follow her. "You want me to weigh and measure you?"

"Listen, don't worry about it. I can find my way around." He left her standing there.

In California, cute women had always ignored him. They never looked past his shaved head, sideburns and tattoos. They never gave him a second glance, if there was even a first. As a way of protecting himself, he'd rationalized their behavior as ignorant or short-sighted, but that had hardly eased the frustration. They had expected him to be who they'd carelessly assumed he was, and he'd become too much that. They hadn't looked beyond his looks and attitude to his inner person. He'd said, "Fuck 'em," the same way he'd addressed many things of an exclusive nature where he was the outsider.

He located the free weight room. It was the antithesis of the one out front—empty of patrons, the walls dirty unpainted cinderblock lined with multiple squat racks. The floor was planked, six weight benches, a dead lift platform dusted in powder and spent amyl-nitrate cartridges, two heavy bags with two speed bags in one corner, no music except the distant thump of the bass beat through the one recently erected chipboard wall. He admitted it reluctantly: his kind of gym.

He kept on his black jeans and boots—he wasn't one for shorts and sneakers—and hung up his leather vest near the bench press closest to the boxing bags, then slid two forty-five pound iron plates onto the bar. During the first few reps he monitored his mended arm. It felt okay. He'd always had strong tendons.

He heard sounds. When he saw who it was he stood, keeping the bench between himself and the three approaching guys. No mistakes this time. He'd keep them distracted; curiosity took precedence over a lot of things. Two buddies surrounded Slag, the guy who'd blackjacked him and a new one, all three looking a little weary today, probably on empty this early. Regardless, Slag came right up to him.

"You? What're you doing here?"

"Nice place."

"I asked you a question."

"Answered."

"What the fuck're you doing in my gym?"

"Member, paid in full. Got my cast off." Jimmy held up his arm and flexed his hand, wanting to punch the bastard. But that would mean blood and cops.

"I want *you* outta here."

"This the way you welcome new members?"

"Listen, asshole, didn't you learn your lesson? You need another?"

Jesus, the guy needed to attend one of those male drumming-circle retreats or go to a spa or something; he was wound way too tight, coked or uncoked. Now that Jimmy was finally confronting Cloutier, his emotions shifted and he felt an edge of giddiness though he knew how stupid he was acting. Some things you couldn't help no matter what you understood.

He backed until he was under one of the speed bags. He pulled the gloves out of his pocket, put them on, the unused leather feeling stiff when his fists tightened around the metal shanks; it was like gripping a roll of dimes. Slag started to move toward him as he began rhythmically punching the hanging teardrop, the slapping sound echoing through the room. Cloutier hesitated and then stopped. Jimmy sped the tempo, dropped it back down, then doubled the beat.

"Shit," said the blackjacker, coming up beside Slag, "Dude sure can hit a speed bag."

"Big fuckin' deal, Bernard."

"I'm only just saying."

"Yeah, well—shut the fuck up. I don't need your moronic commentary." Keeping the three of them in view, Jimmy walked over to pound one of the heavy bags, starting with quick flicks of his left jab, the arm extending from the shoulder like a blurred piston, a clean *pop* from each impact. He brought the right into play, the bag lifting into the air with the upper cuts and overhands, the hard bite of leather to canvas echoing through the room, the punches shaking the whole steel structure that suspended the bag from the ceiling. The anger at his present situation was released into the bag—his heart pounding, his lungs burning, his tension receding. He dropped his hands, a glistening sweat on his arms and face. He looked at Slag, emptying his face of any emotion.

Cloutier stared back. The new guy said, "Slag, he's some damn professional. Did you see that? Did you *hear* it?"

"I got to tell you to shut up too? You're like a buncha fuckin' old hens jabbering away."

Jimmy took a step forward. It was difficult not to pop the guy with a quick jab.

Slag glanced at the others, back at Jimmy. "You think I'm scared of you?"

Jimmy shrugged.

"Fuck you, asshole." The chest inflated, the veins appearing on his huge neck. No doubt about it, Slag was one big guy.

Jimmy took another step forward.

Slag backed. "Jack him, Bernard."

Bernard glanced at Slag, his face surprised. "What's with you, man? Let's see the shit you're always talkin' about. Dude is obviously calling you out."

Jimmy could see by Slag's eyes that it was already over.

"This asshole's gone crazy," said Slag wrenching his cell phone out of his pocket. He glared at Jimmy. "You want me to call the cops?"

Jesus, that's all he needed. "Cops are gonna arrest me for joining your gym?"

After a moment the phone returned to his hip. Everyone had his eyes on Slag. "Fuck this." He jerked around, stopped at the doorway, his face livid. "I don't have time for this shit. I got things to do. I can't be wasting another second on this asshole."

The new guy joined him. Bernard continued to stand there. There was a long silence, the music thumping through the wall. Then Slag was gone, the new guy in tow.

Jimmy turned to Bernard, his arms loose but ready; he remembered the dull crack to his skull only too well.

Bernard lifted his hands from his sides as if to indicate a truce. "I been meaning to tell you something." He glanced quickly behind him toward the doorway. "Man, look, sorry about that other thing."

"Other thing?"

"You know, by the car." Bernard made a blackjacking motion. "Forgotten."

"You serious?"

Jimmy nodded.

"No shit?"

"In the past."

Bernard grinned. "Man, you got one hell of a punch. I mean, fuckin' A, dude. I've never seen Slag like that. 'Bout goddamn time too." Bernard cautiously extended his hand.

Jimmy slipped off the glove and shook it. What else could he do?

Chapter Nineteen

After Jimmy finished working out, he was restless and some of his tension returned. Though he'd momentarily settled with Slag, it had been an inane thing to do; pride was a dangerous emotion. And the Claire issue remained as unresolved as ever. Vicky had placed him on the defensive by lying. What a mess. Maybe he should simply get out of this town and hole up somewhere else? After all, what did it matter where he hung out? He'd already paid his homage to Chevalier with the months in Maine; now there was no reason not to go wherever he wanted.

When he walked past the young woman at the desk, her ponytail and gum motionless for once, she didn't mention his membership card or a refund. Actually, she wouldn't even look at him, but he didn't care. There was no sign of Slag's SUV in the lot. He drove up into the graveyard, but after only a few minutes of looking out over Scoggton, trying to decide what to do and where to go, he was back in the Impala headed down into town.

As he approached the Den, he pulled over. The Pabst neon was glowing and both doors stood open, one wedged by a large plastic salt pail. The Den wasn't a bar you could look into and see anyone; regardless, he hoped to spot Claire. Instead, a drunk staggered out trying to light a cigarette. The guy cuffed his ankle on the salt pail, glared, kicked it, then wandered off. Jimmy hated drunks. They were all basically the same—boring or nasty and always selfish. He got out of the car and crossed the street.

It took his eyes a moment to adjust. No Claire, no Slag, same bartender. Jimmy took the same corner stool, but before he could order, two drafts were set before him.

"On me," said the bartender.

Jimmy nodded calmly but on the inside he was surprised. Why would that guy buy him a beer let alone remember his having ordering two? The TV flickered with a Fenway game, half the ballpark still bright with evening sun, the Red Sox at bat, the camera alternating between the shadowy infield and dazzling green grass and wall of the outfield. Jimmy glanced around. The other patrons kept eyeing him, but that wasn't unusual for Scoggton. He drained the draft, the cold beer delicious after the workout, his body clean after the steam and shower. Only his mind was muddled and a bit anxious. He had no illusions about Raymond Cloutier or what he'd started. And for what? To impress Claire? Show Doris who he really was? What if the cops got involved? Luke would never forgive him. Actually, he'd never forgive himself. Jimmy raised his finger to the barman.

"On Roger," the bartender said as he placed the beer.

Jimmy looked down the bar. The guy he supposed was Roger offered a grinning salute. Now Jimmy was really wondering what was up.

By the time the untouched beer had gone flat, the bar had bought him nine drafts, and not knowing quite why, he'd drunk them. He signaled the bartender.

"Yeah, Bob. Whaddaya need?" *Bob?* The guy even knew that?

Jimmy slapped a hundred on the bar and lassoed the air with his arm and finger. "Everybody, and you're?" The bartender stared blankly. "Your name?" Jesus, he was beginning to feel the beers.

"Oh. Clyde."

Clyde scooped the bill, went over and pulled the cord on the brass bell attached to the back wall; the chime echoed through the place like factory-quitting time. He began filling drinks. Then Jimmy noticed a blur of intense color parking behind his wagon. Neon violet. Whenever the Impala was out in public he tried to keep an eye on it if he could.

She walked into the Den and everyone turned. The squirrel nest was elaborately tousled, and a low-cut turquoise top tested the fabric's tensile strength to its limits. White jeans tucked into white cowboy boots, a filter cigarette held low. Though people greeted her, she ignored them and aimed straight for Jimmy.

"A party and you didn't invite me?" she said.

"Wanna drink? I got this round."

"I don't usually come here." She wrinkled her nose. "I saw your car."

"You're here, you want one or not?"

"Are you always so *rude*?"

"What's rude about buying a drink?"

"I want a margarita, but they sure as hell don't serve 'em in this dump. Come on, let's go some place else."

He patted the stool beside him. "Take a seat." He needed her cleavage at a less direct angle; the squirrel could be hiding in there and no one would know. She sat, but it didn't help much. "Wanna shot of tequila?" He raised his hand, but Clyde was still busy filling everyone's drinks.

"What're you doing in here anyway?" She glanced around with distain.

He stared at her. Too much lipstick on plump lips that looked as chewed as Terri Coal's nipples, too much eye shadow around porcelain blue eyes, definitely too much sweet perfume—but still, what a goddamn body.

"Are you gonna leave your hair like that?" she said.

"Light-socket look."

She giggled and stabbed out her cigarette. "Well, *hello*. Ever heard of a haircut? You'd be surprised what I could do with that."

Clyde set down Jimmy's change. Three twenties and a fan of bills. Jimmy held up a twenty. "Two tequilas. This is yours."

Clyde grinned, took the bill, and rang the bell again. Jimmy supposed certain tips got the chime as well.

"So it's true," she said.

"What?"

"Your money."

That stopped him, slapped him upside the head. He couldn't believe it. And she'd promised! He felt suddenly sick to his stomach. "You told Claire I asked you out. Why?"

"She told you that?" For once her voice lost its languor. "I can't believe she told you that."

"I didn't ask you out."

"But you wanted to, didn't you?"

He picked up his fresh draft. The question wasn't worth answering. The tequilas arrived, filled to spilling.

"What should we drink to?" she said.

"Back stabbing?"

"Are you mad about that?"

"Just drink the damn thing." The Den didn't bother with salt and lemon.

"Hey there, Vicky." A short guy, balding with ponytail and neatly trimmed goatee, stood there with a bottle of beer. Roger. "You don't greet me when you come in. What's that about?"

"You don't come into the salon anymore either."

"Twenty-six bucks for a cut? Too much."

"That includes the shampoo, scalp massage and blow dry." She winked.

"From eighteen to twenty-six is too much jump."

"You always were a cheap prick."

Roger shrugged at the insult. "You know our hero here?"

Jimmy swiveled. *Hero?*

"Hero?" she said, reaching into her bag for another smoke.

"He didn't tell you?" She shook her head. "He bitch-slapped Slag in his own place. Total showdown and Slag is terrified, goes running out of there in tears, screaming for the cops. 'Bout time someone took down that big asshole."

Vicky rotated back. "You did that?"

"Not exactly," he said. So that was what this was all about. It was worse than he'd anticipated, magnifying his apprehension that he should've left it alone.

Roger stuck out his hand. "I'm Roger Gagnon. How you doing, Bob? Bob, right? A real honor to meet you." They shook. "Thanks there for the beer."

"You beat up Slag Cloutier?" Her eyes on his. "I thought he beat you up?"

"Nobody beat nobody up."

"That's not what I hear," said Roger. "Bernard said your hand move so fast no one see it. Just the sound, *slap, slap*, and Slag's face bright red, and then him backing off. You were a fighter, a boxer, maybe even a champion, but you fought under a different name—Jimmy something. That's true, right?"

Half the bar was listening now, staring at him with what could only be fascination. The beer sponged his brain, the tequila torqued his blood, Vicky's eyes continued to appraise him. "Had a buncha different jobs," he said. Other customers stood and began to crowd toward him with their drinks. Jimmy drained his beer, pocketed his change, slid off the stool.

"Where you going?" said Vicky.

He brushed past a few faces he didn't recognize, the entire place watching him.

"You leave a full beer here on the bar," he heard as he neared the doorway. Knowing it was ridiculous, Jimmy nevertheless wanted to say something impressive before he exited, a good parting line for his new fans, but at the moment he was a blank. All he managed to do was escape.

Jimmy angled onto True Terrace, the valley of the city in blue shadow, the sun still ochre on the hilltops. It reminded him of the ballpark on the TV. He berthed the Impala carefully and headed for the front door. It opened before he reached it.

"Robert! You're finally home. I have news."

He stopped, a narrow band of sunlight hitting his eyes and blinding him. He moved his head, Doris's face coming gradually into focus.

"They finally relented. I think they were teasing me all along. I knew they'd have to give in eventually." Her glasses tilted aggressively at him. "Robert, are you listening to me?"

He nodded.

"The city finally remembered who I was and what the Callahans did for Scoggton. They didn't forget. The Callahan name still means something around here, by golly." Her face reddened, her eyes tightening with anger. "Regardless, I won't *ever* forgive them for treating me so rudely. After all, I'm almost seventy, and there is no reason for badgering an elderly woman of my position to that extent. But at least it's resolved now, it's over."

"Good news."

"Yes, it is good news. It's the best possible news. I thought perhaps we might have a whiskey to celebrate my victory."

He nodded again. Jesus, when it rains it pours.

"You won't have to move now, but I might be forced to increase your rent fifty more dollars." She gestured for him to enter and didn't even comment when he caught his boot toe on a step and tripped. He followed her down the hall and into the kitchen. "My house is mine again," she said as she reached for the juice glasses and brought out the Bushmill's. "I can't tell you how good that feels."

They lifted their drinks, and he silently drank to Rebecca Hines. She was a good woman after all. She'd complied with his instructions, writing the letter to Doris that he'd suggested. He made a mental note to give her another Ben.

Chapter Twenty

The next day Jimmy phoned Claire.

"Hey."

"Hey."

"Are you still mad?" he said.

"I heard she came after you at the Den. Now I don't know what to think."

"Did you tell her about me?"

"What do you mean?"

"Money."

"About you being rich?"

He grunted, reached down and scratched Yellow.

"Are you really that wealthy?"

He hesitated. "Maybe."

"How much? Like a hundred thousand?"

"Way more."

"Twice as much?"

"Listen, can I come over?"

"When? Now?"

"Yeah."

"I just got home from work. Let me take a shower. You want something to eat?"

"I'll pick up some steaks. The kid like steak?"

"Brandon eats pretty much anything."

So the kid would be there. "In an hour?"

"Okay."

He pressed end on his cell. She hadn't answered his question, had she? Hearing her voice made him forget everything, threw him off balance. How could a mere voice do that? He was supposed to be pissed at her, she'd broken her promise, and now he was bringing her steaks. Great.

He fed the cats, headed to the second floor and down the front stairs. And stopped—

"Robert. I've decided to raise your rent only twenty-five dollars. It dawned on me that you've been giving me grocery money every week and that makes up the difference." She paused. "Where are you going?"

"Out for dinner."

"The way you've been acting lately, I almost think you don't like my cooking." Her glasses glinted. "Is that true?"

"Like your cooking." He choked slightly saying it. "With the cast off"—he waved his arm gleefully as if to prove it—"I can make my meals. Besides, not fair to put you to all that trouble."

"It isn't *that* much trouble."

"Nice of you to say, but I know it is." He strayed slowly toward the door, got his hand on the knob.

"Are you going out with that Constantine girl again?"

"Yup, and I'm late." He opened the door and bolted. Doris never followed. At least that. Once he managed to get outside the house and off the steps, he was a free man. She kept to the confines of her home like a watchdog keeps to its yard. But he probably shouldn't be comparing her to a dog. But if he did, she would definitely be a terrier.

Jimmy picked up some steaks, beer, tulips, and made one other stop at Renys, the discount store. He parked on Claire's street and just sat for a minute, trying to sort out his feelings. Then he gave up, gathered his purchases and mounted the stairs. It was damn convenient having two arms again.

When she answered the door, her eyes looked different. It concerned him. Her eyes had always been wary and a little lost, but now there seemed to be something broken there. He held out the tulips.

She embraced the flowers for a long moment, then asked him in.

He followed her into the kitchen and set down the packages, her place just as neat as the first time. When she turned, he noticed tears in her eyes. They stood a moment, awkwardly, and then it was Claire who came into his arms.

"I missed you," she whispered, her lips against his earlobe.

There was no way he was going to get aroused again, so he pulled back. "Where's the kid?"

"Poolroom. He'll be in later."

"Brought him something."

"You didn't have to do that."

"Nothing much, just some car kits."

She looked in the bag. "All these?"

"Didn't know which he'd want, so I got a bunch."

He reached in a different bag and pulled out a rack of beer.

"You got the Canadian kind," she said.

"Want one?"

She showed him her glass. "I think I'm going to stick with wine."

"Shoulda brought some, but I don't know nothing about it. Tell me what kind you like, and I'll get it next time."

She went to the fridge and poured herself another.

"Shit, forgot to take off my boots."

"It doesn't matter so much this time of year."

"You sure?"

She nodded, still looking a bit teary. He handed her the wrapped steaks.

"Got these at this butcher place off Acadia. Guy cut 'em up for me. T-bones."

She set them inside and closed the door; even the fridge was orderly. "I don't know much about steaks."

"I'll cook 'em then. My stepfather taught me. About the only thing he showed me. You broil each side until it catches fire, making sure the middle stays raw. If you don't burn the house down, you eat 'em." He waited. "I'm joking."

Her expression dropped further. "I heard about what you did. I guess I was wrong there too." She walked into the living room and settled on the sofa. As he sat beside her, she said, "He's going to go after you, Jimmy. It isn't good. He's become a real vindictive bastard. I know, I've spent a lot of time trying to stay on his good side."

"He have a gun?"

"Every guy in Maine has at least one. I know Ray has a couple shotguns and rifles. He hunts."

"Hand guns?"

"That I'm not sure of."

"He's going to need one."

She turned toward the window, then back, her ponytail flouncing. "I still don't know anything about you, do I?"

"Come on. You know a bunch about me. More than anyone."

"Are you going to go out with Vicky?"

"What do you think?"

"I don't blame you. Men always want her because she's *so* sexy." She sipped her wine. "My mother was beautiful. I guess it's what did her in. My father got her pregnant when she was still a senior. She blamed him that she never had a career on the stage. After a while she had all these delusions that she'd been in movies, and it was my dad who'd forced her to quit just when she was about to make it. All she'd ever been in was a few high-school plays. I used to comb out her hair. She was very proud of her hair. Then one day she cut it all off right down to the scalp, plucked her eyebrows out, pulled all her eyelashes out. That's how it started. Can you imagine how I felt when I walked into her room and saw her like that? I was only twelve but I sensed things were going to turn bad. Neither of my brothers would come home to help, not that I blame them. Soon she wouldn't leave her room anymore, so I cooked and cleaned for my father." She stood. "You want another beer?"

He nodded, wondering what the hell was going on. He'd never seen her so vulnerable and self-deprecating and didn't know what it meant. When she returned, he said, "I think you're beautiful, really beautiful."

She slowly handed him the beer bottle like he might bite her fingers. "Thought it from the moment I saw you in the Den."

"I almost think you're serious." She studied him. "Jimmy, *no one* has ever thought I was."

"I do."

"Shit!"

"What?"

"What are you trying to do to me?"

"*Do?*"

"You can't even see it, can you?" Her voice was getting louder.

"See what?"

"I'm sorry about what happened. I don't know why I did that. Those drugs made me feel like anything was possible."

"Claire."

"No, you probably think I'm some kind of a slut."

He just sat there, his insides turning to acid.

"I know you want Vicky. I mean, why would you want me? She has everything I don't have, except brains. At least I'm a lot smarter than her."

"Why are you doing this?"

"Is it because she's so tall? Her tits? That's it, isn't it?"

He shook his head, setting the beer on the coffee table.

"Then tell me one thing. Wouldn't you prefer it if I had big tits?"

He stood, her intensity scaring him. "You gonna stop this?"

"My mother had nice breasts, not huge, but okay. I don't know why mine are so small. And then I got this leg too." She stretched it out to show him. "Crippled titless Claire. And you think I'm beautiful? Why are you doing this to me?"

Ten minutes later, about the longest ten minutes he'd ever been through, he banged down the stairs and outside into the twilight and then didn't know where to go. He felt like punching something again. Hard. As her rant had continued, he'd been so close to taking her into his arms, kissing her wet eyes. Had wanted to lick her nipples, caress her foot, feel himself deep inside her. Nothing he'd said had helped, and she'd just gone on and on and on, running herself down until there was nothing left. He couldn't stand her talking like that; it destroyed everything. As he'd listened to her, one worry kept prodding him. Was she going crazy like her mother? Maybe it was just beginning? He wasn't sure what he'd seen in her eyes, but he didn't think it was insanity. Maybe this was for the best though? He could break from her now. He had his excuse. He could focus on what needed to get done—killing Wendell Alden.

But when he ignited the Impala, he couldn't seem to drive off. His eyes kept straying to her upstairs windows, and he kept hoping she'd come down onto the porch. He would swing open the car door, she'd climb in, and they could just drive off somewhere, his arm around her delicate shoulders. But the apartment building remained as dead as a favorite roadside bar he'd driven hours to reach only to find it closed. The June dusk dampened the trees, the first glow of streetlights barely discernable against the sky.

When he parked near the Den, he scanned quickly for the violet convertible, then entered, the doors open again, the evening air warm. Four or five patrons, including Roger, glanced over and then looked quickly away. Finally he'd garnered equilibrium—neither villain nor hero. It was a relief. He took his window perch and lifted a finger to Clyde. No response.

He waited a couple minutes. "Hey, how about a draft over here?"

Nothing. A few at the bar snuck a glance, the others deep in their drinks. "Clyde," said Jimmy, "Thirsty over here."

Clyde walked over, too slowly. "I can't serve you."

"Can't serve me? I'm a Finn, not Irish, for Chrissake." Jimmy winked but immediately regretted denying his mother's side for the joke.

Clyde shook his head. Jimmy locked eyes and the guy's face flushed. Clyde leaned forward and said quietly so the other patrons wouldn't hear: "Bob, if it was up to me, you'd have three drafts sitting in front of you right now."

Jimmy tapped the bar top with the side of his fist. "No problem. Another time." He slid off the stool and left. Jesus—what was that all about? Maybe Slag had something on Clyde and had called in the marker.

He was hungry, but he didn't dare head home. The day had sucked enough without a plate of Callahan Boston boiled dinner steaming poisonously at him. The Broadway seemed like a reasonable option. It would be good to see Henry—at least someone sane in this goddamn town—and he felt like a steak. Those thick custom-cut T-bones he'd abandoned at Claire's haunted him.

Phyllis's goldness went white when Jimmy entered the Broadway. She blocked the entrance like a diaphanous bouncer. "We're closed," she said abruptly.

"Closed? At seven-thirty?"

"I'm sorry, but we closed early tonight."

"You too? Jesus." He didn't bother to ask or argue. Instead he brushed past her to wave at Henry who was mixing cocktails behind the bar. Henry waved back, a slight smile lighting the skeleton. At least that. As he expected, there were some diners who had just sat down. He rotated and headed for the exit. As he walked under the multi-colored neon, a nasty thought crossed his mind, but his hands were empty. Besides—it wasn't the sign's fault.

He returned to True Court after all, parking with as little noise as possible, tiptoeing into the house. It was wasted effort.

"Robert, I need to talk to you."

He sighed. "Not now, okay? Cats need to be fed."

"You can do it after; I must talk with you." She'd never sounded this serious.

He sniffed apprehensively for cooking odors and followed her into the kitchen. Reassured that nothing was bubbling on the stove or warming in the oven, he took a chair. Without prompting, she retrieved the whiskey and poured them two, the bottle three-quarters empty now. She set a glass in front of him.

"You know who called me today?"

He shook his head though he could guess.

"Raymond Cloutier."

"Why?"

"He insisted I evict you. Said you were a troublemaker who had been terrorizing his son."

"The *father* called?"

"Didn't I say that?"

"Thought you meant Slag."

"Now why would he call me?" She was examining him through her glasses. He pulled at his whiskey. "Tell me the truth—are you a troublemaker, Robert?"

"Sometimes I am."

That slowed her. "Fred told me about what happened in the gym. I guess you are rather tough after all."—he could only imagine what version of the story she'd heard—"I apologize for making those comments about hiding behind your tattoos. They were ill-informed."

She took one of her signature sips. "Raymond Cloutier told me if you weren't removed, I wouldn't have a prayer keeping this house."
"He can't do that."
"He said I'd be out in the street with nothing."
"Bull."
"So I called city hall to find out if he had any leverage. I demanded some answers. Paul Bilinear would only admit that an anonymous person had settled my taxes. Finally, Becky Hines told me the truth."
"What truth?"
"She told me what you did and how you asked her to write that letter. You made a fool out of me, Robert." Doris glared at him with a look he couldn't meet.
"Didn't mean to." At least he hadn't given Rebecca the second hundred. Or maybe that was the problem.
"Was the money you paid my taxes with stolen?" she said.
"No."
"Do you promise?"
He nodded.
"Word of honor?"
He nodded again.
"I called him back. That idiot should get his facts straight before he threatens people. You know what I said to Mr. Raymond Cloutier?"
He shook his head.
"I told that big bully he'd have to remove me in a pine box before I evicted you."
He focused on his whiskey.
After a moment she said, "You know, you're the oddest person I've ever known, but I must admit, I'm getting a mite fond of you."
"You're not so bad yourself."
"And now I'm going to cook you the best meal you ever had. How's that?"

Chapter Twenty-one

Another morning, another day.

As he woke, yesterday's calamities began to surround his mattress like evil grinning imps. It had been so much easier when he was a kid: on a summer morning, silently letting himself out of the trailer at dawn, the wooden sword carved from a birch stick in hand, long socks pulled up piratically on his calves, he would head down the hill to the forbidden grounds of the mill. Everyone would be asleep in Happy Acres, only the mill humming below him, a monstrous dragon. And here he was, over twenty-five years later, wanting to get on with the dragon slaying. The delay continued to weaken him; there was no doubt about that. He'd e-mailed Luke last night:

L—We got to move sooner. I need to get this done. Wing has healed. J

He rolled out of bed and checked his e-mail, but there was nothing except the usual spam. Luke was probably asleep; it was three hours earlier out there. Jimmy fixed coffee, started some bacon and sausage, fed the cats, did his exercises, doubling his normal count although he was already viciously sore. He opened *My Life* and stared at it. Bypassing the pathetic phone call to his father in San Francisco had destroyed his momentum. Now he didn't know what to do with the rest of the story. He'd just have to tell the truth about his father and move on to his Santa Cruz days. As he sat there staring at the screen, the idea for a poem began to rumble in his head. A poem? He'd never written one, didn't even read the stuff. Most of it bored him painfully. He gave it a try anyway.

You open up a beer
with the right bottle opener
and it makes a noise
like a bullet going
into a gun.

He smelled something. He leapt for the stove, grabbed a dishtowel, ran cold water on the burning pork. After Doris's culinary monstrosity last night he needed something soothing, but he decided to eat later and returned to his desk. After an hour, he had this:

OBJECTS

When you open a beer bottle
with the right opener
it makes a sound
like a bullet loaded
into the breech of a rifle.
And in some ways
there is truth in this,
depending on who uses it.
The gun or the beer.
When stakes get high in life
most people, they stiffen,
it's called a choke.

Objects seem straightforward.
A can of beer
A car key
A bullet
Boots
I prefer beer in cans,
I drive a 1965 Chevrolet,
I wear boots with steel toes,
I don't give a damn
how fast they run.
And I don't like bullets,
don't have any use for them,
I still like to do things
with my hands.

Jimmy read it over a few times. It didn't rhyme, but it sounded pretty
good, though he supposed some of it didn't make complete sense. But
wasn't that what poetry was all about? He wanted to show it to Claire,
see what she thought. She hadn't called him, and he wished she would.
He didn't want to have to call first. But what *was* he going to do about
Claire? What had seemed clear last night had evaporated by morning.
And now he had daddy Cloutier trying to freeze him out. He needed to
protect himself. He went to the closet and hauled out the suitcase,
grabbed a couple garbage bags; there had to be a shovel in the carriage
barn.

He was interrupted by a hollow knock at his door. Doris must have a problem; she never bugged him up here anymore. He closed the suitcase, quickly checked his teeth in the bathroom mirror, and headed down the steep stairs.

"What?" he said.

"Open up, I can't talk through a door."

Doris stood in the hall with a wry grimace, her glasses winking. "You're certainly getting popular," she said. "There's a girl out front. She insisted I page you."

"Who?"

"Vicky Lattrell."

"Fuck."

"*Robert!*"

"Tell her I'm out."

He heard a voice at the bottom of the front stairs.

"Bob, I gotta talk to you." Vicky's hair showed first. Her top was pink and much too close to flesh colored, the rest of her clad in spangled blue nylons under a short purple leatherette skirt.

Doris swiveled. "I was getting him for you," she said with an angry frown. "You can't just barge into people's houses, go wherever you want."

"It's important," said Vicky.

"Important or not, it's appropriate to show some manners."

"Sorry, but I need to talk to him." Vicky disregarded Doris. "Is this your place, Bob? Can we go up?"

They were both eyeing him. He stepped aside and gestured. Vicky slid past smelling of too much perfume and cigarettes. At least she'd put the thing out before coming in. He imagined her high heel scrubbing it dead against the front stoop, and knew Doris would insist he remove the butt.

"Thanks, Doris," he said, ignoring her sour expression as he closed the door. He followed Vicky's clacking heels, not looking up her skirt.

"What'd you do, burn your breakfast?" She walked to the windows and—*Jesus*, what a walk, her ass cheeks like a clock pendulum. "I got to say, Bob, this is actually like, pretty decent. You can really see the town. My house sucks for a view though it's brand-new." She turned and walked up to him. "You should come over some time. I just hot-topped my driveway and planted all these flowering bushes. The yard looks real nice now."

"Hot topped?"

"Yeah. It's like this sealer you put on so you won't get cracks and shit. It looks good too—*smooth* and even and really black. It's pretty easy to lay on."

"*You* did it?"

"What do you mean?"

"You did it yourself?"

"They wanted like five hundred, so I said fuck, I'll do it for that. You use these big brooms and these squeegee things and just push this sticky stuff around. It comes in five-gallon cans."

She was standing too close, and he backed up a step. There was something about the way her upper lip couldn't seem to cover her teeth. Claire was right: she was annoyingly sexy.

"I painted the whole inside of the house myself too. I got this really great paint on sale. They're mixed to match eggs. Like, colored eggs, but all natural shades from real actual egg shells, you know what I mean? My front entrance and living room is this really cool blue, feels like an ocean cottage or something. I think that one was from a robin egg or a sparrow or something—can't remember. I just love colors." She took a step toward him, her hand inching upward like a man-eating plant. "I wish you'd let me do your hair."

"You needed to talk to me? I doubt it was about a haircut."

She poked him in the chest. "I almost forgot, didn't I? You got anything to drink up here?" She checked her watch. "Noon already and I'm dry."

"Not working today?"

"I let the girls take the shop on Wednesdays. Hey, you know what I'm going to do? Open a nail clinic in part of the shop—manicures, pedicures, *and* maybe even paraffin."

"Paraffin?"

"Hot wax to lubricate your hands." She demonstrated with her fingertips. He looked out the window, trying to ignore her. She moved away from him and started touching—her nails black today—along the edges of his worktable, computer, from the back of a chair to the mahogany TV to the horsehair sofa. "What's with the old suitcase?"

"Just a suitcase."

"Actually, everything up here is old, really *old*. Are you into antiques or something?"

"Doris's stuff."

"I guess she was kind of pissed at me for walking in. Why don't you buy yourself some new furniture and get rid of this old junk? This place could be nice if it was dressed up a bit."

"I like it this way."

"You do?" That slowed her, but it was only a speed bump. "You should let me take you shopping. T J Maxx has some great deals right now. So, how about that drink?"

"Wanna beer?"

"You and your beer. It's *so* low class to drink beer. But sure, I'll have a beer if that's all you got."

He pulled two from the fridge and snapped them, handed her one.

"*Cans?* Can I at least have a glass?"

He retrieved a glass from the dish drain and handed it to her. He drank half his can in one pull; she was really bugging him.

"Am I making you thirsty?" she said as if she'd read his mind. "You don't talk much do you? But you're tall. Most men in Scoggton are so short."

"What did you want to see me about? Got to get some work done today."

"Oh, your book? Claire told me you were writing a book about your childhood."

"Anything she didn't tell you?"

She sipped her beer. "Girls talk, you know. After all, we've been friends our whole lives."

"Then what are you doing here?"

Her eyebrows went up. "You don't have to be that way about it. I came over here to warn you, so there."

"Warn me?"

"Yeah." She took another sip, scowled at the beer as if it was fish-tank water. "Mr. Cloutier is after you. Slag must have told him something, and now Mr. Cloutier is on the warpath, big time. He has a lot of pull in this town. A lot. See? I'm just trying to help you out. I'd be screwed if he knew I warned you."

"Where's he work?"

"He's in everything—insurance, real estate, banks."

"Where's his office?

"You know the Drummond Insurance building?"

"Ugly cement place by the bakery."

"What are you talking about? They just built that."

"He works in there?"

"He owns it."

"With all those mills empty, he built that thing?"

"No one wants to be in those drafty old mills, Bob. You are *so* difficult." She sauntered into the kitchen and set her glass down in the sink. It was a sip shy of full.

"Didn't like the beer?"

"Let's go out to the Ramada for a real drink."

"Beer is the real drink. Been around for thousands of years. Created civilization."

"Come on, it's my day off."

"Got to get some work done."

She rolled her eyes. "Will you meet me later?"

It took him a moment. "Maybe." Why had he said that?

"What's your cell number?" Somehow he couldn't not tell her. She headed for the stairs. "I'll call you later, okay? Like a few hours. Work well and then we'll have some fun."

He walked her down the two flights, watched her climb in the violet convertible and rev up, a long arm waving as the tires spun and she shot down True Terrace. When he got back upstairs, her smell, the stale tobacco and the sweet perfume, was so strong that he plugged in a fan Doris had loaned him for the hot weather. It whined and clumped as he sat at his desk. Jesus, what was he going to do about her? He couldn't stand her, but annoyingly he wanted to see her naked. He'd never touched tits like hers before, tits that must be damn similar to Terri Coal's. Women like Vicky had always ignored him, and the temptation was obvious as much as he resented it.

There was the jingle of an arriving e-mail, and he clicked on the dancing envelope.

H—I got a guy watching A. I know you hate that but I was in Nam with this guy. No worries. If A moves sooner I'll know in hours. Hang in there. L

He wrote back:

L—What the fuck! J

Within ten minutes:

H—Relax. He goes out with the girl that handles A's travel. To good to pass up. Let me handle my part you fuck. L

Jimmy had to smile. Luke was the best. If anything really got messy in Scoggton, all he had to do was make one phone call. And then it struck him that maybe Luke felt about him the way he felt about Chevalier.

Chapter Twenty-two

Doris brought him an envelope with the arrival of the afternoon mail.
Two door-poundings in one day. "I hope you're not going to be letting
all these women in here at night, Robert. I'm not running that kind of
place, no matter who pays the taxes."
He reassured her. Spinsters!
He trudged back up his stairs and opened the letter.

Dear Jimmy,

*I have never felt about anyone the way I feel about you. When I first saw
you in the Den, I was immediately compelled to talk to you. I don't
usually just go up to strange men, even when I'm half drunk, but with
you, I just had to. I did say to the others that I thought you might be a
cop, but the truth is that I was drawn to you and wanted an excuse to talk
with you. There was something about your eyes, and the way you sat
there, you seemed so lonely somehow, the kind of loneliness I have
always understood. But under that loneliness I also sensed a true
capacity for joy.*

*As I've gotten older I've come to believe that much of the beauty of the
world is in the inexplicable, those moments when you see or experience
something that cannot be rationally understood until so many years
later, if ever. But it's allowing these things into your heart that can
change you, give you the magic of being alive. You gave that to me
again after I had closed myself off to it for way too long, and I will thank
you for that forever. Is it hope, a belief in possibility, the courage to risk
everything for love, a simple willingness to really live? I felt it in you
from that first moment in the Den, and I still feel it in my prayer for us. I
believe it is the one thing in life that allows us to forgive what we've done
to others and what they have done to us.*

*But then so much of what you said to me seemed to be a lie, or at least
you seemed to be hiding something. I keep trying to ignore it because of
what I sense in you, but maybe I'm too old for lies, Jimmy, and I'm not
holding up well under the strain as you might notice. I need you to be
honest with me. So the other night, I wanted so much to believe you, but
how can I? And then I overreacted, and part of it was being scared,*

scared that you really did mean the things you said. Having the dream so close is in its own way terrifying because of my fear that my intuition is false. I'm not sure I can handle another disappointment. More than a few times I've told myself simply to retract from you and be done with it, go back to my mundane life. But I can't yet. I guess what I really want to tell you is, that if you want to try again, I'm willing.
Yours,
Claire
P. S. Brandon loved the car kits. He was very touched by your generosity and wants to thank you in person.

He placed the letter on his desk and picked up his cell.
"Claire."
"Hey."
"Can you give me twenty-four hours?"
"What're you talking about?"
"Just give me twenty-four hours, and no matter what you hear, no matter what happens, just trust me. Okay?"
"Jimmy, what are—"
"Please."
She paused. "Okay."
"No matter what that Vicky says either, okay?"
"All right."
"Thanks."
He set the phone back, grabbed his vest, the bag gloves, and headed down the stairs.
When he arrived at Super Flex, there wasn't a red SUV in the lot. He went in anyway. The girl with the ponytail stood up the moment he walked in, shaking her head emphatically.
"You can't be in here," she said.
"I'm a member."
"I can't let you in. Listen,"—her ponytail darted nervously—"you got me in *a lot* of trouble already. I almost got fired."
"You sign a new member and you get fired?"
"You said you were Slag's friend."
"I did?"
"He comes in, and I'm all, 'a friend of yours just joined, he's out back,' like he'd be pleased. Instead I got, like blamed for the whole thing. Like how was I supposed to know you were here to beat him up, that you were a professional fighter?"
"Tell you what. I'm due a refund, right?"
Her head was gyrating again. "No way! I can't do that. You'd have to

talk to *him* about it. No way can I do that. I'm not getting in—"
"You know where he is?"
"I shouldn't even be *talk*ing to you."
"Let me clear the hassle I caused. You keep my refund."
She considered this a moment. "Whaddaya mean?"
"I'm due a refund: I paid and now I can't work out. You keep the money."
"You serious?"
He nodded.
"But it's like eighty bucks or something."
"Buy yourself a new leotard."
She smiled, then frowned. "This isn't a *leotard*." She rubbed her hands over her hips. "You don't like this outfit?"
"Won't hurt to have a few more."
He drove toward the smell of the bakery. Parked in the Drummond building lot, left the bag gloves on the seat, and aimed for the panel of glass doors. *To solve a wasp problem, head for the nest.* The building was basically a giant cinderblock, each floor alternating orange and brown paint, with undersized square windows; the architect, if there'd been one, should have been sealed in the foundation. A directory by the elevators—Raymond Cloutier Enterprises was on the fifth and final floor. As Jimmy rode up he almost wished he was wearing the Callahan suit jacket. Make it official. What a jerk Cloutier was trying to scare an old lady, threatening to evict her from her home, only because his son was a coked-out bully. The elevator door slid open and he approached the woman at reception. She was fiercely middle-aged, reminding him of a particularly mean gym teacher he'd had.   "Can I help you?"
"Bob Gray. I have an appointment with Cloutier."
"*Mister* Cloutier?"
He nodded.
"Just a moment." He could tell by her expression that she didn't believe him. She spoke into her headset and her look changed. "Mister Cloutier will see you. At the end of the hall."
He walked down the long hall wondering if anyone else even worked here. It all looked unused and smelled synthetic. The air seemed laced with an invisible poisonous dust and he coughed. When he arrived at the door, he purposely didn't knock, but entered, closing it behind him with a click. Cloutier didn't even glance up, just sat there studying some papers. He looked even larger than his son, late-forties early-fifties, dressed in the usual gray suit and acidic-yellow tie. The walls held a few football and hunting photographs, the obligatory one with a past president, the white paint bright in overhead fluorescent glare, desk and chairs gray

metal, the whole effect Spartan. The room stated that its occupant was a man of action, no frills or compromise.

"Came to talk to you about your son," said Jimmy.

The head still didn't move. This obvious technique to intimidate was boring him, but he waited patiently.

After at least two minutes the face looked up. The eyes were lost in florid flesh, the big shoulders and neck bunching the expensive cloth of the suit coat. He looked like a gin drinker. "What do you want?"

"There seems to be a problem between me and your son."

"No problem anymore."

"No?"

"You're finished in Scoggton."

"Finished?"

"You should've left well enough alone when Ray first asked you to leave town."

"You want to know what really happened?"

"Ray told me what you did. Now, get."

Jimmy started to laugh. He couldn't help it. "What is this—a Western? You the sheriff?"

Cloutier straightened in his chair, his eyes narrowed and his face got redder though it didn't seem possible. "Get out of my office and stop wasting my time." The voice was cruel. Jimmy knew cruel.

"Let me tell you my side of it. We can clear this up."

"Nothing to clear up."

Jimmy tried to hold back his temper, but he'd heard this same condescending crap too many times in his life. "Came here to solve this."

"I said all I'm going to say." Cloutier's head went back to the papers.

"You might think you're a big deal, but you're only running a piss-poor mill town in Maine. This isn't a backwoods football game where you're the big man and you're sure to win. You're gonna lose." He felt only slightly embarrassed saying this. He needed to get this resolved though he hated how personal it had turned. "You're out of your league, Cloutier."

Now Cloutier's head jerked up and he got to his feet, moved around the desk. "You think a punk like you can walk in here and talk to me like that?"

"A punk?"

"You're a nobody, a scum. I ran your name. A nothing. I hire guys like you to shovel shit, and when I'm done with losers like you, I throw them on the shit pile."

Jimmy nodded slowly. This sucked. His temper was raging. "I bet you were always a bully. Fucked everyone over. Took whatever you wanted and never gave a thought to who you destroyed. Always the big fucking man, right?"

Cloutier pointed. "Out. Now!"

"Fuck you."

"What did you say?"

Jimmy said it again, very slowly.

A jolt of disbelief showed in Cloutier's eyes. "You've got to be kidding me."

"Come on," said Jimmy, his hand motioning. "Come on."

It took a few seconds. The bull charged.

Jimmy pivoted and took out a knee with one quick kick. It was simplest. Besides, the guy was huge and he couldn't take chances. Cloutier collapsed, sliding like a derailed train along the floor almost to the doorway, ending up on his side, both hands around the ruined knee. The building was solid, Jimmy had to give it that. He approached, leaned over, flicked the side of his hand into the exposed Adam's apple. Cloutier began to choke and gag. Better than him screaming.

"Can you hear me?" Jimmy said, kneeling behind him, composure back. Nothing but gurgling. "Nod if you can hear me." Still nothing. Jimmy grabbed the neck and pressed the carotids closed. When the face was a horrible color and the arms and hands went limp, he released. Waited a few minutes, the life in the body gradually returning. "Nod if you can hear me?" It took a while but the movement came. "If you fuck with me again, your son dies. Don't be stupid about this; my people will destroy everything it's taken you a lifetime to build. You have too much to lose. The men that will come after your family have nothing to lose. They will enjoy destroying you only because I asked them to. Is that worth the gamble? Think about it."

Jimmy waited a moment, worrying for a second that the guy was going to have a stroke or worse. Weren't gin drinkers prone to strokes? He continued anyway. "Run your little mill town, but call off your skunkshit freeze-out and then everything will be fine. You understand?" Movement again. "I'll tell your secretary you slipped showing me a football move and hurt your knee." Jimmy stood, shifted the body slightly so he could open the door, and left.

He was irate with himself for losing his temper. He prayed Cloutier wouldn't be a fool.

Chapter Twenty-three

Now he had to wait. Guys like Cloutier either moved immediately or the rage passed and they got some sense. Jimmy was getting weary of this kind of shit though. He'd felt repulsion choking Cloutier—the thick arteries of blood straining under his thumb and fingers, the rank odor of spent booze, sweat, and fear, and how easy it would have been to kill him. Even threatening him had sounded sickening somehow. He had nothing against Cloutier—the man was just a type, trying to take care of his family, unable to face up to having a spoiled lout for a son. Maybe Slag had been different in high school when everything went his way, but college or something had turned him. And the father, like the son, was just one of the many people who wanted too much, spent all their energy trying to get it and keep it. Jimmy knew. Hadn't he been pretty much that way? Now he wasn't so sure what he wanted anymore, although he still had Alden to do. Wendell Alden was different than Cloutier. Much different. He'd murdered the only truly good person Jimmy had ever known and for that he had to die. But it was even bigger than that in his mind. Those in power had to realize that they couldn't get away with it anymore. It was his duty to send the message.
Chevalier had changed Jimmy's life. Chevalier had seen something in him, something he hadn't known was there. Chevalier'd trusted him without hesitation. It had changed everything. And then a thought hit him: would Chevalier want him to kill Alden? He'd never considered that and rejected it immediately. Alden had to die. Period. Everything he believed in was based on that.

He stared out the garret windows as twilight shimmered over Scoggton, the dark mills, the streetlights, the traffic. Somewhere out there was Cloutier. Jimmy knew they wouldn't hurt Doris. If Cloutier came, and he wouldn't come alone, Jimmy wanted to be easy to find. There was no point in hiding. Better to get it over with. He just hoped it wouldn't be cops.
Damn it! He'd forgotten to bury the money near the graveyard because Vicky had distracted him. He retrieved the carbon-fiber case from the old suitcase again, tiptoed in his socks down to the second floor and

looked around. Finally he hid it in a tiny back room under the bottom drawer of a built-in linen closet. The dust was so thick that no one must have been in there for twenty years. Then he headed back up and sent this e-mail:

L—If something happens to me, Raymond Cloutier is who you want. Cash in 2nd floor back closet should go to Claire Constantine. J

It was convenient that they had the same name. He knew that if anything happened to him, Luke would take them both out just to be sure.

Most of Jimmy's money was in two safe-deposit boxes in different California banks, but he wasn't ready to tell Luke that although he was the beneficiary. If Jimmy died it would be in his will, and Luke would find out soon enough. Hiding his cash probably wasn't necessary because he doubted Cloutier would come. There was nothing for Cloutier to gain, and among other things, he'd have to admit to whoever assisted him that he'd been defeated, beaten up by a punk. A punk. That killed him. He got a beer, the Canadian kind, and picked up his cell. He noticed he had a message. Must be Vicky. He'd forgotten about her afternoon of fun. He fingered in a number.

"Hey."

"It's only been twelve hours, so are you sure it's okay to talk to you?"

"Funny. What time do you get out of work tomorrow?"

"You want to come over?"

"Will the kid be there?"

"You want him to be?"

"Rather see you alone. To celebrate."

"Celebrate what?"

"We'll think of something. Okay?"

"Jimmy, are you going to insist on always being this way? You and all your mysterious twenty-four hour stuff? You haven't mentioned my letter."

He didn't say anything. She never gave him the chance to do things his way, as he saw it, the stylish way. She was always rushing things.

"Did you get it?" she said.

"Yup."

"And?"

"Called you, didn't I?"

She was silent.

"Meant a lot to me, okay?" he said.

"It did?"

"Claire, of course it did. It was a beautiful letter. Most amazing letter I've ever read. Okay?" Silence. "Tomorrow then?"

"Tomorrow."

This time he brought roses, two-dozen red, along with champagne, two six-packs, and a small narrow box. He felt like a sherpa heading up the stairs, climbing slowly because he didn't want to get sweaty and spoil his shower; his teeth were immaculate. He wore a fresh black T-shirt and a pair of delicate black loafers he'd picked up that afternoon on Acadia Ave in the one remaining shoe store. The selection had been dusty and grim, but the old guy who fitted him was somewhat like Henry and that made the difference. He still wasn't sure he liked the shoes. They were so light, the leather sole so thin that he didn't feel connected to reality although sensing the ground with every step. More of a dance slipper than something a man wore. Usually he only shopped for black multiples of six: T-shirts, jeans, vests, boots—but there was no way he was going to buy a half dozen of these.

When she opened the door an odd dizziness struck him between the eyes, and for an instant he worried he might stagger. She'd never looked more fetching, and it couldn't be just the perfectly ironed white cotton shirt, or her slim pale gray slacks, or the hair in a single braid resting on her shoulder. Her eyes were excited and wary at the same time. They opened wider.

"My God, Jimmy—roses."

But when he held them out to her, somehow the champagne slipped and like a bomb the bottle dropped, the thick rim of the end connecting squarely with his toes. "Damn!" he yelped, trying not to lose anything else. The bottle rolled noisily along the maple floor of the hall and stopped.

"Are you okay?"

"Fine," he muttered. He *knew* he shouldn't have bought the shoes. This was why you wore steel-toed boots. "Take these." He passed her the flowers. Held onto the door jam with his freed hand while desperately trying to ignore his toes and his rising stomach. There was no way he was going to be sick in front of her again.

"Are you sure you're okay?"

"Fine." The surge of pain and ensuing nausea were beginning to abate.

"God that must've hurt."

"I'll get the damn wine." He limped over to retrieve the bottle, and for an instant almost chucked it at the wall. He struggled back. "Do I have to take these off?—they're new, the soles should be okay."

"You better sit down."

He ignored the suggestion and followed her into the kitchen. She put the roses in water, beer and champagne in the fridge, and poured two drinks. They moved into the living room.

"You're limping like me," she said. "Are you sure you didn't break a toe? That was a vicious thud."

"That's what beer is for." He could feel what he suspected was blood pooling in his shoe. He didn't care; it was the last time he'd wear these damn things.

"Hey, you should have one of your pain pills. What did you call them? Mister P?"

"You want one?"

"After what happened last time?"

"I liked last time."

"You did?"

"You know I did." He fished two Percs out of his vest pocket, handed her one.

"I'm supposed to chew?"

He nodded, extracted the narrow box and passed it. "Got you this. Kinda to thank you for your letter." The jewelry store clerk had been a bit aloof with him at first, but once he told her what he wanted—the most expensive kind—she'd done a nice job wrapping the gift. Claire undid the dark blue foil paper. He sipped his beer nervously, hoping she'd liked it.

"Jimmy, it's beautiful."

"They said it was a good one."

"My God, it's solid platinum."

"They had a gold one, but I figured Phyllis has gold covered. The nip thing is still gold though. They're all like that."

"I've always wanted one."

"You can do more writing now, maybe. I thought that letter was something special."

"Do you know how much this means to me?"

He shrugged, embarrassed now; she was looking very serious.

"I never told you, did I?"

He shrugged again.

"I wanted to be a writer too, you know. Everyone tries it once, maybe only keeping a journal or something, but I really tried. When I got out of high school, I wrote at least five hours every morning, then worked in this pizza place, my dad babysitting Brandon. Every night in that kitchen, always unbearably hot in there with the ovens, but it gave me time to write and be with Brandon during the day. It took a few years, but I finally finished something that I felt was great. A short story about Jeremy and our friendship, ending with what he did to me."

She was staring at him, her eyes so vulnerable and appealing it killed him. "Jimmy, I knew it was a strong story. I was sure of it, so I sent it out to maybe two-dozen different magazines. After waiting months with all this intense hope—almost positive I would get published—half a year later, a copy finally comes back. You know what was scrawled across the first page?"

He shook his head.

"'If you intend to write, write what you know. This obviously would never happen.' I mean, fuck him! What would he know about being raped? After that I couldn't write anymore. Stupid but there you have it." Her eyes were wet. "Maybe with this pen I'll try again. What do you think?"

He had no idea how to respond to all her emotion, so he just nodded. What he wanted was to touch her.

Then she started giggling. "God, every time I do one of these pills I start confessing."

"Do you still have that story?"

"I tossed everything."

"That's too bad." He didn't really believe her but realized the subject was still tender. He understood about that.

"You know the second thing that happens, don't you?" She was grinning now, and he could almost feel her mood flip.

"Whaddaya mean?"

"After one of these pills."

She stood and moved toward him. He came to his feet to meet her. His arms went around her waist and she stretched on her toes. The tenderness of the movement killed him, and her lips, her smell, the surprise of her tongue. He pulled back playfully, a little overwhelmed, waited for her to find him again. The tip of his tongue outlined her mouth as if he were licking on lipstick. He found his hands untucking her shirt, that clean scent of laundry on a line: where did she hang her clothes out? And then he broke away from her.

"Brandon?"

"A friend's . . . he won't be back till late." And her mouth was there again.

Her shirt was off, no bra, her unusually full nipples erect in their dark circles, her breasts a gentle arc like two dessert dishes. "I'm sorry they're not larger."

"Your nipples are so perfect." His tongue proved it.

"They are? Really?"

He left her breasts and quieted her with a kiss, his mouth moving to her ears, her neck, her shoulders.

After a while they stopped—he to get a beer, she for the bathroom. Somehow it was easy between them for the first time. Then they were on the sofa, the evening beginning to mute the room, the sunlight excluded by trees and walls. He sat and looked at her, wanting to take his time, his eyes now where his tongue had been: her neck, the roundness of her shoulders, the flare from her waist, the delicate tapered cylinders of her arms, the balance of her torso.

"Will you strip for me?" he said. Only her pants were left.

"I'm too shy."

"Please?"

She stood. Reached for his beer and drank. Handed it back and began to move. For him it was like a heaven-bound candle flame in a still room. She released her pants and slid them down slowly. "I can't really dance too well." She kicked them away, stumbling slightly. "My panties too?" He nodded and she hooked her thumbs in the white lace and drew then down. "I have a scar."

"We all have scars," he said. She rotated a little. "Jesus, your ass is perfect too. My God you're beautiful."

"There you go again."

"It's true."

She watched him and he couldn't tell what she was thinking. At the moment he didn't care. "Lie down."

"Here?"

He nodded again. She lowered herself onto the rug, and he walked over to her, kicked off one loafer; the other was stuck. He reached down and pried it off, that sock staying inside the shoe. He unbuckled, freed himself with one quick pull, shrugged off his vest and T-shirt.

"Close your eyes," he said. "Don't open them." Lowering himself so that his body was over hers but not touching, he brushed the tip of his erect penis along her thighs, over her breasts, up her arms, the head running with clear fluid; he explored her whole body—her forehead, the side of her face, her neck, dipping into her armpits until she giggled, reaching even her toes and the instep of her misshaped foot, his wetness leaving a dashed glisten wherever his penis had touched her. Only her center he avoided. He wasn't ready yet. It made him nervous—how would they fit, how would it feel, would they be bound forever?—and he decided to save it.

Her body trembled, and he wondered if it was from pleasure or if she was just ticklish. He wasn't even sure why he was doing it, dragging his erection over her, except that he felt so ridiculously happy. He struggled with his damaged toes, trying not to let them touch anything, oddly delighted to feel her pain just once, his arm muscles burning from keeping his body above her for so long; he rested some of his weight on the knee with the hurt foot, sensing it was bleeding again. Dusk began to fill the room like a slow syrup.

"Oh God, Jimmy, please," she said, and spread her legs.

He brought his mouth toward her center, breathed in her smell, that which he'd longed for finally his, his body trembling now as well. The tip of his tongue found her clitoris, flicking and nudging until she cried out; then he held it with his entire tongue as if protecting it, soothing it; her whole body shuddered again.

He moved up her. His chest sliding across hers, his mouth to hers. She arched her back to meet him. He rubbed his penis along her wetness, allowing the head to spread their juices from her anus to her clitoris, back and forth, back and forth, hesitating. Her hands grabbed his ass and tried to pull him into her. He fought her for a few moments, knowing what it meant, overwhelmed and uncertain, then gave way. As he entered she cried out again, the sound piercing him, his own searing pleasure blinding him, his eyes wet.

It was dark when they separated. Only one streetlight pasted a rectangle of vaporous milk on a wall. He kissed her gently on the lips, crawled over to the sofa and leaned his sweaty back against it. She propped her head on an elbow, watching him. He snagged the beer off the coffee table and drank.

"Warm," he said. "Wanna cold one?"

She nodded.

When he got back, trying not to limp, she'd switched on a light, settled on the sofa, shaken out her hair and put her shirt back on, leaving it unbuttoned. He handed her a beer. And she started laughing. For a moment he didn't know why and then he knew. Fuck—he'd forgotten to put his T-shirt back on. She continued to laugh, almost bubbling over.

"I was only eighteen," he said, sitting beside her. "Seemed like a great idea at the time."

"It's incredible. I love it."

She bent at the waist, the shirt spreading. She kissed the headlight, the bell, then up to the smokestack with its coil of burning coal, licked down to the cowcatcher just above his navel, kissed every freight car all the way to the caboose and the horizon, which bisected his nipples. "You really are funny, you know that?"

"Took forever too."

154

"I want a tattoo."

"Not sure steam would be right for you. Maybe a diesel?"

She poked him. "What's that?" She reached down and wiped her fingers along the floor.

"Sorry about that."

She examined his foot for a moment. "Wait right there."

Jimmy leaned back and sipped his beer. He felt so light he almost expected to start floating around the room.

She placed a bowl of warm water beside him, lifted his leg and began to wash his damaged toes. The water turned dark immediately.

"Stacking firewood," he said, "Dropped a mook on my foot—"

"A *mook*?"

"Big piece of firewood. You don't call 'em that?" She shook her head. "My big toe swoll up bad, but I didn't want to tell my stepfather; he'd get so pissed if I had to go to the doctor. But after a few hours, my toe was all purple—really throbbing. He was in the trailer drinking beer with this guy from the mill, my mom was still at work, so I finally showed them my toe. The friend heated up a paperclip over the gas range and burned the hot end right through my nail. Blood went everywhere."

"It must've hurt."

"Actually it didn't. My toe felt much better."

"Doesn't this hurt? Your toes are pretty mangled."

"Claire, I don't think anything could hurt me right now."

She stopped washing. Took the towel she'd brought, and wrapped his foot in it. "So what happens now?"

"Whaddaya mean?"

"Was it . . . okay?"

He glanced out the window, the streetlight forming a white-green nimbus in the tree leaves. "How can you ask that?"

"Jimmy, I just—"

"Come here." He held out his arms and she nuzzled against his chest. "I have to ask you something," he said. "I shoulda asked you this before. Can you get pregnant?"

She lifted her head. "You mean, can I have another child?"

"I mean from today."

"Oh."

He waited. "Can you?"

"You want children?"

"Never really thought about it. So?"

"You don't have to worry," she said quietly.

He was relieved. "Speaking of kids, when is Brandon coming back?"

She glanced at the clock on the bookshelf. "Not for another hour."

"He wouldn't be early, would he? I'm not exactly dressed to see the kid."

"Hey, are you hungry? Shall I make you something?"

"I think I'll just eat you." He chewed on her ear, and Claire started to giggle.

When Jimmy left the apartment, at the bottom of the last flight of stairs, he stopped. Through the door's window, he saw a figure lurking in the shadows of the porch. Cloutier? Wrong size. One of his henchmen? Wrong stature. He opened the door cautiously, ready for an attack from his blind side. The figure moved into the porch light.

"Mr. Gray."

"Brandon."

"Hey."

The kid looked even stranger than usual. He wasn't moving. "You have a good time at your friend's?"

"Naw. His dad was drunk and got in this big fight with his mom. I came home."

"You just get in?"

"Naw. I've been here like a couple hours—at least."

Jimmy paused. "Were you upstairs?"

"Kind of." The kid looked out at the dark street. "I heard some noises and I just wanted to make sure my mom was okay. I came right back down though because I knew she was with you."

Fuck! Jimmy studied the street too. "Sorry, Brandon."

"That's okay Mr. Gray. I like you."

"Forget the Mr. Gray. Let's go with Jimmy." He couldn't believe it, but the kid smiled a little. Jimmy didn't know what to say next. But he had to come up with something. "You like trains?"

"I guess. I don't know much about 'em."

"You know that big abandoned rail yard south of town?"

"Yeah, I guess."

"How about you and me go out there some time? I'll show you around, you know, explain some stuff." He owed the kid something.

"When?"

"How's Saturday?"

"Saturday'd be great . . . Jimmy."

"I'll pick you up around ten, okay?"

Brandon nodded. Jimmy could tell the kid didn't believe him. "Later then." He headed down the porch steps.

"Jimmy?"

He turned.

"Thanks for all those car kits. Maybe Saturday, if we go, you might want to see my models?"

"You got it . . . and Brandon?" The kid waited, those earnest eyes watching so carefully. "Maybe you should tell your mom you just got home a few minutes ago."

The kid smiled again. Awkwardly, but it was a smile.

Jimmy gave his low wave and walked to the Impala. He started whistling. A Goth Metal tune, so it wasn't easy to whistle. He stuck with it anyway.

Chapter Twenty-four

Around nine o'clock on Saturday morning—one of those perfect June days—Jimmy left True Terrace and headed for Cartier Street. Claire had invited him for breakfast. He'd asked her to have the kid look out for him because he needed help with something, and now, as he pulled up at her curb, Brandon was already standing on the porch. He shot down the steps and approached the rolled-down window—in a black T-shirt.

"Hey, Jimmy."

"Hey yourself."

"Mom said you needed me."

Jimmy pointed behind him. "Think we can get that upstairs?" He hopped out and slapped down the tailgate, slid out the rolled up package by yanking on one of the loops of rough cord that bound it.

"Ready?" he asked the kid.

Brandon nodded. "Is it a rug?"

"Yeah, a real beaut. Wait till you see it."

They grabbed it like a dead body, each hefting one end, and headed up the stairs, Jimmy taking up the rear so it would be lighter on the kid. Brandon staggered up the last flight, the bundle slipping a bunch of times, but he regripped each time and kept hauling stoically, barely making it. Claire opened the door for them. "What's this?"

"A—rug," said Brandon, out of breath. "Wait—until—you see it."

"A rug?"

Jimmy leaned in next to her ear. "It's a gift. I got blood on your other one." He turned to the kid, held out his car keys. "You mind closing the tailgate and locking my rig?"

"Sure." He snatched the keys and started off.

"Hey," Jimmy called after him. The kid froze running like in a cartoon. "There's a long black case in the backseat. Bring it up, okay?" A nod and he was gone.

"Brandon's been excited all week," she said.

"And you?"

"And me."

They embraced, kissed. He was tempted to slide his hand between her legs, but the kid had witnessed enough, or at least heard enough. Besides, he was eager to unveil his gift. "Let's unroll it," he said, and they separated. "You won't believe this rug. You know the place over by the mills?"

"Marden's?"

"They have this rug-fabric outlet for discontinued stuff. Doris told me about it." He flicked open his jackknife and ripped through the cords. "I couldn't believe it when I saw this baby. I guess no one else spotted it—it was under a bunch of other rugs, like the last one in the pile." He kicked the roll and the rug began to show itself, a puff of dust at each turn. "All handmade," he said proudly.

"My God," Claire said when it lay flat.

"Yeah, I know. Incredible, isn't it? You wouldn't believe the deal I got on it either."

She kept staring at the rug.

"You're not saying much."

"I'm just overwhelmed, that's all."

"Yeah, I know. I got no idea what castle it is—they didn't know at the rug place either."

"It's certainly a *big* castle."

"Yeah, look at all those turrets. *Got* to be Middle Ages. Sometimes I think I shoulda been born then."

"The sunset is something too."

"Maybe a little bright. It didn't look quite so bright in the warehouse."

"Even a moat *and* a drawbridge."

Something in her voice stopped him. He examined her. "You don't like it, do you?"

"I like it."

"Not really though."

"Jimmy—I like it."

"I guess I got carried away. Forget it. We can get something else."

The door banged open and the kid shot in. He handed Jimmy the case, his face flushed. "I locked the Impala."

"Thanks," said Jimmy. He handed the case back. "Yours."

"Mine? No way."

"Open it up. Hope it does better than the rug."

"What's wrong with the rug?" The kid walked over to look. At first he was silent. "Whoa." His mouth opened again but nothing came out.

"Let's forget the damn rug, okay? Open the box."

Brandon set the case on the coffee table, snapped up the two brass closures and lifted the lid. He stared at the cue, then at Jimmy, back at the cue. "Holy shit," he said. "This is a McDermott. *Mom*, see the green four-leafed clover with the *M*?" He pointed. "That's how you can tell. Jimmy, I can't believe this. This is totally unreal."

"They said I should get the nineteen ounce when I told them about you."

Brandon carefully removed the stick and screwed the two parts together. "This is really mine?" He felt along the shaft, his fingers caressing it.

Claire leaned against him, smiling. "What are you, Jimmy? Santa Claus?"

He put his arm behind her. "No. Robin Hood."

That stopped her. "Robin Hood?"

"Well, more than Santa. I mean, who the hell wants to be Santa Claus? A fat guy in a dorky red suit."

"Are you still upset about the . . . ?" She tipped her head toward the rug.

"We'll talk about it later. I'm hungry. Brandon, you hungry?"

"What?" He was preoccupied with fondling his pool cue. "Sure," he said, looking up.

After breakfast—griddle cakes with Maine maple syrup, fried potatoes with onions, coffee and fresh-squeezed orange juice—Jimmy said: "You have no idea what I've been goin' through."

"Going through?" she said.

"Yeah, I've been under siege."

She waited.

"It's been a rough time." He rubbed his stomach. "I've been eating Doris's cooking for months. Not that I don't like the old girl . . . but her food—yikes. I can't tell you how good that just tasted. I feel like a lumberjack."

"And you look normal. No red, no bloating," she said. "You're getting used to my cooking."

"Easy now." He turned to the kid. "You ready?"

Brandon jumped up. "Sure."

"You wanna bring the stick? We'll try it out, shoot a few games after our walk."

"Okay. Sure."

"And I'll look at those cars when we get back."

"This is how the railroad turned locomotives," said Jimmy. "Course they ran power to the thing. Would've been a big electric motor under that shack there, with a gear running on a toothed track. Too bad they scrapped everything for the iron during world war two. Fucking Goodyear wanted everyone on rubber."

The sky and the sunlight held them in a vibrant blue grace. They walked through spent dandelions, thistle, burdock bushes, ragweed, a variety of grasses; much of the old track bed had weeds coming up through the cindered gravel. Scoggton, just the tops of the two hills visible, was lost in the haze of summer noon. A half fallen-in engine house brooded in the heat behind the turntable, its multiple bays like the mouths of some ancient creature that could no longer feed itself. Jimmy pointed out the cement foundation of where a water tower had once stood. It wasn't easy being with the kid. He had no example except Chevalier who had said little, was always just honest and direct, and he sure wasn't going to use his stepfather as a model. But Brandon seemed delighted by everything, so he stopped worrying for the most part though the kid's all too apparent adoration made him uncomfortable.

"So you really rode freights?" the kid said. "That is so awesome. Maybe we could do it sometime together, if you had, you know, the time that is. You must be busy with writing your book and all."

"I rode twenty years ago. I'm not sure how it is now. Hey, look here." Jimmy bent down and pointed to something in the center of a railroad tie the color and texture of driftwood.

"What is it?"

"Date spike. Railroads used 'em so they knew when the tie was put down. Maybe we can find one with your birth year." They started looking. Jimmy was sweating in the sun, but he wasn't ready to take off his T-shirt though the kid would probably like the tattoo. Jimmy watched him—prancing nervously on each tie with short awkward steps, his skinny neck pointed down searching, his hair in his eyes, sneezing every so often. Funny fucking kid.

"Jimmy, what's your year? I think these are too old for mine." He told him, and within minutes the kid had found one with the last digit correct. He wanted that one. Jimmy dug the spike out—it was more an oversized nail—with his jackknife. "Can I have it, you know, like a memento of our day?" *Memento*—the kid was too much. "Thanks. This is *so* awesome. We'll pretend it's your year because it's only off by ten, okay?"

They walked farther from town along the abandoned line until they came to an old switch welded closed long ago against the shiny rails of used track. Here the gravel was granite-gray and weedless, the ties dark with creosote, some liquefying in the fissures of the wood. The smell brought memories.

"If a train comes by, can we hop it?" said Brandon.

"They got to be going pretty damn slow to jump 'em. You need open boxcars too. You don't see many empties anymore these days."

"But we could ride it all the way out west together, couldn't we?"

"Your mom might not like that."

"Yeah," the kid said with disappointment. "I'm just dreaming, that's all."

In the distance was a vague cadence.

"Train," said Jimmy.

"No way. Really?"

Jimmy reached in his pocket and handed the kid some change. "Put these in the center of the rail. Put a few on top of each other."

Within minutes, the track was humming. Jimmy showed the kid how to put his ear to the rail to feel the vibration. When the headlight showed, he said, "Okay, stand back." It wasn't much of a train. Two tired sooty Grand Trunk diesels, a listless wave from the engineer, about two dozen boxcars with the doors sealed, and no caboose, just a flashing red light attached to the back of the last car.

"Wow," said Brandon. "That was wicked sweet." He started hunting the coins. "Look!" He held one up. "Here's another one." He ran over to show him. A penny was indented with the impression of a nickel, the softer metal yielding to the other. A quarter was twice its normal size.

"You know a lot of cool stuff." The kid was grinning at him a bit insanely.

"More mementos, right?"

They parked in a dirt lot, opened a metal door with a rain-wrinkled paper sign billiards masking-taped to the center of it, climbed the stairs to a second door. Another abandoned factory, the room was enormous, dark—just a rough plank floor, unpainted walls, exposed pipes; in the far corner the bathroom door was open, a row of tall porcelain urinals gleaming in the one hanging fluorescent light. A section of the room had been partitioned off with a plywood wall, carpeted only under the pool tables, a modern jukebox blinking, one buzzing beer neon in the window reading *BOLEHCIM*. Steel pillars painted tan bisected the space, four pool tables to a side. No one was using the tables. They approached a glass-topped counter that might have been dragged out of an old jewelry store. Brandon was in the lead. "Willie, this is my friend Jimmy. Look." He set the cue case down and snapped it open. "He gave it to me. It's a McDermott."

Willie glanced at the stick, then studied Jimmy with his liverish bagged eyes. "This is one hell of a cue. Lot of cue for a fourteen-year-old."

"The kid's serious about the game."

"Not the point."

"Oh yeah, what is?"

Willie brushed back his long white hair. "It's a hard game, takes a long time."

"Then he needs a good cue."

"I wouldn't want him to lose it."

"What's that mean?" Jimmy had taken an instant dislike to the guy.

"Don't mean nothing. You want a table?" He slapped a tray of pool balls on the counter. "Number six."

Brandon picked up the plastic tray, and Jimmy followed him to the pool table. "How long has this place been here?" said Jimmy.

"Just a year. Willie moved because the rent was cheap. Or that's what he says. He lets me clean the place in exchange for table time." Brandon was racking the balls. "You want to shoot eight-ball?"

"What do you usually play?"

"Mostly I practice, but sometimes Willie plays me Nine if it's quiet."

"I'll just watch."

"You sure?" He looked disappointed, but Jimmy hated playing pool. He could never make a damn ball except the white one, and he didn't want the kid to witness that.

"Try out the cue. I'm gonna get a drink. You want a pop?"

"Sure."

"What kind?"

"Root beer."

Jimmy walked back to the counter. "What was that crack about the cue?"

Willie didn't move for a moment, then very quietly: "That's a three or four hundred dollar cue. Does Brandon know that?"

"Wha'd the crack mean?"

"You don't need to look at me like that."

"You gonna tell me?"

Willie glanced out the window as if checking on the weather. Jesus, this guy didn't scare at all. Some old guys were like that: they didn't give a damn if they'd been through enough.

Willie turned back. "Do you know his mother?"

That stopped him. "Do I know Claire? Why the hell would I be with the kid if I didn't know her?"

"Just asking."

"One more time: what did the crack mean?"

"Brandon's a good kid, but he doesn't have a lot of friends. If some of the scum around here learn about that stick, they'll steal it. That's a given."

"I had you wrong."

"I guess I had you wrong too."

"How's that?"

"Let's leave it there."

"You got beer?" said Jimmy, liking the guy's style. First impressions could be wrong.

"What kind you want?"

"Ballantine's."

Willie shook his head. "Where're you from?"

Jesus, here we go again. "New Hampshire." He heard the pool balls break and enjoyed the sound of the echo. There was something appealing about the empty room.

"We got every kind, but we don't have that. That's an old man's beer. I used to drink that forty years ago. No one drinks that anymore."

"I do. You got any Canadian beer?" The head shook again. "Just give me a beer then, as long as it's cold, and a root beer for the kid."

"You ever wonder why they call it root *beer*, but ginger *ale*?" Willie reached down into a long refrigerated locker—it was obvious his back bothered him—and brought out two bottles. He church-keyed them. "Three dollars."

Jimmy tossed a five on the counter. "Buy you a beer?"

"It's a little early for me."

"Never too early to drink away a misunderstanding."

"No, I suppose it isn't." He bent to the locker and opened a beer for himself. "They still make Ballantine's?" Jimmy nodded. "I'll get some then. It's a taste I miss."

They sipped the beers. Jimmy turned, watching Brandon sink a few shots. "He's good."

"He's real good for his age. A natural."

"He play a lot of the guys in here?"

"No. I play him sometimes, show him some stuff."

Brandon noticed them watching him and came over. "Jimmy, I can't believe how this cue shoots. It's just unreal, *so* sweet. I can't believe it's actually mine. Willie, can you believe that I got a genuine McDermott? You got to try it."

"Here's your root beer." The veined hand slid the drink.

Brandon leaned the cue, as if it were made of glass, against the counter. He took a thirsty pull on his soda, then dug into his pocket and fanned his hand to Willie. "We were in the freight yard. A train came by and look."

"I used to do that as a kid. Lot more trains back then. Scoggton was a railhead in those days."

The three of them worked their drinks for a moment.

"Is it okay if I practice some more?" said Brandon when he'd finished his root beer. Jimmy nodded, and the kid took his cue back to the table. They watched him sink a few balls. He looked over and smiled.

"You made that boy real happy," said Willie.

"You got a pencil and paper?"

Willie reached for the pad on which he jotted down table time, handed it over. Jimmy wrote his cell number. He pushed the pad back, leaned over the counter. "I'm gonna level with you. I like his mom a lot. If anyone touches that kid, or messes with his cue, I'll go after 'em. You spread the word. Bob Gray. I rent from Doris Callahan on Brackert Hill. That's my number if you ever need to get a hold of me."

"I'll do what I can."

"That's all I ask."

They clinked bottles. The jukebox as if on cue burst out with a tune. It was a sappy country song though, and Jimmy didn't like it much, didn't hum along.

Chapter Twenty-five

". . . and he's flying over this island, right? On the beach he sees Wonder Woman lying down there with her legs spread wide and her pussy all open." Jimmy pushed the head of his penis back in; it felt as if there was almost a suction. "Now, Superman gets all excited by this. Jesus, he thinks, look at that." Jimmy opened his eyes wide, showing the whites, and below him Claire started giggling. He stroked in and out a few times gently, adjusting his body weight on his stretched-out arms. "So he decides to give her a real surprise. She's obviously really horny, her ass jumping around on the sand. So Superman flies real low along the beach, his Super hard, all out and ready, and he aims right for her. Wham,"—Jimmy thrust deep into Claire and she grunted, her breath touching his neck—"he glides right into Wonder Woman, pushes her along the sand. It's the best thing he's ever felt, and he has this Super orgasm. He can't believe it, it's so good. A moment later he's lying beside her, panting, happy as hell, right? He tells her how fantastic it was, and asks her if it was as good for her." Jimmy looked at Claire, trying to hold back his grin. "And she says: 'I didn't feel a thing, but the Invisible Man musta loved it."

But she wasn't laughing. Not in the least. She was upset. He stopped moving and pulled out. "It's only a dumb joke."

"I'm sorry," she said.

"No. It's really dumb."

Her eyes dampened, one tear building, then breaking surface tension and gliding off her cheek, those lovely cheekbones.

"Come on, it wasn't that bad, was it?" He eased down beside her, staring up at the ceiling. Her bedroom was as stark as the rest of the apartment, the bed some kind of Japanese thing. Comfortable though, he had to admit. It was about two weeks since they first fucked, and they couldn't get enough of each other. The pool cue had turned out to be a smart gift: Brandon was at Willie's all the time now, and so far, apparently, no one had bothered the kid about it. "Why're you crying?" he said.

"I'm just being silly."

"Come on, tell me."

"I can't."

"Please."

She shook her head.

"Claire, please tell me."

She glanced out the window, the light glistening across her wet cheeks.

"I guess, I just don't want this to end."

"Why would it end?" Jesus, was she clairvoyant?

"It's just a feeling. Sorry." She yanked a tissue out of the box on the bedside table.

He didn't know what to say. One minute you're fucking, having a great time, now this. Neither spoke. She blew her nose.

"Has Vicky called you?" she said.

He was stalled for a few seconds. "A couple times."

"And?" she said.

"And nothing. Is that why you're upset?"

She shook her head. "I really thought she was my friend. There are people you know all your life—but you don't *really* know them. You just accept them as a constant, so you figure you must be friends, because you've hung out together for over twenty years. Now I realize she just used me. She claims she was only curious about you and wanted to test you and make sure you were honest."

"Honest?"

"Yeah. She says you're not telling me the truth, that you're a big deceiver, a scammer, and I'm falling for it."

There was a silence. He'd didn't want to go near that one. Especially after her letter, which he'd reread many times. And then with sudden inspiration he thought of something that might divert her. "Hey. I brought something for you." He got off the futon and picked up his vest. He handed her a folded piece of paper and settled back beside her, praying it would work.

"What's this?"

"Something I wrote. A poem. My first. Since you used to write I figured you might wanna read it."

She sat up, wiped her eyes and arranged her hair behind her back, opened the paper and started reading. The window screen snapped, then bellied in and out with the noon breeze, the sunlight beginning to find the room. After what felt like a long time, she looked up. "*I still like to do things with my hands.* This is a bit scary."

"Scary? How?"

"Is it supposed to be from the point of view of a killer?"

He glanced at the screen again, every strand of the weave bright silver.

"You think I'm a killer?"

"No, of course not. That's not what I meant."

He stood, his back to her.

"I shouldn't have said that," she said.

He turned, watched her, wondering if she could sense something like that. First the joke, then the poem, now this. Some days you fell into a ditch no matter where you walked. "It's only a stupid poem, okay? It's supposed to be funny."

"I guess I didn't see the humor. Don't be mad."

"I'm not."

"Come on and sit down. You're all red."

He sat. A car honked in the distance, and then a huge fly started buzzing stupidly at the screen, trying to get out.

"You know what the rumor is around town?" she said. He shook his head. "Cloutier is on crutches. People are saying you did it, though he denies it."

"Slag?" Though he knew well enough.

"The father. Did you hurt him, Jimmy?" He couldn't answer. "Will you tell me the truth? *Please*." He still didn't say anything. "No one will ever hear it from me. On my son's life. I need to know."

"I went to talk to him, trying to fix this Slag thing. He attacked me."

"And you won the fight? Without a scratch on you?"

"Kinda"

"My God. Why isn't he coming after you? Or sending someone after you?"

"I talked to him. I reasoned with him."

"And that stopped him? That's hard to believe."

"We'll see."

"Jimmy? What are you really doing in Scoggton?" She said it almost as a sigh. Of resignation? Of fear? As always, she sat with perfect posture, her nipples pointing at him, still erect.

"You got to give me a little more time," he said.

"More *time*?"

"Yeah, more time." He said it louder than he'd intended. "Okay?"

She looked away. "Brandon thinks you're a god, you know."

"The kid's all right."

"You like him?"

"He's okay."

"Even if he's kind of different?" She searched him.

"What do you mean different?" He got up and slapped at the screen. The fly was driving him nuts. He missed again, and it flew into the other room. And he was supposed to be a killer?

"Nothing," she said.

"What?"

"I just said, *nothing*."

"Oh. Hey, what time is it?"

"The clock's right there." She pointed.

"I think it's time for a beer. You want one?"

"Do you always drink beer?"

"If I can, yeah, I do."

"Jimmy?" He turned to face her, and it didn't look good. "I have a real problem," she said so quietly he barely understood. He waited; the fly returned to the screen. She sat up even straighter. "I'm completely in love with you—and I'm terrified you're going to disappear and I'll never see you again."

He moved across the mattress and took her in his arms. He'd get a beer later.

Chapter Twenty-six

Hakken sat in front of his computer screen. For once he was relieved there were no e-mails from Luke; his mind was on other things these days. Maybe that's why *My Life* hadn't progressed. He'd stalled, unsure of what to do with the interval between his Santa Cruz gym days and his start with Chevalier and BioTel. There was a lot of crime involved, and he wasn't eager to write it down. Besides, everyone knew about stealing cars and chop shops or doing collections; it was boring. He wondered if they could prosecute based on something like that, on something you'd written. Most guys who wrote that stuff were already in jail or were obviously making it up. Jimmy still hadn't shown Claire his book, but he was considering trying out that writers' group to see what they knew. Couldn't hurt. Now that Claire had told him she'd been a writer he was too embarrassed to show her his novel. It wasn't as if the poem had gone over great. He wanted to write about his mom, but since that happened before he left home, he wasn't sure how to work it. Flashbacks or something, but how?

His mom had loved holidays. Every Christmas the trailer was covered in a net of multi-colored lights, his stepfather half-drunk and awkward on the ladder, complaining with each strand. "I got to pay the electricity for all these damn things. Every goddamn year you gotta add more." When it came to their finances, he ignored the fact that Jimmy's mother worked and earned almost as much as he did. But then he overlooked everything that didn't serve him. His mom would say nothing and continue decorating. There were two huge plastic candles glowing on each side of the door, a worn Rudolf with a blinking nose. Each year his mom would have such hope, getting her hair done fancy, a new dress, baking a big turkey with bread and mushroom soup stuffing, telling him everything was going to be fine this time around. Of course it never was. His stepfather would get really drunk, sing lewd renditions of carols, stumble into something—a lamp, a present, the tree—and ruin it. His mother would try to hold things together, then end up crying. One Easter when he was six, some time after the holiday, he'd found a foil-wrapped chocolate egg in the low crook of a half-dead birch tree— his mom said a squirrel must've hidden it there—and it cheered him for an entire week. He kept it in his room and didn't eat it. Funny the odd things he remembered. Now he knew who'd hidden the egg, and how much she'd tried to make things nice for him. She never said much, her lanky body drawn up in a chair, smoking cigarettes and listening to his stepfather who was always ranting about someone he thought had cheated or slighted him. That ignorant know-it-all voice. How Jimmy had hated it. The wrong kind of sound could drive you—

His cell phone. He reached. Didn't recognize the number. "Yeah."

"Bob, are you avoiding me?"

"Why would I avoid you?"—for an instant unsure who it was.

"I couldn't imagine why," she said. He didn't respond. "Rumor is you took care of Mr. Cloutier, so I guess I didn't need to warn you after all. What'd you do—buy him off?" He heard the low husky laugh. Jimmy wasn't sure why, but he couldn't seem to get away from Vicky Lattrell, and it was obvious she was nothing but trouble. "So, when are we going to have our drink?" she said.

"I don't drink."

"You're pretty funny, you know that?"

"Vicky . . . I thought Claire was your friend."

That stopped her but only for an instant. "She *is* my friend. I just think you're interesting. If that's such a big goddamn deal, let's forget it."

"No need to get pissy."

"Yeah, sure. I mean, my God, what's one little drink?"

"And that's what you're talking about?"

"You shouldn't be so sure of yourself."

"I thought women liked confident men." He couldn't seem to help it. With her the cocky lines just seemed to pop out.

"You know, you're really impossible." She paused again. "So, are you going to call me when you're ready?"

"I suppose."

"I'll be here. Hey, you know that song?"—she began to sing—

"*Whenever you call me, I'll be there; whenever you want me, I'll be there; whenever you need me, I'll be there—I'll be around.* You remember that?"

He was surprised. "You sing good."

"Thanks. I got big lungs—it helps."

Jesus.

"Good-bye, *Bob*."

He hated to admit it, but she was giving him partial wood. Nothing was ever simple, was it? And then almost immediately his phone rang again. He answered without looking: "You again?"

"What's that?"

"Who is this?"

"Jimmy, it's Brandon Constantine. Sorry, my mom said it would be okay if I called you. Is this a bad time?"

"What's up?"

"You sure this is a good time? I could call back later. Are you writing?"

"What's on your mind?"

"It's kind of stupid, so I thought it would be easier to say on the phone."

"Fire."

"Huh?"

"I just mean, tell me."

"Oh. Right." There was a long pause. "I was wondering if you might, like, be able to teach me how to be cool like you."

"*Cool?*"

"I know it sounds really dumb, but I thought, you know . . . you might give me some pointers. You probably realize I need them." He made a sound that might have been a laugh.

Jesus, the poor kid. "I'm not sure I know that much about it."

"Jimmy, come on—you're totally cool."

"For starters, you never admit to being cool. You show things, through actions, but not with words."

"Really?"

"Yeah, that's one thing. Like if you did something cool, which usually has risk, you don't say nothing about it. See what I mean?"

"I think so."

"Like if you made a great pool shot, don't go: 'Wow, did you see that shot? Wasn't that something? Aren't I the best?' Instead you say nothing, like you can make them anytime you want. Then if some guy says something, just give a nod."

"Hey, I think I get that. Like when you wave, you just give a little flick with your hand."

"I do?"

"Yeah. It's way cool. I've been practicing it, but I've been too nervous to try it out."

"Are you nervous a lot?"

"You can tell, huh?"

"Naw, not really."

"I guess it shows big time. I'm always nervous people won't like me, and I try to be extra nice, but it doesn't help much."

"And you can't whine if you're going to be cool."

"Sorry, I probably do that a lot too."

"And don't ever apologize for being you. Fuck 'em if they don't like you."

"Really?"

"Yeah. Why not? What're they gonna do about it?"

"But that's you. I'm not so sure it would work the same for me."

"This might help. If someone looks at you, like they're trying to intimidate you or something, keep your eyes on theirs, but look bored, look right through them. Never try to look tough or mean."

"Really?"

"If someone is trying to act tough, it means they're posing like, and probably scared and trying to cover."

"No way."

"And if you want something and you're getting a hassle, just keep repeating what you want real simply and quietly with the look. Works every time."

"But you look tough even when you're smiling. I'm not so sure it would be the same for me."

Kid might have a point. "You ever work out?"

"I run sometimes."

"Your arms and chest."

"Like with weights?"

"You want me to take you to the gym sometime?" He tried to imagine that and vetoed it immediately. "Or tell you what, if I got you some weights, would you use them?"

"You mean it?"

"Done."

"Huh?"

"Done. Means it's going to happen. Another thing about cool, if you don't get something, just ignore it. If it's important enough, people say it again."

"Got it!"

"You're getting it."

"Jimmy, I can't tell you how much this—"

"Whoa."

"Right. Sorry. I mean, right."

"Later, Brandon."

"Later, Jimmy."

It was going to take a lot, but what could he expect—kid never had a father.

Chapter Twenty-seven

"I can't believe what's happening to him."

"Whaddaya mean?"

"You're turning him into a hood." There was the clank of iron from down the hall. "I raise him to be a polite kid, and now he mumbles all the time, won't answer questions, and does that low wave thing of yours in response to everything."

"He's turning into a teenager."

"I suppose that's your excuse."

Jimmy started laughing. It was finally sounding more natural. "Yeah, must be my excuse. Listen, I never had the chance to be a damn teenager."

"I guess I didn't either."

"So let him alone. Brandon's going good."

"According to you."

"He needs toughing up."

"I don't want a tough son. I have you."

"Come here." She curled up next to him on the sofa. He massaged her feet. "When is the kid done with school?"

"Next week, why?"

"I want to take you guys to the coast," he said. She leaned back slowly and examined him. "You know, a vacation—a real vacation. We'll stay somewhere nice, some cabins on the water, swim in the ocean, get some rays, get out of Scoggton, eat lobsters . . . "

Her strange look intensified. "For how long?"

"Week, ten days. Think we can stand each other for that long?"

"I don't know if I can get the time off from the shop."

"Well, check." He couldn't figure out what might be wrong, but he sensed something in her. What could be the problem with a vacation? Everyone loved vacations, didn't they?

"When do you want to go?"

"In a couple weeks?"

"I'll ask."

Jesus, if she wasn't excited by the idea, maybe Brandon would be. He called down the hall. There was a clunk, and in a few moments the kid appeared in the living room, his face flushed, the armpits of his black T-shirt soaked. "How's it going in there?"

"Did my curls. I'm up to six reps with the fifteens."

"That's what it takes. Listen, how would you like to go to the coast for a vacation?"

"Are you serious?" When Jimmy nodded, Brandon started jumping around, "Vacation, a vacation," then stopped. "Sorry, I mean, yeah, sure, whatever."

"Okay then. We'll rent some cabins, barbeque steaks on one of those grills you put the coals in, the whole bit."

"That would be so unreal. Maybe we could visit Mitch and go out for a ride in the lobster boat."

"No boats, no cousins." Brandon looked a little hurt, but what kind of cousin was it who only saw the kid once in his life? "Okay, back to your workout."

"I'm almost done."

"Back to it. No shirking." Brandon reluctantly headed down the hall. Jimmy slid his hand over Claire's knee. "See? The kid wants to go." But she looked even more sour, and here he'd thought she was going to be so pleased, really excited. "You did a good job with him, you know that?"

"And you're too good to be true, aren't you?"

He ignored the comment. This was heading in a wrong direction again, and he didn't like the feeling. "I got something to ask you."

"Oh, oh—sounds serious."

"It is." She tensed, straightened. At least he had her full attention. He lowered his voice: "I think you should tell the kid who his real father is." She glanced out the window. "Why are you bringing this up now?"

"I've been thinking about it."

"Why?"

"Why what?"

"Why would I tell him that?"

"Because it's the truth."

She rotated back. "Do you hate Raymond that much?"

"Nothing to do with it."

"Why then?"

"If you were Brandon, wouldn't you want to know?"

"It's more complicated than that."

"Wouldn't it be better to have an unknown father than one who didn't give a rat's ass about you?"

"I guess." She didn't sound even remotely convinced, but he knew the answer to that only too well.

"Tell him his real father disappeared. Don't tell him you were raped."

"You've got it all figured out, haven't you?"

"Don't look so sour, come on. We're going on vacation, right?" He rubbed her thigh; she pushed his hand away. Now he was really worried about what was up with her though he knew nobody liked to be told how to raise their kid. "Has Slag tried to get in touch with you recently?" She shook her head. "His father didn't come after you, did he? I'm surprised. I mean, Ray is a blow-hard, but his dad is the real deal. You must've terrified him."

"He gains nothing by going after me, and he risks everything if he does."

"Is that really true?"

"What do you think?"

"I don't know what to think with you. I wish I did."

"Let's not worry about it, okay? We been over that enough. Besides, we got better things to do. We got this vacation to plan up." Her expression wasn't improving.

"And how am I supposed to pay my part of this famous vacation?"

"I got it covered."

"Are you going to pay for everything?"

"Yeah, why not?"

"Jimmy, if you're so rich, why do you live like you do?"

"You think I'm lying?"

"Why do you do this to me?"

"Do what?"

"Put me in this position."

"I'm not *putting* you anywhere."

She stood up. It always took her an instant to get her balance. "I better start cooking if you want some supper."

"Don't be pissed."

"I'm not *pissed*—"

"You look pissed off." Though it wasn't exactly true. He couldn't read her expression.

"I'm not."

"Then what is it?"

"I'm confused. What else would I be? I don't understand any of this." Her voice was getting louder. "You show up in this town from nowhere, like this tattooed biker tough-ass. But then I look into your eyes, and I feel there's something more, some deep sadness or hidden joy, or something, I don't know what, but I can't help but be drawn to it. And first you're Bob, and then you're Jimmy. God knows who or what you really are. But who cares, because before I know it, you're this goddamn knight in shiny armor, befriending my son, buying him pool cues and weights, buying me thousand-dollar platinum pens, fixing neon signs, beating up the guy *no one* messes with, who does absolutely nothing to retaliate, and now—"

"Mom!" The kid stood there trembling—Jimmy hadn't even noticed him enter the room—"Mom, what're you doing? Can't you ever just be happy?"

Claire spun toward Brandon's shrill voice and almost fell. She looked as if the kid had slapped her.

"Just once. *Please*! Can't you just accept something good that's happened to us? Just say, 'This is good, I'm going to accept it and be happy.' Just once? Just one damn time?"

"*Brandon*." It was a desperate plea, her eyes that of someone caught in headlights approaching at terrifying speed. Then she turned away from both of them.

Jimmy stood, the tears now on Claire's cheeks, the kid still trembling, staring at his sneakers. "Your mom doesn't trust me yet. Don't blame her. This stuff always takes time, and trust is a funny thing. Listen, we're going to have a great vacation, a perfect vacation—okay?" He waited, but neither of them responded. "I've never been to the coast. I've always wanted to go—my whole damn life. We load up the wagon, right? We'll need some coolers and towels and shit, and we'll drive over there, rent a cabin, and so on. Just the three of us." He glanced at Claire but she hadn't moved. "It's nice there on the ocean, right, Brandon?"

The kid was crying now too. "Yeah," he said in a choked voice. "It's really nice."

"Good. Then we'll have a great time."

Chapter Twenty-eight

Her tongue licked the salt stuck to the rim of the glass. "I was so glad when you called—I thought you were scared of me." Out it came again. Jesus, it was long. Everything about her was oversized. "You don't talk much do you?" she said.

"You wanna 'nother?"

"Wow, *two* drinks. What big balls." She rattled her ice. *Just like the snake.* "So, what are you, a Scorpio?"

"Huh?"

"When were you born?"

"December." He signaled the waitress.

"Ohh, a Sadge. December what?"

"Sixth."

"Oh, my, God! That's my dad's birthday. That's such a huge coincidence. No wonder I was drawn to you."

He sipped his beer. Some Mexican thing—tasted horrible. "What's he do?"

"He's a dentist. Together we got half the head."

He grabbed a chip and shoveled it into the salsa. It tasted pretty good—the chips crisp and slightly warm. "Shit."

"Aw-oh—your nice leather vest and T-shirt." She leaned over with a wet napkin and started rubbing, the cleavage on cinemascope. "Do you always wear black?"

He took the napkin away from her.

"Why?" she said.

"*Why*?"

"Yeah. Why always black? Don't you like colors?"

He flashed to the castle rug. They'd given him his money back, but the guy who sold him the thing had seemed disappointed by the return. Claire had gotten the blood out of the other rug anyway.

"So, you going to tell me or not?"

"About what?"

"Why you always wear black. You should have your colors done. I bet you'd be a lot less gloomy if you wore something bright."

"I'm not gloomy." He glanced around. The restaurant was dripping in plants, straw hats, crossed marimbas and ponchos that made his castle rug almost dull by comparison. He hated this kind of place, but he needed to find something out and Vicky was the only person he could ask.

"Don't you ever just wanna have fun, act silly?" she said.

The waitress dropped off another margarita and a beer. He thought of exchanging it for a different brand but didn't really care; a few lousy beers wouldn't kill him. Then he felt something against his foot. He was back to his boots so at least his smashed toe was protected. The nail had fallen off and the new one was taking forever to grow back. Vicky was giving him a look. He moved his boot, and her high heel started traveling up his leg.

"Cut it out," he said.

"See—gloomy."

"I got to talk to you about something serious. I can't do it with you kicking me."

"You think that was kicking?" Her grin flipped vicious.

"Ouch." Jesus, right on the shin.

"Hurt?"

He shook his head.

"Shall I try again? You're supposed to be so tough, I figured you might like it."

"I'm not so tough."

"Sure. So, what do you want to talk about?"

"Claire."

That finally slowed her down. He took a pull from the second beer. Tasted just as skunky.

"What about her?" She sounded gloomy now and that cheered him.

"Is she okay?" he said not sure how to phrase it.

"What do you mean *okay*?"

"You know, normal-like."

"*Normal*? She's not as smart as *I* am, but I guess she's normal."

"You think you're smarter than Claire?" He couldn't believe it.

"Well—I have my own business, I live in a brand-new house, I drive a brand-new car, and what does she have?"

"You think owning things makes somebody smart?"

"If being successful and getting what you want isn't smart, then what is?"

"We're off the subject."

"Got you there, didn't I?"

"Listen, are you going to answer me or not?"

"Go ahead."

She looked pleased now, but he continued anyway. He wanted to get this over with. "What I mean is: do you think Claire is at all like her mother?"

"Oh. You mean nuts?"

"Not crazy, just maybe very emotional-like."

"Women are emotional, Bob. Especially when we don't feel secure. Do you think Claire feels secure with you?"

"Why wouldn't she?"

"Oh, I don't know. Why don't you guess."

"You still talk to her?"

"Sometimes. She doesn't see this the way I do. And that made her kinda pissed off."

He tried the Mexican again. "So why do you wanna go out with me?"

"Hey, what're you talking about? You called me."

"I suppose I did."

She stirred her margarita, the ice whirling. "You know, I don't think you and Claire are right for each other. I told her that."

That stopped him. "What the fuck does that mean?"

"Now don't get all huffy."

"You don't know anything about me."

"Don't be so sure."

He waited.

"Girls talk, you know. Besides, Sadges and Virgos never work out; it's a fire and a water sign. You need a Leo like me. And you're too tall for her. We're a perfect match size-wise, don't you think?"

"Look, this is stupid."

"Let me ask you something since you asked me so many questions." She reached up to twirl one of the strands of her hairdo. "Do you want to have kids?"

"*Kids*? I've never even thought about it."

"They're great. A house full of kids—playing, laughing, running around. They're what makes life worth living."

"I don't notice you've got any."

"Never met the right man, as they say. I was married once for like six months but there was no way I was gonna have his kids. Besides, I still have plenty of time. But, think about it—wouldn't you love to have a family? At least a son to carry on after you?"

He thought about it. "Maybe."

"Well, you asked me if she was nuts—"

"I didn't say that."

"Whatever. Claire has always been negative and depressed. You know why?" He shook his head. "At first it was always her foot, but she mostly got past that, then it was her mother. Then Slag wouldn't marry her. Then it was slaving in the pizza place and being a single mom. But what really did her in was—at least this is my theory—she can't have any more kids."

"She has Brandon."

"Yeah, Brandon. You know what they call him in school?" He didn't move.

"*Fag*-don. He even got a hard-on in the showers after gym class." Her finger illustrated, the long nail wagging. "And you know what? I think Claire knows and does nothing about it. Now is that the kind of family you want?"

Chapter Twenty-nine

". . . just tell me one thing: did you fuck her?"

"I can't talk to you if you won't calm down."

"How the hell do you expect me to *calm down*!"

He glanced out at the town—the darkness, the lit bridge. His cell phone weighed a hundred pounds and Claire's voice burned his ear.

"Are you going to answer me?"

"Claire, this is ridiculous."

"I knew"—she said between sobs—"I knew this was all too good to be true. Brandon said, 'Mom, don't worry,' but I knew."

"What are you talking about?"

"You went to her fucking house. I can't believe you went home with her!"

"You got to stop screaming."

"I'm not screaming." She quieted a little. "What did she say to you?"

"She just wanted me to see her place."

"Oh, fuck it." A pause. "Jimmy, I just want you to know one thing: I really loved you. I mean *really* loved you." She was crying again. He felt like punching something. "I got to go," she said.

"Claire, wait, hold on a second." But she'd already hung up. He threw his cell phone. It bounced off the baseboard and skidded across the floor. He whipped around, took a few long strides and ripped open the fridge door. The entire machine teetered forward. He slammed it back with his shoulder almost losing his balance. A can of beer fell out, rolled under the stove. He grabbed another. Snapped it. Drank.

When he was on his third beer—downing them far too quickly —he heard the shriek of brakes in front of the house. He thought he knew the sound of those brakes. From his windows he could only see the swath of the headlights but there could be no doubt who it was. He raced for the door, unintentionally banged into a cat, slid madly down the steep stairs in his socks, shot along the hallway, and down the front staircase. The distance had never seemed so ridiculously far. As he wrenched open the street door, he heard the engine scream as if it had been grabbed by the testicles, the tires chattering across the cracked pavement. It didn't seem possible to burn rubber in that car, but she was doing it. He stopped at the bottom cement step and yelled in the direction of the taillights. When she didn't slow, he ran halfway down True Terrace, waving his arms madly, the loose gravel spearing him through his socks. As he trudged back, cutting across the yard to avoid the sharp rocks, he punched one of Doris's prized oak trunks.

And there she stood in the open doorway. She was wearing a plaid nightdress and her head was festooned in pink and lime plastic curlers. With her thin hair he wondered why she bothered. Everything seemed like a waste of time to him.

"Robert, this is hardly the time of night for all this ruckus."

"Sorry." He barely managed the word and attempted to warn her silently not to say much more.

"Who was that?"

"Claire."

"And what was she doing here at this hour?"

"I don't fucking know. Okay? For Chrissake, not everything has an explanation."

The old woman froze. She began to turn away but faced him again. "I didn't realize you were so upset, but there is no cause to talk to me in that manner."

He plopped down on one of the steps. Held his head in his hands. He hadn't cried since his mother died and he sure as hell wasn't going to now.

"What's this?" she said. She'd come out of the door and was nudging something along with her slipper. It made a dry sandpapery sound against the stone. Reluctantly, he turned to look. It was a narrow box, dented on one corner, missing only the blue foil paper. Doris bent over stiffly and picked it up. She held it out to him.

"I don't want it."

She settled on the step beside him. "Robert, did you and Claire have a tiff?"

The dampness of the June night made him shiver. He should have grabbed a T-shirt.

Doris tapped the box against her kneecap. "You've hurt your hand."

He glanced at his skinned knuckles, blood running along his wrist. He wiped it off with his other hand.

"You should clean it so it doesn't get infected. Do you want to end up in the hospital again?" She adjusted a curler that had flopped down. There was a long silence. "You can talk to me if you want to. You probably think because I never married that I don't know about some things."

He groaned. The last thing he needed was a lecture on love from a spinster who had probably only read two-bit romance novels.

"Robert, just allow me to say this. It's the heart that either has the capacity for love, or it doesn't. That's what makes the difference. And two hearts that find each other, two loving hearts—nothing can keep them apart if they're meant to love each other." She set the box down between them. "This problem you have with Claire will work itself out. You'll see."

He brought his head up. Out past the glare of the porte-cochere bulb, there was a single firefly pulsing in the bushes. It was probably searching for a mate, sending out its feeble light—*love me, love me, love me*. Jesus, the stupid bastard. "It's over," he said.

"Why? Claire has a good heart. I can see it in a person's eyes. I saw it in yours that first day we met."

"You did?"

"Why else would I have allowed you to live in my home?"

He glanced at her.

"There's more to it than just money, Robert. Remember, I lived without taking in a boarder for my whole life."

The firefly was heading for the heavens now. What did it expect to find up there? "You don't think we're wrong for each other?"

"You and Claire?"

He nodded.

"Who said that?"

"Vicky Lattrell."

"Oh *her*. She thinks she's too good for this town, but she'd be lost anywhere else. Are you seeing her too, Robert?"

"I did yesterday. Claire found out."

"No wonder she's angry. And to think Vicky is supposed to be her friend. But Vicky is one of those women who knows what she wants and goes after it. She married some unsuspecting guy just for the divorce settlement. She doesn't care who she hurts."

He glanced at her again.

"I know you think I'm just a prideful foolish old woman, but I know some things. I know you and Claire would be good together."

"You think she might forgive me?"

"We almost always forgive the man we love. God knows I had to."

Doris had a lover? Then he remembered her father. "She might not love me anymore."

"She still loves you. You can count on that. Look what she just did."

There was a distant siren heading over the bridge, the mournful cry of the thing giving voice to what he was feeling.

"I'm gonna go and call Claire," he said.

"Yes, do that."

He stood up on the step below her, wanting to tell her how much he appreciated what she'd said, but, "Thanks," was all he managed. She looked up at him, her eyes lost in the glasses, and he almost held out his hand to shake, but decided that would be too ridiculous. Suddenly her right hand jerked up and covered her mouth. Her face turned away and she started shaking spasmodically. She seemed to be having some sort of fit. "Are you all right?" he said. Jesus, that's all he needed, Doris dying right in front of him. He didn't know shit about CPR. "Doris, talk to me. Are you okay? Hey, come on now."

She opened her eyes, took off her glasses and wiped her eye sockets with two fingers, then held the bridge of her nose. "Oh my. Oh dear. I'm *so* sorry, Robert. I just couldn't help it. Please forgive me. And I thought the stuff on your *arms* was strange." She pointed at his chest and began giggling again. "Choo-choo," she said through her laughter. "Choo-choo."

Jimmy slumped in front of his computer in the darkness. It was hugely annoying, but on top of everything else, he was extremely horny. Terri Coal's breasts hung in the screen—how could a million pixels of prismatic light be so mesmerizing?—and it was true, they were somewhat similar to Vicky's, but only somewhat. He reached for his beer can.

Vicky had shown him around her house. Every room was a color, and every color had a weird name, like puce, or coral, or magenta, or plum, along with the bird-egg ones. His castle rug would have fit right in. Only her driveway was black. She'd whirled through the rooms, a tequila and tonic attached to one hand, the other gesturing with a cigarette, pointing out the different features as if she were a real estate agent. And then at the end of the tour she'd set down the drink, put out the smoke, and said, "Have I ever shown you these?"

Her hand had unbuttoned her blouse, and she'd shrugged her arms out of it, and then she'd reached behind her, and the bra—a lacy ivory white—fell forward. God dammit, he should have turned around right then, but instead his hands had lifted with a will of their own. And he couldn't stand Vicky Lattrell. After a moment her tongue had filled his mouth, attacked his mouth reptile-like, and he'd almost gagged at the taste of tequila and dead cigarettes. It was only then that he had come to his senses and recoiled.

Now he felt sick. He felt like a complete ass. He hated himself. And how could he tell Claire what had really happened, or actually not happened? She had all those small breast worries. How could he tell her Vicky's had felt more soggy than appealing, and that they weren't firm and cleanly defined like hers? And that she'd smelled pungent in an unpleasant way. The difference between fantasy and reality could be so harsh. Besides, Vicky meant nothing to him, and Claire everything. A moment of weakness and look at the mess he'd created.

He glanced at the chipped and cracked cell phone resting on the desk, but he knew it wasn't any use. He'd tried repeatedly and nothing was going to revive the thing. He considered waking up Doris and asking to use the one in the kitchen, but there was no way he was going to have her listening to every word. But it wasn't only that. He felt exhausted, played out, as dead as his damn cell phone.

Chapter Thirty

Hakken glanced up at the dark apartment house for maybe the hundredth time. He was parked on Cartier Street, and nothing had moved for an hour except his drinking hand. Earlier, stranded in his stuffy rooms with the fan rumbling, sleep had been out of the question. He'd tiptoed downstairs, pulled on his boots at the cement steps, ignored the laces. He'd scanned for the firefly but the poor unloved bastard was gone. Then he'd driven through town—nothing like a three a.m. mill town for appearing dead and lonesome—and ended up here, the vortex of his emotions. Jimmy worried the kid might spot him—Brandon was weird enough to be an insomniac—but he couldn't seem to move either closer to Claire or away from her, even though the last thing he wanted was the kid running out onto the porch just to say Hi. He snapped another ale. He didn't even want to keep drinking but couldn't seem to stop either. Where had his discipline and control gone? What the hell had happened to him over these last few months?

As the first misery of dawn blanched the sky he finally woke the Impala with a twist and drove to the graveyard. The gates were closed. He considered walking in with a rack of beer, but then the cops might notice the stranded car and come prowling. Brokenhearted was one thing, blatant stupidly was another. He eased downhill back into town, circled the empty oak-laden park, drove up Acadia past the cold Broadway neon, Willie's poolroom, and the bakery. It alone showed signs of life, but there was no smell of fresh bread as much as he craved something uplifting. He headed out of town like a broken limb swirled helplessly adrift in a senseless current.

He had held something perfect and fragile.
It had been handed to him with trust.
And he'd dropped it.

Jimmy drove south along the river; the high crown of the narrow road seemed to be nudging the wagon, pulling him toward the murky water. He had to eat something. The dozen cans of beer he'd drunk were making his stomach groan, and his head was dull from emotion and no sleep. Within twenty minutes of guiding the Impala carefully along the twisty macadam, the pallid rectangle of a diner sign floated out of the blue morning, and he swerved into the dirt lot.

He pulled open the restaurant door, and those diner-cooking smells surrounded him like friendly relatives. A mound of potatoes hissed on the grill, the coffee machine leaked a steaming stream into a Silex pot. He chose a stool at the counter.

"Mornin', dear, you want some coffee?" He nodded. "Be ready in a sec. I unlocked only a minute ago." The clock on the polished stainless backing read a few minutes past five.

Jimmy ordered the hunter's breakfast: sausage, eggs, hash, and potatoes. When his meal arrived, other patrons began to file in— farmers, truck drivers, drunks, the usual early-morning mix. The food eased his stomach but did nothing for the pain under his ribcage. Why did he feel so bad? He'd made no promises to her. He'd been so careful not to, but somehow he'd let her down anyway. It was the unsaid that got you into trouble. Chevalier had talked to him about that. About unwritten unspoken obligation. About knowing in your heart what was right and what was wrong. About being called on to do something that could cost you everything only because it was right. But where had it gotten Chevalier?
Dead.

Yet somehow he wasn't.
Chevalier had not been willing to put on the gloves and spar. He'd said, "That's all behind me now. I wasn't much of a boxer anyway. I just liked the workouts." Chevalier still had the pipes though. And always wore the same blue T-shirts. The CEO of BioTel and he wore T-shirts and jeans. And he never raised his voice. But didn't have that simpering soft-spoken thing either. He just talked straight at you, as if you were in a bar, discussing baseball, or bikes, or a kind of beer you liked. He was always honest and kind but perfectly cool no matter what happened. How could someone consistently manage that?
Jimmy stood up and tossed a bill next to his plate. The waitress headed over. "That'll be six-fifty," she said, sliding the twenty off the counter. "All set," he said.
"Why, thank you, dear. How nice."
"Later."
He aimed for the door. By now the sunlight was in the flowered curtains that spanned the bottom half of the windows. It blinded him when he walked to the Impala, his shades still in the apartment. He thought of grabbing a toothbrush from the glove box and going back into the diner

to brush but didn't want to return. Besides, what the hell did his teeth matter? As he headed for Scoggton, he sipped at the last can of warm beer. It tasted like bile. He pulled over beside the river and poured it out. For a moment he thought he was going to vomit, his hangover already descending.

"It's dead all right. If you'd purchased the insurance package, we would have replaced it for free, you know that? Why did you say it failed again?"

"I didn't."

The salesclerk, who reminded Jimmy of Barney Rubble without his Ritalin, frowned. "Well, if you don't mind me asking, how did it come to fail? We like to keep a survey on the performance of our equipment. Failures on this particular model are very infrequent."

"I threw it at a wall."

Barney paled, his hand juggling the spent cell phone. "That explains the crack." He pointed it out to Jimmy. "We don't recommend throwing our phones, but I'm sure you know that. Well . . . our new phones are all on display over there." He pointed again, his eyes glancing everywhere but refusing to meet Jimmy's. "The features are listed on each phone, feel free to test them out. If you have any—"

"Which would you get?"

"Oh, I don't know, that's not an easy question. It really depends on your needs in a phone. We do have a special this week on the new Nokia for two hundred and ninety-nine dollars. It has some outstanding features like—"

"Look, bud, get me a phone. Any damn one that works. Okay?"

When Jimmy got outside into the mall parking lot, he grabbed the phone from the plastic bag and started to key in Claire's number. He stopped. He wasn't sure what he could say at this point. If only he could be with her in person, it would be a lot easier.

He drove past the frame shop and tried to see if she was working. But even if she was there, it would be awkward. A customer was bound to barge in before he could say anything, and he'd have to stand around like an idiot while matte colors or some stupid picture were discussed. Then he remembered this was the night of that weekly writer's thing, that meeting where people read their stuff. She'd be there. Maybe he could simply walk in, read some of *My Life* and maybe she'd like it and soften towards him a little. Afterwards, he could ask her if she wanted to get a beer or something and . . .

With a fresh feeling of hope, he pointed the Impala over the center bridge.

Doris wasn't around when he climbed the stairs. The old woman was much more complex than he'd figured. But wasn't that always the way with people? He scratched and fed the cats, went to the fridge and drew out one of his last green cans. His drinking was getting out of control, yet this wasn't the day to suffer a hangover. If only he had some P, but Luke hadn't been sending. Come to think of it, he hadn't heard from him in weeks. Where was Luke? Why hadn't he been checking in? He set the beer aside, flossed and brushed, then checked his e-mail. Nothing. Claire had given him the number of the guy who ran the writing thing. He found it, walked to the window, focused on his view, and dialed.

"Eliot Barclay?"

"Yes, this is he. Who is speaking please?"

He almost gave his real name. Goddamn hangovers. "Bob Gray."

"Are we acquainted?"

"I'm a friend of Claire Constantine."

"Oh, how delightful!"

"Huh?"

"Excuse me?"

It took him a second. "Say again."

"I meant, being Claire's friend is a gratifying and agreeable circumstance. *Now*, how can I help you?"

"She coming to the writing meet tonight?"

"Are you referring to our writers' group get-together?"

"Bingo. Claire coming?"

"I expect she'll attend."

"What time?"

"Are *you* a writer?"

"Kinda. Been working on this book. Claire said you might help me out on it."

"Is this fiction? We only allow fiction."

"Kinda."

"Well, Bob, the usual procedure for our group is that you'd be invited to join us on a certain predetermined evening; you'd then read us a chapter from your novel or perhaps a short story, hopefully something around fifteen pages—some chapters, of course, having more brevity, some being quite verbose. After you read, we'd critique your work for you, as you would do ours for us. Then at the next meeting, our membership would vote on whether to include you in our little gatherings, or whether it might be better for you to find another group more appropriate to your needs and talents. Fit is so important in these matters, now isn't it?"

"I'll be there."

"Bob, that might be rushing things just a smidgeon. How—"

"You still meet at the library?"

"Normally we gather there in the upstairs reading room."

"Time?"

"Well, everyone is usually there by six o'clock. But, Bob, if I might—"

"Bingo."

Jimmy pressed end, took a long pull from the can. Jesus, the things we do for women.

Chapter Thirty-one

Hakken lumbered into the reading room a little after six. Every head turned—except the one he wanted to see. "Where's Claire?"

A stocky guy with a prow of a chin stood up, slowly. "You must be Bob Gray." He spoke as if his mouth was full of walnuts and he didn't want anyone to notice. "I'm Eliot Barclay."

"Hey," said Jimmy, accepting the hand, a surprisingly firm grip. "Claire late?"

"Affirmative. She called me this afternoon to inform us that her mother's in some kind of *situation*, and that she'll be detained. She'll arrive somewhat later, I presume. Allow me to introduce our little gang. This is Suzette Fredrick." A stick of a woman with a dingy brown Afro blinked absentmindedly behind thick glasses. Eliot Barclay continued to gesture around the heavy oak table. "And this is Janet Turnblatt." Large with something dark over her lip who sneezed into a Kleenex. "And our poetess with prose, Alice Bromley." Aggressive blue eyes, tanned stevedore arms, hair wrenched back into a bun. Though they had all nodded politely to Jimmy, and Alice Bromley had actually shown teeth, they were eyeing him now like a reject from a Petri dish. And he'd showered, shaved, brushed, flossed, and put on his best leather vest. He remembered why he'd always shaved his head—his hair was one continuous cowlick.

"Please, sit down, Bob, and tell us about yourself." Barclay settled, smiled benignly. All he needed was a goddamn briar pipe clenched between those teeth.

Jimmy sat. There were plenty of chairs around the table. He chose the one furthest from the sneezing Turnblatt. "You sure Claire's coming?"

"There's every indication that she will, but of course, no guarantee."

Jimmy aligned his printed text with the table edge.

"Bob, please, tell us about yourself—your major impetus as a writer, your influences, your heroes and heroines, your *raison d'etre*."

"My what?"

"For instance, how long have you been writing?

"I started in November, but I read a lot as a kid."

"Ahh. And where are you from?"

"New Hampshire." For once it made no impression.

"Where in New Hampshire?"

"North. Irving."

"I'm afraid I'm not familiar with Irving. And where did you attend university?"

"I dropped out of high school. Listen, when do we get to the reading part?"

"You're eager to read then?"

"Maybe. If Claire gets here."

"Ahh. Well, it's actually my and Alice's evening to read, but I'm happy to forgo my slot, Bob. You're welcome to take it."

"Eliot, you read," said Alice. "I've only got a short piece this week. It's still a little rough, and I wouldn't mind some more time to revisit it."

"Are you certain?"

She nodded.

"Then I'll proceed. Thank you, Alice." With both hands he smoothed his gray hair behind his ears. "Bob, I'm reading from my new novel, which has a pub date for next year. I fear you'll be entering in the middle, through a side door, shall we say, but hopefully the context won't be too baffling for you. Just allow me to explain that the dateline is the late nineteen-sixties, the arena California." He slid some sheets from a briefcase onto the table, adjusted himself, and began:

"Chapter six. Morning." A pause. "The resplendent beads of light sparkled, nay twinkled, radiating brilliance from each precious dew-soaked leaf. Chuck Daffney hailed the dawn with every expanding fiber of pleasure in his soul. Little did he know what awaited him in the coming hours! He sauntered back to his steel steed, sashayed his behind along the cracked leather seat, fingered the bright stub of the microbus's ignition key, and the familiar green smoke soon ballooned into the blistering morning air. Ah, to be in the desert again! To have the whole glorious day before him, stretching its gilded crown magnetically to the shimmering vault of the horizon.

"Chuck Daffney spotted the hitchhiker, imagining at first that she must be a mirage. He nudged the bus toward the berm cautiously. And was glad he did! She virtually pulsed in the desert sunlight. Oh, Venus limed in delicious *contrapposto*, eyes irradiant, hinting at gateways of depraved intimacy, her stupendous breasts hammocked in tie-dyed cloth. 'You going my way?' she intoned, her splendid lips quivering. 'Oh, y-yes,' he managed to stammer. Once she was positioned in the seat beside him—an art of quivering motion too delectable to contemplate—he pondered the delicate architecture of her nasal orifices, the petite cartilage armature just visible beneath her very white skin, the glistening cream of her faultless cheeks."

Eliot took a deep, meaningful breath, and Jimmy tuned out. He just wanted Claire to arrive so he could get on with it, though he was starting to think *it* had been a bad idea. If Claire liked this guy's writing, he was a goner. Jesus, the guy was still describing the hitchhiker. Now he was going on about her smells. ". . . exuded an odor as complex and gratifying as an aria, the sublime syncopated meshing of the pure feline feminine . . . " And at least five minutes later: ". . . thighs not quite plump, traveling precipitously toward the frowning cherubs of her finely crafted knees, the stretched highlights as colorless as white marble."

Now they were having a discussion—Chuck and the hitchhiker, Gwendolyn. Finally some dialogue, but they were both talking the same way, and sounding like Eliot. Jimmy had never heard people talk like that. For that matter, he couldn't believe Eliot spoke the way he did. Was he trying to sound like English royalty?

Ten minutes later, Eliot finally got the bus moving. " . . . and into the crushed ochre berm, across the scalded macadam of the brittle highway, drizzled the thin line of transmission fluid, like an artist's inspired brush stroke, like a euphoric child dragging a narrow stick in the placid sand as he feels his way up an endless beach, so this wet streak followed their path along the desert road, drying inexorably in the searing sun, a hieroglyph decipherable only by the gods."

Eliot slowly lowered the manuscript.

"Lovely," said Janet, "simply divine." She sneezed again. Jesus, why would anyone go out in public with a cold that bad? "I loved the analogous context of the line of automobile fluid. Here they are striking out on a relationship, but Chuck leaves a string, a map line if you will, to find his way back if everything is not as he hopes. And the fact that it's a secretion . . . lovely. The term wordsmith is over used these days, but you, sir, are a *wordsmith*."

Eliot nodded contentedly.

"Yes, I agree," said Suzette. "Some of your best description, and allegory, and so sublimely cunning the way the prose continues to fold back on itself in cadence *and* in melody. The irreverence is, of course, transcendent. My one concern was the triple alliteration of *steel, steed*, and *sashayed*."

"Too much?"

"*Sauntered* is in the same clause."

"Metal steed?"

"Yes, try it. It might be better."

"Thank you, Suzette."

Alice folded her sunburned arms across her chest. "The writing is, as usual, your toned filigreed prose. And as Suzette said, some of the rhythms and echoes were simply tantalizing. I, however, felt the ogling of Gwendolyn might be over the top."

"*Ogling*?"

"My God, Eliot. Chuck practically fucked her with words."

"But isn't that the point? To penetrate deeply?"

Janet Turnblatt began to snicker.

"That's disgusting," said Alice.

"Thank you." Eliot looked to Jimmy. "Bob, do you have any insights? It would be enjoyable to experience the thoughts of a male."

"Insights?"

"Yes. Whatever came into your mind. I'd say penetrated, but Alice seems to have *issues* with the word."

Alice jerked her head away.

"The leaves," said Jimmy.

"The leaves?"

"I'm not sure what desert it is, but would there be wet leaves? Not many trees in most deserts. And what was up with the green smoke?"

Eliot's voice changed. "As I understand it, those old Volkswagens smoked copiously."

"Engines can smoke blue, black, or gray. No green."

"Ahh." Nothing but his lips moving. "Never green?"

Jimmy shook his head. "And what's this woman doing out in the middle of a desert, half undressed?"

"Does there need to be a reason? Mystery is compelling in a novel."

"Just wondering. Then why isn't she sunburned? You said she was white as marble."

Eliot rubbed his forehead with his middle finger.

Jimmy ignored it. "Ever hitchhiked in the desert?"

"Anything else?"

"If the car's leaking tranny fluid in a line, it's not going to get far before the tranny seizes. Worse in that heat."

"Bob, perhaps you'd like to grace us with your offering now."

Jimmy glanced toward the doorway. "I'll wait for Claire."

They were all glaring at him. Jesus, maybe he'd said the wrong thing. He was just trying to help the guy out. Why did Eliot want to write about stuff he obviously knew nothing about? And use words like *contrapposto*? What the hell was a contrapposto? At least there hadn't been any dead kids in it—yet. Everything he read lately had a dead child in it.

Eliot said, "I think you should proceed. We're all eager to hear your offering, I'm sure."

"Yes," said Janet. "Please do."

The others nodded. He scanned the door one more time. "We're waiting, Bob."

He picked up the sheets. What else was he going to do? Maybe she'd walk in while he was reading, which would be perfect. "My Life," he said, skipping over his real name just in time. "The night I planned to run away from home my stepfather caught fire. I get out of my sleeping bag to pack some stuff for my trip, pissed I got to leave it behind. It's a black and yellow cotton thing, covered in flying ducks. I'd gotten it two years ago on my fourteenth birthday from my mother, and the bag was a gem, but no good for the road. Rolled, it stands as high as my waist. I have a wool blanket to sleep in instead. As I'm packing, my mother cries out from the other end of the trailer. I run." As Jimmy continued reading, he felt as if he were sinking into mud. He could tell they didn't like it. Eliot was fidgeting and examining the ceiling. Janet had stopped sneezing, and was writing notes. So was Suzette. Alice was squeaking her fingers along the edge of the table. All the movement threw him off, and he kept screwing up. Reading it out loud, his writing sounded really dumb. Finally, it seemed like an hour though it probably wasn't ten minutes, he was nearing the end. Still no Claire. Maybe that was for the best after all. He read the last page of the chapter:

"'I'm going to find my father.'

"She hesitates at this. 'Where's he?'

"'West Coast.'

"'Why so far away?'

"'He's a sailor. Soon he's going to be a mate, just under the captain.'

"'On a sailboat?'

"'No. A huge tanker with giant steam engines. San Francisco is the home port.'

"'Really?'

"'Yeah. I'll probably get a job in the engine room as a mechanic or something. We'll go all over the world together.'

"'You're too young to be a mechanic.'

"'I can learn, can't I? And I'm willing, ain't I? I'm willing to do whatever it takes to make it.' I look out the window of the bus, not wanting the girl to see my eyes, and I know it's true."

Jimmy dropped the manuscript on the table, then aligned the sheets with the edge as he waited. No one moved. No one was looking at him either. For an instant, he almost bolted. He was stunned he cared so much.

Eliot cleared his throat. "A coming of age novel, I take it? Has a few interesting bits, even if it's very over the top." He glanced at Alice. "And, of course, alcoholic characters like the stepfather have been done and overdone until they smell kind of burnt." A coy pause. "I appreciate your intent with the stepfather, to generate sympathy for the protagonist; however, it lacks verisimilitude."

"Vera-*what*?"

"Truth, Bob, truth. It's simply not believable. Sensational, yes, believable, no. And, of course, your writing is very neophyte—too many misplaced modifiers, extraneous description as with the sleeping bag for instance; why would the reader care about the sleeping bag since it's being left behind? These mistakes are to be expected, considering your education, and the duration of your efforts—"

"I rather liked it," said Alice. "I thought it had a rawness that's lacking in much of today's prose. Very David Copperfield. The young hero strikes out. And he was so tender with his poor, broken-down, battered mother—touching. I agree that the burning stepfather was too obvious a fabrication, though the dialogue with the girl on the bus was more real, if not quite believable. Still, it held my interest and I would be willing to continue."

"I would beg to ask—" Janet stopped to sneeze. "What possessed Bob to invent that passage? I found it rather vile."

"The stepfather as malodorous pyre?" said Eliot.

She nodded. "I think it could be omitted with no great loss to the senses." A smirk.

"Well, Bob. I'm sure we're interested in your elucidation." Jimmy glanced at their faces. The four smug expressions. "That's what happened. Why the fuck do you think?" He gathered up his papers, slid back his chair.

"Ah," said Eliot. "A memoir. I was under the assumption it was fiction."

Jimmy was already halfway to the door.

"Touchy, isn't he?" he heard Janet say.

"Beginning writers are always like that."

"If we deem to call *him* a writer."

A snicker and then there was only the sound of his boots on the stairs. A bar! Jesus, he needed a whiskey.

Chapter Thirty-two

But he didn't go to a bar. He was too exhausted: the fight with Claire, drinking all night, the lack of sleep. He went home instead, shoved the Impala into its spot, plodded through the cooling dusk and up the stone steps. It all seemed so familiar his throat tightened. The little gang could shove it. Who were they to ridicule his childhood. What the hell had he been thinking, going to a writers' group? Never again. He hadn't really understood why Claire had quit writing because of mere rejection. Now he did! And where was Claire anyway? God, he felt defeated.

He opened the front door, Doris missing as well. He trudged up the stairs to his rooms, and even the cats ignored him. Only Yellow lifted his head, gave a cursory look, and went back to sleep. Jimmy visited the fridge, and after a few long drains, the ale began reviving him a little. Jesus—the existence of beer was one of the only proofs that God loves us. Ben got that one right. Maybe a good night's sleep and everything would seem better by morning? He doubted it, but what the hell. Some days you were just a metal duck in a shooting gallery.

His cell startled him. Claire? Please let it be Claire, no matter how pissed she was. She'd probably shown at the library, and the little gang had told her what a shitty writer he was. He didn't recognize the number, but pressed the button. "Yeah."

A jumble of static.

"What? Who is this?"

"—will—poolro—rand—"

And then he thought he recognized the voice. "Willie? That you? I can barely hear a thing."

It cleared slightly and the voice was louder. "Brandon's in trouble."

"There?"

"Yeah."

"Bad?"

"Yeah."

"Did you call the cops?"

"Not the way it—" The phone went dead.

Willie wouldn't sound like that if it was only about the cue. This was something much worse, and the timing really sucked. He was too worn out to deal with anything else right then. Jimmy downed the ale and stood motionless, breathing deeply, hoping to find what he needed. But what choice did he have?

He grabbed his bag gloves, keys, and shot down the stairs, his boots hammering on the tread; for once he was unconcerned about the noise. He ran past the fieldstone foundation of the house, ignited the wagon, roared backwards, spun the wheel—the car listing like a boat broadsided by a wave—and shot down True Terrace. He was doing sixty over the center bridge until traffic slowed him.

The red SUV was parked in the poolroom lot. He left the Impala unlocked and ran for the door. He took the stairs two at a time, bolted across the empty first room. He heard no one playing pool, the jukebox dead. As he entered the pool table area he spotted Slag Cloutier and two others at the far end of the room. They were clustered in a loose half-circle around Brandon who stood shivering, his pants around his ankles, his white briefs with a wet stain at the crotch. Slag had a new gang of henchmen. One had Willie trapped behind the glass counter, the old man holding a bloody handkerchief to the side of his head. Jimmy'd worry about Willie later. He moved between the pool tables toward the kid. Slag rotated on his sneakers, a windbreaker over the usual sweat suit. "Hey, boys, looky here—if it isn't my old pal Bob come to join the party." His voice was disturbingly calm. "You musta been who Willie called. Saved us the trouble, didn't he?"—Jimmy was close enough now to see that Slag's eyes were bugged and red, maybe something extra mixed with the coke tonight—"Turns out though, you're not Bob at all. Fag-boy here calls you *Jimmy*. Told me not to mess with him because you're tougher than anyone in Scoggton. Can you believe that?" He chuckled and adjusted his ball cap. "A lot of fuckin' surprises around here lately. Turns out fag-boy isn't my son either. Is that some hilarious shit or what? The bitch gets me to pay for a bastard I never had. Isn't that a kicker?" He slapped his thigh, his whole body quivering. Jimmy didn't like this new confidence. "Makes sense though. I mean, why would Cloutier blood produce a faggot? So we're testing him. Find out how much of a fag he really is." Jimmy could see Slag's body changing, rage entering with sickening intensity. "Maybe you don't know this, but we're not big on fags around here." Slag yanked off his cap and slapped Brandon across the face with it. The kid didn't move though a red welt appeared on his cheek. "Or lying cunts. Or dickheads like you." He pulled his cap back on and stepped toward Jimmy. "Why'd I know you were gonna show up?"

"You shouldn't've touched the kid."

"Scary, Bob. Fucking scary." He nodded his head in an

exaggerated manner. "Everyone's scared of you. Even my father told me to lay off. Can you believe that shit? My own damn father. But you know what? I ain't fuckin' scared of you." He took another step toward Jimmy as if to prove it.

"You shoulda left the kid alone," said Jimmy. Something in Slag was really bothering him. This wasn't all bluster, there was something truly dangerous under the surface. He snapped the bag gloves out of his back pocket, quickly pulled them on.

"The fucking gloves." Slag laughed. "You know what? I got something for you too. See if you can outbox this, dickhead." He reached under his jacket. Nothing quite has the presence of a gun. Everyone in the room stiffened, the two henchmen backing slowly. They obviously hadn't known about the automatic. Luke had told him it doesn't always hurt too bad getting shot. Sometimes the bullet passes right through, depending where you're hit. Of course, some bullets open you up, the soft metal tip spreading and tearing away everything in its path, the exit wound a foot or larger in diameter. No one survived those. He knew Slag would shoot him. He had that look. No bluff this time. And from this close, he couldn't miss.

"Maybe I'll start with fag-don's nuts. Put him out of his misery. Then we'll see how tough Mr. Boxer really is. Reggie, cover the downstairs door."

Reggie raised his hands. "Slag, I don't want nothing to do with shootin'."

"Cover the fuckin' door before I kill you first."

Reggie backed away and then they heard him on the stairs. The door banged.

"Fucking pussy," said Slag.

Jimmy eased to the left, Slag tracking him with the automatic. Out of the corner of his eye, he saw the kid reach down and pull up his pants. Smart kid; now he could run. Jimmy couldn't see Willie behind the counter. The situation simply sucked and he felt dread. He should never have gotten near anyone in this goddamn town. Now he would probably die here. He kept inching in the direction of Brandon, trying not to let the fear get the better of him, expecting the explosion and the impact of the bullet at any instant. When he got himself almost between the kid and the gun he said, "Brandon—*RUN*."

"Touching," said Slag, his face demented, a trickle of spit hanging from his lip. "Fucking touching. Faggot here's been telling everyone you're his father. I didn't believe the little shit, but I guess it must be true if you're willing to take a bullet for him."

There wasn't a sound from behind him. The kid hadn't moved. He was probably frozen in terror. "Run!" Jimmy said again, his eyes locked on

the disgusting face. "Brandon, *just* run. You'll be okay. No one will hurt you." He'd keep his body between the kid and the weapon.
"No," said Brandon, his voice barely a croak. "I'm fighting' with you."
"A fuckin' hero," said Slag. He stepped toward Brandon, the black barrel still pointed at Jimmy's chest, the three of them forming a triangle now. "Maybe faggot here wants to suck my gun. Huh, Fag-don? Before I blow your nuts off. Would you like that? Show us what a big hero you are? The cunt's puny fag bastard."
Brandon lunged at Slag, his stick-like arms flailing madly in front of him. Slag's face deteriorated into confusion and his aim wavered for an instant, his outstretched arm caught between the two of them, the gun pointed at nothing. Jimmy drove his fist into Slag's shoulder. No punch had ever sprung more violently from his body, the bag glove adding weight and force. There was the dull crack of bone and the arm fell like a severed tree limb. Slag staggered backwards; before the gun clattered to the floor, a right uppercut exploded his jaw. The rest of his body seemed to liquefy, landing on the carpet as a lifeless heap of sweat clothes, the cap knocked off, blood puddling at his mouth.
Jimmy glanced at the kid. "You all right?" Brandon nodded, his body shaking violently, tears in his eyes, but silent. Jimmy turned to the other guy, slipping off the gloves and sticking them back in his pocket. "It's over," he said. He reached down and picked up the automatic, slid out the clip, stuck it in his vest pocket, tossed the gun into the corner. "Get him out of here. He's gonna need a hospital." The guy nodded to the one guarding Willie, and the two of them moved toward Slag cautiously, hoisting him up by each shoulder, the damaged arm dangly horribly.
"Don't let him drown in his own blood," said Jimmy. "Keep him on his side." Jesus, the guy was bleeding like something slaughtered. "And listen." They stopped dragging the body, stared at him. "Tell the father. Tell him the truth about what happened tonight. Tell him I could've driven his son's nose bone into his brain. He should be thankful I held back. Next time, I'll kill him. I got no more for this shit. You got that?" They seemed to, and then continued hauling the body laboriously to the stairs. Slag sure was a heavy bastard.
"Stupid fuck," Jimmy muttered. Now that the adrenaline was wearing off, he felt sick. This had all gone way too far, gotten ridiculously out of control. He'd almost been shot, Slag's arm would probably never work right, and his face was a lopsided mess. It all seemed so inanely senseless and sickening.
He looked at the kid. Poor kid was still shaking badly, just standing there, his cheeks wet. Jimmy needed to calm him down. He'd been through a lot. Who knew what it would do to him. "Come on." He held

out his hand. Brandon jerked forward and took it. His hand was like a
dead bird. They walked up to Willie, and Jimmy let go of the hand—
holding it made him queasy. He heard a few loud thumps coming from
the stairwell, then a groan. Jesus, they'd kill Slag before they ever got
him to the hospital.

"You okay, Willie?"

"Yeah, just a dent. More blood than hurt."

"I think we need beer."

"Now you're talking. Quite the night." The old man turned, reached
down and pulled two out of the locker.

"Three," said Jimmy. Willie nodded and brought out another, setting
them on the counter and working the key.

"No shit—Ballantine's. In the bottle." The sight of the beer cheered him
considerably, made everything seem more normal again.

"Got 'em in for ya. I was surprised they still make it."

"Here." Jimmy handed one to the kid.

"Is it all right?"

"*Is it all right?* You save my life, and wanna know if it's okay to drink a
beer?"

Brandon looked down at his shoes and shook his head. "I didn't save
your life." It was barely above a whisper. He took the beer though,
grabbing it awkwardly by the neck.

"Fuck you didn't save my life. You got guts. Real guts. Here's to ya."
Jimmy tipped back the bottle, downed two-thirds of it. He needed it.

"Not many men can charge a loaded gun. Right Willie?"

"Damn straight."

Brandon wasn't shaking as badly now, it was more a trembling. At each
sip a little beer dribbled down his chin. "You mean it?" he said. "I did
all right?"

"Whaddaya think?" said Jimmy. He asked Willie for another round
though he was the only one even close to finished. He took off his vest,
slid the bullet clip out and clunked it down on the glass counter; the vest
he held out to the kid. "Here."

"I'm okay," said Brandon. "I'm not that cold."

"I know you're okay. I'm givin' it to ya."

The kid stared a second, his lips twitched, and Jimmy worried he was
going to start blubbering. "Here," he said again. "It's yours."

"Mine? Really?"

"Now whaddaya think?"

Brandon took it and put it on, repeatedly rubbing the front smooth with
his hands. It hung on him like a priest's shawl, but somehow it looked all
right. "Thanks, Jimmy."

The kid was smiling at him, a nervous crooked smile, something glowing in his eyes that made Jimmy ridiculously uncomfortable.

"We did all right, didn't we?" Brandon said in the same uncertain voice. "I mean, together like."

Jimmy nodded and then had to turn away. He studied the beer neon in the window for what felt like a bit too long. For some damn reason he was getting choked up.

Chapter Thirty-three

Yellow was nudging him on the forehead and licking him on the nose. The room was overly warm with sunlight, his mouth like dry paste, his head dull from too much sleep. He staggered slightly as he stood, flicked on the fan next to the open window, the metallic breeze displacing some of the stuffiness. No wonder Yellow was concerned; it was past noon. Jimmy let the tap run cold, downed two glasses of water, fed the cats, did his hundred pushups and attended his teeth.

Brandon had ended up drinking three beers in the poolroom when Jimmy decided to cut him off, and the kid was a little drunk when they pulled onto Cartier Street, but his trembling had stopped. He seemed reluctant to get out of the car, and the two of them sat there. Jimmy glanced up, the third-floor apartment dark. He couldn't tell if Claire was home or not. He wondered if she'd heard about what happened yet. In Scoggton bad news seemed to travel faster than light. At least Slag would be out of commission for a long time, if not for good; the father he was still concerned about. He'd just have to wait and see. He glanced at Brandon. "Doesn't look like your mom's home yet."

"Maybe she's still with Grandma."

"You all right alone?"

"Sure. Thanks f'r the ride."

"No problem."

The kid was searching him, still not getting out of the car. "Jimmy . . . about the other thing, about what they, you know, called me, I—"

"You don't need to say nothing."

"But I don't wan' you to think . . . "

"Brandon. None of that matters a damn. It's what's inside that matters." He'd tapped his chest. "You proved that tonight, bud."

Brandon'd glanced down a moment. "It was really *you* who saved *me*."

"Like you said, we worked it together. Now get out of here. I need some sleep. Tell your mom I'll call her tomorrow." The kid's face was so open and trusting it was hard to look at.

"And the other thing I said, about you being . . . you know, my dad and all. I'm *really* sorry I said that, I just figured—"

Jesus, the damn kid was relentless. "Don't worry about it. Okay?"
"And this vest, I can't believe you gave it to me. Unless you need it
back—"
"Brandon—git."
He'd grinned and opened the door. "Later."
"Later, kid."
Jimmy'd wheeled it out of there.

Now he stood naked in front of the fan and wondered if he should call
Claire before he ate breakfast. She was probably at work. Or was this
one of her days off? He couldn't remember. Had she forgiven him at
all? Maybe he'd gained some points last night if the kid had told her
exactly what happened, but maybe not. Who could tell with her? He
dialed, his stomach reacting. She answered.
"Claire. You're there."
"I got home a couple hours ago."
"Is this one of your days off?"
"I called in."
"You okay?" She sounded tired.
"Yeah." She paused. "No, not really. Mom tried to commit suicide last
night."
"Jesus! What happened?"
"She'd been acting strange all afternoon, or stranger than usual, so they
called me. I sat with her a long time listening to her talk crazy, but
finally left to get something to eat. When I got back she'd ODed.
Apparently she'd saved up all these pills. Funny how you can be crazy
and still be clever."
"Is she gonna be okay?"
"I guess. She came around early this morning. At least her vitals. It was
amazing what she ingested. She's healthy as a goat." She sighed, her
voice dull with resignation and exhaustion.
"I'm sorry." His heart when out to her, his arms and chest wanting to feel
her against him.
"Brandon told me what happened to you guys. Quite the night for
everybody, wasn't it? Every time I think about Ray and that gun, I get
sick. I just can't get it out of my mind. Fucking Ray! He's completely
lost it. Brandon told me everything you did. Jimmy, I owe you big
time."
"So you're not mad at me?"
"Mad?"
"Yeah."
"Oh, that. It seems so stupid now, doesn't it? Besides, Vicky came to the

hospital last night. She finally confessed and told me what happened between you, that she tried, but you said no thanks. I shouldn't have been so jealous, but Vicky seems to always get what she wants and I was terrified I'd lose you. God, I'm so tired. Sorry I sound so dopey. It's all been a bit too much for me."

"You should sleep. That stuff with your mom musta really drained you."

"Brandon said you'd call. I didn't want to miss it so I stayed awake."

"Listen, why don't you get some rest, and then we'll go out tonight, the Broadway, sky's the limit. Snails, snakes, flaming swords, champagne—anything you can think of, it's yours. We can take the kid if you want. We'll put all this behind us."

She started laughing. "Sure—okay—I'd love to."

"So call me when you wake up, all right?"

"Yeah. And Jimmy"—her voice painfully tender—"thanks for what you did."

"You got a hell of a kid there. The heart of a goddamn lion. I tell him to run, so what's he do? He charges the gun and saves me. Iron balls, let me tell you, fucking iron."

"I get sick every time I think of it. Both of you might have been shot."

"Without Brandon I probably would've been."

"You mean it?"

"Damn straight. What've I been saying? I never woulda guessed the kid had it in him."

"Brandon's really growing up. At first I thought telling him the truth about Ray was a huge mistake, but it seems to have freed him somehow. He admires you so much. You have no idea. You've made such a difference in his life."

He grunted, not knowing what to say.

"I was so scared you wouldn't accept Brandon."

"Because of that?"

"Yeah, I guess. Did you know at first?"

"Vicky told me."

"That *bitch*."

"She's just Vicky. A steamroller. A big colorful one. Wanted me to have my colors done. Can you believe that?"

"Are you defending her?"

He was silent.

"I'm only joking, okay?"

"Claire, I'm really sorry I did that to you. Talk about stupid."

"We all do stupid things, don't we? The point is getting past them." She didn't say anything for a moment. "Brandon's been parading around in that vest all morning, looking at himself in the mirror, saying, 'Mom, you think my muscles are getting bigger?' Here I'm a complete wreck imagining him shot, and he's worried about his arms like nothing happened. He wants tattoos now too."

"A locomotive?"

"Has he seen *that* one?"

"For your eyes only."

"I can't wait to see it again."

He paused, feeling himself stiffen, his penis beginning to angle toward the fan blades. "Maybe we can get some time alone tonight?"

"Maybe I don't need a nap?"

"No, you sleep. We have plenty of time, plenty of time." His eyes roamed over the Scoggton skyline, the railroad bridge by the falls. "Hey, when we first went out, you told me that story on purpose, didn't you?" Jesus, and he'd told her that stupid superman joke. No wonder she'd reacted.

"Which story?"

"About those two they threw off the bridge."

It took her a second. "I suppose so."

"You worried even then, didn't you?" There was a knocking at his door, and he missed what she said. "Sorry, someone's knocking. What'd ya say?"

"Not important. Answer your door. I'll call you when I wake up."

"Sweet dreams."

Jimmy clumped down the stairs and opened the door. Doris was holding a cardboard box completely mummified in shiny packaging tape. "This just arrived for you. UPS overnight. It's obviously urgent."

He held out his hands. It was a little heavier than he expected. When he confirmed the handwriting, a dagger of concern passed through him. He tried to brush it aside not wanting Doris to notice.

"What's in it?" she said, her glasses blinking.

"How would I know that?"

"Well, Robert, usually when someone sends a package, they call beforehand to let you know they've sent it, what the contents are, and when it might be likely to arrive."

"They do?"

"Certainly." She frowned. "Did you hear about Raymond Cloutier?"

He hesitated. "What?"

"He was in a horrible accident and he's all mangled. When they took his blood at the hospital, the doctors found enormous quantities of all kinds of drugs. His father can't hush this one up, and he's irate with his son. Apparently, when he's well enough to walk, he's being sent to a clinic somewhere out west to correct his bad habits, though I doubt any clinic will fix *him*. Must have been some car wreck." She said this gleefully. "Even more ghastly than when Dolly Kimball killed all those poor people when she drove through the supermarket."

"It's dangerous driving in this town."

"Robert, truer words were rarely spoken. That's why I'm happy to stay home."

"Did you get all this from Fred?"

"Now from whom else would I hear it?" Jimmy waited. "How are you and Claire faring?"

"Great. We're going out tonight."

"I'm glad." Though she didn't look it. Maybe Doris was only sweet if you were wounded. "She was always a nice girl, if a tad plain."

"Later, Doris." Fred must have missed Claire's mother's suicide attempt somehow. There was hope for the town after all.

"Okay, Robert. Remember, your rent is due next week. Not that I'm particularly worried, but I thought it best to remind you."

He closed the door.

Upstairs he didn't open the box. Instead he quickly checked his e-mail.

H—A is in motion. You get your wish. Flying into Bangor at 7:10 PM June 30. Box with Art will be there same day. L

Jimmy broke into a sweat.

Chapter Thirty-four

Art—Artillery. Luke had a bunch of odd expressions like that. He'd shipped two handguns and what was probably a couple extra clips in a quarter mile of bubble wrap. There was also Doctor P. Jimmy put the pills aside but didn't unwrap and examine the guns. Luke always had some fancy new weapon he thought was the greatest ever made. They were usually some exotic import from Italy, Germany, or Israel whose special characteristics he'd explain in numbing detail. Though Jimmy didn't like guns, he knew they'd need them for this. This wasn't as simple as threatening two Cloutiers.

Five hours and Luke would be at the airport. Just like him not to call. He decided to cell and make sure.

"It's me," he said, hearing vague noises over his cell.

"Box-sin?"

"What?"

"Is the *box* in?"

"Yeah."

"Good."

"You in the air?"

"Naw, fucked up route. Three stops. I'm in Denver, sittin' on my ass. Should be on time though. Bring beer. We head for F tonight. Gotta run."

Jimmy snapped the cell closed, set it on his desk, and stared at it. Last night he'd told Brandon that what mattered was what was in your heart. Chevalier had said the same thing to him: "It doesn't matter what you come from—it's what's inside you, now, that counts." And what was inside him now? Was he weakening, backing away from what he knew was right? Wendell Alden had to pay. He'd murdered a great man and he had to die. It was justice. It was that simple. Jimmy had to kill him. It was completely different than the stupidity of getting involved with the Cloutiers. He made a fist and pounded the desk.

But what about Claire? Hadn't he just told her an hour ago that they had plenty of time? What had he been thinking? He'd drifted away from his goal, from his promise, from his vow to himself and the memory of Chevalier. How had he allowed himself to become so distracted? He chewed a Percocet, washed the taste away with a beer. Then he prepared to leave town.

He sneaked down to the second-floor hall and retrieved his case from behind the drawer; if Cloutier had used cops, at least they wouldn't have gotten the money. He knew old man Cloutier was finished and no longer a threat, but the outcome was still depressing: what father wanted to admit to having produced a fucked up son like that?

He sat at his computer.

Dear Doris,

      If you are reading this, I didn't make it. In the closet you'll find a suitcase. Under a panel in the bottom is a carbon-fiber attaché case. The combination is 12666. (Don't panic, just my birth date.) You'll find about a quarter of a mill. It's not stolen. It's yours. Get the house fixed and painted. It needs it and deserves it. There are also two safety deposit boxes in Santa Cruz, California, with about 2 mill each. Also not stolen. It's from the sale of BioTel stock. Check if you want. (I've put in a business card from each bank.) I leave half of that to Claire Constantine and her son Brandon. The other half goes to Luke Delamar. He'll find you, don't worry. So this is a last will, and you are my executor. If I'm dead, they'll ID me and know who I really am, and Claire and Luke can claim the money.

Doris, thanks for everything, sharing your home with me, and cooking all those dinners.

The last bit wasn't easy to add—just the memory of the biscuits and boiled dinner almost choked him—but what the hell, she was only doing her best. He deleted the part telling how much was in the safety deposit boxes. Claire and Luke would find out soon enough, and there was no reason to tempt anyone though he trusted Doris. He printed it up, signed his real name, sealed it in an envelope, wrote *Doris Callahan* on it, and stuck it under his pillow. Then he began packing the extra suitcase.

Since he always wore the same thing, it was easy. He tossed in his vests, T-shirts, socks and jeans—a black mound only differentiated by texture. Actually, he and Luke were going to need some of those dorky flannel shirts if they were going to pose as fishermen. He remembered guys fishing in New Hampshire and they always wore those plaid shirts. They could stop somewhere on the way south and buy a couple. He fanned through the two six-inch stacks of hundreds he'd removed from the case before hiding it again. It would be enough to cover Luke's pay and any extra expenses. He thought of Luke, the P beginning to tingle.

Luke had this funny routine during a job. "Buddy," he'd say, as he held down the security guard, or whoever, which at his size was never difficult. "Buddy, you and me are juss workin' stiffs, men with guns. We coulda fought back to back in Nam. Think about that. Now you make this easy, I give you one large when I leave. You don't, you gonna die. It's your choice." They always made it easy and never seemed to give the cops much of a description though Luke was simple to describe: a huge black bear. Jimmy had asked him once, "What are you anyway?" "Whaddaya mean?" "You Italian?" "*Italian?*" "Well, what then? Black, Greek, Cherokee? You got to be something." Luke had said, "My family didn't go in for that kinda shit. I'm American. Maybe God beat me with the ugly stick, but I'm just an American, nothing more. What more do ya need?"

He packed two digital tape recorders, fresh batteries, put in the guns and clips still mummied in bubble wrap, filled his toilet bag with brushes, floss, soap, and a razor. He spent some time organizing and cleaning the apartment, emptying the fridge, forcing himself to throw out the last of the mushrooms, taking down the garbage, chewing another P and drinking a beer as he finished the job, relieved to have the Doctor onboard. Then he went down to find Doris.

She was writing a grocery list at the kitchen table. "Robert, this pen writes very nicely." She held it up to show him, the platinum glinting in the fluorescents.

"I need it back."

"But you said it was mine, and I quite like it. It just glides along the paper."

"I got to get it back to Claire."

"As I understood it, she didn't want it."

"That was then."

"She's changed her mind, I suppose."

He nodded. "It's hers. I bought it for her. Besides, it's a symbol."

She frowned, but slid the pen across the table. "I've never had such a nice pen, but I'll concede to your decision. But only reluctantly. If she doesn't want it, I'd like it back."

He picked it up and stuck it in his pocket. He'd be damned if he was going to give Doris a thousand-dollar pen to write grocery lists. "I came down to pay my rent."

"Would you care for a cup of tea?"

The second P was beginning to coast in. "Doris, I think the occasion calls for a Bushmill's."

"What occasion? Paying the rent? Have you gone mad, Robert? It's the middle of the afternoon."

"I'm leaving town for a bit."

"Leaving? For where?" The concern in her face surprised him.

"Just a week or so."

"Oh. Well, that's not so bad. Where are you off to?"

"A fishing vacation."

She went back to her frown. "Fishing? Frankly, Robert, you don't seem the type. My father fly-fished, did you know that? But I can't see you fishing."

"This is dangerous fishing."

"Don't be ridiculous—fishing is hardly dangerous. Maybe I still have some of his tackle and fishing poles. They must be somewhere. I'll go look after a bit."

"I just thought we'd have a drink, to good luck."

"Tea is as beneficial for luck as whiskey, maybe more so."

"I doubt it. Besides, it's not traditional." That slowed her. "And I got a toast. A special one, for you."

She reluctantly brought down the bottle. He noticed it was a fresh one she must've hauled up from the basement. She broke the seal and decanted two. "Okay, I'm waiting."

He held out his glass. And couldn't seem to say anything. He was getting flustered, the P and everything else numbing him. What if he never saw her again? This weakness horrified him. What had happened to him over these six months?

"Well?" Her lenses were expectant disks.

"Doris, I lost my mom when I was sixteen and . . . I never had much family. And being here, in your house and all—" This was sounding kind of stupid but there was nothing to do about it now. "I just want to thank you for everything and stuff."

"That's very nice of you to say." She downed her whiskey. "My goodness. It burns a little on the way, doesn't it?"

"You could try sipping it." He did.

"My father always said to just drink it off in one swallow. Shows spirit."

"You definitely have spirit," he said.

"Thank you, Robert. That's a nice thing to say." Her eyes were watering slightly. The way she drank, no wonder. "When are you departing then?"

"A few hours."

Her head twitched a little, the glasses on him again. "That's certainly sudden."

"You got to go when the fish are biting."

"I suppose that's true. Shall we have another? For the success of the fishing trip?" He nodded and she poured.

"What happened to the other bottle?"

"I figured I might as well finish it. No point in keeping that shallow remnant, was there?" She sipped this time. "I won't have you bringing back any fish to clean. I have no interest in gutting dead fish and removing scales."

The thought of fish a la Callahan was mortifying. He could just imagine it added to the boiled dinner. "I have a favor to ask you."

"And what would that be?"

"Can you look after the cats till I'm back?"

"What would it entail?"

"Just feeding them twice a day. I'll put out plenty of fresh litter, so you don't got to worry about that."

She examined him suspiciously. "Is that why you've been plying me with liquor, Robert, and making all these touching toasts?"

He reached into his pocket. "Here's the rent money, and here's something for cat food."

"A hundred dollars for cat food?"

"Get the good kind."

Jimmy climbed the stairs, up the worn runner, each creak like a familiar note plucked. He'd never thought about what he planned to do after he killed Wendell Alden. He'd never envisioned a life after that. It was just the one thing that had to get done, a commitment with no way around it, a sort of ending point without a future. For the first time he started to consider what would happen afterwards. And stopped himself. This could only lead to more weakness. It was time for business, and time to stop fucking around. But Claire. What was he going to do about Claire? He had to at least see her and tell her. And it was going to suck.

He celled her apartment and got Brandon. The kid said she was still sleeping, and Jimmy asked him to wake her, that he was on his way over. He filled the cat's water bowl, scratched them good-bye, and hauled the suitcase downstairs. Doris was waiting for him by the front door.

"I found them." She pointed to an ancient bamboo rod and a dull metal tackle box. "I want you to utilize these."

"That's okay. I wouldn't want to mess them up."

"Please, Robert."

"I'd rather not."

"My dad would want you to take them."

He noticed her expression and winced. Why did this have to be so difficult? "All right. I'll take them. I'd be honored."

"Where is *your* fishing gear by the way?"

"Going to pick some up."

"You're not really going fishing, are you?"

He didn't respond.

"I don't care, Robert. I just hope you're coming back. I don't find it easy to say, but I must admit, I've grown very fond of you, and I'd miss you terribly if you didn't come back. . . . Are you coming back?"

He put his arms around her bony frame, her balding head reaching only the bottom of the locomotive boiler under his vest and T-shirt, her hands barely touching his back. They separated quickly.

"Well, now," she said, obviously flustered.

"Yeah." He knew just how she felt. He gathered up the fishing equipment, his suitcase, and headed for the Impala.

As he drove past the porte cochere, she was still standing in the open doorway, her father's huge dilapidated house surrounding her like an irredeemable obligation. She waved and he honked.

Chapter Thirty-five

He climbed the stairs to Claire's apartment and for the first time had nothing in his hands. His heart was another matter. Without the P he might not have been able to make it. He considered taking another, but tapped on her door instead, waiting restlessly, tempted to flee. She opened it wearing only a white terrycloth robe, and he smelled her shampoo again.

"Hey, eager beaver, I just got out of the shower." Her smile killed him.

He attempted to match it.

"Don't just stand there looking glum; give me a kiss." Her mouth tasted like peppermint and her hair was still damp. He loved the way she stretched on her toes to meet him. The robe slipped open and her cool flesh was against him. "God, I've missed you," she whispered in his ear. Her hand found him and began to rub.

"Where's the kid?" he said.

"He'll be back. I figured you couldn't wait. I can't either."

"Claire, I got to talk to you."

"Later—I need something else right now. Words won't cut it." She grabbed the tail of his vest and pulled him into the room, kicking the door closed with her foot.

"We should talk first."

"It can't be that important." She kissed him again. "God, I love you." She reached down and unbuckled his belt, pulled open the buttons on his fly. His jeans soon bunched around his knees.

"Wait a sec."

"I can't."

His penis ached for her as she stroked it. Maybe it would be easier to talk after. "Let me get my boots off." He hobbled awkwardly to the sofa. She followed, the robe left on the floor, the whole polished glow of her skin around him as he unlaced. She slid the vest off his shoulders and lifted his T-shirt. "My train," she said. "I don't want anyone to know it's here but me." She licked across the tattoo, gently bit his nipple, and he twitched. "My sensitive tough guy."

But it didn't seem right. "Claire, I *really* got to tell you something."

She stretched him out on the sofa, her tongue moving up his thigh. Her mouth found the head, circling it with a wet tip. Then she squatted over him, gripped his penis with her hand, flicking him rapidly across her soaked vagina lips, then she slowly eased herself down, inch by inch, the tightness almost painful. "God you feel good," she said. "I've missed you so much."

She rode him, bucking against his pelvis, all of him deep inside her. When he felt her vagina squeeze and pulsate, he thought he'd never seen anything as beautiful as her open mouth, her glistening face and chest spreading with redness. They lay together on the sofa, the evening breeze just beginning to meander through the screened windows and across the drying sweat of their joined bodies. He didn't want to move. Movement meant change, confession, confusion. He wanted this quiet moment of happiness to last forever. Why? Why does it always have to be so difficult?

"You're still hard," she said. "Didn't you come?"

He moved. "Claire." His tone broke the bond, and she sat up. "I can't take you to the Broadway tonight."

"Just because you didn't come?"

"I mean it."

"You run out of money?" But she wasn't smiling.

"I got to go do something."

"Do something? Like what?" She sat up straighter.

For an instant he almost told her the truth. "I'm going fishing."

"*Fishing?* Tonight?"

"It's something I committed to a long time ago. Before I met you."

"Fishing?"

"Yeah. I know it sounds stupid, but that's what I got to go do. Doris even loaned me her dad's gear."

"You *have* to go fishing?" Her voice cut him again, and he wished he'd done the third P.

"Yeah. I gotta go."

"How long? Overnight?"

"I'll be gone about a week, maybe a bit longer." Maybe a lot longer, but he couldn't start thinking of that or he'd never make it.

"You can do a lot of fishing in a week," she said. He didn't answer. "Alone?"

"I got a partner."

"Is it a drug deal?"

"Claire, it's fishing—no drugs."

"You can't tell me?" she said. He shook his head. "Is it dangerous?"

"A little." He saw her face. "Not really. Don't worry, okay?"

A tear broke loose and she brushed it away quickly. She was shivering now, and he took his vest and placed it over her shoulders. "Do I get a vest too?" she said, and tried to smile.

"Just a week and I should be back."

"Should? *Should?* Jimmy, I can't lose you. I know you've made no promises about anything, but I can't lose you now. We're just starting something real. Can't you see what we could have together? If we gave it a chance. Even if we only tried it for another month. Can't you put it off for just a month?"

"It's gotta happen now."

She reached up and pulled back her hair. "Why don't I go with you?"

He studied her. "You'd do that for me?"

"Anything."

He glanced away. Any more of this and he was a goner. "Look, sorry, but I'm already late." He stood and gathered up his clothes, putting them on, lacing up his boots. It was killing him, but he did it anyway. "You want the vest?"

She shook her head and handed it to him. "I want you."

He picked up the white robe and tossed it onto the sofa next to her, but she ignored it. "One week," he said.

"Oh, fuck." The *fuck* was a sob.

"One week. Okay?" He leaned over and kissed her, held her naked shoulder. There was no response. "I can't promise anything, but you got my word, I'll do everything I can to get back as soon as possible."

"I knew, all along, I knew there was something. I guess this was it. Jimmy, if this is about money, don't do it. I don't give a shit about money. I've always done without, and I'd rather have you."

"It's not about money. It's about friendship."

"Friendship?"

He nodded.

"How about love?"

"Love too." He almost choked saying it. He had to get out of there.

"And you really can't tell me anything?" she said. He shook his head again. "Just tell me one thing. Are you going to be okay?"

He paused. "I'm gonna be okay. You say some kinda crazy prayer for me, right? Then I'll be just fine."

She was crying now, but she nodded, her black waterfall of hair in a slow sad dance.

He was getting in the Impala when Brandon came up behind the car. He did his best to pull himself together. Kid had terrible timing.

"Jimmy, how's it going?" The kid had the vest on over a black T-shirt, his posture different, straighter, his hair brushed back from his face. He actually looked kind of cool for the first time and it cheered Jimmy slightly to see it.

"Fine. How you runnin'?"

"Pretty sweet. School's out. I was just over at Willie's. I know I'm not supposed to talk about this kind of stuff, but everyone is treating me weird now. I think they know you'll kill 'em if they fuck with me. Sorry, I mean, *mess* with me."

"Brandon, I got nothing to do with it. You can take care of yourself, believe me."

"You really think so?"

"I know it."

The kid blushed and glanced into the back of the wagon. "You going somewhere?"

"Fishing."

"I thought you didn't like boats?"

"This is land fishing."

"Oh. Wow, look at that old pole. It looks like wood or something. You sure are fishing with some ancient stuff." He aligned the vest. "We going to the coast when you get back? Remember? The vacation and all that."

"Yeah. Listen, I gotta run. I'm late."

"Okay, sure. Good luck or whatever you say for fishing. Hope you catch lots of big fish."

"Right. Later."

"Later, Jimmy." He gave the low wave.

Just as Jimmy pressed the accelerator, his eye caught something on the seat. It must've fallen out of his pocket. He tapped the brake, stopped the car, glanced back. "Hey."

The kid ran up to him. "Give this to your mom." He handed Brandon the platinum pen.

Finally, he punched it and shot down Cartier Street.

Chapter Thirty-six

Luke plowed through the other disembarking passengers like a bulldozer. He was wearing an American flag do-rag, and only his sunburned nose and cheeks were visible in all the black greasy hair, gray beginning to take over the beard. His hand, the size of a spade, shot forward.

"Hack, ain't you a sight for sober eyes. Freakin' planes, man. Goddamn security delays. Like that's gonna catch terrorists. And this dumb-ass jabbering over the intercom trying to make everyone suspicious. What retards. You bring beer? Damned if I was gonna pay five bucks a can. Can you believe that? Five bucks for a can of Bud? Pissed me off so much I said fuck it."

Jimmy told him not to worry, he'd picked up a case. He'd grabbed it leaving Scoggton, wanting to make sure he could get Ballantine's. This was for Chevalier after all. "Bags?" he said, pointing at the carousels. Luke shook his head. They turned toward the exit. "No bags at all?"

"I need anything—we'll buy it." They crossed the entrance road—a few cars loading luggage and passengers with flashers blinking—and they entered the parking lot. "So this is Maine. Don't look like much, do it?"

"It's got some good things."

"If you say so." They approached the wagon. "Fuck me, if it ain't Chevalier's old sled." Luke slapped the hood. "Chevy really made a car then, didn't they? Steel, real honest American metal. Can't beat it. This'll get us down south in style."

"I considered a rental." Jimmy hopped in and reached across to lift the lock.

Luke settled onto the bench seat and rubbed the dash. "Paper trail. Forget it. It's good you got Maine tags. Old Bob Gray workin' out?"

Jimmy nodded. Luke was rarely so talkative. Maybe he'd been lonely? The thought surprised him.

"I'd be too cramped in a rental anyway. I fit better in this beast." Jimmy pointed behind him, and Luke popped open the cardboard case as the

Impala started moving. "Sixteens, good man." Luke handed him one, tilted his, grinned, though with the beard it was hard to tell. "Road trip, man. And some action—*finally*." He slapped Jimmy's shoulder with a giant paw.

Jimmy wound his way out of the lot, and they rolled through the outskirts of Bangor, a magenta band of light under the gray cloud cover to the west. Within minutes they were on Interstate 95 and up to speed. He held it about five or ten over the limit; that was the least conspicuous.

"Man, this old boat cruises. Real smooth, you know that?" Jimmy didn't respond. "One thing about Maine, the air smells good—fresh like." He breathed it in with a massive snort, filling his lungs, looking around. "Lots of pine trees and shit up here, I guess."

After a few more minutes, he said, "Hack, you okay?"

Jimmy glanced over at Luke, framed in the sunset. "I'm fine," he said though he felt like hell. He couldn't get Claire's face out of his mind.

"You're pretty cute with this hair, I'll say that. Now you won't have to kick the shit out of skinheads for calling you a skinhead." Luke chuckled in his strange subwoofer way. "You get the P?"

"Yeah, thanks. Need any?"

He patted one of the many pockets in his olive-drab pants. "All set. Seems like you could use some."

Jimmy ignored it. "What's our timing?"

"Alden'll be in Florida tomorrow. There for three days. No idea why he's going, but let's pray it ain't a crowd. I cased the boat approach and rental. A cinch. Two guards at the most, probably one; his digs ain't as big as some of them down there. The key is to get to him before any alarms. If it's the early evening, they shouldn't be set. I still think you should shoot the fucker—*stomach*—just like they done Chevalier, but it's your play. I'm stoked about this fifty large, man. You know I woulda done it cheaper."

"You deserve it."

"Been eyein' this chopper. Guy did it up right—old school, no gimmicks. Big bucks though. Juss the way it is now with every yuppie asshole wantin' a hog."

"How's the black Panhead?"

"She's my baby, runs like hot oil. 'Nother?"

Jimmy handed his empty and nodded. Luke reached back. "What's with the fishing pole?"

"I figured it'd be good cover in the boat."

Luke nodded. "No shit. Good thinkin'. Wha'd you do, buy that in an antiques place?"

"We'll stop at this store down on the coast, pick up some more gear."
"Won't it be closed?" Luke checked his watch, the same one he'd always carried with the stainless steel band. "We got nine now."
"It's open twenty-four hours. We need flannel shirts too. Those plaid ones fishermen wear."
"Too funny." He chuckled a moment. "Hack, I think it's goin' be way warm down there for any fuckin' flannel shirts."
Jimmy worked his can. "I suppose you're right. I just wanted to see you in one."
"Humor. Good man. 'Bout fuckin' time. That *Scagg*-town must've bummed you out. What've you been doin' for six months, shovin' prunes up your ass?"
"If I told you, I don't think you'd believe it."
"Try me."
"Maybe later. It's a long trip."
"You're the boss, bub." He took a sip and frowned at the can. "You know what, Hack? This is some nasty-ass tasting beer."

"What type of fishing do you fellows intend to do?" The clerk smiled at them with perfect teeth, dapper in his green shirt and trousers. The store was as big as a warehouse, even had its own trout pond with bubbling waterfall.
     "Regular kind," said Jimmy. "From a boat."
     "Damn," said Luke, looking around. "You guys got a lot of fishing shit. I had no idea it was so complicated."
     "It's not really. There's fresh water and salt; ocean, lake, and stream; fly, lure, or bait."
     Luke nodded. "I've hearda that fly one. That's where these dudes wave a fancy pole around and act all snobby about it. Seen 'at in a movie. We're salt and bait men."
     "Good enough. We have something for everyone. Follow me, please."
     When the clerk told Luke the price of a graphite rod he was outraged. "You got to be shitting me. For that skinny little thing. You got anything cheaper?" Luke relented when the guy showed him a nylon one, considerably less expensive. Soon they had fishing gear. Jimmy picked up a long-billed cloth cap in neon orange. Luke lost it when he put it on, so he bought it.
     "Tape," Luke said to the clerk. "You got tape?"
     He told them it was in a different part of the store, and began explaining how to get there.
"Too complicated, bub. You show us."

They followed the clerk who continued to be unflappably polite. Luke bought a half dozen rolls of duct tape, the kind with the camo print. "If you don't mind my asking," said the clerk, "Why do you need so much tape?"

"Boat leaks. Never know, right?" Luke swatted him on the back and almost knocked him over. The clerk caught himself agilely on a counter. A flicker of concern from Luke. "Sorry, bub, this fishing stuff gets me all excited like."

Soon they were on the highway again, Luke searching for the ocean in the darkness. "Shit, you'd think you'd smell the salt or something." He was studying the map in the glove-box light. "It's right over there—somewheres." He tossed the map back in and flipped up the lid. "Fuck, Hack. I'm glad I didn't waste money on a toothbrush. Whaddaya, collect the damn things?"

They crossed the Piscataqua Bridge and left Maine, the lights of Portsmouth shimmering in the inlet. "There it is," said Luke. "The ocean. Finally. Hey, we need to pick up some surgical gloves. But we got plenty of time. You see our guns? Cool, huh?"

"I left them wrapped."

"Wait till you see 'em—somethin' from the past, somethin' from the past."

By midnight they were cutting across Massachusetts. They passed Worcester, the freshly paved lanes like a black river between the silver guardrails, and Luke began to snore. Jimmy paid the toll for the Mass Pike, stared out at darkness. He couldn't stop thinking about Claire. Without Luke to distract him it was worse. He tried to imagine her in bed, asleep or not, he couldn't tell. He wanted to phone her, but what was there to say? Or what could he say that would make her feel better? And then he might have to explain it to Luke if he overheard the conversation, and that was out of the question. And Luke, so damn cheerful and animated. He needed to pull himself around. After all, in less than a few days it would be over. One way or the other.

When Chevalier had been murdered, Jimmy was shattered. He realized that now. He'd been in much worse shape than he'd thought at the time. First there'd been disbelief: it didn't seem possible that he could lose someone else, and Chevalier—the man was simply too vital to die. He'd built up BioTel with such energy and fairness, hiring his crew of misfits with unerring vision. All except Duncan Henlic, but Jimmy'd taken care of that mistake. It was the only thing he'd been able to take care of to honor Chevalier. Then the rage had set in, and Jimmy'd become obsessed with revenge. All he thought about was strangling Wendell Alden. He wanted to feel that one life drain out through his fingers. No one had ever deserved to die more. But then what? That's what upset him now, as he piloted the Impala up and down the gradual hills of western Connecticut in the damp June darkness. What then? And what if he didn't make it? Things can always go bad. Things usually do. Would Claire ever find out what had happened? Would she hate him because he wanted to execute someone who deserved to die?

He stopped for gas, ridiculously over priced, Luke muttering in the blaze of the fluorescent canopy but not waking. He could sleep through anything. Did nothing bother him except the price of beer?

The interstate was almost empty, only the occasional pair of headlights flashing past in the opposing lanes. He reached back and snaked out a can of ale, but it was too warm. He sipped at it anyway.

Had he promised Claire anything? With each mile south, Scoggton seemed less and less real. What had he been doing in that town anyway? He'd gotten stupid, that's what. Befriending Doris, throwing his money around, threatening Cloutier, fucking Claire, and getting involved with that weird kid—all of it attracted attention and could've led to disaster. He had to put Claire and Scoggton out of his mind if was going to get this thing done right. And then the memory of that skinny kid charging the gun forced him to smile. And Claire, with all her crazy emotions, those eyes always searching him, and her hair, her smells, her nipples, her limp, the way she talked to him, and the way he felt when he was with her. So different than with anyone else. Could he simply give her up and forget her? He wiped his eyes, stuck his head out the window, the cool blast refreshing him. After he crossed the Tappen Zee Bridge into New York State, he found a rest stop, took a piss, woke Luke, and they exchanged places. Luke barely had the car rolling and Jimmy was asleep.

When he surfaced, the sun was just breaking horizon. "Where are we?" he said, flexing his legs and hoisting himself up in the seat.

"It lives." Luke had a lit joint sticking out of his beard, aviator shades on his turnip of a nose. "Beer's gone warm. And we need some tunes, man. This sucks without music." He took his hand off the wheel and inhaled the joint like a blast-furnace bellows. His other arm was draped out the window.

"Jesus, how fast're we going?"

"Yeah, suppose you're right." His voice was constricted, holding in the puff. He backed off on the gas and the wagon calmed. "This sled moves nice, Hack. I dig this ride. Eights, you know what I'm talking, right? Eights own it." He honked the horn and exhaled. "Hey, you hungry? Man, I'm famished."

"Warm beer isn't a good enough breakfast for ya?"

"Good man. Cheering up?"

"I'm fine."

"Yeah, yeah, Mr. Fine. I know you're the grim reaper, but last night you were sad sack. Hey, Sad Hack, dig that! Rhyme." Luke subwoofered, it turning into a cough. "You still haven't even told me how you broke the arm."

"Jesus, let me wake up a second, will ya?"

"Fightin' man got to be ready anytime. Hack, you know the drill." He pitched the last of the roach out the window. "I used to swallow those, but I guess I'm getting old. Almost fifty. Can you believe that shit?"

Luke wanted drive-through, but Jimmy insisted on a sit-down place that wasn't a chain. He wanted to brush his teeth for one thing, and chains depressed him with their orange plastic seats and generic food. They found a place a few miles off an exit outside of Dover, Delaware.

"This takes extra time, Hack, you know that?"

Jimmy pointed his finger through the curtained window. "But we can get a case across the street at that packie."

"Good man. That's why you're the boss."

"And we need a cooler, since it must be ninety degrees out, even this early. Is it always this hot down south?"

"Hot? Just wait."

They'd ordered breakfast steaks with sausage on the side, along with all the trimmings. "Can't believe they don't have those crabs." Luke had argued with the waitress about it, and he couldn't seem to get over it.

"It's a diner, why would they have soft-shelled crabs?"

"They're supposed to be famous around here. I wanted surf and turf."

"First you wanted fast food."

"At least they have beer." Luke pulled at his Bud. "And not that green stuff you brought. That's some nasty shit."

"It's Ballantine's. An ale. Chevalier had talked about it. His favorite." That stopped him for a moment, his expression turning serious. "Sorry, Hack. Don't mean to disrespect the man's beer." He took another sip, and his face was immediately back to normal. "We'll get those crabs for lunch. I've never had 'em, but they're supposed to be good with beer."

Jimmy was drinking coffee. Luke could drink a lot more beer than he could. Even the bottle in his hand appeared half size.

The steaks arrived. "Here we are." She set down the loaded plates. "What else can I get for you boys?" she said. They shook their heads. "You sure? All right then. Now you enjoy your breakfasts."

"They sound kinda dumb around here," said Luke around a forkful. "But at least they don't bug you about eatin' good. In Cal now they stare at you like you're a leper when you order two kinds a meat, like I can live on that sprout and whole-wheat shit. That's bird food, man! If meat weren't good for you, how'd the caveman survive, tell me that? And they had it a lot tougher'n us."

Jimmy paid the check—as far as he knew, Luke never ponied up for anything—and he took a toothbrush into the restroom. Luke wasn't big on hygiene either.

They'd decided to follow the coastline and stay clear of as many cities as possible. Luke wanted to see the Atlantic, and it also had the benefit of keeping their cop exposure to a minimum. Jimmy took the wheel since Luke couldn't seem to hold the wagon anywhere near the speed limit, usually letting it creep up to over eighty. By noon, they were crossing the Chesapeake Bay on an endless bridge, miles and miles of highway suspended over the gentle chop of ocean.

"Hack, check that shit. Looks like the road goes right into the water. Weird trick, huh? They call that a *mirage*, you know. You ready?" Jimmy shook his head, and Luke dredged another Bud from the cubes, the icy water dripping on the mat of black hair covering his chest. Luke wasn't big on shirts either, and with the amount of hair covering his torso, he didn't need one. "Someone should make a cooler you just plug into the cigarette lighter. 'Course we got the blaster plugged in there now so we'd need two sockets." He drummed the dash. "*Electric* Jimmy. Fucker could work that thing." He had Hendrix decibeled to distortion on the huge CD player they'd bought at Circuit City leaving Dover. He'd spent forever in the mall, picking up about every imaginable thing in the place, including a pair of two-hundred-dollar sunglasses, waiting for Jimmy to pay. Jimmy hated malls.

"Turn that down a little."

Luke glanced over, stopped drumming on the dashboard. "You had that zombie dungeon metal crap 'bout this loud."

"Yeah, but this is the fourth time you played that."

"Hack, it's James Marshall Hendrix. He wasn't a mortal, he was a god." But Luke thumbed the lever, the volume retreating infinitesimally. Suddenly, he grabbed Jimmy's shoulder. "That's a tunnel up ahead."

"Yup."

"I ain't so keen on tunnels. You better pull over."

"What do you mean?"

"Just that. I can't handle tunnels."

"Can't *handle* them?" His shoulder was starting to throb.

"No way I can go through that tunnel. It's a Nam thing."

"You serious?"

"Dead."

Jimmy eased their speed. "Can you let go of my shoulder?" He released it and feeling began to return to Jimmy's arm.

"Hack, we gotta go back. Turn around."

"It's hours and hours."

Luke nodded, clutched his beer, and continued to stare at the tunnel mouth. "Tell me this! Why the fuck would they drop the bridge down into a tunnel in the middle of the ocean? That's juss crazy. What's wrong with keeping the bridge above? Tell me that."

"This way the boats can get across."

"Fuck the boats!"

"It's only a short tunnel. Can't you close your eyes or something?"

"It's under water for fuck's sake! Goes right into the damn ocean." Luke's face, for Luke, was blanched, and he was breathing as if his breath were choking him. "Hack, I was buried alive over there. Seven hours before they found me."

Jimmy turned into the visitor's center parking lot as far away as possible from the stone building that housed the tunnel entrance. He shut off the music and arranged the brand-new beach towel—it had a Bud girl in bikini printed on it—over the cooler. Who knew when a cop might show up? He asked Luke for the map and studied it, calculating the distance. "Six hours." He began tidying up the car—beer bottles; CD wrappers and CDs; four different chopper magazines; snack bags for chips, beer nuts, Slim Jims, Gummi Worms, and Cheese Waffies; boombox packaging and plastic mall bags—and carried the litter to a trash bin. Luke sat there, his eyes still fixed on the darkness, not even drinking his beer. With the wagon reorganized and the oil checked, Jimmy slumped in behind the wheel again, the sun near noon, burning, but the breeze from all the open water cool. Motorists kept pulling in and parking, whole families disembarking near the visitor center.

"Let's head back," said Jimmy. "It means going through Baltimore, D.C., and Richmond though."

"Hack?"

"Yeah."

"I think I can do it, man. It's just about a minute, right? One fucking tunnel."

Jimmy stayed quiet. He wasn't going to say a word. Luke rolled a spliff the size of a small megaphone. The end when ignited looked like the taillight of a finned Cadillac. He worked it down, the breeze carrying the dense clouds out the window. Some of the tourists probably thought the wagon was on fire.

"Okay, Hack, I'm ready, man." He gripped the door handle, his eyes blinking madly, moisture glistened along the sides of his nose. Jimmy started the Impala and goosed the accelerator, the car leaping across the lot. He careened onto the highway right in front of a truck, air horn bleating angrily, and hammered toward the black orifice. He avoided glancing at Luke. "Oh, fuck," said Luke. "Mother of God." They blasted down into the tiled cocoon and Luke screamed, one prolonged roar of terror. Then they were headed up and into the sunlight again, and Jimmy eased his foot on the pedal. Luke lay back in the seat panting, sweat beaded in his heavy brows and chest hair, dripping from his nose, his do-rag wet. A nasty armpit funk assailed Jimmy's nostrils.

"I did it. Hack, I did it! But I tell you what brother—*never* again." He was beaming now, started to laugh, slapping his knee. "How 'bout it? Home free. The sun never felt so good." He inhaled the air as deeply as a prisoner released from solitary after ten years. He reached back into the cooler, twisted open two frosties, handed Jimmy one, and nearly drained his. "It's amazing what you can overcome if you set your mind to it, man, but that nearly killed me." He rotated for another beer, wiped his brow with cooler water, turned back forward. His face crumbled and he dropped the unopened bottle. "No fucking way!" Jimmy slammed the accelerator to the floor. Luke only muttered as they charged the second tunnel.

By early evening they were passing through Myrtle Beach. Or rather, they were stuck in dinner traffic, surrounded by air-conditioned vehicles, a few teenagers giving them the thumb-and-little-finger salute, which pissed off Luke at first, until Jimmy explained what it meant. "Oh. Thought it's like the evil eye or some shit." Luke had the boom box pulsing again. "Hey, Hackster, maybe there's a good ban' playing 'night?" Luke had been celebrating his tunnel survival double hard. Even for Luke, he'd put away the beers. They'd stopped for another case, and that was about gone.

"Every band you like has been dead for thirty years."

"The Stones, man." He drummed the dash again, a dent beginning to appear in the vinyl pad. "Howz about the Stones?"

"Never heard of 'em." Twice, Jimmy had told Luke to lay off pounding the dash.

"Dass cruel. I don't say nassy shit about that funeral crap you like."

"Look at this damn place. It's like the biggest gasoline alley on earth." Jimmy checked the rearview mirror. "Cop at six o'clock—keep your beer low."

"Hey!" Luke pointed. "Taco Bell, man. Pull over."

Jimmy kept driving. When they'd stopped for supper, Luke had eaten enough to give an elephant bloat. The waitress had never seen anyone eat so many crabs. Then he'd ordered two poor-boy sandwiches to go, which he'd eaten in the car, sauce dribbling onto his hairy belly.

"Juss a couble Taco Supremes, Hackster. Come on now, bro', don' be mean."

Jimmy had witnessed enough falling food. The vision of Luke attempting to negotiate a taco was too much.

They finally broke free from the traffic, the congestion and consumerism ending abruptly, replaced by tree-lined highway, grassy fields, Spartan farmhouses on cinderblocks. Luke's head rolled back near the doorpost, mouth opened, and the snoring started. Jimmy was relieved. He shut off Neil Young and removed the beer from Luke's hand—only true drinkers can fall asleep and not spill their beverage. Luke slept going through Charleston, the snoring thundering metronomically even when Jimmy slotted a Dirge CD. The sky reddened with a mottled cloud cover, the dusk hot and hazy.

At the fall of darkness, near a swampy stream crossing under the highway, there were hundreds of fireflies, an iridescent swarm of pallid yellow-green covering the moss-draped trees. Claire. How he wanted to show her. Her image was there again, riding him, gazing down as her body filled with pleasure and her skin bloomed and her eyes closed. He sniffed his fingers hoping to find a last trace of her.

With the orange glow of Savannah visible in the low clouds above the interstate, rain began to dot the hood and windshield, blowing in through the windows. He let it, wondering if it would wake Luke. Maybe it would wash him? He felt lonely around Luke, and that was odd to discover, though they'd never spent this much time together, this close. What Luke had done for him by going through the tunnels, that meant a lot, had really touched him, but Jesus the guy stunk. Of course in this heat he was ripening himself.

There was a moan and a sputter. "I's drownin'." Luke shook his head, droplets of rain spraying the interior.

Jimmy waited until he woke up. "Let's get a couple rooms, tomorrow's a big day."

"Where're we?"

"Florida. Outside Jacksonville."

"Might's well. Can't sleep with dat damn death rock goin' anyway."

Chapter Thirty-seven

Someone was pounding on his motel-room door. The digital clock read 7:12. A voice: "Hack. Let's go, man."

Jimmy untangled the sheet and pulled on his jeans. When he opened the door, there stood Luke, his mouth moving somewhere in the middle of the beard. "You sleep a lot, don't ya? I been up for an hour anyway. Hundreds of channels and nothin' on that damn TV but an exercise show. What's wrong with porn in the morning, tell me that? Besides, I need some breakfast."

"Did you shower?"

"Shower? What the fuck for?"

"'Cause I'm not payin' ya unless you shower."

"That bad?"

"What do you think?"

"All right, all right. Gimme ten."

They found a restaurant, Luke at first suggesting a Taco Bell, Jimmy ignoring him. Actually Luke ended up enjoying the southern breakfast—catfish with hot sauce, country ham, cheese grits, extra hush puppies, sweet iced tea.

"Okay, you were right. I just had this taco thing in my head for some damn reason."

"You wanted them last night."

"I did?"

"Until you passed out."

Luke gave him a frosty stare. "Hack, I don't pass out. Come on now, man"—he continued to glare—"don't piss me off. Maybe I took a short nap."

Luke drank about a dozen iced teas. The waitress finally brought him a pitcher. "No beer this morning?" Jimmy said.

"Hell no! Workday. Who do you think you hired, a beginner? I always party before a job, you know that. If I go down—I had a good day."

"Did you?"

"That second tunnel was rough."

"Thanks for that."

Luke tossed back another hush puppy. "You're almost like a teetotaler now, Hack, what happened? You used to be a distance man, now you barely get through the sprint."

"Preoccupied."

"Yeah, I hear ya. Thinking about strangling that fucker can use ya up. I still say gut shot, but either way, soon you can relax—it'll be done."

Jimmy finished his coffee; he'd drunk enough tea with Doris to last him. "You ever think of having kids?"

Luke set down his fork. "Where'd that come from?"

"Nowhere."

Luke frowned. "Come on, let's hit the road."

Jimmy paid and they walked out of the sub-zero AC into the blazing hot morning. It was like a wall of steam, their sunglasses fogging instantly. They turned the Impala's wing vents backwards to maximize the airflow, but it didn't help. The sky was viscous lead and everything looked soiled in the humidity. The interstate couldn't have been flatter or duller, the only variant being giant billboards.

"Scorcher, as my dad used to say. The jungle was hot too, lemme tell ya."

"Kyle's Qwik Bail Bonds," read Jimmy.

"Check the brothers out. Should I take down the number?" Luke batted him on the shoulder. "Just kidding. Check out Billabong. Look at that bitch. Now that's my kinda sign."

The heat increased, the haze thickened, Jimmy felt as if he could barely breathe. Bugs clogged the windshield like in a horror movie. He hated bugs.

"Ugly, isn't it?"

"Why's that?"

"Just look at all this shit."

"Better than nothin' but pine trees."

"At least it's not this fucking hot in Maine."

"You got that."

"Why do so many people wanna live down here?"

"It wasn't so bad a couple months ago." Luke glanced over. "Hack, you're all in black. You got jeans on for Chrissakes." Luke had bought a pair of tan shorts in an army surplus place across the street from where they breakfasted. "And those boots? Come on, man, whaddaya expect?" The same store had supplied sandals with soles from recycled tires. Of course, Luke had calves that looked implanted—no one could have calves naturally that large—and Jimmy's, no matter how many reps of leg raises he'd done, still reminded him of a new-born colt.

"We'd die without shades, man." Luke had picked up another

wraparound extra-dark pair at the surplus store, waiting at the counter until Jimmy had paid for everything. He calculated that Luke's extraneous expenses were over six hundred by now. Luke still hadn't opened his wallet.

"The ganja helps. *Keeps you cool, mon.* Too bad you're not a puffer."

"You ever get hangovers?"

"I heard of them once. What're they again?"

"Figures. You wouldn't."

"Actually, Hack, I do. Man just don't mention that shit. To tell you the truth, this morning was none too perfect. P and all that tea helped. Hey—rhyme."

"You ever get sick of the guy thing?"

"What guy thing?"

"You know, bein' a hard-ass all the time."

"What's a hard-ass?"

"I mean it. Always having to be tough."

"You serious?"

"Sometimes I get sick of it."

"But what else you gonna do, Yoga?"

Jimmy held the Impala in the right lane behind a line of semis, as late-models with closed windows streamed past in the other lane, their occupants probably freezing. "Can I ask you something?"

"You just did."

"This is important."

"You wanna get beer!"

"I'm trying to talk to you about something."

"Shoot. I'm all ears."

It took Jimmy a minute to phrase it, wondering why he was bothering. "How would you feel if you had a kid who was gay, like a son?"

"A fag?"

"A cool kid, but gay."

"Hack, fags wanna suck dicks for Chrissakes. I mean, what's up with that? And it don't stop there."

"But that's just the way they are, right? It's not their fault."

Luke shook his head, obviously dumbfounded. "Man, we got to get you some other clothes. Your brain is burning up. Let's get off this freakin' pike and see if it's cooler over by the ocean."

"At least there'd be something to look at besides this shit."

It wasn't cooler on Route 1, but Jimmy had to admit, the loose Hawaiian shirt and bare feet helped. The jeans he kept on. He'd never worn shorts and that was the end of it, even if he sweated to death, even if Luke couldn't understand why. Luke had chosen a shirt with choppers and palm trees, and insisted Jimmy buy the one with Chevys and palm trees. Both were monochrome-challenged. Vicky would have been pleased. If he ever saw her again, he'd hint that Luke was filthy rich but refused to show it. The filthy would be true. They could discuss hot topping. Luke had terrified most California women, and Jimmy had never seen him with a girlfriend, but Vicky . . . she could give him a full makeover, do his colors. This heat was making him nasty, and he had to quit being so edgy. He had to stop worrying about Claire and focus on the job at hand. He didn't used to be like this. He glanced at Luke.

"Let's get some beer."

"Hack, I thought you'd never say it. Good man."

"But I'm done drinking that damn Bud."

"Whatever you want, brother, whatever you want. As long as it's cold I'll drink it—even Chevalier's brand." Luke tapped the outside metal of the door and jerked his hand back. "We never thought of this rig not having AC, did we?"

"I had no idea it could get this hot in America."

They plunged south, through Titusville, Melbourne, and Vero Beach. If anything the air seemed to get hotter, the horizon growing dark with humidity. The beer helped, and they stopped for orange juice. Luke insisted. "Vitamin C, man. We gotta keep our strength up. Besides, it's Florida, *home of the orange.*"

"You'd make a good tourist."

"That's the idea. *Float like a tourist, sting like the reaper.*" Luke frowned. "No rhyme. Hack, you're gonna feel a lot better after you kill this fuck. Then we can get back to old times."

"You know what Chevalier told me once? Lemme see if I can get this right. 'People with power never have the humility to use it correctly.'"

"No shit." Luke nodded. "That Chevalier was about the smartest guy I ever met. Tough fucker too. Remember when he took that shot in the arm but took out those two thugs?"

"They still got him in the end."

"Hack, anybody can be got. You know that."

"Yeah, but the wrong people always seem to die."

Luke bottomed his beer. "This one buddy of mine in Nam, Stony Jones, he said to me once, 'Luke, you know what I'd like to do? When the brothers riot'—this was right around that time—'I'd pull up in a big bus, load everyone on board, have beer, whiskey, ribs, and drive them to where the super rich live, crash right through the gate or whatever and park in the middle. Say, "Brothers, these the motherfuckers you want," and juss open the doors.' He had a point. Know what I mean?"

"Kinda messy. You might get the wrong ones."

"Wrong ones? Hack, what the fuck. Better'n looting a bunch of poor shopkeepers. Sends a bigger message too."

"You think any of it ever makes a difference?"

"Got to do what you can, got to do what you can."

"You think we could've protected Chevalier?"

"You're still eatin' yourself alive with this shit, aren't you?" He turned in the bench seat. "Hack, Chevalier died but he lived clean, followed what he believed. He was like a Viking or some shit. We all die, right? But if we live good and serve our code, it's as it should be. Now it's your time. Kill Alden, be done with it. If you got to strangle him, do it. I still say one gut shot is a lot cleaner. I got some big bore pistols with soft tips. You're in and out, a few minutes tops."

"He's got to confess."

"Complicated."

"I got to know for sure."

"Hack, you think too much. It's fuckin' with you, man. I say—"

Suddenly a fire hose opened from above. The storm had been mounting, but the fury of it surprised them. Rain jumped two feet off the pavement, exploded against the windshield, the wipers fighting hopelessly. "'Bout time," said Luke, allowing the water to strike his face. "Don't that feel nice." Jimmy slowed the wagon. Some other cars pulled over to a halt, flashers blinking. "See, God has spoken. Guilty and he must die. No confession needed." Luke slapped Jimmy on the shoulder and began to woofer.

Chapter Thirty-eight

"Hack, why ya wavin' your hands around so much?"

"These Florida mosquitoes. Kinda insane."

"What—the bugs? Ignore 'em."

They'd rented a boat for a couple hours. Luke wanted one run by to see if anything had changed. No surprises. They'd loaded in their fishing gear, Jimmy insisting on his neon long-bill, and they set out an hour before twilight. The boat crawled up the torpid inlet as Luke studied the topographical map, Jimmy for the moment mesmerized by the symmetrical reflections along the shore. He wasn't used to being on the water.

Luke folded the map. "Okay, think I got it." He pushed the throttle forward and motored toward the waterway. As they rounded the tip of the land-fill peninsula, the chop began, and he punched the throttle, the canvas canopy flapping above them, the muggy wind on their faces. Jimmy gripped the seat and fixed his eyes on the horizon, bug bites a secondary concern.

"How long we gonna be in this kinda water?" he said.

"Whaddaya mean, *this* kind?"

He pointed. "With waves."

"You call them waves? Just wait."

And sure enough, as larger craft roared by, the rolling wake attacked their boat. It lurched madly, and Jimmy felt as if he were on a carnival ride. A demented one. He wasn't sure if it was because of his unruly stomach, but suddenly everything felt unreal: the heat, the shrieking bugs, the boat, the pulsating tropical twilight, even Luke. *Jesus*, had he really come all the way from Maine to this strange place to kill someone?

"You okay?" said Luke, after ten minutes of turbulence.

Jimmy nodded, didn't dare speak.

"You look a little tweaked behind that mustache." Luke chuckled. "That thing is too funny. You should see yourself. You look like a Mexican bandito vacationing in Hawaii. Hack who only wears black. Hey—rhyme." Jimmy also wore a long-sleeved shirt to cover his tattoos, jeans and boots, the whole getup itchy, sweat running from his armpits.

Luke rotated the wheel, the boat leaned precariously, and Jimmy almost stuck his head over the side. "Hack, you aren't seasick, are ya?" Jimmy shook his head, slowly. "You sure? You damn well look it. Kinda green like."

"You got tunnels—this is mine."

"Gotcha. For a second back there I worried it was the yips, but I know you better. Hang on, almost there, buddy."

Within minutes the water was calm again. The lights of a few estates jiggled gold lines into the inlet, the humid early dusk closing in with a drape of ultramarine and rose. Luke slowed the craft, and the dissonance of bugs intensified. Jimmy let the mosquitoes feed.

"Feelin' better?"

He nodded though if there was any improvement it wasn't readily detectable.

"Good man. Hack, I didn't know you had any weaknesses." He throttled back even farther, the engine a muted chug. "Lights are on, flag is out. Good sign. Must mean he's home. No flag two months ago."

"So that's it?"

"That's it."

Wendell Alden's house was a confused array of dormers, too many windows, balconies, columns, and angles, painted an ugly pink with white trim, some kind of tile on the variety of roofs, the whole water edge of the property fronted by about three hundred feet of sturdy dock, probably teak. The landscaping was unnaturally pristine—the lawn around the lighted pool like a fresh crew cut dyed a synthetic green, fronded plants spraying from enormous terracotta urns the only sign of life, even the American flag hung limp at the pole which was a fake schooner mast. Just seeing the place and thinking of how Chevalier had lived—the couple of rented rooms in San Francisco, the decrepit house on the Oregon coast—it made Jimmy want to get the thing done, now. Everything seemed clear again.

"No guards," he whispered, "and it looks like he's in. Should we hit?"

"We don't have the art."

"I don't need it."

"Patience, Hack. Tomorrow."

He was letting emotion confuse him. The memory of Chevalier did that. "Besides, there's a guard somewhere."

As if on cue, one appeared out of the pool house. He walked toward them and came out onto the dock, folded his arms across his chest, making the bulge of his gun obvious. "You're not allowed here."

"Sorry," said Luke, keeping his face down. He turned the boat, goosing the motor a little. When they were out of earshot, he said, "Fuckhead. Now I got something to look forward to tomorrow. And the tide'll be perfect. We're lucky."

They headed back out into the channel, Luke assuring Jimmy he was keeping the boat as level as possible. As they reached the inlet for the rental place, the swell eased and Jimmy said, "You think Alden'll be there tomorrow?"

"Got to be."

"And if he isn't?"

"We wait. He's gotta sleep at some point. It's just a chance we got to take. What're we gonna do? Call and say we got a flower delivery, is Mr. Asshole at home? Everybody knows that ruse by now. This is risky, but it's clean. Besides, with you wearing that mustache, we gotta have God on our side."

Chapter Thirty-nine

The next day just after sundown, they motored away from the boat rental place, up the same inlet, Luke at the wheel, Jimmy amidships. The gun was jammed into the waist of his jeans. It wasn't the modern automatic he'd first imagined under the bubble wrap, but an ancient .375 revolver out of a Dirty Harry movie. Luke had explained. "It's for Chevalier, man. He dug old stuff, so I got these. Besides, I ain't dropping an expensive weapon into no ocean. But don't worry, they've been cleaned, oiled, tested, and they blow a monster fuckin' hole." What Jimmy had thought were clips were bullets strung together with masking tape. Luke obviously liked tape.

That morning they'd switched motels from the night before, choosing The Pink Palm so they could walk to a second boat rental place, parking the Impala behind the building out of the way. They'd unwrapped and loaded the guns, Luke insisting they keep the top chamber empty for safety. Still, he didn't like the feel of the cold barrel jabbing into his back. Nothing felt right at the moment. He hadn't slept well, the moaning air conditioner barely working, the humidity keeping him awake. Lying there on the damp gritty polyester sheets, all he'd thought about was Claire. Would she still love him if he was a killer, no matter how noble the cause? Would she know? He hated the question, but couldn't resolve it. It seemed to be lodged just under his ribcage like a burning iron ball. The only response he had was that he'd given his oath and he knew his cause was just. Why wasn't that enough? A few months ago it had been all he'd lived for.

"That bug shit helping?" said Luke.

Jimmy didn't answer.

Luke steered the boat into the waterway and accelerated. "Bugs all gone now, brother."

Luke had suggested he take Dramamine, but he couldn't risk being drowsy. He hadn't puked yesterday during the recon and he doubted he would today. Luke had rented a slightly bigger boat, figuring it might help. Fifty thousand or no fifty thousand, Luke was a good friend although his constant good humor was irritating. Or maybe, with Luke there, he felt he had to go through with it.

"How you doin', Hack?"

"Fine."

"Good man. We get this done, we're on a flight outa here. All we gotta do is sell the car. The Cubans'll cream for that ride. By the time the cops trace it, if they ever do, it's a dead end, right? It'll be a freakin' lowrider." Luke reached over and batted him on the shoulder. "Lemme tell ya, no beer for twenty-four hours is killin' me, and we're goin' make up for lost time. We party on the plane—even at five a can—we party in Cal. I'm gonna twist up the biggest spliff ever rolled. A Titanic. We'll make a new man outa ya. Not that you've ever been exactly jolly." Luke was chuckling again. Jimmy knew he was trying to relax him.

They entered the mouth of Alden's inlet just at dusk. The two estates on the right leading in were as dark and vacant as the evening before. They passed the row of palms and could see Alden's house. Luke snuffed the boat lights. "Perfect. Enough light to see but not be seen. And looky there—flag's up, windows lit, tide just right." Luke glanced at him. "Ready?" Jimmy nodded. "Okay, take the wheel. And remember, only one shot if you decide to cap him." Jimmy knew: people hear a distant shot, they listen for a second. If there isn't one, they always explain away the first.

They motored by the dock twice, hoping to lure the guard, Luke holding a fishing rod in his hand like a skinny club, Jimmy at the helm. Finally, the same guy as the evening before appeared and sauntered down to the edge of the dock. "You're not permitted here," he said, in the same bored tone. Jimmy steered along the dock toward him. "Did you hear me? I thaid, NO BOATING," the voice loud over the garble of the motor. Jimmy continued, closing the distance, watching to see if he reached for his gun. "Hey—" Only a few yards separated them now. Luke dropped the rod and leapt onto the dock, the hull lurching, surprise bursting across the guy's face, his hand now grabbing for his weapon. Luke head-butted and bear-hugged him in one rapid motion, Luke's enormous weight flattening the guy, the dock reacting with a dull thud. Within seconds, Luke wound tape around the guy's head, covering the eyes. That was all Jimmy needed to see. He parked the boat at the far end under some mangroves, killed the engine, looped the bowline around a cleat. He removed his silly hat and shirt, leaving the mustache. After pulling on a pair of surgical gloves, he slid a roll of tape onto his forearm. Then he walked up the dock, joined Luke and the downed guard.

"He's coming to," Luke whispered. He'd secured tape around the wrists and ankles; a Glock lay on the boards a few feet away. The guy began to gasp for breath, his nose running blood, his shirt front a napkin of black in the duskiness. Jimmy glanced up at the main house, but everything

seemed quiet except the infernal insects. Luke leaned over, his beard by the guard's eardrum, most of the ear under duct tape. "You a hero or a workin' man?" Luke waited and tried again. "You wanna die, or you wanna make one large?" No response. Luke pulled his gun and stuck it in the man's mouth. Jimmy could think of nothing worse, being blindfolded and having that oily rusty steel barrel jammed in there. It gave results but bothered him. As if hearing his thoughts, Luke removed the gun and straightened, looking down at the guy. "Hero or workin' man? You and I got no issues. We're just men trying to do our jobs. All I want to know is: how many in the house, is the system on, where is Alden? You tell me, I pay you. You lie, I kill you. So what's it gonna be, bub?" Luke winked at Jimmy. He was enjoying himself.
The guard's voice was strained. "Don't kill me."
Luke turned to Jimmy. "Why do they always have to say that? Like it's gonna help." Then back to the guard. "Answer the three questions."
"Juth don't shoot me."
"What's your name?"
"Dennith."
"Dennis, I'm gonna wait two more seconds."
"There'th only the cook, Charlene. Thecurity comes on automatically at nine. Mr. Alden is in his thudy."
"Good man. Nice work. Where's the study?"
"Down the hallway."
"Right or left?"
"Left."
"Street side?"
Dennis nodded.
"He's telling the truth," Luke said to Jimmy. Luke must've already had some of this from the recon.
Luke reached down and taped over the mouth. Dennis sputtered insanely, the guy's body lurching. Luke ripped the tape off again. "What?" said Luke.
"Can't breathe. My noth eth all blood."
"Good point. But if you make a sound, any sound, I shoot you, dig?" Dennis nodded vigorously. "In no time you'll be a grand richer and we'll be gone. Oh, and Dennis, by the way, anybody can fish here if they want. Even rich fucks don't own the ocean, not yet anyway. Remember that."
Luke tossed the Glock into the inlet with a plop. "What a waste," he muttered, "but never trust another man's gun." He rolled Dennis off the dock onto the grass. Luke stripped off his colorful shirt, both in black clothes now. They walked up the edge of the property along a row of

palms and a hibiscus hedge, through the murky twilight, mosquitoes swarming them. They walked normally, slinking or running would only draw attention, Jimmy forcing himself not to swat at the bugs. "Nice pool," whispered Luke. "I wouldn't mind a pool like that. Get one of those inflatable rubber beds with a beer cooler built in. They must have those, right?"

Jimmy didn't answer.

"Okay, Hack, here we are. I'll take care of the maid, disable any cameras, destroy the tapes. Don't waste time, the security system fires soon." Luke clutched him on the shoulder. It said everything.

Jimmy eased open one of the many sets of French doors off the porch and entered a huge room. Everything was white, a few fans rotated high above in the vaulted ceiling, soft classical music emanating from everywhere, the space a shock of cool dry air. His sweat began to evaporate, the mosquitoes left outside. As he moved through the empty room and down the hall, he heard Luke faintly in the distance, "Charlene? Where are you? I'm hungry, sweetheart." Knowing Luke, he'd probably get her to make him something to eat.

The hallway was white as well, the floor some kind of pale marble. The first room was shelves of books, tufted leather easy chairs, everything dim with the twilight. Jimmy continued down the hall, sensing it was the next room. His heart pounded, the dead weight of what he was about to do intensifying under his ribcage. He slowed, drew the .357, and slid around the edge of the doorway.

Wendell Alden sat at a desk, studying some papers under a green glass lamp, a softly lit garden with a dark pond through large windows in front of him. He didn't turn but Jimmy made out the face in the glass, recognizing him from the internet photos, something unreal about the man as if he might be a body double. And the setting was so appallingly tranquil—the immaculate view, the generic strings and piano, the ornate antique furniture. Jimmy stuck the gun back in the waistband of his pants as he approached the lavender dress shirt, their reflections appearing together in the window. Alden was smaller than Jimmy had imagined, a bland face behind gold wire-rimmed glasses. This was the man? This had murdered Chevalier?

"Dennis, I believe I told you not to disturb me." The head began to lift. Jimmy stripped a section of duct tape—Alden's head jerking around at the sound—and he quickly wrapped the eyes, glasses and all. Alden attempted to jump up from the chair, his arms flailing behind him. Jimmy chopped him in the side of the neck. By the time he came to, Jimmy had him taped across the chest to the chair back, each wrist locked to an oak arm. Finally he could remove his stupid mustache; he stuffed it in his pocket.

Alden's head and body fought the restraints for a moment, then settled. "Who are you? Where's my guard?"

The face below the silver tape sickened him—the delicate straight nose, the strong cleft chin, the thin lips. The intensity of the moment made him feel weak. He hadn't expected this.

"Who are you? Tell me what you want."

Jimmy waited, wanting him to suffer, tempted to shoot and run.

"Is this a robbery? I keep very limited capital in the house. There is nothing here for you. I've already deployed the alarm system. The police will be here momentarily."

"You have one minute to confess your crime."

"What is this?"—the voice losing only a modicum of confidence.

"You have a large-bore revolver pointed at your stomach. When I fire, you will suffer for hours before you die."

"Who the hell are you?"

"Do you confess?"

"Confess to *what*? Are you insane?"

Jimmy reached into each vest pocket, looked carefully and pressed down the buttons, having just enough feel with the thin rubber gloves on.

"You're Wendell Alden. Is that correct?"

"You obviously know who I am."

"Nine months ago, you contracted the murder of . . . " Jimmy didn't trust himself to say the name. The anger flamed for an instant until he thought he'd choke. He attempted to control his voice. "The head of BioTel. Do you confess?"

He watched the body react at the word BioTel. Immediately, he knew it was true. It was almost impossible to control responses when you were blinded.

"Just tell me who you are. I'm sure we can work this out." His tone had changed.

"If you lie again, I'll fire." Jimmy removed the .375 and thumbed back the hammer. Alden jolted at the metallic click.

"Please. This is crazy. I have a family." Sweat was showing even in the air-conditioning. "What do you want—money? Tell me how much. I'm sure we can find a way out of this."

"You have thirty seconds. Remember, just one lie."

"Don't shoot, *please*, God, don't—"

"Confess."

"I'll give you a hundred thousand."

"This has nothing to do with money."

"Five hundred thousand."

"If you mention money again, I'll fire."

"My God, what do you want then?"

"I told you. You have twenty seconds."

Alden strained against the chair as if he were having a seizure.

"Fifteen."

"We tried to reason with him. Believe me, he refused to be reasonable."

He spoke frantically, the sweat at his arm pits a darker lavender.

"And you killed him."

"You must realize what was at stake. A whole way of life was at risk. Sometimes things have to be taken care of that are distasteful. There's no choice. Any intelligent person realizes that and assumes the responsibility. That's just how the world works. You make a decision— are you going to let just anyone take away everything you love and believe in?"

"Ten seconds."

"God, stop counting. If you don't want money, you must want something. Everyone wants something. Name it."

"Confess."

"To what?"

Jimmy almost fired, his hand trembling.

"*Please*! He had to be sacrificed. There was simply no alternative."

"His name?" Jimmy stretched out his arm, pressing the barrel into the soft stomach, the hard curve of the trigger against the glove; Alden screamed.

"One second."

"Oh God."

"Name."

"Chevalier. His name was Jay Chevalier."

Alden collapsed, the head hanging. Jimmy supposed it must be pretty awful—blinded, taped, imagining a bullet blowing your stomach through your spine at any instant. He lowered the gun, stared at the limp body. The shitty classical music droned on oblivious.

Alden revived, his head twisting spastically as if he was trying to hear better. "What're you doing? I confessed! I did what you said. Don't shoot me, *please*. Don't kill me . . . I have a family, a daughter and a son, a loving wife." He was on the verge of sobbing.

"You know what? I got a family too, and you're not worth them."

Jimmy released the hammer and stuck the gun back into his pants. Then he reached into his vest and checked the two digital recorders. They were still running. He shut them off. Almost to himself, he said: "You sicken me. You and your kind and your skunkshit lies. All the damage you do to everyone else. You're so lucky I didn't kill you. If you'd been here a few months ago, you'd be dead." He couldn't say a word about Chevalier; he might have changed his mind.

Alden was hyperventilating. Jesus—he'd probably have a heart attack. Or a brain explosion like that Henlic asshole.

"Calm down, will ya. It's over." Jimmy glanced out at the last twilight. "I just recorded your confession. If you make any attempt to track me, or one of my people, not only will copies of this tape go to all the media, but one of my people will kill everyone in your family. You understand?" He looked over, sickened by what he saw and smelled. Pathetic. All he'd wanted for half a year was to kill this man, and now all he wanted was to get away from him. "Do you fucking understand?" he said too loudly.

The voice was desperate. "You're not going to kill me?"

Jimmy didn't bother to answer. He went to find Luke.

Chapter Forty

"That cook was mean, man. She kicked me right on the shin. Alden shoulda had her as the guard. Probably woulda thrown us both in the pool. I said to her, 'Sister, what the hell? What you doin' attacking one of your own?' She said, 'What the hell *you* doin' comin' in my kitchen with a gun, Rambo?' Took me a while to *contain* her ass. Frisky, and she had to be my age. Too bad we gots-ta go tonight. I liked her. Gave her five bills."

They walked together toward the inlet, a few lights from other estates winking through the palm fronds, insects shrieking, the heat surrounding them like a wet curse.

"So you didn't shoot him after all. Strangled the fucker. You're one tough-ass, Hack. Not sure I could slowly choke somebody to death anymore. Takes way too long, the body jerkin' around the whole time. Kinda sickening."

Dennis was still taped up beside the dock, looking miserable lying in the grass, covered in deliriously feeding mosquitoes. As Jimmy went to retrieve the boat, he could hear Luke.

"Dennith, my man, how's it goin' out here?"

"Okay, I gueth. Bugth an' anth are killin' me."

"You didn't tell me Charlene was a hellcat."

"Theeth a bitch."

"Now, now, Dennis."—The engine gurgling, the bowline loose, the boat moving, Jimmy heard a yelp—"Easy, bud, I'm only stickin' five bills in your pocket. You don't wan 'em, say so."

"You're really going to pay me?"

"Didn't I say so? I always do what I say, remember that." A ripping sound. "I gotta tape ya now. I'm puttin' a slit so you can breathe." Dennis began complaining as Luke ducted over his mouth. "You gonna be okay? . . . Fuck, your nose is workin' fine." Luke stood back up. "Now Dennis, here's the rub—you identify us in any way, you gotta give me a refund and then I kill ya. Got it?" Luke gathered up his shirt, strode across the dock and hopped onboard. "Tho long, Dennith." Jimmy moved over and Luke took the helm, wicked open the throttle.

"How come you only gave Dennis five?" said Jimmy.

"'Cause I gave Charlene five."

"But I reimburse you."

"So? Besides, that Dennis was a whiner. You'd think Alden would hire somebody a little tougher. That guy was an embarrassment. You think it was his bloody nose?"

"What?"

"The funny way he talked."

"I think he just has a lisp."

Luke glanced at Jimmy and saw he meant it. "Fuck. I guess I shoulda given him the full K then." Suddenly he stiffened, backhanded Jimmy's arm. "What's that?" He pointed his beard up the inlet to the mouth of the waterway.

"A boat turning."

"Let's get our shirts on. Damn—the lights." He reached down and snapped on the running lights.   Jimmy grabbed a fishing rod. "Stay on course. No . . . no guns yet."

"Man, just when you think it's over," Luke whispered.

The other boat continued to bear down on them fast. Then Jimmy heard the motor slow. He couldn't get a read on the three figures on board. "Evenin'," someone called.

"Hey," said Jimmy. "How's the fishing?"

"Is that what you're doin' down here—fishin'?"

"Sure."

"You boys catchin' anything?"

"Just a bunch of freakin' rednecks," muttered Luke under his breath, but he throttled back. Then to the voice: "No. You?"

"We're gettin' a few sheepsheads. Caught 'em on Silver Minnows." Their boats were closing now. "They don't usually let you fish down here."

"We learned that."

"What kind a lures you usin'?"

"We're bait men."

"Shrimp?"

"Yeah, but we sure as shit need some cold beer to go with 'em." That brought a chuckle.

"You might wanna try a line in that rod. Helps when you're fishin'." This brought another.

"So that's it. Knew it had-ta be somethin'." Luke pushed the lever, the boat responding. "Later."

"Take 'er easy." The sound of laughter following them.

"Whaddaya think?" said Luke, looking over his shoulder as the other boat turned around.

"We're okay."

"Nosy, weren't they?"

"They had a point on the line. And we forgot the damn lights."

"Everybody's looking for terrorists these days. Everybody wants to be a hero. If they only knew. I shoulda taken out the cannon and started blasting the water. 'See fellars, we don't need no fishin' line.' See what kinda heroes they are then."

"We better get you some beer."

"Hack, you got no idea." Luke gunned it toward the waterway. "I suppose we gotta dump the art. Seems a shame, but whatcha gonna do?"

At least the waterway was free of wake; no other boats now that it was night. "I just need to get off this damn thing."

"Right. Gotcha." Luke glanced back. "If those assholes report anything, we'll be long gone. I doubt anyone'll find Dennis till morning. And Charlene ain't goin' nowhere. Man, I tell ya, nothin' but that five hundred calmed her ass down."

He couldn't concentrate on what Luke was saying. When his stomach was on the brink, they docked and tied up. The rental place was closed as expected; he'd prepaid, slipping the guy an extra hundred for overnight. He gathered their gear as Luke quickly rinsed the outboard with fresh water and ragged off any prints, gloves or no gloves. Then they started walking along the highway, traffic whooshing by in air-conditioned numbness. Soon, out of the hazy heat, a pink neon palm tree pulsed. "Beer!" said Luke, the fishing pole over his shoulder, towing a cloud of bugs, looking like an oversized hairy Huck Finn. "'Bout fucking time."

"I'll meet ya in your room in fifteen."

Luke searched him. "You all right?"

"I'll be over and we'll crack one. I got something to tell you."

"Okay, bud. Remember, all clothes in the garbage bag—anything you had on in there, even your boots. This new DNA crap is a nightmare as you know. Can't be too careful. We'll hit a dumpster headin' to the airport."

Jimmy gripped him on the bicep. It was like grasping a ten-pound bag of flour. "Thanks, Luke. You're the best."

"Now don't be gettin' all emotional on me. We'll kiss after I shower. I know how you are about sweaty stinks."

Jimmy entered his room and closed the thin door, the air only moderately cooler, but mosquitoless. What a dump the room was. The rug was like a map of too many nights gone sour, the furniture revealed plywood at

the edges under a chipped brown plastic veneer, the ocherish walls moldy with one clinically depressed clown falling out of his frame. Quite the contrast to the way Alden lived. But not anymore. Alden's unblemished sanctified days were over. He opened his suitcase, picked up his cell phone, and sat on the bed. He punched in the number.
"Claire?"
"My God—Jimmy!"
"Did I wake you?"
"I haven't been sleeping much. Where are you?"
"Claire, it's so damn good to hear your voice."
"You're safe? You're okay?"
"Yeah, I am. Real good. Never better." He paused, feeling her breathe, imagining her in the bedroom in Scoggton, sitting up straight. It felt too far away. "Listen, I got something to tell you."
"I'm here." Her voice was wary and uncertain.
"My real name is Jimmy Hakken." He waited—only silence. "I won't ever lie to you again. Okay?"
"You won't?"
He could hear her gentle crying.

Chapter Forty-one

Hakken rapped their code on the door to Luke's motel room, but when it opened, a stranger stood there. Jimmy almost yelped but held himself back somehow. It wasn't easy. The man was as big as Luke, but he had an enormous bald head. The burnt turnip of a nose and cheeks clashed with the pasty skin below—an ashen gray color tinted with blue, rarely seen on a live human. The ears were like wings. A raised pink scar straddled the jaw line, the lips like partially chewed fruit. Jimmy wouldn't worry about his chin ever again. This one was similar to a frog's.

"Pretty bad, huh?"

Jimmy got hold of himself. Luke had done this for him, after all. He forced his expression neutral. "When the tan evens out, it'll be fine. We could get you some of that tanning-cream stuff at a drugstore, if you want."

"Forgot about the tan thing. I haven't shaved since Nam. Kinda weird seein' my face again."

Jimmy almost said: "You're telling me," but instead: "I need a beer." He entered the room and was assailed by pot smoke. He didn't blame Luke a bit. Jesus—what a face. The man could sub as a gargoyle, no problem. Even the principal one right over the holy trinity. The Catholic church would be safe from demons and the devil forever.

Luke pointed at the cooler. "If anything could taste better, you tell me."

Jimmy snapped one, lifted it to Luke. They drank.

"I guess you won't be kissin' me any time soon, will ya?"

He looked at Luke again—bumpy thick red lips sticking out of the gray pallor, the deep-fried nose, those enormous damn ears—and he completely lost it. He couldn't help it. He tried to cover his grinning mouth with his beer, but it was hopeless. His whole body was shaking with laughter.

Luke glared. "Hack, don't piss me off now."

"Sorry."

"You got seconds to cut the shit."

"I'm—sorry." He bit his lip, his body still shuddering. "It's been a long—few days."

"At least that fuckhead is dead. We got the thing done. Chevalier can rest in peace, God love him." Luke exhumed another beer out of the ice.

Jimmy stopped laughing. "I got to tell you something."

"So you said."

"I didn't kill him."

"What?" Luke turned like he'd been shot, his beer hand lowering like a semaphore.

"I couldn't get it done."

"Fuck me! All that?" Luke walked crookedly over to the bed and sat down, the springs groaning. "Hack." He banged his forehead with a fist. "You don't get second chances with shit like this."

"I got a lot to tell you."

"What the hell. I can't fucking believe this. You?" He shook his head slowly. "We gotta get out of here now. This changes everything." Luke stood. "Can he ID you?"

"He won't want to."

"What're you talkin' about?"

"Listen." Jimmy pulled one of the tape recorders out of his pocket, pressed play, set it on the end table next to the bed.

You're Wendell Alden. Is that correct? . . . You obviously know who I am. . . . Nine months ago, you contracted the murder of . . . the head of BioTel. Do you confess? . . . Just tell me who you are. I'm sure we can work this out. . . . If you lie again, I'll fire. There was a metal click. *Please. This is crazy. I have a family.* The tape continued. Then: *One second. . . . Oh God. . . . Name. . . Chevalier. His name was Jay Chevalier.* A pause. *What're you doing? I confessed! I did what you said. Don't shoot me, please. Don't kill me. I have a family, a daughter and a son, a loving wife. . . . You know what? I got a family too, and you're not worth them.* Jimmy reached over and shut it off.

Luke stared at him. "Hack. You're a goddamn genius. We can extort millions out of the fuckhead. *Millions!* We can ruin 'im. That tape is worth a fortune." He stood in his excitement. "Think of it! Alden can't go to the cops, or the FBI. He can only turn to whoever set up the hit and they'll know he's a risk now. He'll even have to silence Dennis and Charlene. And best—no one is after us. That's a huge fuckin' relief. And here I'd thought you'd lost it." He was grinning, at least Jimmy supposed it might be a grin. Suddenly Luke's face darkened—a nasty storm. "I didn't need ta shave! You fucker." Luke lunged. Jimmy was stunned at how fast he moved. He didn't even have a microsecond to react. The beer shot from his hand, banging against the wall. Luke had him hammer locked and he was completely paralyzed. Then Luke started tickling him. "Laugh now, you fucker." Then Luke stopped abruptly and backed away. "Wait a minute. Wait just a freakin' minute. *Family?* You said you had a family. You serious?"

"Yeah."

Luke slumped onto the bed again.

"I met a woman in Scoggton. She has a son."

There was a long wait, only the fickle grumbling of the air conditioner intruded. Luke went to the cooler. Pulled one, faced Jimmy. "The one in the e-mail?"

He nodded.

"I was worried about that, but then you said nothin' so I . . ." Luke's face was horrible. "You're not coming back to Cal with me, are you?"

Jimmy shook his head.

"So now I'm so freakin' ugly a whore won't touch me *and* I lose my best drinkin' buddy?"

He still couldn't say anything.

"Shit, man. I thought it was gonna be old times again. I figured, we get this behind us, and . . ."

"We'll see each other. You'll come visit."

"Maine? Fuckin' Maine. You're gonna stay up there with all those stupid pine trees and shit?"

"We'll see."

"Scagg-town? Hack! It snows and shit. Ice! Remember ice? All over the goddamn ground. You told me yourself."

"You'll visit."

"What girlfriend of yours is gonna put up with me?"

"Claire would. Brandon will think you're the best."

"The kid?"

Jimmy nodded.

"How old?"

"Almost fifteen."

"Good kid?"

"Great pool player, and he's as tough as you."

"No shit. And her?"

"She's simply the best. A heart the size of California. Most beautiful eyes I've ever seen. They're like . . . poetry or something."

Luke sipped his beer as if it were poison. "You're a lucky man then." He searched Jimmy. "Is she why you didn't strangle Alden?"

"Probably."

"I knew you'd changed."

Jimmy picked up the tape recorder and handed it to Luke. "A

250

gift."

"Hack, this is worth millions."

"I got one too."

"No shit?" Luke was smiling again.

"Wanted to make sure I got the confession so I used two. Never trust just one machine."

"We both go after him?"

"I'm not gonna."

"*What?* Are you crazy? We're talkin' millions here. *Millions!*" He whispered it reverently.

"I'll give you one month. You get whatever you can. Ream the bastard. Drain him. Then I'm sending copies to every newspaper in the country."

"Can they prosecute from a tape?"

"Who knows. It's probably coercion."

"What's it matter. It'll totally ruin 'im anyway. His wife and kids'll hate him. Everyone'll hate the bastard. People loved Chevalier and since his death he's become like a god. They'll probably stone fucking Alden. Wouldn't that be great?" He took a drink. "One month?"

Jimmy nodded.

"You're driving back up there, aren't you?"

"I got to see her."

"All that way again. All those miles."

"At least you won't have to go through the tunnels."

"Hack." He looked down, the shaved head gleaming in the lamplight. "I'd do anything for you. Even those tunnels again. But you know that, don't ya?"

They sat together, not speaking, sipping their beers. Then Jimmy:

"I'll drop you at the Miami airport. There's a five-twenty to Oakland. I've got your fifty large in my suitcase, plus whatever you got in expenses."

"Can we drink a few beers before you go? For old times sake."

"You better believe it." They started laughing. "But let's get out of this dump. Let's go somewhere ice cold."

"I hear you, brother," said Luke, standing up. "Man, do I hear you."

Chapter Forty-two

Hakken was whistling. And why not? No bugs, every mile was
fractionally cooler, at least in his imagination; he was out of Florida,
Georgia, South and North Carolina—Luke would be back in Santa Cruz
by now, probably already working on the Alden sting—and Claire was
waiting for him. He loved the feeling of moving toward her, for her.
What man doesn't like driving toward the woman he loves? Even the
wagon was running better now that they had left the extreme heat behind.

He motored onto the Chesapeake Bay Bridge-Tunnel, the
incredible openness and the evening breeze off the water a perfect fit
with his emotions. After the second tunnel, he pulled off and parked. He
opened both front doors and rested his head on the back of the seat.
Across the road was the lot where Luke had reached inside himself and
found his decision to continue. What a heart the man possessed. It was
something to have a friend like him. Jimmy celled.

"You back?"

"Hack, where are ya?"

"At the tunnel."

"No shit. I had this funny feelin' that's juss where ya were."

"Everything go smooth?"

"I told the stewardess I'd been shooting a movie, about cavemen
and dinosaurs—a new Spielfinger thing with Brat Pimple. She says, 'I
didn't even *know* they made movies in Miami. Do you all know Brad
Pitt? Is he in it? I'd juss *love* to see him as a caveman in one a them
loincloths.' I told her the fake beard was itchy in the heat. She
sympathized. Got a few free five-dollar beers out of her."

"You know, you're a funny man."

"You think so?"

"Maybe you should do standup?"

"Easy, Hack. Till the beard grows back I'm *very* vulnerable."

"This is a nice spot. The sun is just setting. Big red wobbly ball.
Really something."

"You gonna ask me to marry ya?"

Jimmy gazed out across the water, the dying light of another day
in his eyes. Sometimes Luke could be almost clairvoyant.

"*What?*" said Luke. "I say the wrong thing?"

"I got something serious."

"Hack, hold a minute." He paused. "I know it wasn't the best trip for ya. I sensed that even if you think I didn't. But, buddy—I loved it. Just hangin' together again, and the way you set up Alden was really something. I know it sounds lame, but I knew the risk we were taking by killin' 'im. I was fully behind ya, you know that, but I knew the cops was gonna look for us a *long*-ass fuckin' time. They woulda had the FBI on us, and those fucks never quit. Life wasn't ever gonna be the easy way again, I knew that. This is one big ass relief, and I can't wait to milk that fuckhead. Can't wait. I'm gonna be a rich man."

"You know the weird thing?"

"What?"

"Chevalier would have wanted it this way."

"You know, ain't that strange, I was thinking the same damn thing myself. Hack, that what ya wanted ta tell me?"

"I got something to ask you."

"You don't want the tape back? Bud, I figure a deal is a deal."

"Nothing like that."

"Thank fucking God." He sighed. "Then shoot, brother."

"If Claire says yes, will you be my best man?"

Luke didn't say anything right away. When he did, his voice was odd. "You gotta be kiddin' me. Me your best man? Stand up there beside you? Hack, I'd be honored. Man, would I be honored."

"We're on then?"

"Fuck." A pause. "I gotta go." His voice was even odder.

"You all right?"

"Juss gotta go."

"Later then."

"Later."

Jimmy had never thought of Luke as someone who could get choked up. Jesus, who knew about anybody when you got down to it. Maybe when Luke's beard returned, and with a few of Alden's millions, Vicky would go for him. She'd never find a more loyal guy, if Luke liked and believed in her, and he was sure tall. He reached into the cooler and hauled up an ale. The ice was gone but the water was cold.

As he sat on the bench seat in the nearly empty parking area, he poured it out onto the hot tar, the sky now webbed by glowing fingers against cool tones of dusk. It was the first time he'd been able to think of Chevalier's death and not become enraged. Instead, there was a strange peace, a calm he'd never known before. Jesus, maybe things would be okay after all? And then he thought of his mother. Her kind face with that worried hopeful smile. She'd always tried to be so damn positive, but never had anything but bad luck. Maybe she would even forgive him? He dredged another ale and called Claire.

"Where are you?" she said.

"Chesapeake Bay."

"God, I miss you."

"I'll be there for breakfast. A late breakfast. Or we can go out if you want."

"It'll be the best breakfast I've ever done. Waffles, French toast, bacon, sausage, fresh-squeezed orange juice, coffee, whatever you want. You just tell me."

"Jesus, I'm getting hungry right now."

"Guess what's for dessert?"

"H-m." He imagined her above him and felt it below. He almost got out his penis but decided to wait. "I'll be driving ninety."

"Don't get a ticket."

"Might be worth it."

"Get going then."

"I'm on my way. Then we're going to the coast. The three of us. Okay?"

"You still want to do that?"

"Damn straight. We planned it, didn't we? I promised the kid, and I got all this fishing shit—never used with actual fishing line. Maybe Brandon can figure it out and catch something."

"Jimmy, I can't believe this is all working out."

"Believe it. Sometimes even people like us get lucky."

And so Jimmy Hakken plunged into the closing darkness, up the Maryland peninsula, the lights of towns and the approaching headlights becoming fewer until the glow from Philadelphia showed on the horizon. He passed New York City way off to his right as if it weren't there, crossed the Tappan Zee bridge again, and finally collapsed in the early morning, pulling over and sleeping a couple hours on the bench seat, waking with a dream of Claire still pulsing inside him. It was only vaguely night when he rumbled the wagon back onto pavement, the cool air of New England laced with wet grass and pine rushing through the open windows like a balm. Here we are, he thought as he blasted across Connecticut toward the dawn, one tattooed arm draped over the wheel, ignoring the speed limit same as Luke, here we are always fleeing something or charging toward something—a place, a person, an idea, the past or the future, it doesn't matter which—there's always something burning in our fucking hearts.

Epilogue

Jimmy watched her eyes move out to the sea. The sky was July-afternoon clear, that shade of blue that all others are compared to, and the sea breeze was just coming up over the cliff. They sat at a warped picnic table between the cabin and ocean, the bit of yard mostly weeds, a hedge of wild roses along a decrepit fence barely preventing anyone from falling off the edge, Brandon somewhere down below on the rocky beach, fishing. He'd had no trouble stringing the line and tying on hooks. "You sure you still okay about the small wedding?" he said.

"We don't have enough friends for a big one."

"Yeah—no shit."

"I'm glad you invited Henry though. He said he gets to wear his tux before they bury him in it. And my dad. Nice of you to ask him for my hand. It meant a lot to him. And if he doesn't deserve *something* after all he's been through . . ." She brushed away a bug and started laughing. "I still can't believe Doris was spending your money. What did she say again?"

"'Robert, what in God's name are you doing here? You're supposed to be dead.'"

"You got her accent. She must have ransacked your room an hour after you left, had the carpenters and painters there the next day. Can you imagine her face when she found the money? How much did she spend?"

"About thirty."

"My God, that much? She must have had a great time shopping after being poor for so long. She'll probably have a nicer dress than mine for the wedding."

"That damn cousin even bought a new cab—that was over half of it. Doris said she was 'sick and tired of riding around in that smelly old thing.' I told Fred he had to take it back to the dealer and I wanted every penny. Fuck him."

"And Doris?"

"Ah, what the hell. How's she gonna get twelve grand? Tell you the truth, she was reluctant as hell giving me back the rest of it. 'You left it to me, Robert.' 'That was if I *died,* Doris,' I told her. She looked at me like that was a damn good idea."

"You left everything to her?"

"I wrote up a will, you know, in case."

"And you left it *all* to Doris?"

"Claire—just the cash in my bag."

"Oh."

"I figured she could use it."

"Obviously. At thirty grand a week, it wouldn't have lasted long."

"It always bugged her the house looked so shabby. Her grandfather built it and all. She probably got carried away and then just felt bad about the whole thing—"

"Crazy! I told you that in the beginning."

—"and was embarrassed. She's got a lot of pride."

"*And* she's tweaked."

"She has her good moments. When do you start?" he said to change the subject.

"Wait a minute," she said.

"What?"

She took his hand, snuggled closer to him. "Are we sounding married already?"

"What're you talking about?"

"I don't know. I guess."

"Tell me."

"I just don't want us to become dull and too normal."

"I thought you always wanted security. I thought that was your—"

She reached up and touched his lips. "Don't say anything for a minute, okay?"

He waited as she held him, the silence, her nearness, the clean smell of her shirt and hair making him consider taking her into the cabin again. But the kid was bound to be back any second. After all, no one could possibly fish for more than a couple hours, could they?

After a while she said, "I just needed to be with you."

He didn't know how to respond to that.

She sat up straighter, rubbing his hand. "They're not really sure."

"Who's not sure?"

"The job. They said it would probably be some time in September."

"You don't have to work, you know."

"I want to. I *really* want to do this. My God, I should have done it sooner instead of that stupid frame shop and copyediting."

"You know I think it's great what you're gonna be doing. As long as you don't teach them that Barclay guy's stuff. 'Salivating on the cherub orbs of her dented knee.'"

"Maybe I'll be reading them Hakken one day."

"Cruel."

"You might be surprised."

"I had to kill the time doing something. You're the one who should write again. You already got the pen." He let his hand fall between her legs. "It'll be okay working there. All that marble and stuff. Carnegie was a bastard but at least he gave us those."

"Maybe I will write again. I'm seriously considering it. There's a story I've been thinking about that might make a pretty good novel."

"What would ya write about this time?"

She looked at him. "You."

He laughed.

A gull was turning out over the water, the wings very white for an instant. It flew toward them, low, gliding just over their heads. There was that distinctive high-pitched cry. "It sounds like it's pissed off at something," he said.

"You think?"

"Maybe it's just hungry."

"Maybe it's saying something."

The gull landed at the edge of the grass, head cocked, eyeing them disdainfully.

"Hey, I talked to that lawyer again yesterday. He still thinks he can get me off easy. Turns out they don't have any real evidence, and according to him, the DA doesn't give a shit anyway. It'll be good to say good-bye to Bob Gray. Then maybe I won't have to pay that fucking three-hundred-and-ninety-dollar speeding ticket I got in Connecticut. Jesus I hate that state."

"You were never a Bob."

"There wasn't a single car on the highway—except her. Female cops are the worst."

The gull flew off and he stopped rubbing her thigh; Brandon had appeared on the path from the ocean. The kid was wet, but fishless. He looked better than a few months ago, wearing a black T-shirt, some kind of calf-length baggy black shorts, his face and arms beginning to tan; they'd both gotten haircuts from Vicky before leaving Scoggton, and Jimmy had to admit, she gave a descent cut. Brandon waved, came and sat at the picnic table.

"Nothing?" said Jimmy.

He shook his head. "Doesn't matter. You gotta be patient if you're a fisherman."

"Bud, let's get the fire going. We got steaks to cook."

"Righteous."

"Go get the charcoal, okay?"

Jimmy'd bought the natural hardwood kind from Quebec. In the cabin's outdoor grill similar to a miniature brick fireplace, he showed Brandon how to stack up the charcoal in a pyramid with newspaper underneath; he'd checked it out carefully online to be prepared. "This way there's no poisons from that lighter-fluid stuff getting in the meat. It's the preferred method by barbeque experts," he told the kid with a wink, trying to sound confident. When the damn coals wouldn't light, Jimmy got annoyed and syphoned a little gasoline from the wagon. As he tossed the match, the blast of flame almost set him on fire.

"Wow, that sure as hell got it going," said Brandon. "Jimmy, you all right?"

He was rubbing his face with cold beer.

The fire settled down, and the three of them gathered around the fireplace on rusted metal chairs. The sky over the ocean was a vibrant evening blue, a bell buoy chimed every so often, the smell of salt and low tide was rising on the beginnings of shoreline fog.

"Damn, if this isn't the life," said Jimmy. "The best." As if to punctuate, the fire snapped and a large ember rolled onto the grass. It sat there at his feet, glowing. Checking to see if Brandon was watching, Jimmy quickly picked it up and tossed it back onto the coals.

"Wow," said Brandon. "Mom, did you see that?"

"Yeah, but I don't believe it."

"Jimmy, how'd you do that? I mean, that thing was red hot."

"You just have to believe. It's all about belief."

"Let me see your hand," said Claire.

He showed her. "Not a mark." He took her hand in his. "It's only a trick. You lick your fingers good and wet first when no one's watching, then you grab it gentle and quick."

"No way," said Brandon. "That's so awesome."

"There's a trick to everything." But because of what was in her eyes, and she could put an awful lot into them, he thought better of it. "Well, just about everything."

Then she smiled.

THE END

Made in United States
North Haven, CT
08 June 2023

37530337R00157